PAUL TAKES THE FORM OF A MORTAL GIRL

PAUL TAKES THE FORM OF A MORTAL GIRL

ANDREA LAWLOR

PICADOR

First published 2017 by Rescue Press,
Chicago, Cleveland, Iowa City

New edition published 2019 by Vintage Books, a division of Penguin
Random House LLC, New York, and in Canada by Random House
of Canada, a division of Penguin Random House Canada Limited, Toronto

First published in the UK 2019 by Picador
an imprint of Pan Macmillan
20 New Wharf Road, London N1 9RR
Associated companies throughout the world
www.panmacmillan.com

ISBN 978-1-5290-0766-4

1 3 5 7 9 8 6 4 2

A CIP catalogue record for this book is available from the British Library.

Printed and bound by CPI Group (UK) Ltd, Croydon, CR0 4YY

Visit **www.picador.com** to read more about all our books
and to buy them. You will also find features, author interviews and
news of any author events, and you can sign up for e-newsletters
so that you're always first to hear about our new releases.

In memory of Gene Blanc, 1945–1995

People if you like to believe it can be made by their names.
Call anybody Paul and they get to be a Paul . . .

—GERTRUDE STEIN, "Poetry and Grammar"

PAUL TAKES THE FORM OF A MORTAL GIRL

I.

Like a shark, Paul had to keep moving. He slept only when necessary. He had business with the world, codes to crack, so many questions. Tonight, for example, Paul needed to know what fucking was like for girls.

Snow piled up outside the house on North Gilbert Street, piled up on the porch, covering everyone's bicycles. The insolent fake spring of the last week was missing, presumed dead; little pink buds glittered in their ice caskets.

Paul paced the second-floor apartment in various states of unsatisfying undress. He supposed his roommate, Christopher, might, against all odds, have one nice article of clothing squirreled away. But there was Christopher, clad in a collarless linen shirt, meditating sanctimoniously on his bed. Silence equals death, thought Paul, as he repaired to his own room to dress.

Paul cast about for ways to look more bad. He did have those black vinyl pants (stolen from Trash & Vaudeville, back in New York) but he'd worn them out and about here five times already, enough to wear off the charge. He wanted to telegraph the word *fetish* far and wide, from Coralville to Cedar Rapids all the way to the Quad Cities; he'd spent the afternoon searching the Mennonite thrift shop for uniforms or glitter-stitched girls' shirts. He liked to elicit swears from the frat boys. He enjoyed his various reputations (freak, party boy, bisexual, New Yorker) and liked to keep them fresh, but his badness was incidental, really.

He'd seen a flyer at Gabe's Oasis announcing bands on

Tuesday night. A local girl band was opening, then a dyke band from Seattle. But who would go with him to see a dyke punk band they didn't know on a Tuesday night in the middle of the Iowa winter? Christopher just laughed. Paul began calling around to his so-called friends.

"Um, no."

Paul required a partner for his mission, a girl who admired and offset him, who bolstered his girlishness. Even rock chicks went to bars in pairs. He tapped Jane's number into the kitchen phone.

"Come on," he said. "It'll be fun. They're from *Seattle*." He drew the word out exotically.

"I don't think so," said Jane, who was studying for her comps. "I have to read this book on the Gaze."

"This will be exactly like studying," said Paul.

"I'm actually busy, Paul," Jane said.

"Please," he said. "I need you."

"I can't," she said.

"Your loss," Paul said. He *preferred* to go alone.

He rooted around in his blue footlocker and found the vinyl pants.

"Christopher," he called out. "You really should come. Everyone's going."

Christopher called back something about a "working group."

He appeared in Paul's doorway. "Remember? The emergency meeting?"

"Just come after," Paul said.

"Perhaps you want to borrow this?" Christopher leaned into the room with a sparkly pink tank top dangling off his

ostentatiously limp wrist. When he spoke his beard moved, mesmerizing Paul. "I wore it at Short Mountain to *great* effect."

"Ooh yeah," said Paul. "Gimme."

"*Greedy.*" Christopher dropped the shirt at Paul's feet. "I want it back."

Paul bent to fetch. For a second, he wished he too had a beard, to offset the sequins. He loved that look. But he'd never grown a beard, wasn't even sure he could. Plus that wasn't the story he was telling tonight.

"Thank you," he said, with the cool dignity of an ambassador's daughter borrowing cab fare. He took the sparkly shirt into his room and popped *Horses* into his tape player. He shut the door between his bedroom and the kitchen so Christopher wouldn't see him change.

First he needed good underwear. He decided to break out the unopened European-style briefs his old sociology professor had inappropriately brought him back from Spain last summer. They looked enough like girls' underwear and wouldn't disrupt the line. He dropped his swishy loose army pants and his shoplifted French-cut boxers, and stared at his penis until it shrank, tucked itself into the tight little crawl space of his former balls. He stepped into the black briefs and admired his smooth front with his hands and eyes, then found the red lace bra he'd borrowed from that girl in New York. His skin shivered all over, belly and back and thighs. He stared down his skinny chest until it obediently softened, grew, filled out the bra. Not too big. It was like that TV show *Manimal* where the guy changed into a panther and other animals, a miracle of special effects, only that guy couldn't control himself. That guy was more like

the Hulk. Not Paul. Paul stopped at a 36C. He was going for *regular but hot.*

He stroked his throat until the bump relented and then he checked his look in the full-length mirror. How could he look so pretty? His black engineer boots and snug Levi's jacket, big fur-lined Lenny Kravitz coat—every detail was good, was right. Who *was* he? He was Ginsberg and Streisand and Kim Gordon rolled into one. He was the girl he wanted to fuck. He clumsily applied silvery pale-pink lipstick. He raked black mascara through his lashes. He tugged his shaggy hair past his shoulders, then experimentally flipped this new long hair, but he didn't have the knack and he hurt his neck slightly but looked good. *Now*, he thought, as Patti Smith serenaded a girl called Gloria.

"Bye, Christopher," Paul called out, clattering down the stairs.

"You are a *big nasty bulldagger*," said Christopher from the kitchen table, without even turning around. "You are so butch."

Stupid queen, thought Paul. All who see me tonight will know I am a girl.

He left the house, alone in the blue night of snow and streetlights, air like paper cuts. Paul decided, as always, to go the pretty way. He cut over to Linn Street, which glittered blue and white, fairy snow in the trees. He walked with his hips deliberating: back and forth, back and forth, careful solid booted steps on the ice.

Paul passed by all his landmarks—Tuck's Place, Cozy House, the expensive sandwich shop, the QuikTrip, Seashore Hall—and then through the causeway by the chemistry building to the yellow lights of the empty downtown. A pack of frat

boys spilled out of the Que and crossed the street, headed his way.

"Hey sweetheart, where are you going?" one of them called. "Do you need an escort?"

Paul tossed his head and kept walking, like he'd seen girls do. This was a first. Now they could actually admit they wanted to fuck him.

He turned the corner and quickly stomped down the rest of the lonely side street to Gabe's.

Inside the warm basement of the bar, a row of pinball machines glowed orange light and glass. The jukebox blasted "Black Hole Sun" into the wood paneling. Paul liked to be early for things, to gain the home-turf advantage—he liked to watch his ducks from a blind. He took a place against the bar and observed with amusement and pride every dyke who walked up the stairs to the room where they had shows. My sisters, he thought.

When he'd seen enough people come in, he paid his cover and walked up the black-painted stairs himself. The black walls were covered in crinkly aging band posters: Sugar, Iowa Beef Experience, 7 Year Bitch, Mike Watt. At the bar in the back of the hall stood five or six dykes with chains on their plaid pants, tattoos on every surface, fucked-up hair. Paul stood by the door, oddly shy to walk in alone, but he saw one familiar face, then another. He made his way to the bar, and the room filled in the time it took to cross it. All of Iowa City punkdom straggled and pushed and posed into the center of the space. Paul bought and drank a beer quickly, just to shake off the awkwardness. He recognized a few people who did not appear to recognize him. So far, so good.

Jane walked in. She'd come after all. He caught her eye and waved her back to the bar where he'd set up headquarters.

"I'm Polly," he said, rehearsing his coy look.

"Okay, Paul," she said. "You look amazing, by the way. It's actually uncanny." Jane emphasized *uncanny* in her graduate-school accent.

"Aren't you glad you came?" Paul said, nodding at the band.

"Oh my god, they're hot," said Jane. "There's so much hotness here I'm parched."

At the bar a fair young punk emerged from the forest of plaid, caught Paul's attention by sucking on one of those fake beers, an O'Doul's. Paul was shocked and oddly turned on. Now, that's tough, that's really beyond the pale, he thought.

"Can you get me a whiskey?" he muttered to Jane, and made his way to the bathroom.

Blisterhood is sourful, he read off the door as he sat to pee with his exciting new vagina. Am I a feminist? he wondered. How could someone so beautiful drink fake beer? Don't forget to wipe.

He found Jane near the stage, flirting with the androgynous line cook who worked at the Hamburg Inn. Often Paul and Jane met at the 'Burg for the $4.95 dinner special of fried chicken, green beans, mashed potatoes, gravy, and biscuit, and to stare at Jane's crush. Just *go* for it, he'd think, eating Jane's drumsticks. Everyone's attainable. Studying Jane confused him. Fruit was hanging low. And Jane—most people in fact—walked through it like it was nothing.

Paul watched Jane now, from miles above, buffeted by the opening band's wall of sound. His body stood next to Jane silently. I am a stuffed bear in Jane's bed, Paul thought. Jane's

mouth moved; the other girl slid closer. What was that *like?* He felt angry for a moment; then the whiskey spread out. Paul realized he also knew the bass player, from Intro to Film Theory, which explained why he thought he'd just heard them sing the words "Maya Deren." He enjoyed and was aroused by this proximity to fame. He nodded to the music and danced in place in such a way as to feel his breasts bounce.

Alan from the coffee cart came up and stood nodding next to him. Paul smiled his special smile.

"Hey," said Alan. "They're pretty good, huh?"

Paul bit his lip, inclined his head slightly, and looked up through his eyelashes.

"Yeah," he said, still nodding to the beat.

Alan leaned his rusty stubbled face close to Paul, who thought *lion cub* and *I could have you.* Alan breathed in, sucking at Paul like a drain emptying.

"I have to get a drink," Paul said. He walked off abruptly to send Alan a message. He scanned the room for the fake-beer drinker. She was close-talking a ponytailed waitress but looked up when Paul passed. Fake beer, he thought. *So perverse.* He got a new whiskey and returned to the warm pit of bodies.

Then the second band came on and Paul let himself surge with all the other girls to the very front. The fake-beer drinker was onstage with a guitar and yellow-green animal eyes, staring right at Paul.

Paul stared back. She was clearly the band's pin-up, scrubbed clean under the torn tee shirt and jeans, a stoic masculine beauty. Girls in the audience screamed as the band ripped into a cover of "Fox on the Run."

It's cold outside, Paul thought. That guitar player better

fuck me tonight. He stood quietly amid the screaming girls and watched. Then he screamed too. It was fun to be a fan.

Jane caught his eye, smirked from on top of a table against the far wall. The line cook was climbing up next to her. Things were getting raucous. The whole room sweated in unison, one steamed-up mind thinking *this can't end.*

Paul very smoothly removed his lacy bra from under his shirt and moved breasts-first closer to the stage. He stopped to dance in front of Alan as he passed, and felt the lump in Alan's pants. I did that, he thought.

Just as the last song ended, Paul threw his lacy bra right up onto the stage. The beautiful young butch guitar god leaned into the microphone for the first time all night and said, "I'll see *you* after the show."

Paul cast his modest virgin eyes toward the ground as all about him girls slathered their envious glances upon him. The heat of a hundred barely postadolescent bodies swaddled him. The lights came up, and Paul's sweat ran cold under his shirt. A roadie opened the fire door and the band began to carry their gear down the stairs. The guitar player packed Paul's bra into a guitar case, eyeing him significantly. Paul hung back and let himself be eyed. All in good time, he thought.

Jane walked up to the stage, minus the line cook, to invite the band to a huge after-bar at somebody's house on Brown Street she'd just heard about.

"Come in the van with us," said the guitar player, looking at Paul.

They all piled in. Jane sat on the lead singer's lap in the passenger seat giving directions, and the surly bass player drove.

Paul took particular pleasure in crossing the party's threshold in the company of a famous band from Seattle.

"Does this place have an upstairs?" said the guitar player, taking charge in such a way that Paul understood he was with a true rock star, not just a scene star.

Paul nodded and they set off to explore the house, one of those sprawling mansions on Brown Street formerly inhabited by university presidents or famous writers, and now, somehow, rented to a group of gay men who had full-time jobs and a lot of CDs.

The rock star opened door after bedroom door, judging something Paul couldn't see, choosing after all that deliberation the sparest room: no piles of clothes or books, no framed Patrick Nagel prints—only a bed, high off the ground, its thick green comforter bright in the street light through the window. Paul stood near the bed, waiting to be directed. The rock star closed the door and walked up very close to Paul.

"Are you going to kiss me now?" Paul whispered.

"I'm gonna do more than that, little girl," growled the rock star, pulling Paul's hair from the nape of his neck. Paul let himself fall back onto the bed and the rock star fell on top of him like a high-school quarterback, lithe with purpose, grinding expectantly into Paul.

"What do you want?" the rock star breathed into Paul's ear.

Paul couldn't think. You tell me, he thought.

The rock star stuck her hand down Paul's special vinyl pants, under his black panties, into his cunt.

"You're so wet," she said. "You want my cock so bad."

Paul nodded. It was true. He was very, very, very wet. He

could smell himself. His cunt was gaping and his stomach was gaping and his mouth was kissing, kissing, kissing. He whimpered as the rock star unbuttoned her jeans and pulled out her plastic cock, black and shiny to match her rock-star shininess. I am being penetrated by punk, he thought as she thrust into him, pushing his legs apart, collapsing onto him like a pistoning flesh blanket.

Inside Paul something tight released: a rusted nut turned *finally* around its old bolt. White sheets were thrown off moldering couches with a fanfare of dust and sunlight. Then the release stopped, as if it never was.

"What are you doing?" Paul panted. "Don't stop. Please."

The rock star's face looked princely, beatific, hovering over Paul.

"I'm not," she said, and slid her hand into Paul, then sat up in a crawling sort of crouch over him. He wanted her to read his mind, touch his clit, not stop. This seemed very important so he said it again.

"Don't stop, okay?" Paul said. "Don't stop."

<div style="text-align:center">×</div>

Paul walked up the slushy middle of Brown Street in the pastel morning, saw the colored Christmas lights still glowing in his second-floor window. He found Christopher in the kitchen eating oatmeal and reading what appeared to be a botany textbook.

"What are you doing up?" Paul said.

"I have class?" said Christopher. "In some cultures, people go to things called classes or jobs in the morning and sleep in the nighttime."

×

Paul slunk into Logic with a large coffee and no textbook. Where was he supposed to get fifty-nine dollars? Other people had parents who bought them books.

"Can I look on with you?" he whispered to the girl next to him.

"Nice of you to join us," the professor said. "Do you have something for me?"

Oh right, thought Paul. The weekly problem sheet. That made three he owed. He really needed to pass this class. But he was there, right? Didn't that count for something?

He flipped open his marble composition book and entered the professor's outfit (stained gray pants with an elastic waistband, yellow button-down, brown poly-blend V-neck sweater, shoes that could only be described as brogues) into his fashion log. English and film professors obviously ranked highest, broken down by period: Modernists, then film production professors, then feminist film theorists, and so on, with the occasional medievalist throwing off the curve. The outlier medievalists were usually Marxists, of course, and Marxists or queers in any period shot to the top. Paul didn't trust anyone in the sciences—hard or soft—to dress themselves, and he had the data to make the argument. This was the gift of gen ed requirements, Paul thought: exposure to so many different aesthetics.

After class Paul walked to the Linn Street Café for his afternoon shift. He arrived only five minutes early. In the kitchen, he tried out his new system for washing crème brûlée ramekins. Sugar crystallized around the rims, requiring long soaks—impossible during the dinner rush—and the chef forbade steel

wool. Paul's innovation was to apply the full industrial force of the spray hose to the rim, tipped at just the right angle, which resulted in clean ramekins, if a wet shirt. Whenever Amanda, the most junior server, brought in half-eaten appetizer plates, she and Paul snacked on bits of leftover smoked trout pâté. Eli, the line cook, made Paul the Moroccan lamb special for his staff meal. By the time Paul finished the last dish, mopped the kitchen floor with bleach water, and got tipped out by the waiters, he was full and dry.

He changed into a clean tee shirt in the walk-in, carefully rolled the sleeves of his Viyella shadow-plaid above his biceps like the picture of Jean Genet on the cover of that new biography, and stuck a clean faded green bandana in the left pocket of his 501s. Tony Pinto had found that bandana outside the Anvil and given it to him, called him a hustler. Paul shrugged into his River Phoenix coat, dark blue corduroy with fleece lining, and walked out of the kitchen like he was walking into Studio 54.

He leaned over the bar to request his shift drink. Angelic Hans poured hefty glasses of single malt Scotches, to see if they could tell the difference.

"Part of the job," Hans said.

"You bet," said Eli.

"Absolutely," said Paul.

A visiting writer, famously Appalachian, sat alone at the end of the bar, smoking a Swisher Sweet.

"You boys want to come to George's with me after you close up?" he said.

Paul nodded. He liked the writer's books; they weren't clever, but offered man realness, the authenticity of the sen-

sitive country boy, a view inside the inscrutable straight-guy mind—unexpected, like a talking dog.

"I just have to get rid of these people," said Hans. "Give me a minute."

Hans raised the dining-room track lights almost imperceptibly, and the beige carpeting revealed its cheapness. Then he changed the tape behind the bar from Charlie Parker to the Hi-NRG remix of "Jolene." Department heads and lawyers slurped down their ports and signaled for their checks.

The visiting writer stubbed out his tiny cigar and shrugged on his jacket. Paul wondered idly if the writer was looking at him, if he thought Paul looked like someone from another decade, maybe the writer's high-school years. Paul knew he had that effect on people. He'd heard the writer was married, with a difficult wife, maybe. She'd either left him or died; he'd heard something.

Finally they were out the door into the manly night, crossing the street not fifty yards to George's, which was like a cozy railroad car stocked with waifs and the heroin chic. Three or four of Paul's crushes were tucked into booths, a vending machine of possible evenings. He slunk to the bar while he tried to figure his various odds:

- The waifish taxi driver who was with his waifish brother and another guy: 20%
- The Steve McQueen–looking poet who was alone but didn't look up when Paul passed: 10%
- The poet who was with her boyfriend but gave Paul the hot eye: 50%

• The front booth, obscured by a cloud of intrigue, where a loud group of Paul's regulars from the 620 had grabbed his ass when he walked in: 40%

• The comp lit grad student who was leaning on the jukebox, obviously drunk: 65%

Paul accepted another bourbon from the visiting writer, and considered him for inclusion on the list. Paul wanted to *fuck* someone tonight, after the business with the rock star, but could come around to the idea of sucking off an older writer with a beard, maybe in the bathroom?

He stared at the wall clock, briefly fixated by the original 1950s Hamm's beer running waterfall—he never tired of the magic. It was only 1:30.

"I've been awake for thirty-six hours," he announced.

"Showoff," said Eli.

"Okay, thirty-four and a half."

"I hear there's an after-bar at the Blue House," Hans said. Hans always liked to go to the gay parties, where older men stared at him, whispering "Pierre et Gilles" to each other.

"Yeah, but it's so far," said Paul, the pleasure-seeker.

"There's something at that house next to the Foxhead," said Eli, who always knew the cool straight parties.

"Better," said Paul. At least half the people in town he was interested in would probably be there and it was only three blocks away.

"We should go to the Foxhead first," said Hans. "See who's there."

The visiting writer was now one of them.

"Yeah, let's go now," he said.

Paul pulled on his Prairie Seed knit cap and pogoed in place briefly, buoyed by the thought of leaving a room full of crushes in order to hunt in another room.

Eli led their little pack past the dark windows of Paglia's Pizza, past the frozen scraggle-grass of the empty lot, and up the two concrete steps of the Foxhead. Paul strode next to the visiting writer as if they were firefighters.

"The Foxhead," said Eli with a lion tamer's flourish, and held the door open. Inside the bright island of glass and mahogany-stained wood were stands of MFA students playing pool or chalking their names on a list to play pool or admiring each other's cashmere scarves.

Paul knew most of the poets from bartending. Poets partied and fiction writers stayed home to work. Someone had told him that one drunken afternoon—a handsome young gray-haired poet who liked people to think he was gay. Paul walked to the bathroom as an excuse to say hi to everyone in the booths.

When he got out he saw the visiting writer had been accosted by grad students. The taxi driver, minus the boy and the brother, had also appeared. A good sign. The taxi driver stood in front of the jukebox, swilling a gin-and-tonic through a straw and listening to a beefy blonde guy in a skintight pink tee shirt.

A little before three, Hans gathered Paul and Eli and the visiting writer, true comrades all, into a preparatory huddle for their next move—the party next door. They buttoned up their coats and swallowed their drinks and crossed the street to buy sixes of Special Export at Dirty John's and then crossed back. Offerings in hand, they lined up behind Eli, who opened the door to the dark house.

"Are you sure there's a party?" said the writer.

"Yeah," said Eli, brushing off his pants.

The four of them walked down the dark quiet hallway. Eli opened the first door and they found a group of art students sitting on a bed, passing a ceramic pipe and listening ironically to Jethro Tull. Hans saw a girl he knew, and they lost Hans.

Paul and Eli and the writer pushed on. In the kitchen Eli's twin brother, David, balanced badly on a skateboard while the taxi driver's brother mixed screwdrivers.

Paul said his hellos and kept going with the bearded writer. Up the stairs, more rooms full of people whose faces he knew. They entered a bedroom with nothing but five framed paint-by-number horses and a bare futon.

"We should hide our beer," said Paul, as much to have a conspiracy as to hoard.

"Yeah," said the writer, and laughed a barking laugh. "The oven's always the best place, but the closet will do."

Paul nodded. This man was no fool, and his twangy accent made Paul feel unreasonably happy. He took the temperature of the situation, considered cutting the space between himself and the writer, and thought of things he could say like, close the door so I can suck your dick. He rolled the words around in his mouth but couldn't get them out.

Then Maisie came in: Maisie, the drug-dealing girlfriend of the famously fucked-up son of the famous poet; Maisie with her dykey haircut and bad-girl jeans; Maisie who Paul had forgotten he wanted to hit on.

"Hey," said Paul, swiveling toward the glitter of the girl.

The writer exhaled noticeably, which Paul tucked away for future reference or anecdote.

Ray, Maisie's boyfriend, walked in, his left arm in a cast.

Paul offered two of his valuable beers to Maisie and Ray in preemptive placation for thinking thoughts about Maisie. The writer was now gone. Ray disappeared. The night was magic, Paul was magic; he saw secret doors everywhere.

Maisie stood in the room and he picked up the message on the airwaves.

"Hey," he said out loud.

"Hey," she said.

They drank from their beers at the same time.

"Were you at George's before?" she said. "I thought I saw you."

Paul had nothing to say to Maisie. He stared her down and she stopped talking, her cool-girl mouth slightly open.

"Let's go downstairs," he said.

They toured the party together like assassins, checking all the rooms for people they knew. By unspoken pact they pretended not to see their friends.

"Who are all these people?" said Maisie, a haughty bored flapper.

"*Really*," said Paul.

"Come with me to the bathroom," said Maisie, like Paul was a girl.

"Okay," said Paul.

They got new beers on the way and waited in the hallway, throwing bottle caps at each other. The music got louder and louder, weird French man-singing.

"Is that Serge Gainsbourg?" said Maisie.

"Yeah," said Paul, who didn't know.

The writer visited them in line and offered sips from his flask.

"He was like a wizard, giving us the magic potion," said Paul when the writer disappeared again.

"Yeah," said Maisie. "What did it turn you into?"

That is called voluptuous, thought Paul. He was glad to give the word some work. Maisie had light brown hair, which had been dyed blue, green, platinum, and several other colors over the months he'd been watching her. Strains of pink showed at the choppy edges. When he had first started noticing her waitressing at the 'Burg, he thought she was a few different girls until Jane set him straight. He came back to the hallway from his interesting mind.

"It turned me into a dog," he said, and he growled and bit her arm. He was glad to be a known homosexual—it allowed him a daring way with girls.

The bathroom door opened and the taxi driver and his brother stumbled out. Heroin. Paul was pleased with his ability to parse visible highs. Heroin had begun taking Iowa City by storm again in '92, he'd heard. Not that anyone had offered him any.

Maisie stood in the dark bathroom doorway and pulled on Paul's corduroy arm. Better to be in snug places. He closed the door behind him and Maisie pushed him back up against it, mouth on mouth. Paul handled her tits through her shirt, then underneath. He had his hand down her pants without thinking, fingers up inside her, and out, and up, until she came all over his fingers. He covered her yelps with his mouth and wet kissing.

A peremptory rat-a-tat on the door startled them both.

"Oh shit."

She'd started to unbutton his fly, he realized as he stood

up. He'd cum in his gray cotton boxer briefs and now his dick was swishing around and his jeans were wet on the front from her too.

"Shit," Maisie said, her face flushed.

She opened the door to a line down the hall and Paul tried to act like somebody who had been doing drugs.

Ray was second in line.

"Hey, Ray," Paul said, thinking *shit shit shit*.

Maisie kept walking, like she didn't know Paul or Ray.

The visiting writer was lurking by the stairs, maybe taking notes in his head.

"Let's go smoke," said Paul.

×

Outside the town was quiet and white. Like the whole state, Paul thought. White as far as the eye can see, people and highways and pig houses and soy fields under murderous quilts of snow. Paul buttoned up his corduroy jacket and thought about hitchhiking, about truck drivers in rest-stop bathrooms. He stamped up and down on the porch.

"Cold," said the writer, shoulders near his ears.

"You want to go see something?" said Paul. "You ever see the angel in the cemetery?"

"Sure," said the visiting writer. "Let's go. My car's behind George's."

Paul looked for a pickup truck, probably a faded blue Chevy.

Inside the visiting writer's maroon hatchback it smelled

like dog biscuits and orange soda. Paul pushed hamburger wrappers off the passenger seat.

"The radio work?" he said, turning the dial. Jazz came out, and Paul left it. That's just what professors listened to, he figured. Even visiting writers.

"Here," said the writer, fumbling for a tape in the glovebox, his forearm brushing Paul's thigh. "My wife . . . She listened to all that."

He pushed a homemade tape in and the Stones came on.

"Is she . . . are you . . . do you not like jazz?" said Paul.

"Don't talk for a minute," said the writer. "I can't see."

Paul held his breath until the cemetery, tracing letters on the passenger window as they rolled down the snowy night streets.

The writer parked outside the cemetery gates.

"Do you like the Smiths?" said Paul, and he stepped through the snow like a delicate horse.

"Not really my thing," said the visiting writer somewhat abruptly. "So where's this angel?"

They wound through the headstones in the snow until they found the monument, an angel looking down, wings folded in like a vampire's cape.

The writer crouched and dusted snow off the base.

"Apparently it's in Czech," said Paul, shrugging. "A young Czech boy died, and his mother commissioned a bronze angel from the most famous sculptor in Czechoslovakia, but when the angel arrived the bronze had turned black because the angel was so sad that the boy had died."

"Hmm," said the writer. "I was expecting a better story. Something more spooky."

"Supposedly if you touch it you'll die," offered Paul. "I also heard if you kiss it you'll have good luck, but if you kiss somebody in front of it in the moonlight you'll both die."

The visiting writer snorted through his beard.

"We're all going to die," he said.

"Yeah," said Paul, embarrassed to be caught out in gothicness.

The hatchback was freezing when they got back in.

"It'll take a minute to warm up," said the writer.

He handed Paul the flask, stretched back in the driver's seat, and closed his eyes.

Paul swigged the last bit of whiskey, and wondered what River would do.

The writer nodded his head in time, faintly smiling, still with his eyes closed. Paul dropped his hand on the writer's leg, and didn't get punched.

He proceeded up the writer's jeans, and thumbed into his button fly.

"Who was that girl at the party?"

"Friend of mine," said Paul, clearing away denim and long-john material.

He pulled out the writer's dick, foreskin almost entirely receded, and covered the purple head with his mouth. The writer groaned and cupped Paul's head to his lap, and Paul felt like a young skier or mechanic in a Falcon video.

"Did you screw her?"

Paul shook his head without looking up. The writer's cock thickened, so Paul breathed through his nose.

"Did she suck your dick?"

He shook his head again. He did the special thing with

his tongue he knew how to do and the writer stopped talking. The writer's crotch smelled like high school. The car got hotter. Paul bobbed his head and began to enjoy the crick in his neck and the writer bucked into his face again, hard then salty. Paul sat up and tried to subtly remove a pubic hair from his tongue.

"I hate the next song," said the writer, flipping the tape and turning on the engine.

"Me too," said Paul.

They sat listening.

"I just live over on Gilbert," said Paul.

Maybe the writer was going to freak out now. Paul hadn't been with too many older straight guys. He didn't know how they behaved after you blew them.

"I'm hungry," said the visiting writer. "I'm starving! You hungry? Country Kitchen makes some pretty decent grits."

"I'm always hungry," said Paul.

×

"Are you ready?" said Christopher, who'd been up for hours, banging around the kitchen passive-aggressively.

Paul did not understand Christopher. Look at him right now, for instance, with rice-cake crumbs in his beard and a Patty Larkin tee shirt, which not even Paul, had he wanted to, which he did not, could have re-signified as ironical. Hopeless.

"I'm not awake," Paul said, slumping illustratively over the kitchen table. He lay his head on a placemat.

"We have to go," Christopher said. "The rally starts in thirty minutes and I have the signs."

"Plenty of time," said Paul, yawning.

"Also, you have messages on the machine. You can't just not check your messages ever."

"Okay," Paul said.

"Some guy has called, like, five times. Tony something?"

"*Okay*," said Paul. "I will listen to my messages. Is there coffee?"

Christopher held up one of the hand-lettered poster boards, which accounted for the pleasant chemical fog of Sharpie in the apartment. *Stop Violence Against Gays and Lesbians Now!* the sign read.

"Too much?" Christopher said. He looked worried. "Should it be 'Lesbians and Gays'?"

"Not too much enough," Paul said. "What about 'Queers Bash Back'?"

"But we don't want to advocate violence as a response," said Christopher. "We don't want to alienate people."

"I do," said Paul, more and more awake. "Fuck those queer-bashers. Fuck all those fucking breeders. Write that!"

"Jesus, Paul."

"What? They don't worry about alienating us when they're beating the crap out of some baby drag queen."

Christopher stacked the signs in the foyer, wooden handles up. Paul realized he'd better hurry or he'd have to walk. He threw on his old Pink Panthers Street Patrol tee shirt and toted a load of mealy-mouthed pacifist signs to Christopher's ancient red Volvo. He hoped Jane remembered about the rally, so he'd have someone with whom to share his various critiques.

Downtown at the ped mall, Paul separated himself immediately from Christopher, who, with his earnest friends from Queer Nation/Iowa City, planned to hand out chant sheets, of

all things. Chants were spontaneous eruptions of clever queer rage, Paul thought. Nobody in New York used chant sheets. The Church Ladies *practiced* before singing "Oh, I'm a homophobic socialist, homophobic through and through" to the ISO guys at Pride. He remembered the ACT UP bus to Kennebunkport, how he and Tony Pinto had laid coats over their laps and cum into each other's hands while mouthing "health care is a right." When they got off the bus, they knew the chants.

Paul made a quick lap of the perimeter, ostensibly looking for Jane but really sizing up the crowd in case there was a kiss-in. He saw the two out queers in the Writers' Workshop; like Paul, they wore their East Coast tee shirts—one *No Glove No Love* and one *Queer N'Asian.* He saw a few closeted gays he knew, standing on the sidewalk as if they'd just happened to be in the neighborhood, getting a cup of coffee, and oh, what was this?

There was a clatch of fresh-faced white girls with their radical-for-Iowa bobbed hair whom he recognized as women's studies majors. There were a few day-shy regulars from the 620, on lunch break from their short-order-cook or gun-store jobs. And there was Jane, resplendent in her knockoff Chanel suit over a Dyke Action Machine tee shirt topped with fake pearls. At least he thought they were fake. Thank god for Jane.

The speaker—a local politician—made her remarks, a pony-tailed bisexual man stood up and read a poem, Christopher led the motley assemblage in a few rounds of "Two four six eight, stop the violence, stop the hate," and everyone dispersed to make it to their next class. No rage, which was disappointing, and no kiss-in, which was just as well if you looked at the available talent.

The women's studies majors had hung a clothesline of

solidarity between two trees: strung-up tee shirts with the puffy-painted names of all the queers murdered in the last year. Transvestite hookers in Chicago, street kids in the Meat-packing District in New York, sissies in Washington, DC, boys strangled by johns, girls shot in the face, and then, of course, that kid in Ottumwa, just last week. All the queers who weren't as lucky as Paul.

"Coffee," Jane said, coming up next to him.

"Out of the streets, into the café!" Paul said.

"You look tall today," said Jane. "Are you wearing lifts in your shoes? Bold!"

"I am tall," said Paul. He might have given himself just a little height this morning, so his pants would fit better, but he hadn't thought anyone would notice. Lately Jane had been positively nosy. Should he just tell her? he wondered for the hundredth time.

<div align="center">×</div>

"And then?" said Jane. She sorted her index cards into neat piles (psychoanalytic, deconstructionist, feminist) and then re-sorted them (French, American, postcolonial), but she was listening.

"We fell madly in love, of course, and he's asked me to marry him, and of course you'll be my maid of honor," said Paul, sipping his milky tea. He threw his scarf Frenchly over his shoulder and sighed. "Nothing. He's old. He's like thirty."

"You don't even know how lucky you are," said Jane. "It is virtually impossible to get a girl to have a one-night stand even, let alone just hook up in a car, without having a whole conversation."

"That is such a lie, Jane, and you know it," said Paul, pushing his chair back from the table and taking one last look around the café. "You have one-night stands all the time. The butch girl from Toronto? Or that poet with the teeth? I have to be at work. Come down to the bar and lie to me more later, okay?"

Jane abandoned her index cards momentarily and sidled up to the counter, where one barista was cuter than the next. She liked that word, "barista," in part because it infuriated Paul, who thought her déclassé when she said it out loud. She ordered a double latte; she had work to do. But the baristas were like television stars up close, so attractive, with such dramatic character arcs. Jane wanted to be in the show with them. She wondered how they talked about the customers, if they noticed her, who was sleeping with whom. She liked the look of the short-haired girl with the glasses. Glasses were always a good sign. She took her latte and sat back down, glad you could finally get espresso in Iowa. She'd been spoiled at Sarah Lawrence; she'd defected to the coast only to end up in graduate school mere states away from her parents and their Folgers crystals.

The espresso replaced Jane's blood with something cold and fulgent, like liquid mercury. She started to have some very interesting ideas about Leo Bersani's article "Is the Rectum a Grave?" but before she could write them down she realized that in fact she could use not only Bersani but also Bakhtin to talk about grotesque bodies in the New Queer Cinema. Bs! She decided to write a paper in which she only used theorists whose last name began with B: Bersani, Bakhtin, Butler, Lauren Berlant. Ooh, and Barthes. Yes! She needed another latte.

"Hey," said the short-haired glasses girl, bussing the table next to Jane.

"Hey," said Jane.

"So, you're friends with Paul?" said the girl.

Jane nodded. Everybody knew Paul.

"Does he have a boyfriend?" she said. "My friend likes him."

"He's very single," said Jane. "You should bring your friend down to the club tonight—he's bartending."

"That sounds fun," said the barista. "Maybe I'll see you later, then."

Jane felt daring, and couldn't concentrate on her index cards. The barista had thick brown glasses, like a German graphic designer, and a haircut that said she—or someone she knew—had even been east of Indiana. She didn't have any of the obvious signs of Midwestern lesbianism (labrys jewelry, Indigo Girls tee shirts, softball haircut) and Jane hadn't seen her at the club or anywhere but the café. Jane experienced a feeling to which she attached first the word abundance, then the word plenitude, and she considered how this might indeed be the best of all possible worlds.

×

Paul could make himself be attracted to anyone. This was one of his virtues. This was one of his virtues *and* one of his skills. He practiced, as a kid and later in life, in elevators, but the game could be played anywhere one was trapped with people. The game consisted of a single question: If you had to fall in love with (by which Paul meant have sex with) one person in this elevator, who would it be? He played the elevator game in every class he ever took, on the bus, in straight bars, in subway cars, in waiting rooms, free clinics, the line at a movie theater, dinner

out with a group of friends-of-friends. He sometimes played the elevator game with Jane, a silent communion of eyebrows and squints or—more likely—a fast-talking, low-murmured loop around the bar, marking targets. Jane was his favorite companion for this; she didn't judge. Most of his life he had played alone.

The game was best when hard, when he had to sell himself on a stranger. He sneaked evaluating looks at shoes, at jewelry, at haircuts; he searched for clues about the sort of lover each person would be. In every single person in the elevator he looked for something he could, if not love, fetishize. That man's hands were so large: Paul imagined the hands covering his small back, pulling Paul into the man's face. That man's eyes were so blue: Paul imagined drinking cocoa at a ski lodge in the man's native country, where they conveniently would be ready for après-ski hot-tub adventures. That boy was so awkward, shifting nervously and trying to cover his tented pants in math class: Paul imagined the boy's secret jerky confidence, pulling Paul's hair and forcing Paul to gag on his long thin dick. That girl's skirt was so short: Paul imagined fucking her with his strap-on, through the leg of her panties, in the stall of the girls' bathroom at a nightclub. That man was so dirty: Paul imagined huffing his armpits while masturbating them both in the stairwell of a construction site. That swaggering butch in the red hooded sweatshirt and black leather jacket— Paul imagined deep-throating her plastic cock at a sex party in a basement dungeon while a crowd of dykes looked on. That fratboy's ass was so round in his black and yellow sweatpants: Paul imagined sliding his cock in between the fratboy's

butt cheeks, holding them apart, and coming bitter handsfree spunk onto his outer ass-ring, eating it because it was his own.

Paul liked to play the elevator game fast and hard. Step into the elevator, maneuver to the side wall, scan each body before the doors closed, choose by the next floor. Sometimes his choice was immediate: there was an actual angel in the box. Paul liked to work for his supper. He believed in *trying* in this life. As a matter of principle (feminist, queer, anti-phony, anti-bourgeois) Paul stared. He smiled at strangers. He held whoever's glance he shouldn't. When they held back, that was an easy point. Paul had practiced eye contact on girls at his high-school dances: look, look back, hold, score. It was all tricks. There was a trick to it all. Why didn't other people know that? Why did people think Paul was so strange, so easy, so lucky? He wasn't. He was just willin', like Linda Ronstadt. Paul had spent nights with men far out of his league in terms of looks and social status: men who were blindingly good-looking, with gym-toned bodies; men with new European sports cars and pockets full of gold-colored credit cards; men whose names and faces appeared in the *Village Voice*. Just look back; that was the whole trick. Everything Paul knew boiled down to this one gimmick: try for what you want. He couldn't always maintain, of course, but if you try one hundred times and you score five times, that's five more times than if you didn't try. And Paul tried for something every day, pretty much. Paul tried for a smile, a look back, an eyeful, a number, some illicit hallway kiss, a blowjob, a romance, a massage, a handjob, a finger up an ass, a free show, a licked lip, a passed note, a present, a surprise, something good, something better than the nothing he had.

Another of Paul's tricks: spot the former fatty, the hot gay man with the soft edges, the man who could have been arrogant but wasn't, who had the credentials for haughtiness but was unsure, who welcomed advances, who was flattered by attention. Like all the most successful attention-seekers, Paul was good at paying out attention, exchanging attention for attention. Attention is a price you pay for services, a currency, a mirror held up to deflect. Paul relied on his ability to attract only the sorts of attention he desired. This was how Paul had avoided the regular beatings he knew other sissy boys had endured, how he avoided the bashings, the police, the hall monitors, the store detectives, the teachers, the informants, the landlords, the bosses.

Paul had honed his skills, and by the time he was twenty-one, he could fairly accurately tell which regular-looking guy in any given elevator would be up for a bit of felching (active) or fingerbanging (passive), which shy girl was secretly dirty and which dirty girl was secretly shy. He could tell within a very close margin of error whose cock he could suck, who would drop to his knees the minute everyone else left the bathroom, which girl would beg him to shove his pussy in her face, which girl would probably expect him to lie on top of her like a man and pump for three minutes before leaking bare sperm into her vagina, that unassailable proof of the heterosexual success of all parties. Paul could tell this last type and he knew he couldn't provide what the situation required. This was the type he generally picked last in the elevator, all other factors (age, smell, gender, relationship to any socially accepted standard of beauty) being equal. Paul considered "not having a type" to be

a point of pride. He was an omnivore, an orange-hanky flagger, an aficionado of all-you-can-eat buffets.

In the elevator Paul just as often imagined the hand-holding, the running down the rainy street with, his hot palm on the striped shoulder of some boy, the being cruised, the reading Proust to, the picnicking, the kissing, the eating take-out, the spending the day in a borrowed bed—not that anyone needed to know that.

×

Paul amused himself privately in Iowa City, budding barely noticeable breasts and walking around town feeling the unfamiliar jounce under his layers, the distracting chafe of nipples against shirt. He spent afternoons at the public library, watching *Taxi zum Klo* and *The Hunger* in open carrels and enjoying the freedom from unwanted displays of public arousal his temporary vagina afforded. He tried on every abandoned prom dress at the Goodwill, a Superman of the changing stalls. He looked for opportunities, his favorite pastime.

His Intro to Film Theory class had night screenings in the new hermetically sealed Comm Studies building, a building so full of charcoal-gray carpet and expensive locked editing suites that Paul always got a little hard when he walked through the heavy swooshing door. Tonight, they were watching *Pink Flamingos.*

It was almost the end of the semester, and the long-haired grad student who TA'd the class said they could bring "beverages," so Paul brought a six of Red Stripe from the bar.

He'd hoped to impress the handsome grad student with his imported taste, but the grad student turned off the lights and left the room. Paul regarded his classmates judiciously, then pushed the cardboard carton toward them.

One of these grateful classmates, a crook-nosed skater boy named Dallas, dropped a folded-up piece of paper onto Paul's chair-desk. Paul unfolded the paper to discover a tab of Alice in Wonderland–themed windowpane. Dallas winked and tucked a similar square of paper under his own tongue, washed it down with beer, and leaned back. He kicked his extra-long legs out so his checkerboard Vans hit Paul's boot. Paul moved his boot very slightly, to see what Dallas would do. Nothing.

Why me? Paul wondered, gumming the paper, which tasted like sparkles—a placebo effect? He didn't know Dallas, but had seen him at Gabe's, at punk shows, at the Kum & Go on East Burlington microwaving cheeseburgers after the bars closed. Paul sat back and let the movie wash over him, a thin umbilical thread of acid connecting him to the skater.

Divine was actually divine, Paul thought reverently. An angry goddess. Filth was divine, not filth. Paul stared at the screen and the perfect gray carpet and at Dallas, who was marveling at his own wrists.

After Divine ate the dog shit, Dallas indicated that Paul should come with him, by which time Paul was in no position to disagree. They walked down to the river and followed it north, scouting for the rabbits who lived along the banks.

"White rabbits," Paul said.

"Rabbit holes," said Dallas.

"Holy *rabbit*," Paul said, and they had to sit down for a few weeks to laugh properly.

Night got cold. Paul rubbed his bare arms up and down many times.

"What do we do?" said Paul.

"I have beer in the place where I live," said Dallas, with some effort.

They left the lit-up riverbank, snaked through campus to Greek Row. Dallas lived in an efficiency near the frat houses, handy for selling dime bags and shrooms.

Inside his apartment, they drank many beers quickly because they were thirsty and because the alcohol didn't affect them.

"The trip is shielding us," said Paul. "We are magic."

"We can't get drunk," said Dallas.

Dallas had jerry-rigged a loft bed like a pillow fort. They sprawled underneath on a beige pleather El Camino bench seat, listening to CDs. Dallas was from Texas, and because of this, Dallas said, he had a lot of Tennessee Ernie Ford and Red Hot Chili Peppers. Paul took mental notes.

"Dude," said Dallas. "That movie."

"Right?"

"Might be cool to have both, though," Dallas said. "You know, to play with both."

They both thought quietly. Paul forgot to breathe. He was forming an idea, somewhat slowly.

"You ever play with both?"

"Naw," said Dallas, pressing buttons on the CD player. "Hey, listen to this song."

Paul listened. And while he was listening he stood with his back to Dallas, ostensibly admiring Dallas's CDs.

"This is a true song. I *feel* easy like a Sunday morning."

"Yeah," said Dallas. "And you know what, it's like—it's like *better* than the original."

"Totally," Paul said. "But it would have been even better if a woman covered it. The best cover songs fuck with gender—like a woman singing lyrics by a man."

Dallas nodded sagely. Paul thought for a moment.

"Sometimes these lyrics contain no explicit gender markers, but in such cases the paratext delivers the thrill. Who can hear Marianne Faithfull singing 'As Tears Go By' without thinking of her also inhabiting Mick Jagger's louche hip-first lean, or Belly's 'It's Not Unusual' without an amusing vision of Tom Jones's beefy confused face?"

Dallas giggled with delight, like a little kid.

"Let's face it," Paul continued. "There really *isn't* anything unusual about Tom Jones's heteronormative male gaze or his whine of dudely entitlement. Tanya Donelly reinvigorates Jones's familiar words, posits an actually unusual expression of desire: a girl's desire—possibly, probably even, queer."

"Yeah," said Dallas, suddenly very serious. "Exactly."

"Some covers deliver the age-old simple pleasures of drag—knowledge, the opportunity to investigate the simulacra and make comparisons, that obscure little frisson of dissonance. Take Joan Baez singing 'Virgil Caine is my name . . . like my father before me, I'm a working man' (which, of course, is originally from the Band's 'The Night They Drove Old Dixie Down') or Cait O'Riordan from the Pogues crooning, 'My name is Jock Stewart, I'm a canny gun man' (from the traditional 'I'm a Man You Don't Meet Every Day'). Joan Baez's contralto can, if you squint your ears, pass as a farmboy tenor; Cait O'Riordan's chalky delivery might be that of a rich ponce."

Paul rubbed his jaw professorially.

"You look like our TA right now," said Dallas.

"Think about it," said Paul. "When women cover songs by men, they don't swap the pronouns. Is this a.) a lack of anxiety about convention, b.) a biologically essential fluidity native to humans with vaginas and/or two X chromosomes, c.) rampant queerness among women singers, or d.) the universal male default?"

"Um, C?" said Dallas.

"Yes!" Paul cried. "It is all that and more. Usually the gender reversal of the singer deliciously implies queer desire, as in Siouxsie and the Banshees' 'Dear Prudence,' The Slits' 'I Heard It Through the Grapevine,' Joan Jett's 'Crimson and Clover,' Everything But The Girl's 'Alison,' or Patti Smith's 'Gloria,' in which her seductive gutterpunk vocals make the Van Morrison original sound as played-out as the locker-room boasts of a high-school football star."

Paul swigged from his empty beer can, and Dallas helpfully handed him another.

"Some covers are queerer than others, approach *jouissance*, like the Raincoats' mesmerizing cover of the Kinks' 'Lola' in which a tranny-chaser's admirably bold declaration of desire pales in its subversion next to the Raincoats' queer-on-queer fantasia of a slightly neurotic but fairly confident British butch picking up a sexy and significantly taller femme. In Suzi Quatro's bouncy 'Born to Run,' Springsteen's working-class lament becomes a queer kid's lusty paean to the joy of getting out of town with a dollop of conquest, persuading the closeted Wendy to come out. But more rarely, a man-type person might cover a song made famous by a woman-type person. Some-

times metal guys—like Megadeth's 'These Boots Are Made for Walkin''—or grunge bands—like Nirvana's 'Molly's Lips'—do covers of girl songs, but mostly these man-type people are super-queer countertenors, you know, Klaus Nomi, Neil Tennant, Jimmy Somerville, Marc Almond, who channel Motown divas or bubblegum pop stars. In these songs, the payoff is always in the uncanny, the repetition-with-a-difference, the photorealism, the *trompe l'oeil*."

Paul paced the room as he'd seen their TA do. He wished he had a chalkboard; he was worried Dallas might miss crucial points.

"Some covers offer even more esoteric delights, for specialists. For instance, in Jayne County's 'I Had Too Much to Dream Last Night,' a portion of pleasure comes from knowing that Jayne recorded the Electric Prunes'—an American band with a British Invasion sound—classic as *Wayne* County, before undergoing a sex change. In the case of the Vaselines' cover of Divine's 'You Think You're a Man, But You're Only a Boy,' the pleasure comes in the form of relief, of danger averted—in the first verse, upon hearing Frances McKee singing Divine's 'you weren't man enough to satisfy me' one naturally worries that one is encountering the beautiful lie of heteronormativity, until Eugene Kelly comes in on the second verse, after the bridge, sounding for all the world like a Scottish Fred Schneider, singing 'you weren't man enough to satisfy me' against a Casio beat. So now we have a woman declaring her dissatisfaction with a man's gender performance—or perhaps even delineating a gender difference between 'man' and 'boy'?—and a man implying it would have been *possible* for another man to satisfy him. Cer-

tainly the implication here is that all gender is performance—a pure Butlerian moment. Or consider Cyndi Lauper's 'When You Were Mine,' which becomes the lament of a girl who'd been fooling around with a straight friend, wanting more, that old familiar sucker, but which of course has its origin in Prince, a lavender menace in his own right. And then again, sometimes the most obviously queer songs—like Pansy Division's 'Smells Like Queer Spirit'—which detourn Nirvana—or Phranc's 'Gertrude Stein,' a play on Jonathan Richman's 'Pablo Picasso'—offer only anthemic live-show rewards: oh, look, we all love this funny reversal! We're all so queer! Let's go hook up in the bathroom!"

Paul glanced at Dallas, whose eyes were bright with awe.

"Yes, Dallas, it's true—maybe covers *are* particular to rock, by which I mean alternative and punk. Other genres use other words and maybe also mean something different: jazz vocalists or musical theater stars perform 'standards' or 'medleys,' and folk and country singers refer to 'traditional' songs in their liner notes, so cozy in their unassailable white straightness and not as concerned with originality or authenticity as those anxious thieving rockers. What about hip hop's obsession with sampling? Take Arrested Development's 'Everyday People,' how Speech sings Sly and the Family Stone so sweetly—almost a cover, but somehow more artistic. Hip hop uses samples as material from which to make art, whereas rock uses covers to foreground identity, performance itself the art. And of course sometimes a cover turns out not to be a cover, like PJ Harvey's 'O Stella,' which I always thought must be a cleverly feminist take on a song traditionally sung by a man, but which the liner

notes reveal to have been written by Polly Jean herself. A perfect Baudrillardian copy without an original, blissfully free of lineage . . ."

Paul was suddenly very tired. He sat down next to Dallas and the two gazed companionably at Dallas's enormous Jimi Hendrix poster.

"Dude," said Dallas.

Paul walked over to the CD player and cued up "Easy" again, hitting auto-repeat for good measure.

"Hey, you want to see something?" Paul put his body in Dallas's way, lifted Dallas's hands to his new breasts.

"Whoa," said Dallas. "Whoa! Those weren't there."

Paul made his dick tiny. Tiny and hard. Dallas fondled Paul's breasts.

"Is your name really Dallas?" said Paul.

"What?" said Dallas.

"Do you want to see something else?" Paul said, grinding his crotch into the skater's hand. Dallas unzipped Paul's cords and cupped his very small erection. My little tater tot, thought Paul fondly. He was leveling off. He drank from a nearby can of beer as Dallas swallowed his dick and balls at the same time. After he spurted on the skater's shoulder, he let his breasts melt away and his dick relax to its proper size as the skater watched.

"What—" said Dallas.

Paul zipped up and cleverly took the CD player off repeat.

"That was a good song," said Paul. "I should probably head."

"You can crash," muttered Dallas, nodding chin to chest just like Matt Dillon in *Drugstore Cowboy*. "This acid is intense."

"I'm cool," said Paul. By the time he got to the door, Dallas was asleep sitting up. Paul stopped by the QuikTrip and

bought three microwave burritos, which he ate cold walking home.

The next afternoon in class, Dallas sat in his usual seat by the door, not near Paul. He gave Paul a polite two-fingered salute and a tight little smile. Paul tried to wave back butchly but Dallas had busied himself sketching Celtic flash in a notebook.

It never happened, Paul thought. Nothing happened. And then under that, parenthetically, he thought, I am a fucking idiot, and *Crying Game*. Dallas might be a drug-dealing skateboard punk rocker right now, but at heart he was an American, at heart he was a normal straight boy. He'd cover all his tattoos with a suit at his Texas wedding. Paul wouldn't even be invited. Paul was repulsive, apart from the human flow of life; Paul was sitting alone outside waiting for a ride that would never come.

He decided not to take any more chances ever again. Ever. He wasn't ready for the obvious question that so far no one had had the opportunity to ask in the sober daylight. What *was* he? Even a film major knew that matter can't be created or destroyed. When he grew breasts, the matter must come from somewhere. When his penis went away, where did it go? Or was it all an illusion, something he could make people see? Could he get pregnant, and, if so, in which body? Could he change the baby? What if he got stuck? Could he turn himself into a tiger or a dolphin? Breathe underwater? How tall could he get—six feet, ten feet? Could he cover his body in hair, give himself a third eye?

"Paul," said the long-haired TA. "Thoughts on the Irigaray we read for today?"

"Sorry," said Paul. "What?"

×

A few miles away from a great state forest there lived a poor bookkeeper with his wife and her two small twins, whom the bookkeeper had adopted. The one's name was Paul and the other's name was Polly. The family had little to eat and no basic cable and then the bookkeeper was laid off. Although the twins qualified for free lunch and milk at school, the bookkeeper and his wife had little food to give them at night or on the weekends.

One evening as he was lying in bed worrying, the bookkeeper sighed and said to his wife, "What is to become of us?"

The bookkeeper's wife said, "If you don't get a new job, how will we pay the landlord? How will we feed the children?"

The bookkeeper replied, "In the morning, we will take the children to the forest and let them practice their scouting skills. They are not very good scouts, and will probably not find their way home, and we will not have to feed them."

"We must not do that," said the bookkeeper's wife. "We should probably not do that."

In the dark before dawn, the bookkeeper's wife awoke Paul first. She pressed a sharp pocketknife and a compass into his small hands.

"I have always loved you best, my second-born," she said. "You must come home to me."

Paul began to cry, although he did not understand his mother's words. He watched her wake his twin, who did not make a sound as their mother dressed her in the beige Brownies uniform jumper and striped blouse with Peter Pan collar and stylish orange ascot, which Paul always wanted to wear and was never allowed to, even though the siblings were the

exact same size. He looked at his own outfit, the drab blue Cub Scout shirt and trousers, the garish yellow neckerchief, and he cried louder.

"Be quiet, Paul," said Polly, when their mother had left their bedroom. "You know how they are. You will only set them off and then we will have no breakfast."

The bookkeeper and his wife bundled the twins into their Chevy Nova. Paul turned around to watch the ranch house disappear out the back window.

"Turn around, Paul," said the bookkeeper. "What are you staring at?"

"My cat," said Paul. "She is standing on our roof. I think she is trying to tell me something."

"Cats do not talk with humans," said the bookkeeper's wife. "You are too old for that kind of nonsense."

The bookkeeper and his wife drove the twins to the state forest. When they arrived at the parking area, the bookkeeper told the twins to get out.

"We will meet you there after we park the car," he said. "Just follow the path as you learned to do in Scouts."

The bookkeeper's wife gave each of the children a peanut butter and grape jelly on Wonder Bread sandwich in wax paper, saying, "Save this for lunch, for this is the last of our peanut butter and the last of our grape jelly."

"Goodbye," said the bookkeeper. "I mean, we will be right behind you."

Paul and Polly walked down the first path they saw, deep into the state forest.

Paul wept quietly as they walked, looking at the blue and red blazes on Polly's Pro Keds through his tears.

Polly led Paul confidently through the state forest. They walked and walked, without talking. Paul thought he might have seen a particular tree more than once, but he said nothing. After a long time, they reached a clearing in the middle of the pines.

"Sister," said Paul. "Let us rest here; our feet hurt and perhaps our parents will find us if we stay in one place."

"Very well, brother," said Polly. "Look, I have matches. We shall light a campfire, as I learned to do in Brownies and you will learn to do in Cub Scouts someday if you pay attention."

Paul gathered a bouquet of small pretty sticks and flowers while Polly made a ring of stones and piled thick branches high in the middle. She lit the fire, and they leaned next to each other against a bench of fallen tree trunk.

The children ate their sandwiches.

"We must beware of wolves," said Polly. "Wolves would like to eat us."

"Where are our parents?" said Paul. He fingered the pocket-knife their mother had given him.

"We have been abandoned," said Polly. "We are unloved. It is just as well."

They heard a noise, which they thought might be their parents. Instead, a pair of hikers passed by their clearing.

"Are you children lost?" asked one of the hikers.

"We are not lost," said Paul. "Our parents are on their way to meet us. They are right behind you."

The hikers were satisfied and walked on.

"Why did you say that?" said Polly. "That was our chance to get away."

"Our parents are coming," said Paul. "They must have gotten lost in the forest as we did. I am sure they will find us shortly if we only stay here."

The children gathered more firewood as the sky darkened.

"Let us sleep here, then hitchhike to Grandmother's house in the morning," said Polly. "Grandmother will bake us cookies."

The twins fell asleep, dreaming of hot cookies as they lay nestled against each other on a mossy bed under a large oak. When Paul awoke, he was cold. He could not see or feel Polly. He heard a loud animal moan in the distance and he hid behind the tree, crying out, "I am an orphan!"

"I am here, brother," said Polly. "Don't cry. I only had to pee."

In the morning, the children were very hungry.

"Let us leave these woods," said Polly. "We will call our grandmother, and she will give us something good to eat."

They walked out of the clearing, pushing away the brush until Polly discovered the red Forest Service blazes painted on the trees they passed. She led Paul back to the parking lot of the state forest, where they called their grandmother from the forest ranger's office. The phone rang and rang.

"We can just walk," said Paul to the forest ranger.

"He means our parents are meeting us at the end of the parking lot," Polly told the forest ranger, who did not feel it was right to let unaccompanied children walk along the highway.

"Well okay then," said the forest ranger, and returned to his paperwork.

Polly and Paul walked down the side of the highway toward the village where their grandmother lived. They walked and

walked, holding hands. Dozens of great violent metal beasts whirred by them without stopping, until one, a van, slowed down.

A long-haired bearded man in a cowboy hat rolled down the passenger window and leaned out.

"Do you children need a ride?" he asked.

"No," said Polly. "We are just picking wildflowers. We do not need a ride."

"All right then," said the long-haired bearded man, and drove off.

The children walked and walked. After some time, a pickup truck pulled over.

An old man rolled down his window. The children could see a slavering dog in the passenger seat.

"Where are you children going?" the old man asked gruffly.

"We are not going anywhere," said Polly. "We live just on the other side of these woods." She pointed to the strip of trees next to the highway.

"All right then," said the old man, and drove off.

The children walked and walked. After another length of time, a red convertible pulled over.

A young woman in very large sunglasses leaned out the window.

"Wouldn't you children prefer to ride?" she asked. "I am driving into the next village, where I am planning to get a milkshake. You will have to share a seat."

"Finally," muttered Polly so only Paul could hear.

She stopped walking and turned to the young woman.

"Yes," said Polly. "Thank you. We would love to ride with you in your car."

The children sat together in the front seat of the red convertible. Paul was by the door and held on to the armrest as they sped down the highway. When they arrived in the next village, where their grandmother lived, the young woman asked if they would like a milkshake before they went home.

"Yes, please," said Polly. "We have not had anything to eat today."

"You poor children," said the young woman. "First we will stop at a diner I know of and we will eat hamburgers. After that, we will get milkshakes, and then I will drive you where you wish to go."

"Thank you," said Polly, and touched Paul with her right elbow.

"Thank you," said Paul.

At the diner, the children ate hamburgers and french fries. The young woman showed them how to dip their french fries in mayonnaise, which they had never seen done before but which Paul thought sophisticated.

The young woman told them she was driving across the country.

"I am driving to a place very far away, where only women and children live," she said. "A magic land. I have provisions and room enough for one of you, if one of you would like to come with me."

"Yes," said Polly. "I will come with you. Paul will only grow up to become a man, and he will have to leave then. I will come with you and never leave."

The woman agreed with Polly's reasoning. Paul wanted to go as well but could not find an argument as fine as his sister's, so he nodded.

"Perhaps it would be best if we left immediately," said Polly. "Paul can call Grandmother from the payphone."

"Okay," said Paul.

"Brother," said Polly, and she placed her left hand formally on Paul's shoulder. He felt a strange current flow through his body. "You will be son and daughter to our parents now."

"Okay," said Paul. "That makes sense."

He handed Polly the pocketknife and compass their mother had given to him.

"Farewell, sister," he said, and watched them drive off.

<center>×</center>

Chicago was only four hours away by Greyhound and Paul didn't know anyone there, reason enough to make the trip, plus he missed starless nights lit by neon, the smell of sidewalks, rooms full of strangers.

A flâneur, he walked from the bus station to Boystown, miles up North Halsted, looking for the gays. After an hour or so, the low-slung warehouses and scrubby lots dissolved into juice bars and vintage clothing franchises, and Paul knew he was close. Chicago was a gray ocean, all concrete and big sky. He began to spot dance clubs, and piano bars, and stopped at a café with a rainbow bumper sticker in its window to change himself into something more comfortable. He'd dressed for the bus—501s and a faded black tee shirt—and in the bathroom of the café he built himself up into a taller, more muscled, and slightly hairier version of himself. He concentrated on his thighs and biceps and chest until his clothes were tight. He was headed to a bar called the Eagle, which he'd circled in the

guidebook tucked in his backpack. He realized now he could hardly take a backpack into a leather bar, so he rifled through the contents and extracted only the paperback copy of *Discipline and Punish* he was reading for school. He could fit it in his pocket, and any guy who saw it would assume it was porn. He neatly tucked his pack under a couch, in hopes that it would appear in the café's lost and found the next day. If not, he could live with the loss. On the sidewalk Paul felt light and tight, ready to see what leather guys did with other leather guys.

At the bar, they didn't even card him, he looked so right. Paul pushed past black rubber curtains, into the techno throb of the nearly empty very dark room. He walked up to the bar and ordered a can of Bud, feeling athletic in his new muscles. He wondered if he was stronger now, or if he just *looked* stronger, like a gym bunny. He hunched his shoulders—was that a deltoid?—in an attempt to flex his pecs. He'd have to work on that. He drank his beer to the industrial beat hammering inside him. A few older leather men gave him the once-over, but Paul ignored them. He wanted to find a hot young top who could show him how to be. He finished his beer, enjoying the slight tingle in his fingers. He'd wait.

The bar began to fill up with the after-work crowd, men who'd gone home from their brokerage jobs in the Loop, changed into Garanimals-style Hellfire jackets and chaps, and come out to watch next year's International Mr. Leather contestants open bottles of beer. Paul was the youngest patron in the bar by fifteen years. The music sucked. No one was being flogged and as far as he could see there wasn't even a back room. He'd somehow thought a leather bar in Chicago would be populated exclusively by young Henry Rollins–looking fire-

men and stevedores who'd immediately invite him to the dungeon. He chugged the rest of his beer and crushed the can in one hand. Super-strength? he wondered. Then again, he'd never tried to crush a beer can before.

"Not bad, little dude," said the barman.

Paul figured the barman used "little" to mean "younger" and also "medium-sized." He considered the barman, who sported a Marlon-Brando-in-*The-Wild-Ones* hat, a leather vest with no shirt, and leather chaps over a yellowed jock strap.

" 'Nother Bud," said Paul, toughly. He laid a five on the bar. The barman pushed it back at him, and Paul knew the score. He nodded a tough nod in recognition of their shared ability to communicate without anything as sissy as words. The barman nodded back, in an actual direction now: behind himself and to the left. Paul noticed a darkness he hadn't seen before, behind heavy black rubber strips, like a carwash, tinged with dim red light. A hidey-hole. He left his new beer untouched and strode into the back.

The room was small, had benches growing out of the walls, everything covered in more dark rubber. Easy cleanup, thought Paul admiringly. The barman was seamless too, his skin and the mesh of his jock and the leather of his clothes all one thing. He grabbed Paul and threw him up against a wall, and Paul stayed there, deciding, his cheekbone pressing up to the leather, which smelled like dildos and head cleaner. He huffed the wall while the barman handled his ass like an aggressive masseuse. He was getting hard and he could feel the barman's cock and he wanted to fight! He pushed himself off the wall and, turning around, pushed the barman down onto a bench. Paul fished a

rubber out of a metal can nailed to the wall. He concentrated on staying hard and not thinking about any of the things he could be thinking about. He rested his knee on the barman's ass, bare in its chaps, while he suited up his enormous new cock in one of the XL rubbers the bar had so kindly provided its all-incredibly-hung studs. The barman struggled and Paul lost control and then they were both standing, Paul with a breeze under his balls. Somebody—all these people—had come in; there were men watching, men twice his age, big men, men who wore the hides of entire cows on their massive bodies. The barman had his own hard dick out, was rubbing their dicks together. Paul avoided the eyes of the men. The barman shoved Paul back up against the wall, and he pushed Paul's pants down and Paul was holding the wall when he felt his ass cheeks pried apart and something, a finger, shoved inside. He let his jeans fall to his boots and arched back, let the barman's rubbered cock plunge into him. He clenched his jaw and his sphincter clenched, and he knew he could make himself bigger to accommodate but he didn't. He wanted this feeling of being rent. He huffed and puffed against the wall and the barman slid out of him so slowly Paul thought his guts might come out too and then in again and he did this twice more and Paul dripped a load of sperm into the rubber he was still wearing. The barman grunted, slid out, unstuck his sweaty chest from Paul, and went back to work. Paul stayed there against the wall, half-naked in the now-cold air. His head was ringing; he was having a hard time keeping his muscles in place. He rolled off the rubber, pulled up his pants, and walked straight out of the bar.

And into the feral night of Boystown, where beefy accoun-

tants and tender satyrs mingled on the sidewalks, on their way to the next wild time. Paul joined the wanderers' parade, alone and not-alone in the street-lit night, strains of deep house beckoning from doors. He felt his ass as if for the first time, getting fucked the answer to *make it new.* Paul thought about his asshole opening up into a cathedral and the smell of the wall and this feeling of being a federation of so many cosmic particles suspended in skin.

He walked up to one of the doors leaking music, a place called Foxy, paid his five dollars, and stood at the edge of the dance floor, thrumming with bass and watching the dancers. It was all red and velvet inside, a red velvet cubbyhole, and the music was the music of the past and Paul imagined all the gays on the Fire Island of yesteryear dancing their Andrew Holleran dances without nostalgia or this subterranean crust of fear. The DJ played "Good Life" and a slow remix of "Elevator Up and Down" and "(You Make Me Feel) Mighty Real" even though or maybe because *Paris Is Burning* had just played. Paul watched a beautiful boy dance with another beautiful boy or maybe girl, and felt happy to be back with people his age, instead of all the old bikermen. The kids had sneaked out! Looking like lions and birds and very young priestesses, maybe vestal virgins. And there were girls here too, dancing with each other in awkward sexiness. Paul thought about how girls used to be the good dancers, but now boys were, and how it must be weird for them but maybe nice to not be the ones everyone looks at. He thought he caught the eye of one of the girls on the dance floor, but she looked through him at another girl. Girls want to be with the girls, he thought. Girls are getting into abstract analysis. His assfuckee adrenaline drifted away with each throb from

the giant carpeted speakers, and he realized from the looseness of his clothes that he'd let his body melt back to normal.

The DJ turned Sylvester into "Got to Be Real" and Paul let himself be swept onto the floor with the ecstatic crush of revelers. He danced with his eyes closed and when he opened them he caught someone staring at him—a black-haired youth, elven in thrift-store denim bell-bottoms and a green lace-up tee shirt. The youth gamboled next to Paul, then behind him, then next to him again, like a dare. This boy was slight, even slighter than Paul, and very fine-looking with those dark eyes, those heavy lashes. Paul had to make an effort not to stare. The remix was extremely extended and Paul dripped sweat. One song became the next, never beginning or ending, and when the youth walked off the dance floor, Paul dangled there alone for a few beats, but he'd lost his rhythm. He knew he'd look desperate if he followed, but he couldn't help himself.

All the bars were dispensing weary drunken kids onto the sidewalk. The youth, alone, nicked down an alley, just in Paul's gaze. Paul trailed, houndishly. At the end of the alley, the kid turned right, and Paul kept pace. They were still in Boystown but heading east, for blocks and blocks until Paul's booted feet ached. The youth whistled now, a tune sad at times, then jaunty. Paul didn't recognize it.

About a half-block from the corner of West Hawthorne and Lake Shore Drive, Paul stopped and stood cartoonishly behind a tree. What was he even doing? He was developing a side stitch. He should go back to the clubs and find someone to take him home, so he'd have a place to sleep for the next few hours. He could see the youth at the end of the block, and he felt again the strange compulsion to follow. But he didn't want

to scare the kid off. He paused for a moment to give himself the appearance of a girl, tomboyish in his jeans but not butch, not threatening. Then he sprinted down the block.

At the corner Paul saw the youth, loping along as if to give Paul time to catch up. He watched the kid dash across the pre-dawn quiet of the first four lanes of Lake Shore Drive. Paul followed, breathing hard. The youth jumped the median into the second lap of the highway and strolled across three lanes.

Paul, trapped in the first grassy median, waited for cars to pass and caught his breath. His quarry jogged across the last four lanes, toward the grass and trees of the harbor park. Paul sprinted. He could hear the youth's whistled song, like a bread-crumb trail. He reached the park and closed in. He was close now, twenty paces behind.

The youth turned back to raise an eyebrow at Paul. Paul recognized, with a start, that the youth was now, without question, a girl. As surely as he had changed, so had the youth.

He stopped running, stood in the bright moonlight and panted.

"Hey," he said, in his own girlish voice. "Hey, wait."

The youth regarded Paul with some curiosity, then sprinted into the trees.

"Really?" Paul said. "Just like that?"

He stood for a few minutes, squinting at the trees, then turned back in the direction of the bus station. As he walked, he tried to whistle what he could remember of the youth's funny little tune.

×

A few hours later, Paul took the first bus back to Iowa City, scoring the three-seater by the bathroom so he could sleep. When he got to town, he walked home to shower off any regrets and/or fecal matter, and to dress for work in his lucky sailor outfit—peacoat, watchcap, tight blue-and-white-striped girl's shirt, and slightly scratchy high-waist wool bells. He liked to look good when he picked up a fill-in shift at the vintage shop.

Bright Iowa sun beating down on his eyelids, Paul walked his special route back downtown, through the causeway then across Iowa Ave to South Linn, to meet Christopher at the Cottage before he got off work. He entered the café, where he knew Christopher would not be, to show off his outfit to anyone interesting who might be about.

"Hey," said the Abe Lincoln–faced boy behind the counter, drawing out the "hey" in the timeless manner of gay gentlemen everywhere. "Christopher's in the back."

Paul couldn't remember the boy's name, but he thought it possible they had once made out in the hallway of one of the family housing projects across the river. Perhaps that boy who'd so artlessly pinched his nipples? Paul smiled benevolently. Bygones, he thought. No one else cute in the place, just frumpy adults discussing frumpy adult matters.

Paul ducked back out and walked around to the parking lot behind the bakery. The back door was propped open, so he poked his head inside.

"Well, hello, little faggot," said Christopher, a red bandana kerchiefed over his brown curls. "Are you hungry after your big night?"

"Yeah," said Paul. "I could eat."

"How about some hot cross buns?" Christopher turned around and spanked his own butt.

"Good lord," said Paul, accepting a bowl of bread pudding. "That is why you don't have a boyfriend. Can we get coffee too?"

After the bread pudding, Paul and Christopher took their free coffees and walked next door to the Record Collector to see if anything new had come in. They climbed up the gray carpeted stairs and opened the smoky glass door. Christopher headed for the Mary Chapin Carpenter section and Paul went straight for the used cassettes by the door. He fondled his options: Nine Inch Nails, Wire, Dinosaur Jr., Patti Smith.

"Who in this world would sell *Radio Ethiopia*?" he muttered. He remembered again that he didn't have any money. He really should get this, though. He was only going to buy it new sometime, and then he'd be losing money. It was financially smart to buy it. He put back the other tapes. The clerk watched him pointedly, which annoyed Paul, who hadn't been planning to steal anything.

"Oh, shit," said Paul. "I'm late. I have to open."

He ostentatiously returned *Radio Ethiopia* to the rack, and bade Christopher farewell. He made it to the shop on time, took the key from Madge, the owner, who was off to scout rural Salvation Armies. Paul settled into the big leather chair to think, because no one bought expensive snap shirts before noon.

Patti Smith—why was she such a genius? The cover of *Horses* was tacked to the shop wall. He tried to imagine the day Mapplethorpe took that picture, what Patti Smith had been thinking. He wished he had a cigarette. He thought about the

smell of piss baking on the August streets of the East Village. He imagined drinking Patti Smith's piss, then Robert Mapplethorpe's. Then Jean Genet's. Then River Phoenix's. He poked through the clothes on the recent arrivals rack, trying on anything that didn't require him to take off his difficult pants. He discovered that Madge's ancient Polaroid had film, and so took a picture of himself, looking almost exactly like Brad Davis. He had a million-dollar idea: he would dress up like every character in Fassbinder's *Querelle* and take pictures of himself. Maybe he could do a photo-essay for his film class instead of a final paper. He shook his picture desultorily while flipping through the racks of dresses with one hand, looking for anything that said Jeanne Moreau. When he unearthed an appropriately baroque dress (black lace on top, clingy polyester underneath), he took a picture of himself in that too, camera tilted down for the most flattering angle. He looked *good*, he thought. People should see these pictures. He could do a zine! When he was sure the pictures were dry, he tucked them into the copy of *S/Z* he was carrying around these days.

Around two, a high-school burnout kid named Zero showed up to talk about comics. They listened to Zero's Pantera tape for a while and Paul said that it was pretty good, which he truly believed while he spoke the words. He gave Zero two dollars to go get him coffee and let him keep the change. At two-thirty Paul counted out the cash box and then paced in front of the full-length mirror trying on hats until three, when Seth showed up for the late-afternoon shift.

"How much you sell today?"

"Just a pair of cords."

"Shit, Madge is gonna be bummed."

Paul shrugged and paid himself out twenty-four bucks. He had the whole afternoon free, and he was locomotive with desire for more more more. He might go back for that tape now, or first he'd stop by the ped mall to talk to the new girl at the coffee cart, or he'd hit the men's room at the Old Capitol. There was somebody he needed to talk to on just about every block and in just about every coffee shop. He established a cover story of looking for Christopher (or Jane, if he found Christopher first) and set out to find what he could find.

<p style="text-align:center">×</p>

Paul sat at the Java House with Jane, drinking a regular coffee out of one of their giant-sized mugs. He felt dainty, liked to look at his slender girlish fingers in contrast to the cup. He sneaked a look at Jane's fingers. Mannish, he thought, unwillingly. Even the femmes are a bit mannish. The minute he had confirmation (besides his own gaydar) that a subject was a homosexual, Paul compulsively searched for the flaws in that person's gender. Every gay had these flaws, Paul thought, although sometimes the flaw was being too perfect. Paul noticed this most often in men. Most women weren't very good at being women, he'd learned when he started to really study them. Like Jane, with her mannish hands. If you didn't notice her hands or know anything about her, you'd see a pretty white girl in combat boots and a Lilly Pulitzer golf skirt. Paul wondered why pretty girls were always doing stuff to look less pretty. He didn't get it at all. The prettier the girl, the more likely she was to dye her hair odd colors, to wear relentlessly out-of-style or ill-fitting clothes, to adopt unnecessary and overbearing eyeglasses. Why

did pretty girls want to hide? What was so wrong with glamour and the days of old? But Jane was different; Jane embraced and enhanced her own glamour. Jane undoubtedly knew her hands were mannish and endeavored to disguise that fact.

"Dude," said Jane. "Dude, seriously."

Paul swiveled like a hairdresser in his chair. He had not been paying attention to the correct thing, in this case Jane's disquisition on wanting-to-be vs. wanting-to-do, which as it turned out when he made her repeat her point had something to do with Barthes's distinction between a *readerly* and a *writerly* text.

Paul was flattered Jane thought he could understand what she was saying, did understand some percentage of what she was saying, and was bored by having to think that hard. He preferred to coast, when he could, on a clever association, a double entendre. He aced his film classes, in part because as a young homosexual he'd seen all the classic Hollywood movies but also because he had a dirty mind. His talent for spotting the door to sex in any situation garnered praise from college professors! He was a natural-born semiotician slash feminist-psychoanalytic reader. The dirty-mind method also worked in English classes, with the younger professors.

"Barthes was really into wrestlers," said Paul, although Jane had not been talking about wrestling.

"I know," Jane said. "Everybody knows that, Paul."

"Oh, burn!" Paul said. He felt good-naturedly dumb. Let Jane be the smart one. She liked that; she was *that* sort of pretty girl.

Jane, he suspected, had actually read all the books on her shelves, but when they went to Jane's department parties, all

the assistant professors laughed at Paul's jokes. He loved being treated as a precocious child and found ways to work into the conversation that he was only a sophomore. No one had to know he'd taken time off, that he was the same age as some of the grad students.

"You look different," Jane said. "Did you get a haircut?"

"No," said Paul, running his fingers through his hair to check. "Oh, wait, no, I did snip a little here and there. Makes such a difference!" He'd actually just forgotten to change all the way back after his encounter with the youth, but he could hardly tell Jane that. He casually crossed his arms in front of his small breasts, hunching his shoulders very slightly in a gesture of elegant repose.

"Want another coffee?" Jane asked. "I'm buying."

Paul nodded. He knew she wanted an excuse to stare at that counter girl up close; he could grant that the counter girl had cute glasses, but she couldn't handle a crowd, always had to ask for your order twice. His mind wandered to the youth he'd seen in Chicago—the youth was one of the thoughts he had on heavy, if involuntary, rotation today. He mentally planned an itinerary for his next trip to Chicago. He'd go to all the places he himself would be likely to go. The youth was like him, must be. Paul would go back to Foxy, would spring for a ticket to see that Pomo Afro Homos show, would see Sister George play at Homocore. He could place a Missed Connection in the *Chicago Reader*, but what would he say? If he could find the youth, he'd know what to ask.

×

Paul was never very good at having friends. If he liked some-
one enough to get to know them, he'd want to suck their cocks
or even just make out after weeks of prolonged staring. That
might be his favorite. Paul perfected his stalking in Iowa City:
on line for ice cream at the Great Mid, on line for the bath-
room at Gabe's, on line for coffee at the Cottage, in the study
carrels across from the fifth-floor men's room of the university
library, in the English-Philosophy building, on the ped mall.
He'd see some sparking boy in a crowd of bodies and he'd regis-
ter that boy's walk, his locks, his red jacket. Now he'd pick that
boy out in any size crowd, out the Cambus window, on bikes.
He'd home in on the boy, ask around for his job, what bands
he liked. Paul would arrange himself to be regularly just at the
periphery of that boy's vision. He'd drop by the café or movie
theater or departmental office where the boy worked and he'd
not say hi. He'd ignore the boy pointedly at shows, in the Stu-
dent Union, at any bar in town. One day, he'd approach the boy
on the ped mall and ask for a cigarette or the time or a dime
for the phone, and the boy would laugh shyly and give Paul
whatever he'd asked for and agree to meet him later at the club.
Sometimes Paul would wait until he saw the boy across a party
or a bar and then he might muscle up to the boy in a small
space and say "Who are you?" to which the boy might reply,
"You're Paul, right?" or "What took you so long?" or "I have to
be at the airport at 5:30; do what you have to do." Paul kept lists
of his crushes by name or identifying feature in a special red
composition notebook. Every few months he'd flip through the
pages, marveling at a time when Felix had been only *The Boy
with the Limp*, Martin Williams *The Comp Lit Guy*, and Ryan

That Girl's Boyfriend. Paul regularly rewrote his lists, both to neaten his printing and to adjust the rankings of his desires. He'd read a novel about a guy who kept track of everybody he'd hooked up with, kept score, and Paul thought maybe he should keep track. But in life, as in the book, Paul had lost count—

×

—At the Old Capitol Mall food court, Paul follows a handsome dark-haired youngman into the men's room. The youngman stands at a urinal, unzips his pants, eyes on Paul the whole time. Paul stands two urinals down, hand on his fly. The youngman watches Paul, strokes his thick cock. He frisks Paul with his eyes and Paul looks away. He's seen the youngman's cards: he—Paul—is desired. The youngman will risk beating or humiliation for the chance to touch Paul, and so Paul has won. Paul tries and fails to remember the very first time a man approached him in a restroom. He has never approached a man in a restroom, or anywhere else, has never given anyone the pleasure of knowing they were hunted by him. Paul is the game; Paul hunts only hunters. He hunts to be hunted.

Paul turns cruelly from the youngman and his thick cock, unzips, and pisses a bus-ride's worth of pop onto the white cake.

"Whatever," says the youngman.

Another man, thin and balding, has noticed the youngman and has taken what would have been Paul's place at the adjoining urinal. A math teacher, thinks Paul. The balding man stares at the youngman's cock, then glances at Paul. Is his expression one of triumph or invitation? What does he think, that he's Paul's competition? That he and Paul are competing for the

youngman? The youngman is competing for Paul and he has lost. That's reality.

Paul is disturbed but he won't show it. He shakes off abruptly, half-hard and fluttering pissdrops. He stuffs his cock back into his low-slung Levi's, admiring his bulge. He broadcasts his disdain as he stands at the sink. He runs a pocket comb once through his hair, putting the youngman and the balding man in their places as he attends to his ablutions. Their sexual activity is petty, worthy of no attention. Paul *is* sex, he is effortlessly sexual, effortlessly masculine.

Paul possesses the sort of masculinity that distracts men and women, that makes some men angry. This has always been true. There is a type of man, often the father of a friend or a coach, who upon meeting Paul disapproves of him and will not say why. There is a type of woman who will not be able to stop herself, who will reach out and stroke Paul's face, who will try to ascertain if Paul is as young as his hairless cheeks make him seem. There is a type of person, man or woman, who will approach Paul on the street and ask him straight out to identify himself. They'll say: What are you, Hispanic? Ay-rab? or Are you a boy or a girl? Paul is accustomed to these reactions, these ministrations; his body is public property, his face a test.

Paul leaves the bathroom and the mall, unsated—

×

"I'm not a fag hag," said Jane. She could tell Paul wasn't listening. "I can't stand that people think I'm a fag hag."

"Nobody thinks you're a fag hag," Paul said, in his soothing voice.

"Ugh," said Jane. "They do, and what's worse they think I'm *your* hag. I can't stand it. I can't *bear* it. Do I have to stomp around town in a three-piece suit? I will do it. I will. Who do I have to fuck to get *seen* around here? These people act like Joan Nestle never existed."

Jane sucked on her straw, considering herself as a possible hysteric. She should put in a chapter on reclaiming the hysterical woman. Or was that too '8os?

"These people have never heard of Joan Nestle," said Paul, with a calm Jane found enraging, a calm that echoed her brothers'—the puerile, penile calm of success. Even the best ones are patriarchal, Jane thought.

They sat in the creamsicle still of the Hardee's on the ped mall, relishing the free air conditioning. Paul claimed to like the free pop refills, but Jane suspected he just liked saying "pop" for trade realness. Frat and farm boys loitered at the other orange tables, scowling at Jane with lust and displeasure. Even before she'd had a conscious sexual thought about a woman, she'd been wrong to men. All her life. Smelled wrong or something. Jane was alternately drawn to and horrified by Darwinism, and often found herself attributing phenomena to the unseeable (hormones, pheromones) despite her strict identification as a social constructionist. This was one of her sore places. Was biology destiny, in fact? That might really fuck up not only her identity but her dissertation.

"There's no one cute in this entire town," said Jane. "I am so desperate for temporary love I am actually considering the Michigan Womyn's Music Festival."

"But you *disdain* Michigan," said Paul.

They left Hardee's and headed to the miniature indoor strip mall of alternative culture shops where they spent most of their student loan money.

"I do disdain Michigan, but there's nobody here. We live in a desert of androgynous softball players. A butchless desert."

"Maybe we should both go to Michigan," said Paul, with an irksome confidence.

"It's daytime too, you know," Jane said. "I'm not saying you don't look great in drag, but . . ."

Paul was unnaturally quiet. They walked into the magazine shop and perused the zines and alternative comics and glossy art magazines and other expensively made limited-edition paper goods.

"Ooh," said Jane, holding up a package of serial killer trading cards for Paul to admire. "Sometimes I wish I did American Studies. They get everything nice."

They moved on to the vintage clothing shop next door. Jane tried on a rabbit fur vest. Paul tried on a moddish white leather jacket.

"Isn't this so Emma Peel?" he said. "Don't I look like a *spy*?"

"It's *darling*," said Jane, and immediately experienced a spasm of impostor shame. She knew she camped it up around Paul, and wondered if he camped it up around her, if they were anxious collaborators in a consolidation of something supposedly shared rather than actual friends. She wondered if anyone had any real friends, when it came to that. How could straight people, for instance, have real friends when their entire lives were an inhabitation of a myth? She felt better, as she always did when she brought herself around to a critique of the het-

eropatriarchy. Paul hadn't noticed anything; he was admiring himself in a large wood-framed mirror studded with antlers. The jacket fit him so well Jane was annoyed, then guilty.

"Okay, we'll go to Michigan together," she said. "It'll be like *Just One of the Guys* in reverse. I'll create diversions so you can pee. We'll get you a bra and stuff it with tissues!"

"I have to show you something," Paul said. He folded the jacket over his arm and fingered a sweatshirt from the 1950s. "But not here."

×

Paul chafed at this second coming out, at being *in* again at all, and so suddenly. Is it endless? he thought, like Russian nesting dolls, with no tiny solid center?

He had begun to read Anne Rice and Octavia Butler books—maybe he was a vampire? or an immortal body snatcher?—with the intensity with which he had once read James Baldwin and Edmund White and checked out stacks of videotapes (*The Lost Boys, Cat People, The Company of Wolves*) from the public library, looking for something, anything, that might speak to his condition. The closest thing he found was *Orlando*, but Paul wasn't some count slash ess who could just instruct the servants in his castle to be cool. He had to think logistically.

He'd sensed his own nascent malleability for years, since childhood. At first, he'd assumed all gays were like him and had quietly decided not to mention that they could choose. But he had pieced together over time, without revealing too much, that he was even to the gays a freak. He was alone in this world. He regarded other gays now with mild condescension. He had gone

through the door in the last adventure in Narnia, and they were like poor Susan with her nylons, stuck on the train (although what was wrong with "nylons and lipstick and invitations" Paul had never quite worked out). For instance, Jane was a Susan. But she was also his friend. And she'd been starting to suspect something, Paul could tell. He'd decided to confide in her; maybe it would feel good, maybe he could relive those high-wire blasts of relief he'd felt in his previous big gay milestones.* Maybe if she knew, she could help him take better pictures for his zine.

Back at Paul's house, Jane smoked a clove cigarette coolly,

* • First admission to self: at nine, after hearing Richie Spagnoletti call the music teacher Mr. Plummer a queer.
• First admission to another human being: freshman year of high school phone call to the Albany Crisis Hotline, while his parents were out to dinner and Ari was asleep.
• First admission to an actual friend: Heather Federson, senior year of high school.
• First gay tee shirt: a white shirt with the words ACT UP!, which he wore under his uniform button-downs the last month of high school. Or maybe the Keith Haring radiating baby shirt Heather Federson brought him back from her weekend in the city? One of the two.
• First gay book: *A Boy's Own Story*, snuck-read in the Troy public library at age twelve.
• First gay friend: Justin Rosenblum, though Paul denied the friendship at the time to anyone who asked.
• First gay handjob received (abortive): from Justin Rosenblum, junior year of high school, in Justin Rosenblum's bedroom with "Free Nelson Mandela" on the record player.
• First gay handjob given (prematurely concluded): to Justin Rosenblum, junior year of high school, also in Justin Rosenblum's bedroom with "Free Nelson Mandela" on the record player.
• First (partial) blowjob received: from Justin Rosenblum, two weeks before Paul's graduation, in the Rosenblum family's poolhouse.
• First blowjob given: to Johnny Pallazola, summer after high school, after three years of Johnny gay-baiting Paul, in the woods at the end of the cul-de-sac where Paul lived.
• First ear piercing: left ear, silver hoop, first weekend at college, 1989.

tapping her ash into one of Christopher's floral-print teacups as she watched Paul take off his shirt and unbutton his jeans' first two buttons.

"I've seen you naked, Paul, and it doesn't do anything for me." She sat back on the futon, narrowing her eyes like a stockbroker at a titty bar, and blew a series of spicy smoke rings.

"Just wait," he said, concentrating. He thumbed his jeans and briefs down to mid-thigh, exposing his pussy to the cold air. His ass clenched a little.

"Dude," said Jane. "You're tucking. Nice tucking."

"No," Paul said. He pulled his labia apart to expose the shiny red skin, his clit, that extra slitted hole whose name he did not know.

Jane, for once, had nothing to say.

He extended his finger to Jane's nose.

"Does that smell like penis to you?"

Jane sniffed his finger, frowning.

Paul let his concentration lapse, let his clit expand back into cock, his hole close up into taint, his labia drop heavily into nutsack. Jane stared, still completely silent.

"You can't tell anybody," he said. He patted his package through his briefs, then pulled his jeans back up.

• First gay kiss: Justin Rosenblum, Homecoming weekend visit to Paul at SUNY-Binghamton.

• Discovery of HQ76: first year of college, Bartle Library, Binghamton.

• First group of gay friends: at Binghamton, the motley gang of sincere, pimply, waxy-skinned boys and girls who'd gather giddily in each other's dorm rooms for John Waters or Joan Crawford film fests.

• First Gay Pride Parade: New York, 1991.

• First official boyfriend: Tony Pinto, New York, July–August 1991.

• First anal sex given: to Tony Pinto, New York, August 1991.

• First anal sex received: from Tony Pinto, Iowa City, December 1991.

"Of course not," said Jane. "If anyone finds out about this, you'll be a total guinea pig."

Paul could practically see the gears turning in her head; she was getting excited about some thought she was having.

"Yeah," he said, emphatically. "And that would suck."

Paul walked out of his bedroom and rummaged in the refrigerator. He preferred to hang out at Jane's house where there was food. He located a single can of Squirt, which he bought for the name. He held it up to Jane and she shook her head.

"But I actually do want to go to Michigan in August," he said. "Don't you want to go with me now? We'll have so much fun!"

Jane picked up her backpack, heavy with library books she was taking home to keep unopened next to her bed for the next eight months.

"I'll think about it," she said. "I don't want to get my ass kicked by a gang of Indigo Girls-worshipping, softball-playing wo-per-daughters with mullets and fanny packs. They're extremely particular about their 'womon-only space.'"

"We won't get in trouble," said Paul. "They'll never know."

Jane looked over the top of her sunglasses. "Maybe," she said.

×

Once upon a time there was a sweet darling young wolf who lived alone in the forest and loved pretty things. Now, this wolf was a strange wolf, quite small, maybe part coyote on his mother's side, or maybe his father was a fox—no one knew. The

pack had reared him after his mother died, as the pack does, but he knew they did not mind his absence, found him easier to miss than accommodate.

Out on his own, the young wolf had been lonely at first but also happy to be in the center of such beauty. The wolf loved the little violets that grew in the grass, the dappled sunlight on soft pine needles, the sharp shiny icicles hanging from the trees, the little thatched cottage where the old human woman lived, maybe even the old human woman herself. He studied her every day, admiring her soft furless skin like fallen leaves, her silver and red hair so like his own handsome coat, her raspy bark, how she gestured delicately with her thin little paws. He watched her read her books by the fire, soak in her claw-foot tub, mate occasionally with a bad-smelling woodsman. What did she think about, he wondered. Why did she do the things she did?

The young wolf struck up a camaraderie with an old fox who also lived near the cottage. Sometimes the old fox and the young wolf watched the human woman together, with no discussion. Did they love her? Want to eat her? The wolf didn't know.

One morning, having gone out of his way to avoid the nasty-smelling woodsman, the wolf found himself near the loud bland human path through the undergrowth. He snacked on a few blackberries here and there, and made one desultory pass at a too-quick rabbit as he wandered pleasurably through the undergrowth. As he neared the path, the wolf smelled something disturbing—human adolescent commingled with old milk, dead meat, smoke, and yeast. He could hear the blundering human sounds: crunching footsteps, a low song. He

crept closer to look, and a child—really a maiden—passed. The maiden was a younger version of the old woman, a sort of pup, draped in a gorgeous expensive-seeming blood-red cloak. The wolf thought he might like to wear that cloak. He felt mysteriously compelled to reveal himself, but he did not know how to do so without frightening the human maiden and so stayed hidden. He consulted with his friend the fox.

"Ah yes," said the old fox. "Hmm. There is more to you than meets the eye, isn't there?"

"I don't know," said the wolf, sadly. "I don't know what I am."

The old fox smiled a dangerous toothy smile.

"I will try to teach you," he said. "You may learn; you may not."

After many days and nights, the young wolf did learn some small measure of the old fox's teaching. When the maiden next came up the human path, the young wolf knew mostly what to do. He revealed himself, and when the maiden went still with fear, the young wolf pounced right into her, just like that. The young wolf stroked his furless soft hands, cuddled into the longed-for velvety red cloak, and set off, weak but tall, to meet his beloved old human woman.

Jane got them through the gates of the festival, though Paul totally could've. He wasn't that nervous. They accepted their work crew assignments, happy not to pay for the ticket, and secure in the knowledge (which Jane had gleaned from her one-night stand with a girl from Toronto) that the cool people at the Michigan Womyn's Music Festival were the workers.

Paul had maybe overdone his outfit. He wore a heather-pink Farrah Fawcett tee shirt with the sleeves chopped off, black leather wristcuffs, cutoff Levi's, a spiked belt, and engineer boots with striped tube socks stretching up his calves. His hair was Tatum O'Neal scruffy (*Little Darlings* era), he wore sunglasses, and he eschewed a bra, for dyke realness. He had heard from Jane (who had heard from the Toronto girl) that going topless was a thing at Michigan. He could go topless. He was feeling pretty liberated.

"Do I look dykey enough?" he asked.

"You'll do," said Jane, who had given herself a flapper haircut before they left and was currently lipsticking an extra-long cigarette holder as she leaned out the driver's window of her hatchback. "Do I look like a tasty morsel for one of those hot San Francisco butches?"

"Um," said Paul. "Sure."

"Let's find the ladies," said Jane, parking.

"Watch out, ladies," said Paul, strapping on Jane's backpack and hugging their two borrowed sleeping bags. "I am feeling

very sex positive, very Gayle Rubin. I have a somewhat Persistent Desire."

"I love that you're a big dyke now, Paul. I really do. But if you cramp my style I will out you so fast your head will spin."

" 'No political revolution is possible without a radical shift in one's notion of the possible and the real,' " said Paul.

"Seriously?" said Jane, distracted by a flat-topped person with an armload of timber. "Ooh, looky!"

Jane gripped the map they'd been given at check-in, and led Paul down a dirt path to a clearing.

"Here," she said, dropping tent and duffel and making small satisfied noises.

Paul set himself to gathering kindling so he wouldn't have to admit he didn't know how to pitch a tent. He hadn't been a Boy Scout. He rested a stack of twigs next to their duffels as Jane expertly erected the borrowed four-man tent.

"Wow," said Paul. "It's palatial."

"I love camping," said Jane, with alienating sincerity. She was sort of *outdoorsy*, Paul realized, as perhaps were all lesbians at heart. How was he going to pass for two entire weeks in the woods?

"I have to pee," he said. "I'm going to find a nice private 'Porto-Jane.' "

Jane gave a reassuring snort at Paul's scare-quotes. She was still his friend; she wasn't a Stepford lesbian just because they were at Michigan and she had all this secret knowledge of tents.

"Go ahead," she said. "I'm going to finish this up and explore for a bit. But I'll meet you at the dinner thing."

"Please," said Paul. "Come with me. I need an escort. It's vegetarian!"

"Just for tonight," she said. "Then I am done babysitting you."

Paul set off. He saw a few clumps of people who mostly ignored him: hippies sporting Deadhead bandanas and patchouli he could smell from fifteen feet, two sensitive shaved-head punks in all black and Fluevogs, and some San Francisco types. Paul wasn't used to being ignored, but he didn't mind the opportunity to scope the scene. He walked around the skeletal paths, down the paved road (cutely called Lois Lane), past various tents with workers already busy inside. He and Jane didn't have work shifts until the next day, and they were on different crews: Paul cooking and Jane working security in a scheme to meet butches. He wanted the lay of the land, as he always did, so he walked and walked, memorizing landmark trees.

Back at the campsite, he found Jane deep in flirtation with Flat-Top.

"This is Frog," said Jane. "Frog, meet my friend—"

"Polly," said Paul quickly, unconvinced of Jane's solidarity or memory. "Nice to meet you."

Frog, conveniently camped one site over and on Long Crew, led them to dinner, impressing Jane and boring Paul, who decided Jane was settling again. Why not look around a bit more? he thought. It's a game preserve.

Over bowls of lentils and brown rice, Frog explained the Michigan lore.

"Y'all are called 'Festival Virgins,'" said Frog.

"Will we be hazed?" said Jane, coyly.

"There may be hazing," said Frog.

Oh gross, thought Paul, and began to look around the area called the Fire Pit, where all the workers had assembled to eat.

He saw the hippies and the sensitive punks from his earlier travels, and a raucous gang of obviously San Franciscan butches and extremely high femmes, but mostly he saw androgynous '70s lesbians, surprisingly appealing in their labrys necklaces and Rosie the Riveter tee shirts. Paul felt like a time traveler, a tourist at a gay reenactment—Hidden-from-History Town.

Frog introduced them to friends from Austin, too many to remember names. Paul was tired from the six-hour drive.

"I've got to go to bed," he said in Jane's ear, as he'd seen girls do all his life. "You stay if you want."

"No, that's *good*," she whispered back. "I'm coming."

They said their goodbyes and walked back to their tent.

"I'm whupped," said Paul. He was glad it was so cold he could sleep in layers, and his own hair was almost as long as his girl hair, so even if someone surprised him in the night with his defenses down, they probably couldn't see the difference.

The next morning, Paul's first big test was at hand: a work shift without Jane. He picked his way from their campsite to the kitchen tent, where he was set to the task of chopping potatoes and carrots for an epic vegetarian stew. The tent reminded him of catering jobs he'd worked at the Troy Golf Club, shucking corn and eyeing caddies. Except the music was better, because somebody had a boom box and was playing L7.

"I love L7," Paul said. Dykes were so cool. What could be more punk than being a dyke? What better way to say fuck you to the Man?

A tall butch in a railroad engineer's cap and two full sleeves of Vargas girls tattoos exhaled derisive air in Paul's direction and hefted a twenty-five-gallon plastic tub of tahini on the metal worktable. Her partner in hummus—smaller, equally

tattooed, and mohawked—chopped garlic furiously and muttered something about Seattle poseurs. Paul realized his mistake immediately.

"I mean, I love L7's old stuff, before they got all big. I'm more into the Sub Pop days, you know?"

Team Hummus gave Paul the collective stinkeye and he decided that silence might be the better part of valor. He purposefully turned back to his potatoes, trying to chop in the most dykey way. Everyone else in the kitchen cut their vegetables so confidently. Paul looked at Sheela, the crew leader, for reassurance that his potatoes were small enough. Sheela was kind, an old-timey lesbian who lived year round on women's land outside Santa Cruz, belonged to the Long Crew, and liked to "nourish all the beautiful women who made the festival what it was," as she'd helpfully explained to new dyke Paul when he first showed up at the tent. Sheela gave a supportive thumb's-up to Paul's potatoes on her way to the pantry.

Paul did a quick nervous body check, under cover of patting down his apron; he hadn't been paying attention, and everything had stayed in place. He was getting good at this.

"You done already? You're a good little worker bee."

Sheela set a ten-pound bag of carrots in front of Paul.

"Same size as the taters," she said cheerfully.

The Hummus Butches disappeared out to the Fire Pit for a smoke, and Sheela popped a Phranc tape in the box.

"This is more my speed," she said, winking at Paul, who felt a brief surge of pleasure at being included.

A brown-haired girl who'd been washing dishes the whole time walked over from the sinks, drying her hands on her pants, and checked something off on an official-looking clipboard.

"I actually like L7 too," she said. "Don't let them intimidate you."

"Thanks," said Paul, pleased to be rescued, to be thought in need of rescue. "I'm Polly."

"Diane," said the girl. "Is this your first time here?"

"Yeah," said Paul. "Pretty obvious, I guess."

"No, I mean, it's mine too," said Diane. "I just came because my friend was coming, but I like it so far."

Paul wondered if she was flirting with him. She was pretty, bigger than the waifs of all genders he often noticed first. She had greasy dark brown hair hanging in her eyes and wore an A-shirt (which Paul had just learned not to call a wife beater), threadbare black workpants, and boots. Diane was road-tripping from Olympia. She'd just graduated from Evergreen (like Kathleen Hanna, Paul thought), where she'd done a concentration in visual arts/sculpture, focusing on ceramics. She didn't know where she lived. Everything she owned was in her car, and she'd come to the festival as a last hurrah with a bunch of her friends from Olympia, including her best friend Zoe, who'd gone on the prowl and left her.

"Oh, that sucks," said Paul, experimenting with the idea that being left by your friend in a crowd of strangers would be a *bad* thing.

"Right?" said Diane.

"Actually, I'm pretty sure my friend ditched me too," Paul said.

"Then we'll just have to hang out," said Diane, and Paul felt a flutter of shyness, a shy girl flutter, the flutter of not knowing if he was making a friend or something else. This was a strange

experience for him, for whom all were prey, and he located the feeling in his new body. He was now having girl-feelings. Weird.

×

After they cleaned up from the dinner rush, Sheela released them into the evening.

"You gals go have a good time now!" she said, as Paul and Diane tumbled out of the kitchen tent and realized eight hours had passed. They stood and looked at each other for a moment in the woodsmoke dusk. Outside, workers from Sec/Comm, Front Gate, DART—all the other crews—reclined in various states of exhaustion, flirtation, and sisterhood.

"Do you want to maybe go for a walk in the woods?" said Diane.

Paul thought for a moment, and was startled to discover that he indeed *did* want to go for a walk in the woods. He hadn't been near any woods since high school, when he'd convince Justin Rosenblum to head as far away from school as possible during free periods so no one would see ambiguous Paul talking to the known fag. Poor Justin, thought Paul, and suppressed a nameless something which threatened to bloom into guilt.

Paul followed Diane past the crowds. She was sort of an *in-charge person*, he realized, but not bossy. She led him down to the place where the official trod-down paths ended and into what Paul couldn't help but consider the wilderness.

"Should we leave breadcrumbs?" he asked.

"Are you scared?" Diane said. She turned and appraised him.

"Of course not," said Paul, and they kept walking in the trees. The August light filtered through the canopy. Paul's work sweat, drying on his back and between his breasts, cooled him in the sweet warm dusk. His skin was electric, buzzing, humming like drugs, like fear, like New York City sidewalks, like any moment before any time he'd ever kissed anyone important. Paul breathed in the walk-in-closet smell of the forest floor and waited for dark, toggling between the pleasures of trusting and fearing a stranger, as they walked and walked.

"Look," breathed Diane, and bridged two fingers to Paul's wrist.

He followed her eyes to a doe. He had forgotten about animals. She pressed his wrist again and he looked to the left, saw another doe, and tried to exhale his pent-up air noiselessly but failed. Both animals shot through the trees. Diane ran after, and Paul followed, into the open, out to a dark purple meadow. The deer were gone to wherever deer go. Paul flopped down in the high grass next to Diane, who was looking up at the darkening sky.

"Smells good," she said.

"Yeah."

They lay in the field, smelling grass and the night. Paul's mind flooded with questions—What was Jane up to? Had any famous performers arrived? Should he be making himself available to meet other possibly cuter people? Did Diane want to kiss him or was he projecting?—and then the flood receded, unusual for him. Diane moved her head to look at him, and he looked away. He just wanted a lark, to pass, to pass among all these women, to sleep with a bunch of people. And now this

girl was looking at him, and seeing something he either was or wasn't.

Diane leaned up on her elbow with a kind of tomboy grace. Paul felt nervous. Paul never felt nervous before whatever variation on what he thought was about to happen. He licked his lips, which seemed remarkably soft to him, softer than his normal lips, which so many men had proclaimed so especially soft. Maybe not that many men, but more than a few. And Tony Pinto. Paul touched his bottom lip with his thumb in a gesture he meant earnestly, which is to say he did not mean at all but which he knew to be—had often deployed as—the gesture of a provocative naïf. Words pattered through his mind, and then Diane leaned over and kissed him, which shut all the words up. How hot her mouth was, and how soft *her* lips! She climbed on top of him, boarded him, lay *atop* him kissing and gesturing on his electric skin, his breasts, his belly through his deliberately thin tee shirt. He felt the rightness of his tee shirt for the moment and the pounding thrum in his vagina, where he could feel Diane's leg, electric. He was lightheaded from lack of air and kissed through his dizziness, miraculously still alive. He sneaked his eyes open and, still kissing, stared at the rosy crepe of Diane's eyelids, until the sleepy pull of the kiss told him that she was lightheaded and sneaking and sleepy too, that they were in league.

"How long do you think we can kiss for?" Diane said.

"Hours," said Paul. "Hours and hours. A hundred hours? Seven hours. I don't know."

They kissed more, with this dare in their heads, and then Paul couldn't take doing nothing else, her hands all over him. He slid his hand down her workpants into the slidey packet of

her, and felt some kind of jittery bursting in his own self, and she jangled out of her clothes to give his hand a better angle to get inside her and he cupped his fingers up inside her, mouth on her nipple, under her pushed-up shirt. His hands somehow knew what to do and he realized that he'd slid his entire hand inside her without asking. She squeezed his knuckles and he tried to tuck his thumb without hurting her, because of how many lectures on safe fisting, and how different could a vagina be? He wondered if she would break his hand with her throbbing and then he surrendered to the immediate need to suck on something and bent to her clit, where he felt exceedingly peaceful for a long time, sucking and slowly moving his fist, so slowly, until she began to come, or come again?, through which Paul just hung on, which seemed to be the right thing. Afterward she smiled at him and they kissed and Paul felt floppy and amped and disturbed in a way he thought might be connected to not having come. Or had he? Things were very sloshy down there and had maybe changed states in some incomprehensible way. Diane was kissing him again, and again this dispelled the thinking and then somehow she had slid between his legs, pulled off his shorts, and was sucking on his girl parts through and then under his hot soaking panties, building to a violent universal bang. Then it was over, and he was just smelling crushed grass and sex and the starry night all over him.

Diane led Paul through the night woods to the main path, and pointed him toward his campsite. Paul wanted to get away from her so he could gloat and also relax his guard, and only after they'd said a chaste goodbye at a fork in the path did he wonder if she wanted to get away from him for some other reason.

He made it back to the tent and collapsed on top of his sleeping bag. Where was Jane? He needed to debrief. He let his body relax into his normal shape, and realized how tired he was from the effort of concentration during sex and over the last two days. His soft penis felt strange in his bought-for-the-trip panties, like an overgrowth. What would Diane think if she knew? How long could he stay a girl without relaxing? And so on, until sleep took him.

×

He needed to piss and—whose body? oh, Jane, phew—white morning light through the tent flap and birds, shockingly loud birds, how loud those birds!—and he was up. In every way.

Paul had always considered the piss hard-on obnoxiously, frattishly sexy in others and a biological imperative in himself, but now it was one more element to control. He concentrated on shifting back into his girl body but couldn't get beyond the breasts. He pulled on his navy blue hooded sweatshirt, glanced at Jane drooling on her pillow of balled-up clothes, and wriggled out of the tent hoping like a middle schooler that his pants were baggy enough. The campsite was quiet, no signs of life from the two other tents. Paul sneaked through the brush to a large tree he hoped was out of sight, pulled down his pants, and squatted with his hand covering his half-hard dick, hoping he could avoid wetting his panties. The more he tried to squeeze out the piss the harder he got. He watched the tents like a sniper, furiously rubbed out a teaspoon of sperm into his palm, buried it in the black dirt beneath him, and then finally, finally the great release. His bladder empty, he found he could let his

vagina return, still dripping piss. The leaves seemed dirty, so he wiped with his hand. He looked up and realized people were stirring at the tents, building campfires, returning from their own peeing missions. He wasn't ready to be discovered; when he'd come into his hand he'd thought, unbidden, of Diane, and he wanted more of whatever was here. He'd need to be careful.

Jane was up, looking like a field hockey player in her sweatpants and creased sleep face. Paul told her so and she punched him on the arm and he squealed.

"You're going to have to rein in the faggotry," Jane said.

"Can't I just be a femme?" said Paul.

Jane rolled her eyes.

"Seriously," said Paul. "I think I'm a femme."

"You're not a femme," said Jane. "Trust me."

Paul wondered if she was right.

They tidied up their tent and headed to the breakfast area, briefly sketching their respective conquests while eyeing the scene. He and Jane were well matched as conquistadors, Paul thought, because neither took the other's wandering eye personally. He felt a surge of appreciation for Jane. None of his fag friends could do that; when he went cruising with another guy he ended up competing with or fucking him. Maybe women *are* less competitive, he thought, and felt a pleasurable second-wave sisterliness.

Early-rising crews of workers roamed the paths, hammering down rugs on the dirt for wheelchairs and shouting into walkie-talkies to prepare for the first day of the festival week. Paul and Jane ate gloppy oatmeal at one end of a picnic table, silently discussing the surrounding talent with a system of eye and eyebrow gestures. Jane had a night shift and headed off to leisurely scope new arrivals, in case she wanted to trade up from

Frog. Paul headed to his day shift. He pictured Diane, moments away, and shivered internally. But when he arrived it was no Sheela, no Diane—just some new shift leader, the Hummus Butches, and women's music. Torture! He sneaked a look at the posted schedule: Diane wasn't due in until the next day. And they weren't scheduled together again until Wednesday. She was probably off right now meeting someone else.

Paul chopped his pile of carrots carefully, languishing in the sad earnestness of the woman who was driving away from something upsetting in a fast car, the one who was closer to being fine, the one for whom life was like a brook, and all the others, those amber divas of lesbian melancholy so different from his gayboy ideas of women who were *every* woman, women for whom no mountain was too high, women who remembered the ways things were. Those hard sneering punks with their chains would never get it, not like sensitive Paul, suffused Paul, Paul of the slow hand and the capacious heart. Where was Diane? Why did he care? He resolved to look around for a better catch once his shift was up. One of the butches (he still couldn't tell them apart) popped a new tape into the box. Paul identified the early strains of Hole's *Pretty on the Inside* just before the shift leader punched eject.

"Oh, come *on*," said the punk. "It's only one guy and all he does is play the guitar."

"No men's music on the land, you know that," said the shift leader. She handed the cassette to the butch and put in Joan Armatrading. "Did you get a break yet, Polly? Go, go! Don't be shy."

Paul, grateful, made himself a cheese sandwich and walked outside the tent for the first time in hours. His shift was almost

over, which was always the best time to take a break anyway. Funny to come all the way to Michigan to work in a restaurant, he thought. He wondered if he'd ever get away from the smell of chickpeas.

Paul finished up his shift without talking to the other workers, and he realized that he'd been uncharacteristically quiet for two days straight. He knew only two people to talk to in the whole state. Why was he even here? He walked back to the tent, got his towel, and headed to the showers to remove the food-service residue. The shower area was quiet; most people were at dinner but Paul was full and antsy. He cleaned up and dressed carefully in everything cut off: tee shirt, sweatshirt, and low-slung Levi's. His hair was rocker shaggy and he wore ball-bearing chains around his neck and delicate wrists. He applied black eyeliner and mascara to make his point, using Jane's abandoned sunglasses as a mirror. He would go see bands, he thought, and hunt there.

Down in the stage area, people crowded in from all sides, cozily, and Paul realized—again—they were all women. They were all women, except him, including him. No one was looking at him strangely. He was being paranoid. He was a girl, just like these girls. And they were all so hot and, yes, beautiful.

He saw Diane standing next to a short curly-haired butch, but she didn't see him, and he looked away, "lost in thought." A moment later he felt her hot hand on his bicep. They looked at each other with impossible-to-hide giddiness. Paul understood the expression "to throw oneself at someone."

"Hey," he said.

"This is kind of amazing," said Diane. "It's like a world within the world."

"Temporary autonomous zone!" Paul said. "Space travel!"

She was taller than Paul, and he followed her as they wended through the tattooed love children, the women's studies professors, the raucous catcallers, the quiet swayers, the breastfeeders, the cliques of the fat-positive and the scent-free, the disability activists and the suburbanites. Paul knew what Jane would say about so much of this. She'd be so full of disdain for those she imprecisely called "softball players," who she thought were lowering the aesthetic bar. Paul wasn't sure how he felt. Jane was angry about something that didn't bother him. Paul was aware of wanting to stand out and wanting to sit down amid the happy throng. He liked being in on the secret. He picked his way around foldout chaise longues and blankets, between coolers and clumps of standers, and stood still.

Diane pressed his hand. There was music but they weren't listening to the music. The music was like a rip in the sky, far and impenetrable.

"Do you want to get out of here?" she said. "I might have just hit capacity of humans."

"Okay," said Paul.

She threaded them away from the stage. Diane was leading him he didn't know where. Paul imagined they looked to the assembly of good listeners like delinquents, and was pleased. On the dirt paths, they encountered other derelicts and evaders, sneaking away from one exaltation toward some other.

They repaired to Diane's tent, where they had sex until the sun came up. Diane raced off to her breakfast shift and Paul headed back to his own tent woozy with adrenaline.

×

They moved Diane's tent to the field where they'd fucked for the first time; they made a fort with a cache of food, a tape player and batteries, and firewood. Paul had maintained his girl body for five days straight now, sleeping lightly until Diane went off to a work shift without him.

Paul woke in their tent alone, still in girl form. He got up to pee, victorious over his erstwhile penis but still urgent. It was very early, pink sky early. Diane was nowhere to be found. Paul squatted at the tree line and breathed in the morning, letting hot urine spill out of somewhere in his vagina, a little turned on by the pressure. Blood pounding in the soft red walls, swelling. Where was Diane? He heard an animal noise somewhere to his left. Flash of brown fur. Bear?

He pulled up his panties and cutoffs and stood up fast, too fast, pee dripping down his leg, and the bear's fur raised up on its neck in spiky tufts.

Those are hackles, Paul thought. And those are teeth.

The bear lowed and lumbered toward him. Paul took a step back, toward the field. Another flash of brown fur, closer to him. A smaller bear. Paul emitted a stench of fear he himself could smell. He wondered if he could change himself into a bear, or a deer, something swift or large, but he was paralyzed.

The cub walked clumsily toward Paul. Paul was fucked. Here was the natural world, the world his cleverness had conquered, and it was in fact unconquered, was instead annoyed, retaliatory, possibly hungry.

Another animal noise, sharp and authoritative, then gentle.

In his fright-blindered vision Paul saw Diane. He couldn't stop her, couldn't shout. He tried to shout with his eyes.

But Diane walked up to the bear. She was the one making the gentle bear sounds. The cub ambled over to its mother, and the mother led the cub away. Paul exhaled.

"Holy shit," he said. "Holy shit holy shit holy *shit*."

"Yeah," said Diane. "You're lucky that little cub decided to leave you alone."

Paul stared at her.

"You weren't trying to pet her, were you?" Diane said.

"I'm not an idiot," said Paul.

"No, but you are a city slicker, slick."

Paul couldn't argue with that and anyway he was trying to work out what was happening. Something was wrong; Diane was trembling, high and heady; she was someone else. He realized for the first time how slow she usually was, how even.

"What did you do to that bear?" asked Paul.

They looked at each other.

Paul wanted to ask her what she was, but the words gummed up in his mouth.

"Thank you for saving my life," he said, to say something. He sat down.

"You're too beautiful to die," Diane said, so Paul guessed he'd said the right thing. "I don't want you to die."

"I don't want you to die, too," said Paul. He hadn't been thinking about death but now he was. He reached for her hand and pulled her down so they were facing each other on the grass. "Let's never die."

"Everyone dies sometime," said Diane. "We'll be in the earth, one with everything. But not until we're very old."

"Okay," said Paul, with a little thrill. "When we're very old."

He'd never said "we" to anyone before, not even Tony Pinto, with whom he'd thought but not spoken words like "we" and "very old."

Now Diane had said the words, and they were bound to each other in this field, like a hippie wedding. He didn't know what else to say, so he pulled her on top of him.

×

"I can't believe I took you to Michigan and you turned into an earnest, monogamous lesbian," Jane said, once they got on the highway.

"Stop," said Paul. "Don't mock. I actually feel like I belonged there as much as anywhere I've ever been. More even."

"*Lesbian,*" said Jane. As usual Paul was having a peak experience and Jane was stuck driving. You won't fuck me and I always have to drive, she thought. Or is it, you never fuck me and I always have to drive.

"I think I might love her," Paul said.

Jane had spent the entire festival chasing Frog, who turned out to be the star top of the Twilight Zone, and, apparently, of the Austin SM scene (who knew they had one!). Frog had been happy enough to act out many of Jane's best-loved, most-read-about sex-positive feminist fantasies. Tied to a tree and whipped? Check. Boot-licking? Done. Public ejaculation contest? But of course. Spend the night? Not Frog's scene, sorry. Jane felt sorely misunderstood. She wasn't trying to *cuddle*, for Christ's sake. She just wanted to stay up all night getting her brains screwed out. She considered the phrase. Yes, that was exactly what she wanted. She wanted to be fucked so thor-

oughly that she couldn't think, but instead she had these souvenir bruises and the second-place ribbon from an ejaculation contest. And the image of Paul in the passenger seat, fondling and sniffing the sweatshirt that girl had given him. Jane had been extremely nice about it, pulled over when the potter had come running up behind the car like some desperate movie lover, sat there watching the digital clock tick off seven minutes while they kissed and whispered against the trunk. She'd even squealed with him about Diane, whom Jane privately thought unclean. That was a hippie thing, Jane knew; she wasn't fooled by Diane's deployment of such punk rock signifiers as bedraggled Jack Purcells, an eyebrow piercing, or cut-off men's pants. Ultimately, *essentially*, Diane was a potter and had BO, which equaled hippie, which equaled earnest, which was the enemy of all Jane and Paul had once held dear. She preferred herself as one of the fags, and now her best friend, her *entrée*, was fucking with her scene.

"Did you ever even *tell* her about . . . yourself?" Jane said, one eye on the gas gauge. She had to remember to get gas money from slippery Paul.

"No," said Paul. "I'm never going to see her again, so what would have been the point?"

Was he about to cry? Oh *Jesus*, thought Jane.

"Are you going to change back before we get home?" she said.

Paul looked at her through smudged eyeliner.

"Yeah," he said, balling up the sweatshirt into a pillow between his shoulder and the car door. He closed his eyes against further harassment, like a morally superior child.

Jane turned on the radio, bored of all the tapes they'd

brought. She flipped from "I'm the Only Hell My Mama Ever Raised" to the tail end of a program on Exodus and New Hope, two quote-unquote ex-gay ministries. Wasn't New Hope a gay resort town? From Grand Haven to Gary, Jane shaped a few murky thoughts under the provisional title "Mama's Boys and Truck Stops: Queering the Evangelical." She really should have done cultural studies.

III.

Paul balanced lightly on the black rubber floor of the Cambus as the bored driver hit potholes and took corners too quickly. Paul was a city person, a bus surfer. He scanned the passengers, assessed then turned away from the high-school kids at the back. He knew in the way he knew things that the kids were discussing him, gathering themselves into a single brave approach. The bravest broke from the pack and kicked Paul's left boot. Paul had seen a lot of fuck-you-freak moves before but he'd never seen boot-kicking. It was amateur; maybe they were in junior high. Harassed by junior-high-school kids—an extra dose of humiliation.

"Hey," said the kid. "What are you? You some kind of freak?"

There it was. Paul didn't answer. If he was with Tony Pinto, oh, the saucy trouble they'd rain down on these assholes! Tony Pinto would definitely agree, yes, they were freaks. He'd blow a kiss, or charge the kids like a bull, or both.

"¿Habla español, freak?" The kid's Spanish came by way of a high school in Dubuque or Ottumwa, Paul could tell, even though his own Spanish was from the movies *(hasta la vista, baby)* and the subway platform (¡cuidado, maricón!). Paul sneaked a look at the front kid's black tee shirt, which boasted a big American flag. These definitely weren't Iowa City kids. He wished he had a good comeback, in Spanish or English. What was he going to say, "Actually I'm half-Turkish, or maybe Greek, but my mom isn't really forthcoming about my biologi-

cal father and maybe I'm just really dark Black Irish, but what if I *was* Latina slash o? Anyway, by the way, yes, I am a giant queer who threatens your pathetic sense of knowing anything about the world, *tiny asshole?*" Not catchy.

The kid stepped up to Paul, leading with his chest and sneering handsomely. The other kids moved closer to watch. Paul tried to catch the eye of the only other passenger, a pink blonde girl in a pink sweatshirt with darker pink plaid Greek letters, but the girl kept her eyes to the front.

"Sorry," Paul said, as the bus lurched to a stop across from the bank. "No habla español."

He hopped off the bus just as the doors closed; he'd go see what was new at the comics shop, or see if anything good had come in to Savage Salvage. And look, there was Jane on the sidewalk by the bank machine, looking, in repose, uncharacteristically indecisive and melancholy.

Paul, in a burst of relief, ran gaily across the intersection, dodging cars, and throwing his arm around her.

"What are you doing? Let's go shopping!" he said, in a tone that refused to brook dissent. He was in very high spirits, he discovered, and he didn't feel like discussing his personal experiences with racism and homophobia.

<p style="text-align:center">×</p>

A contractor and his wife tried for many years to have a child, but no child came. They tried and tried. They wanted a baby very badly, and finally the contractor's wife's belly grew large. They rejoiced, proclaiming their happiness and good fortune

to all who would listen. When the baby came, on a crisp early December morning, the contractor and his wife gazed in wonder at its beauty. They talked of nothing but their baby and their happiness.

"What a well-formed child," they said to each other. "He looks just like you! How strong, how handsome, how sweet-tempered is our baby boy! How intelligently he plays with his toys, how easily he takes to the breast, how peacefully he sleeps through each and every night!"

The contractor and his wife were very pleased with their baby and began to plan a party to celebrate. They invited all their relatives and friends and coworkers from far and wide to gaze upon their beautiful child.

Around this time, a diplomat from the nearby fairy court was returning to his Queen in shame at having failed on his first mission of state. He had been entrusted to negotiate a détente with the next court over. This court, historically friendly to his own, had nevertheless offered succor to an insubordinate water sprite, a particularly belligerent naiad who had used rough language to address his Queen on one of her jaunts to the mineral springs. The insult may or may not have had something to do with certain requests her Highness had made of the naiad's consort. The neighboring court's Queen not only refused to make the naiad apologize or deliver her into the fairy diplomat's custody, but had even intimated that his own Queen was at fault.

The fairy diplomat nudged the haunches of his squirrel, and she slowed to a trot. His Queen was known to possess a temper; no need to hurry back. As they passed by the happy

family's cottage, the fairy diplomat overheard the contractor's wife speaking on the phone to a baby-modeling agency. Perhaps all was not lost. He hurried back to court with a new plan to distract his Queen.

The fairy diplomat knew he must act immediately, as the following night was winter solstice. The Queen's ball began at sundown, and she expected tributes before midnight. The fairy diplomat went round the forest from tree trunk to cave pool until he found what he was looking for: a particularly mischievous young fairy who, as it happened, was part water sprite. The Queen had hidden her little daughter on an island in the forest lake, where she was being raised by a kindly old otter. He caught the young fairy attempting to escape her nursemaid, who threw up her paws in disgust.

The fairy diplomat whistled a little tune, pleased with his own efficiency, as he swaddled the fairy child up in a large leaf to transport her to the happy family's cottage. He swapped out the children, and hurried back to the ball to present the human infant to his Queen.

A few days later, the contractor and his wife began to notice something strange about their baby, who was still beautiful but whose temper seemed to have spoiled. Now the baby cried and cried, and the contractor and his wife couldn't sleep. Now the baby fussed and scowled and refused to nurse. The baby became more and more difficult as he grew older, howling his displeasure when the contractor's wife tried to dress him in a tiny football costume, drinking only strawberry milk, singing strange little songs which unnerved the old woman who ran a day care from her house a few blocks away.

There's something wrong with that baby, thought the

contractor, and he blamed his wife, for her family had always seemed odd to him. A few months later, the contractor left his wife and their squalling child, moved across the sea, and was never heard from again.

×

Paul was broke, as usual, and October rent was coming due.

He sat on the edge of a red-brick planter on the ped mall, next to the coffee cart, and sucked his free iced latte through a straw. Paul had reciprocal hookups all over town, a perk of bartending or personal charm, he wasn't sure which. Alan at the coffee cart was one of Paul's prized contacts.

It was early, obscenely early. 9 AM. The braggart trees flaunted their two weeks of red and orange, the crisp air busked for attention, shop owners unlocked their doors simultaneously as if in a Busby Berkeley number. The entire town conspired to pretend it was fall, right here in River City.

Paul had woken up fourteen minutes ago on the fifth floor of the Holiday Inn, in the room of the Illinois assistant men's swimming coach. He had sneaked out like a Russian spy. Two of his favorite parts of tricking were sneaking and seeing the town at unexpected times.

Another reason to leave was that he couldn't really afford to go out to breakfast, and he couldn't count on the assistant coach paying—he hadn't been a very good tipper at the bar the night before.

Paul looked over at Alan, his scruffy red beard and lanky indie-rock body, an ectomorph in faded black jeans and a *Reid Fleming, World's Toughest Milkman* tee shirt. They'd almost

messed around one drunken Tuesday night last spring, after beers at George's. Alan had asked Paul lots of questions about Being Gay and then casually invited him back to his house to watch a bootleg of *Superstar*. Paul had been legitimately tired, said no, and had immediately regretted it. At least he was still getting free coffees, though, which he might not be if they'd fooled around.

Sucking on his straw, Paul sidled up to the coffee cart. Alan looked up from cleaning the espresso machine after the first morning rush.

"Hey man, you ever see any Kenneth Anger?" he said, in his urgent low husk-voice.

"Sure, like *Scorpio Rising*?" said Paul. "When I lived in New York I saw the retrospective at the Anthology."

"I just saw *Invocation of My Demon Brother*. That shit is out in the stratosphere."

Paul hadn't seen it.

"You ever seen any Jonas Mekas?" he countered.

Alan packed espresso into a little metal cup and hooked the cup into the machine with a tidy wrist flick.

"Yeah, I saw this really—" Alan said, holding a cup of milk over the piston as the machine roared.

"What?" said Paul.

"Here you go, man." Alan presented Paul with another latte, not even asked for. Just bonus.

"Thanks," said Paul.

A film grad student Paul and Jane called "the French girl" stood behind him. They didn't know her name, but she reminded Paul of Jean Seberg in *Breathless*, with her short hair and her signature striped sailor shirt. Diane had a striped shirt.

Alan was already talking to the French Girl, done with Paul. No chance to impress him with having seen Jonas Mekas eat pierogis at the Kiev.

Paul decided to head home; he didn't have to be anywhere until the afternoon and there was a chance Christopher had food. As he walked down South Dubuque he passed the unopened Prairie Lights, the unopened all-pasta restaurant, the unopened Deadwood (where he'd spent many an afternoon playing pinball). The street was empty and the buildings low, like in a Western. Paul walked chest first, hands in pockets, his legs wide as he could make them, checking his stance for cowboy in the black windows of the storefronts. He assessed his financial situation.

He had $3.85 in the bank and $35 in cash in his wallet. He'd spent $50 on Polaroid film and copies for his zine, which he'd called *Polydoris Perversity* and which maybe hadn't been such a good investment. He had copies on consignment at Prairie Lights and at the zine store in the Hall Mall, but he wouldn't see that money for weeks, if not months. His rent was $242.50, due in eleven days. He got paid weekly from the club, which totaled up to about $25 before taxes, plus another $60 for cleaning the bar, which came to about $75 a week, take home. He was rounding down to avoid surprises, but the outlook wasn't good.

The bar was a gamble. On a good Friday night he might take home $100 after tipping out the barbacks. On a bad Wednesday night, $15. On a really good night, like Iowa Pride or if July Fourth fell on a Saturday, he could walk out with ten twenties in his wallet. Thing was, he only had two shifts a week right now. When the club was busy, Paul bettered his odds by putting money in the register without ringing in all the drinks.

When he counted his tips after close, he'd put in five ones, remove a twenty, and so on, until he'd balanced his drawer. He could easily pocket an extra twenty or thirty bucks this way. His philosophy was, keep the theft petty and regular, a ten here, a twenty there, so as to prevent anomalies, which is generally what led to people getting busted. Paul could do this arithmetic fast and casually, under any manager's gimlet eye. He was fairly sure Greg, the manager, had his finger in the drawer as well, but they never discussed it. Greg was a thespian when not at the bar, active in community theater. At 5'3", he was usually cast as "the son" or "the best friend." As a result, Greg advocated tirelessly for shows like *The Fantasticks* or *Pippin*, in which he was assured lots of stage time. His big coup was playing Bobby in *Company*, an actual romantic lead. Paul had gone to see that show with the other bartenders (to be nice—he wasn't into musicals) and they all joked for days about Greg's big Leading Man moment as a closet case.

Paul felt pleasurably tall and even hunky around Greg. Greg had one of those faggy baritone speaking voices (though he sang tenor, with a British schoolboy inflection), a military brush cut, big chest muscles and skinny little legs, and generally wore either a crushed velvet or a metallic short-sleeved buttondown. 1993 is too soon for '80s retro, Paul thought. We're doing '70s now.

But Greg was a good manager; he protected all his nogood workers from the closeted absentee owner. The owner left them to their own devices in most ways, primarily musically. Paul couldn't have worked in a regular gay bar with the booming techno all night long. He'd much rather the Pet Shop Boys

or the disco divas the DJ threw as bones to the queens. Brian, the straight DJ, drove to Chicago a few times a month to check out the record stores and listen to house music in the clubs on Halsted. They played Chicago-style house at the club, lots of traumatized ladies who were going to survive. Greg was particularly fond of Liza Minnelli remixes, which Brian played when he was getting ready to ask for a night off.

Paul had the two nights at the club and the five days, Thursday through Monday, he went in to clean before they opened. That meant $6 an hour before tax, and he had to punch in, so he couldn't drag it out too long if anybody else was there, which he tried to avoid. He could get there any time before four and have enough time to clean before they opened, but if he was bartending he liked to go home, take a shower, and put on an outfit, so those days he cleaned in the mornings. Afternoons he'd help Greg roll kegs to the walk-in behind the bar, which added a half-hour to the clock. Greg was always happy to have extra help, and to dish about the others. Like Paul, Greg had worked his way up from barback and still clung to his underdog resentment of princessy bartenders who wouldn't do side work.

Some days Brian or another DJ (like the dyke who played New Wave hits on Wednesdays) would be there, putting together a set. Paul tried to time it so he was alone. That way he could make mixtapes in the DJ booth, mop and wax the dance floor without trapping anyone behind the bar, sweep the rugs properly, steal a six of beer or some large cans of tomato juice or toilet paper, fix himself elaborate Bloody Marys, eat potato chips and olives, talk on the phone while prepping the Bloody Mary mix, roll up his shirt sleeves and pretend to be a sailor in

Querelle while mopping, listen to Liza Minnelli remixes without being called a hypocrite, and/or bring friends or tricks to hang out and play records while he worked.

Paul got paid Wednesdays, which meant he had two checks from the bar before rent, and three nights of tips, but those usually melted away. He also had two nights washing dishes at the Linn Street, which was the fanciest restaurant in Iowa City. It paid a little better, $5.50 plus dinner plus a share of the waitstaff's tips, usually an extra $15 a night off the books—

As he walked past the chemistry building and hit Linn Street, Paul stopped calculating. He found himself standing in front of the Hamburg Inn. He was too hungry to wait until he got home, and what if Christopher hadn't gone shopping? He sat at the counter and eyed the staff. They had a newish rocka-billy girl and mostly dykes in the kitchen. No Maisie, thank god. He nodded to the platinum-haired short-order cook and liberated a *Press-Citizen* from a recently abandoned booth. He felt an amiable indignation while skimming through an editorial blasting the socialist on the city council. He imagined what Diane would say. He'd had one postcard from her, vintage from Niagara Falls, the message written in boyish block letters: "I am having to do this not like Cousteau with his assiduous team aboard the sun-flooded schooner but here alone . . ." Postmarked Syracuse. An announcement or an opening, he wasn't sure. He'd memorized the words, but had no way to write back. Which made it seem more like an announcement, when he thought it through.

The pink-haired waitress tapped her pen on the counter. Paul looked up.

"Hey," he said.

"Whaddya want?" she said, snapping her gum and looking bored, which thrilled Paul.

"Two egg special," he said, adding a little stutter to the "special" and looking up shyly, like a country boy, he thought. I should go thrifting today and look for some bibs, maybe a cowboy shirt.

"Special ends at eight," she said, gesturing with her eyebrows toward the clock above the booths. "It's lunchtime."

"Two eggs scrambled, then," said Paul, put in his proper citified, sissified place. "And coffee." He wished for the *Times* and a cigarette. He could be a famous director, just in from the coast to scout locations for a blockbuster.

"Oh, could I get some hash browns too?" he called to the waitress in the kitchen.

After breakfast and tip, Paul had $31 in his pocket and the smell of kitchen grease on his denim jacket and in his hair. He headed home for a shower. Maybe later he could sell some tapes downtown. Or he could butch up, lie to the plasma bank, sell his gay blood. He wondered if his blood would give him away, had any special properties. It wasn't worth the risk, the blood bank didn't pay that well anyway.

He walked north on Linn, then cut over through an alley to Gilbert. The alleys between houses were nighttime magic— stolen kisses, mescaline, slugs of Jim Beam shared with people who "just wanted to talk." He wished he could show Diane the alleys, but he was trying not to think about Diane.

He'd been a boy since he'd gotten back, a fag, *himself*, just normal. He was a free agent; it was hunting season. He'd

changed a bit here and there in the last month but he'd always done that. Sometimes in the showers in high school he'd make himself bigger but not too big. Or later, the times he'd fucked guys, to make his penis fit into someone in the most agreeable way. He hadn't even known what he was doing, not really. He thought everyone must do it: stay small in dicey situations, get big on cue. If he concentrated he could do these things through force of will. When he stopped concentrating, regular life resumed: inconvenient boners, whiskey dick, being not-so-hung. Sometimes lately to please a guy Paul would sneakily inquire about fetishes. Like big balls? Done. But he hadn't been Polly since the last day at Michigan. He'd let himself sink back into his normal body and his normal life once they crossed the Indiana state line. The experiment was over, except for the photo shoots for his zine, and that was art and so didn't count.

Paul emerged from the shady alley onto Gilbert, into sunlight, and walked home in a funk. He really should get a Walkman, he thought. Maybe Kostas or his mom would buy him one for Christmas, if he ever called either of them. Or maybe he should ask for a bike. All this walking was giving him way too much time to think.

When he got home, he saw the previous day's mail stacked on the kitchen table along with a pink Post-It from Christopher itemizing Paul's share of the utilities. He ignored the note in favor of the pile's true bounty—a postcard of a whale in midair. He turned the card over and read "think of me by the river I'll think of you by the sea" and underneath, RETURN: GENERAL DELIVERY PROVINCETOWN MA 02657. An opening, he thought. Definitely.

×

Paul sat on his bedroom floor, circled by unsteady stacks of his and Christopher's CDs and tapes. He wanted to explain something to Diane in the only way he knew how. Christopher's music collection ranged from Patty Griffin all the way to Emmylou Harris, plus a few obvious disco compilations. Christopher was more of a lesbian than any actual lesbian Paul knew. He needed Jane for this. Paul packed up his stacks and headed over to Jane's on Christopher's bike.

Jane wasn't home, so he let himself in with her emergency key and plopped down on the ironic purple shag carpet in front of the stereo system. Much better. Jane had tape-to-tape, for one thing, and lots of vinyl, and everything the Pixies had ever released. Fags 0, Dykes 1.

"Ooh," he said into the empty apartment, fondling the Bikini Kill/Huggy Bear split LP before succumbing to the distraction of Jane's mighty cassingle collection.

Diane was definitely going to get the message: Paul was fun and intense. He lifted out his most precious mixtapes from his backpack and lined them up next to Jane's music. Was it cheesy to pass Jane's superior collection off as his own? Or was it a sign of his dedication? He could also go down to the club during the day and use some of the vinyl there, if he wanted dancier songs; that would be really intrepid but maybe too faggy? Yeah, too faggy. He wanted to give Diane things she couldn't get herself, to turn her on to new things, to share his access, to *provide*, to shore up his girlfriendable-ness.

He had 90- and 120-minute tapes, and Jane had some 60s, but you had to be really stuck to use a 60 anymore. And weren't

the 120-minute tapes supposed to be of inferior quality? He'd bought the most expensive ones available, German-made.

SIDE A:
I Am a Poseur - X-Ray Spex
Pretty on the Inside - Hole
Cherry Bomb - The Runaways
What's Inside a Girl? - The Cramps
Rebel Girl - Bikini Kill
Pumping (My Heart) - Patti Smith
Golden Thing - Throwing Muses
Rid of Me - PJ Harvey
Touch Your Woman - Dolly Parton
If I Was Your Girlfriend - Prince
Beauty and the Beast - David Bowie
That's Really Super, Supergirl - XTC
People Are Strange - Echo and the Bunnymen

Paul was happy with Side A, though not entirely sure about that last track. Also, maybe "Me-Jane" would have been a better PJ Harvey track after "Golden Thing" because of the beat, but the lyrics weren't romantic. Paul knew that some people didn't consider the lyrics when making mixtapes, but he always did. Occasionally he'd choose a song for ironic purposes or to say the opposite of what the lyrics said or for litote (for instance, "Rid of Me") but *always* lyrics were involved in the decision. Paul disliked instrumental music. He wanted stories, all the time. He wished he could make a tape of all the moments from films he wanted to show her, but how was that even possible? Maybe if he hooked up Jane's VCR to another VCR and rented

all the movies . . . He felt that old familiar electricity surging up in him, a desire to accumulate and then display a complete collection. He imposed a small measure of self-control and returned his attention to the mixtape.

He would listen to Side A to check the flow, to subject himself to its momentum before he started Side B. Start out strong, pumping, then go for counterpoint with Dolly, then take it to a sexy place, but not for too long (keep the tension), then—maybe the Bowie was too much? He wasn't sure about any of the last three songs, really, but sometimes the songs you weren't sure about were the genius choices. No, he couldn't dismantle the tape now. He made a sandwich, leaving Jane with one slice of bread. She might not notice; she was kind of rich.

Paul tried to imagine Diane listening to the tape on auto-reverse, driving down some street in Provincetown, maybe driving to her new job. Okay, what should the first song be on the second side? You've got that moment where the tape reverses, the antici . . . pation, and so the first song on the second side is the heart of the tape. By that point, you're committed; you've listened to an entire side and you've entered the world of the tape—you've waited, and what are you waiting for? He decided to go for a declaration. Forget subtlety. His tape would be a manifesto of his readiness. He wanted to be Diane's girlfriend, whatever that meant.

SIDE B:
Kinda I Want To - NIN
Birdhouse in Your Soul - They Might Be Giants
Take Me With U - Prince

Paul stopped. Something was wrong. He didn't want to seem queeny, male, obvious. This side was all dudes so far. Jane had a few compilation CDs, so Paul scanned the track listings until he hit gold: Jane Wiedlin from the Go-Gos. Apparently she was a PETA person. He cued up the tape:

Fur - Jane Wiedlin

Halfway through, Paul knew the song was too campy; Diane might think he was making fun of her feelings about animals. He rewound. He could do better. He retrieved a bag of Oreos from Jane's cabinet and took stock of the situation.

~~Fur - Jane Wiedlin~~

Paul considered a tape Tony Pinto had made him, so long ago. Two years ago. Was it entirely ethical to copy a song, or multiple songs, from a mixtape someone else had made you? What if you changed the order? What if the person who made you the mix had copied at least half the songs from *Just Say Yes, Volume III: Just Say Mao*, which you later discovered while looking through their CDs? What if the person who made you the mixtape was in love with you but you weren't in love with them? What if the person who made the tape was in love with you and you had been in love with them, maybe, but you weren't anymore? Was it really even okay to copy *any* songs from a mixtape? Paul decided it was okay if the tape had been given to you in the spirit of true love and had then become part of who you now were. It was not just okay, it was in fact *crucial*,

then, to share this with your new love, so they could understand you. He put the Joan Armatrading on, wondering what Tony Pinto would say about Diane. Or about Paul's new look. What would Diane say about Tony Pinto? Some things were perhaps best not discussed.

I'm Lucky - Joan Armatrading
Caribou - The Pixies
(You Make Me Feel Like) A Natural Woman - Carole King
Kangaroo - This Mortal Coil
Hounds of Love - Kate Bush
Witchcraft - Book of Love
Freedom '90 - George Michael
Kool Thing - Sonic Youth

The last song fit exactly on the tape. If that wasn't a sign, Paul didn't know what was. Diane *was* a Kool Thing. She *did* walk like a panther. They both were like *fuck you* to male white corporate oppression. Paul thought about how hot they looked together in the Polaroids they'd taken at Michigan. He couldn't believe he was one of the hot girls in the pictures but there he was, four times a lady.

He played the finished tape all the way through one last time while hunched over Jane's kitchen counter with an X-acto knife, rubber cement, and a 1955 *Playboy*, collaging two tiny Bettie Pages onto a campfire scene for the tape cover. He listed the song titles on the cassette itself, as he'd seen art students do, using a fine-point silver paint pen, and on the outside of the case he carefully printed the words "VOLUME ONE." He

immediately second-guessed this title and swapped out the case for a fresh one, on which he carefully printed the words "FOR DIANE." Better not to be quite so obvious, he thought.

×

Saturday night the club was still dead at 11:30, which was very bad what with the rent situation. Where was everyone? Paul shorted the register with every other shots order, but even so, he'd be lucky to leave with fifty bucks. Greg was in a crappy mood; he'd already sniped at the barback for not cleaning plastic tumblers well enough, refused to provide the bouncer her traditional rum and coke, and forced Brian to play Erasure twice.

"Whoever closed last night really screwed us all over for tonight," Greg said.

"Wasn't me," Paul said.

"Oh, I know that, honey. You always leave everything just so."

Good. Paul couldn't afford to get on Greg's bad side. Greg might decide they didn't need two bartenders and "give" Paul the rest of the night off. And what would he do then, go home? Linger among the trolls? Check out some other bar in town?

Where was *Jane*? he wondered. Probably with that *barista*, cuddling somewhere. Lesbians. He stretched the bar phone's cord into the keg closet and called Christopher, who refused to leave his studies and come entertain Paul. *Lesbian*, thought Paul.

He returned to his place at the long bar, wiping down the steel-top with the diligence of a midshipman. He poured plas-

tic cups of lite beer, a few pitchers, five or six Long Island Iced Teas. Paul wished someone, anyone, would order a Negroni, or a Manhattan, anything besides these endless draws and well gin-and-tonics. He ducked into the DJ booth, startling Brian, who palmed his lit joint with the studied casualness of a varsity athlete.

"It's just me," said Paul, flipping through a milk crate of EPs.

"What's up, man?" said Brian, exhaling a miniature fog system. "Wanna be DJ for a while?"

"Play something good," said Paul, brandishing the Yeastie Girls/Consolidated 12" of "You Suck."

Brian shook his head. Paul held out the disc in an Oliver Twist pose.

"Not for this crowd," Brian said, unsheathing and brandishing a record. "They don't deserve anything good. I'm going to punish them."

Paul left the DJ booth. "I'm Gonna Get You" turned into "Rhythm Is a Dancer."

"Brian is trying to kill us," said James, the barback, looking up from the sink.

"I know," said Paul. "It's homophobia."

James swiftly dipped a succession of sticky tumblers onto the rotating brush head of the bar sink, like a faggier Little Tramp.

"Will you make me a Long Island, darling?" he said. "It's medicinal; I need to dull the pain."

Paul lined up the rum, gin, tequila, triple sec, vodka, gin, and sour mix on the bar. He wiped down each bottle after tipping it into the shaker, admiring the precision of his wristwork. Was there any other field in which his god-given ability to pour

exactly 1.5 fluid ounces would be so appreciated or so useful? He decided that for the rest of the night he'd concentrate on bettering himself as a bartender. Maybe with enough practice he'd be able to bartend somewhere glamorous, like France. Or somewhere English-speaking and glamorous. He couldn't at the moment think of where that might be.

"You forgot the Coke," said James.

"It's better that way," said Paul. "It's a North Shore Iced Tea." Most of bartending was a con job.

"*Coke*," insisted James, twirling his platinum locks and pursing his lips. "Hamptons-style."

Paul knew James had never been east of St. Louis but subscribed to *New York* magazine and the *Village Voice*, and was disdainful of Paul's decision to leave The City for Iowa.

A pack of new people came in, refugees from another bar or party. The club was open until 2; Paul might salvage the night yet.

The herd clustered at Brian's bar, and Paul serviced the stragglers, mostly hard-up straight guys who'd come with their ambivalent, upwardly mobile girlfriends, who'd followed *their* fag friends, who'd needed a ride or to feel less gay. And in all of that, no one cute. Paul poured a round of Goldschläger for four of James's friends, and made a joke about golden showers, a joke he'd made countless times and which never failed to titillate the hairdressers.

"Oh bartender," called a Hepburnish voice attached to a ten-dollar bill. "I'd like a Negroni."

Paul looked up. Jane, of course, dear good Jane, making him believe in fairies, in the silver screen.

"I'm actually out of Campari," said Paul, pouring her a stiff top-shelf lime rickey. "But thank you for asking."

"No matter," said Jane, inhaling through the cigarette holder she was affecting for the evening. "And you're really going to thank me in about a minute, when you see who walks in."

Paul gave her his raffish Sal Mineo smile and waved away her money. He glanced at the door. Maybe the waifs? Those taxi-driving brothers were still on his list, though he wasn't sure which one he liked better. He actually couldn't tell them apart.

Paul pushed plastic beer cups down on the automatic brushes two at a time. Where was James? This was the *barback's* job.

"Hey Jane," he heard, as he piled the clean wet cups into a tower. Something snagged in his peripheral vision and he finally looked up.

And then there was Diane, out of context and across the bar from him. She narrowed her eyes at Paul in confusion. She looked like she was going to speak but then didn't.

Paul wiped his soapy hands on his pants.

"Hey," he said.

"Hi," said Diane. "*Polly?*"

×

Now Paul had to impossibly finish the night with needy drinkers suddenly five deep at the bar, the tide of camp squeals and synthesized beats rising over his head, the boredom drinks he'd downed earlier cottonballing his response time, and Diane staring at him across two feet of burnished steel—staring maybe not in a good way.

She was beautiful, he thought, with a pinch of anger. He had decided not to remember how beautiful she was, and now he could see her quietly standing in an entirely different plane from the rest of the club, one universe to the left, the universe he'd left behind somewhere on I-80. She stood and stared at Paul and then at Jane, who widened her eyes at Paul over the rim of her tumbler.

"Diane, wait," he said. "James, can you cover for me? Five minutes, I promise."

He poured a double shot of whiskey, ducked under the bar top, and pushed through the swarm toward her, brushing past the ass-grabs of his regulars, drink held high. He dreaded another dramatic revelation scene like the one he'd had with Jane, the kind of scene he always fast-forwarded. But he had to make Diane understand.

"Is it you?" Diane said.

Paul led her outside, and around back, behind the warehouse.

He handed her the soda tumbler of whiskey.

Diane leaned against the corrugated aluminum siding, swallowed the whole drink and bared her teeth, tough-guy style.

Paul shivered in his thin black Pat Benatar *Get Nervous* '83 World Tour tee shirt, trying to resist the pull of Diane. He went to kiss her back into their own good world, but she stepped away.

He knew her feelings about bisexuality, her pride in her Gold Star status. She was seeing him now, nothing he could do about it. He concentrated on changing: emerged his breasts,

receded the lump in his pants, drifted his mild soft stubble into the lightest peach fuzz.

"Look," he said. "I'm like you." He took her hands and placed them on his soft soft cheeks. She touched his face forensically, like an insurance inspector. He searched her face back. What was she thinking? She looked like Colossus, her face and body turned to steel. Where was his Peter Rasputin? he thought. Where are you in there?

"I'm like you," he said again.

"You're not like me," Diane said. "I don't lie."

"It's not that simple," said Paul.

Diane looked at him with her hard Colossus eyes.

"I have to go in," he said finally. "My manager will kill me if I just take off."

"I'll wait," she said.

"You will?"

She nodded.

He began to change back, and saw her face.

"I have to, at least a little," he said. "They all just think I do really good drag sometimes."

"Yeah," said Diane. "You're really good."

She turned to walk back inside and Paul followed. He ducked under the service gate of the bar, poured Diane another whiskey, and began listlessly to take drink orders until James intervened.

"Oh my dear," said James, doing his best Eve Harrington. "Are you entirely okay? Let me help. I can open beer bottles for thirty minutes. You go home now and get some rest."

Paul agreed, although he knew exactly how James would

represent the situation to Greg. He found Diane standing by the pool table, looking so surly he lost his breath.

"Let's just go," he said. "I punched out."

Diane nodded.

Paul directed her, badly, toward his apartment, and they drove in silence past his street and into a strange and depressing cul-de-sac of ranch houses with tricycles and other debris on the lawns.

"I should have told you," Paul said. Even though of course I *couldn't*, he thought angrily.

"Yeah," said Diane, turning the car around. "You think?"

He didn't understand this sarcastic Diane, at once familiar and yet so not herself. He'd brought her to this point, he thought, his fear mixed with a secret surprising pride. He'd broken down her cool reserve.

She didn't speak again until they were in his room. She sat heavily on the floor in a corner by the window, as if to refuse a chair was to refuse Paul's . . . what? hypocrisy? To refuse *Paul*. He crouched on his futon. He pulled his sleeping bag around his shoulders like a cape but he couldn't get warm. They stared at each other, past unspoken opening lines, past comfort or discomfort, and the night opened into some universal parentheses containing everything there was to be said, all the small moments and passing thoughts, all the excuses, explanations, possibilities of being known—and closed again, like a winking anus or a wormhole. It was really a strangely long time, Paul thought. He didn't know if he'd ever been silent this long. His leg began to cramp but he didn't want to move and disrupt what he suspected Diane might consider a new kind of intimacy.

"You're a liar," said Diane finally, into the cold stillness of Paul's room. "You lied. You knew I wouldn't want to be with a man."

Paul looked up at his wall collage of magazine pages and tried to gather his thoughts.

"I didn't fucking lie," Paul said, shedding the sleeping bag like a boxer or a lady aristocrat. "I never fucking lied. You lied to me first—I know you talked to that bear. You talked to a bear! You talked to a bear and then just pretended nothing happened. Plus I don't *know* what I am—so how is that lying? I mean, I'm obviously not some *man.* Jesus!"

"Don't raise your voice at me, Polly," said Diane, her body taut and almost menacingly still. She spoke his name not pointedly but with a great politeness. Paul wondered for an instant if she could turn him into a punishment animal, like maybe a stag.

"I'm not," he said, attempting, and failing, to modulate his voice. "I'm not what you think."

Diane made a noise Paul realized must be a "scoff." She scoffed at him!

"I mean, I *am* what you think, what you thought," he continued, and as he spoke he felt more and more like Dionne Warwick, his words swelling orchestrally, a wave of tears threatening to break. "I'm the girl you met at Michigan, the girl who can't stop thinking about you, the girl who wants to be your girlfriend."

Diane sighed and began to unlace her boots. Paul superstitiously subdued a mental victory yawp, his tears barely a memory. Everything was happening so quickly. He wished he could somehow videotape this entire night, internal and external, to

pore over later, to parse, to own. He couldn't keep up with his own life, he thought. He should really keep a journal.

"Can I use your bathroom?" Diane said.

"It's this way." Paul waited for her in the dark kitchen, pouring glasses of water and hoping Christopher wouldn't wake up and wonder why lesbians were fighting in the apartment. When Diane reemerged, he handed her a glass. She put it down and pulled Paul to her by the incline of his waist, running her rough hands over his hips. Paul tipped his head up to be kissed but Diane mysteriously did not kiss him. She wanted to, he thought. In fact, he was sure she wanted to. But instead she bent her head to where the front of his shoulder met the top of his breast, like a weary knight. He could feel her lank hair on his collarbone.

"Why do you think I drove all the way to Iowa?" she said.

×

They didn't wake up until after two the next afternoon. Thank god Diane had a car. They had to drive way out on South Gilbert to find food, to that all-day breakfast place with the bicycle wheels on the walls and the special vegetarian omelettes. Paul wanted to show Diane everything good about Iowa City and to not see anyone he knew.

Diane, surprisingly enough, drove like a highly caffeinated cabdriver. Paul buckled himself in, discreetly, and tuned the radio to KRUI, chattering happily about the particular charms of Iowa City college radio.

"Very cool," Diane said, accelerating through a yellow light.

She was such a surfer, he thought, admiring how her hair fell in her half-lidded eyes even as she recklessly took a corner without slowing.

The radio played "Atomic Dog." Paul sang along, barking in the pauses.

"Your accent is terrible," Diane said.

"Grrr," said Paul, lazily wondering if she was joking. He slipped out of his seatbelt and curled against the door to better watch Diane. She manipulated the gearshift in the desultory manner of an Italian race car driver, and Paul imagined her manipulating something gearshift-shaped inside him with such grace and purpose. How different this morning was from the night before, he marveled, and was unable to banish intrusive nature metaphors (a calm sea after a storm, a single crocus poking up through snow, etc., etc.) from his mind.

The line of hungover poets, bakers, and seventh-year undergrads stretched out the door, but what did Paul care? More time to canoodle. He was a girl in the daylight where he lived, with his hot lesbian lover who had recently fucked him for *three hours straight.* He saw some dykes he didn't know in line, and they nodded at him, the secret head-nod acknowledgment. He knew they were nodding at him because Diane was tracing patterns on his hand. He could smell her unwashed hair; she smelled amazing. He said so.

"Mmm, *you* smell amazing," Diane said. Then: "Oh! I think . . . Oh, I just figured something out."

"What?" Paul said, bracing himself.

"You always smell the same," said Diane. "You smelled the same last night when I first saw you as you do now."

PAUL TAKES THE FORM OF A MORTAL GIRL

The waitress approached, smiling the smile of liberal toler-
ance, and showed them to a booth, where they sat across from
each other holding hands.

"Really? I smell the same?" Paul said, nodding his desire for
coffee to the waitress. "Don't I smell somewhat less like smoke
and beer after that shower?"

"No," said Diane. "I mean you smell like a girl all the time.
You didn't smell like a boy before. You can't fake pheromones. I
think you're really female. Like, chemically or something."

"That's cool," said Paul. "I think that must be true."

"Did you always know you were a girl?" Diane asked.

The waitress came back, took their order, and left.

Paul thought. Had he always been a girl?—

×

—Paul remembered watching *Bad News Bears*, feeling like
Tatum O'Neal in the face of his gym teacher's surprise he could
hit the ball.

Paul remembered a girl in kindergarten who wore a tee
shirt that said "Anything boys can do, girls can do better!" and
he remembered coveting that shirt.

Paul remembered dressing up in his mom's maroon-and-
lime-green paisley pantsuit.

Paul remembered babysitting his high-school math teacher's
kids, cleaning the kitchen after they went to bed, but pretending
he'd spent the night watching baseball.

Paul remembered playing house with his *Star Wars* action
figures and knowing not to admit it.

Paul remembered always wanting to be the medic when the neighbor kids played war.

Paul remembered Stevie Nicks's voice, how his voice *should* sound, and the promise of her name, a secret way around the problem of what to be called.

Paul remembered Halloween.

Paul remembered the pink extra blanket, huddling underneath and making sparks with his legs.

Paul remembered letting his family call him Pauly well into high school, and discouraging the practice only after the appearance of Pauly Shore, "the Weasel."

Paul remembered Boy George. And Marilyn.

Paul remembered the split second in *Tootsie* where Jessica Lange thinks Dustin Hoffman is a lesbian and *considers* it.

Paul remembered *Rocky Horror.*

Paul remembered turning the channel to *Bosom Buddies* when no one else was in the rec room.

Paul remembered feeling excited during certain parts of *Freebie and the Bean,* the second *Back to the Future, Ghostbusters,* and *Victor/Victoria*—perhaps especially *Victor/Victoria.*

Paul remembered seeing a picture of Patti Smith for the first time, that flash of recognition when he first came across the Mapplethorpe postcard at the gay bookstore in Binghamton, thinking that's what he looked like on the inside, taping that postcard up in every room he'd lived in since.

Paul remembered alibis and secret victories: he remembered dressing up as one of the guys from KISS to wear makeup; he remembered pretending to like punk rock in order to pierce his ears; he remembered New Wave eyeliner.

Paul remembered watching a foreign movie he now knew to be *Fanny and Alexander* on public television one Sunday afternoon and when Kostas and his mom walked in saying he "liked history."

Paul remembered the dollar theater which showed movies like *Some Like It Hot* and *Cabaret* on Saturday afternoons, and telling Kostas he wanted to be a filmmaker.

Paul remembered Stanley's department store downtown, buying the smallest bottle of Chanel No. 5 with his snow-shoveling money one year, "for my mother."

Paul remembered how he kept the bottle in the stomach of his Trojan horse bank, taking it out only if no one else was home.

Paul remembered that paper on being a feminist man he wrote for his first women's studies class; he remembered faking it; he remembered his undeserved A.

Paul remembered Kostas's face when he took away Paul's flea-market Barbie, the socked-away Barbie boa and shimmery evening gown Paul kept in his Hot Wheels suitcase, under the bottom layer of Toreros and Karmann Ghias—girl cars!

Paul remembered the time he had sex with Heather Federson, how jealous he was she got to feel a dick inside her, how she got to feel hands on her breasts.

Paul remembered reading about British public school boys, and how they had to act the girl parts in their school plays, and how it was no big deal.

Paul remembered playing Puck his freshman year of high school, tights and glitter and the pancake makeup hiding his lack of facial hair.

Paul remembered the day in sixth grade the substitute

yelled at him for being in the boys' line for recess, and her mean face apologizing. And the other sixth graders' looks of shame at knowing Paul.

And farthest back in the recesses of time—the first recess, the first freedom!—Paul remembered Paphos, barely, remembered running down the beach in his tie-dyed tee shirt with his long salty hair his mom hadn't cut until they moved back in with his grandparents, and all the old Greek ladies pinching his mom's pretty little darling; Paul was pretty, darling, a girl, yes—

×

—"Yes," said Paul. "Did *you*?"

Diane laughed, delighted.

"Oh yes," she said. "As long as it's permanently unclear what it means, I've always been a girl."

Now Paul laughed. The waitress delivered them their respective American cheese omelet and oatmeal, which they dug into.

"I had you pegged as a kind of a hippie-artist-antitheory person," said Paul. "Maybe even an essentialist."

"Oh, that's nice," said Diane. She reached over and stole a forkful of hash browns.

Paul arched one eyebrow.

"Expropriations," she said, and shrugged.

"I'm not the enemy," said Paul. In his peripheral vision, he noticed Greg and James walk in. *That* was an odd pairing. He slid down in the booth and banked on the likelihood they wouldn't notice girls.

"To each according to her needs?" Diane offered.

"Why can't you stay a few more days?" Paul said.

He drank the last of his coffee and waved unobtrusively for the check. He couldn't invite Diane to move to town, but he didn't want her to leave either. She didn't have a real job or an apartment; she was a renegade traveler; she *was* kind of a hippie. If she thought he was open to it, she might just decide to stay. It was a fine line. He pushed it gently.

"What's so great about Provincetown?"

"My friends already have a house," she said, pulling out a twenty and waving Paul's money away. "And I found a painting job for the off-season but it starts on the first. So I have to get back."

"Yeah," said Paul. "Okay, but what's another couple days?"

"Maybe one more day," said Diane.

"Two," said Paul.

He'd have to tell Christopher something. Or maybe Jane would let them stay in her place and she could crash with the barista? Ugh, now he was saying the dread word. The *counter girl* would let her crash, he was sure of it. That would be good for Jane, an excuse to get laid. He'd be doing her a favor.

He put on his jacket quickly, turning away from Greg and James. Outside, Diane leaned Paul up against the side of her car and stared at him.

"I can't believe how beautiful you are," she said. "I can't believe you want to go out with me."

Paul squirmed under her scrutiny. He leaned forward quickly, offering himself to be kissed, and was obliged.

"Okay," Diane said. "One more day, but maybe you can come visit over your break."

×

Jane unlocked the front door of her studio loudly to avoid surprising Paul and Diane, but they were gone. She took stock—she'd definitely have to do laundry, and, of course, go grocery shopping. She found a pair of lacy panties that must belong to Paul, and she used her salad tongs to pick them up and throw them away. She didn't mind when Paul ate all her food and fucked some random in her bed, but Diane just bugged her. She had never once acknowledged Jane, which seemed at best a violation of the ancient laws of hospitality and at worst a serious misunderstanding of a butch's job. What did she even see in Paul? He was pretty, Jane gave him that.

×

As the semester waned, Paul realized he had a homework situation—three overdue response papers for feminist film theory (a class he loved, so why didn't he just write them?), two other term papers, and a chemistry midterm to make up. He also had a post-office box full of SASEs and looseleaf-wrapped dollar bills for his zine. He should really make more copies and send them out. After the review in *Holy Titclamps* and the mention in the queer zines listing in *Factsheet Five*, he'd been swamped with fan mail and requests for a second issue. Being a star was extremely stressful, he thought. He had the sophomore slump.

More alarming, however, was his cash flow situation in the wake of his last phone bill. Paul studied the *Press-Citizen*'s clas-

sifieds. Nobody was hiring except Mondo's for dishwashers. He needed to make money fast if he was going to take the whole winter break off and go hang out in Provincetown with Diane. He put on his ironic/dirty Iowa Hawkeyes Wrestling baseball cap and biked downtown. Mondo's was a sports bar off the ped mall, across from the creepy parking garage; Paul instinctively avoided this entire block of East Burlington and had never been inside Mondo's (the name alone a deterrent). He said very little to the polo-shirted manager who interviewed him, not trusting his inflections to sound heterosexual. Not speaking seemed to send the right message, and Paul was immediately hired, two shifts a week starting the next night. He wouldn't have any nights off now, with his shifts at the club and the Linn Street, but that was fine by him. Like Alicia Bridges, Paul loved the nightlife, loved the disco round. Working nights let him out efficiently into his own secret world.

The guys in the Mondo's kitchen were very different from the guys in the Linn Street kitchen. The cooks at Mondo's compiled pulled pork sandwiches or bacon double cheeseburgers or plates of nachos with sour cream, green paste from a tube, and bacon bits. Almost everything Mondo's served included pork, a proud nod to Iowa's industry—*the Other White Meat*. Paul pretended not to know Mondo's wasn't fine dining. As a basic safety precaution for his first—and all subsequent—shifts, he stripped himself of style, wrapped a Deadhead bandana over his hair and wore a plain but not faded black tee shirt and baggy jeans. He spoke minimally: he accepted his shift meals, inquired after scores of Hawkeye sporting events (except swimming), and once offered an Iron Maiden tape for the kitchen boom box—all standard dishwasher behavior in

this town. He was particularly proud of the Iron Maiden move; he'd bought the tape for a quarter at the Salvation Army, for the name's camp value. He supposed he could invent a computer science major, but he thought maybe that was de trop.

So he'd go into work, wash dishes furiously for four hours, eat as many fajitas as possible while sitting on a salsa bucket by the walk-in, wash more dishes, and leave. He never stuck around for a shift drink and Truly Tasteless Jokes session with the cooks. He barely spoke to the waitresses, who were all girls, and so were dangerous in a different way. A real dishwasher wouldn't say the things Paul thought, like "Cute side ponytail!" or "I think Brent the busboy is flirting with you!" or "Did you get those shoes at Domby's? Can I ask how much?" Paul kept his mouth shut. He needed more money than he was making at the club and Linn Street combined, and no one else was hiring. Plus, he knew he could just quit without notice; he wouldn't care about burning a stupid sports-bar bridge.

He'd been working at Mondo's for two weeks when Chad announced at a pre-shift staff meeting that the owners were inviting everyone to a Christmas party at Givanni's, their more upscale Italian restaurant. Paul overheard the waitresses sniping about the conceited Givanni's staff. Paul didn't care; he liked a free meal and an open bar. He was allowed to bring one guest, but Jane refused, and he wasn't about to invite Christopher to flame all over him. He'd go alone, be a spy, finally see what normal straight people did when no one was looking.

The night of the party, Paul biked downtown in his dressed-up dishwasher clothes: black pants and a white button-down and a shiny powder-blue Macy's brand tie borrowed without asking (and after a judgmental moment of discovery) from

Christopher's closet. He stood by the bar, trying to get his one free drink. The two girl bartenders ignored him. He saw the cooks drinking shots in their frat-boy dress-up clothes at the other end of the bar. Paul was a bad spy. No one was going to talk to him; he was being frozen out by normal people, kings of their own element. One of the waitresses flat-out ignored Paul's repeated attempts to start a conversation. The cooks looked like a couple of Army guys; Paul remembered with a start how in his world those guys would be considered meat, trade, objects. Paul decided to get one for himself, see what it was all about.

"Hey, Chad," he said to the manager, a former wrestler and current MBA student.

"You didn't bring anyone?" said Chad.

"Oh," Paul said, thinking. "Actually my sister's meeting me here, but I have to go make a phone call. Is that cool?"

"Sure," said Chad. He finished his Molson Ice and released a small belch. "Excuse me."

Paul left the restaurant, and biked home very fast. He felt brave, like Elliot in *E.T.* He changed himself, put on a tight miniskirt and cleavagey striped shirt and strappy platform shoes he'd been hoarding. He called a cab, and was back at the restaurant a half hour after he'd left. No one questioned him at the door. Pretty girl privilege, he thought. He'd heard of it and tonight he was going to test it out.

ABBA came on as he moved to the end of the bar where the cooks stood, drinking their manly ice beers.

"Excuse me," Paul said. "I can't get the bartender's attention. Can you—?"

The cooks sprang into service like two cartoon lackeys.

"What're you drinking?" said one.

"It's free, right?"

The cooks nodded vigorously and exchanged a glance. Paul thought carefully; he needed his drink to communicate his intentions.

"Maybe a Long Island?" He beamed cleavage at the cooks and composed his face into an expression of apprenticeship.

"Have you had anything else already?" said the bigger cook. "You don't want to mix with a Long Island."

"Oh, good point," said Paul. "I had some wine. What should I get? I like sweet drinks." He wondered if his makeup was too queer, too thick.

"Maybe another glass of wine?"

"Ooh," Paul said, inspired. "I want a daiquiri!"

The cooks looked at each other and laughed. Paul knew he had nailed his performance. Now he would take it to the next level.

"Wait—what are *you* guys drinking?" Paul imagined Jane's disapproval.

"Oh, we're doing Jäger shots. Do you want a shot?" The bigger cook leaned his muscular bulk onto the burnished metal bar top and signaled for the bartender, who jiggled her way to him at a speed which made Paul marvel. He'd never move that fast for a hot guy. It sent the wrong message.

A round of Jäger shots magically appeared and were festively drunk.

"Which restaurant do you work at?" the smaller cook asked.

"Oh," said Paul. "I don't. I'm just meeting my brother here, but I can't find him. He works at Mondo's."

"We work at Mondo's!" cried the two cooks.

"I'm Polly," said Paul.

"Dave," said the bigger one.

"Dan," said the smaller one.

Paul was happy to get their names straight for the first time. Even though Dave was probably 6'2" and Dan was maybe 5'8" Paul couldn't reliably tell them apart. Both were ripped, both spiked up their blonde crew cuts with gleaming gel, and both had spring-break-in-Cancun tans. The littler one was hotter: more compact and with Sears-model blue eyes. The bigger one—*Dave*, right—was okay-looking, kind of square. Paul let a crowd coming in the door squish him closer to the bar, in between the cooks.

"Sorry!" he said merrily.

Dan ordered more shots.

"Paul seems like a cool guy," said Dave. "Quiet."

"We're total opposites," said Paul. "He's always been really quiet, and like, *deep.*"

"You're not deep?" said Dave. "You seem like a deep chick."

Paul wondered what he'd done to give off this impression. Was he dressed wrong? Did he say something dorky? Or did guys talk to girls like this?

"Of *course* I'm deep," he giggled and scolded at the same time. They did a second shot and he could feel himself warming. He felt cozy and gregarious, everywhere and maybe especially in his pussy. He weirdly loved these guys. The dinner segment of the party had ended, and the tables had been moved to the walls to make room for a makeshift dance floor. The first song the DJ played was "Disco Inferno."

"I love this song! We have to dance," said Paul. He was just going to let it all unfold. The cooks followed and they

made a tiny circle amid the purse-clutching waitresses and air-punching busboys. The bigger cook was definitely more focused on Paul, and Paul was just a little oarless boat on a stream. He danced closer to the big one. He was *so* big. He wasn't a bad dancer. Dan, the littler one, seemed annoyed, and Paul began to wonder if *he* liked Dave. Ha, Paul thought. I bet! That's why he's not into me . . . Dan excused himself to find the bathroom, which Paul took as confirmation of his analysis.

"Disco Inferno" ended and the DJ paused, then played "YMCA." Paul watched his coworkers make nostalgic letters with their arms. Probably thinking about swimming lessons, he thought. He stopped dancing in protest.

"Do you want to go outside where we can talk?" Dave said.

"I can't hear you," Paul said. He did not want to talk. "Let's get another shot."

Dave nodded and led Paul back to the bar by the hand. They were now on a date, it seemed. Dave gently pushed Paul right up to the bar and protected him from the outside world with his bulk. Paul took this in, feeling Dave's body whispering close to him. Dave took care of everything, ordering shots, fending off other people, whatever needed taking care of. Paul twisted his body around so instead of his ass brushing Dave's pants, they were face to face. Paul felt very private in the lee of Dave's body and the protective cover of drunk girls on barstools all around him. He let his wrist dangle and bump Dave's pleated pants. No one could see a thing. He looked Dave in the eye and let the backs of his fingers drum the hard line of Dave's fly.

"Let's go outside and get some air," Dave said. It wasn't a question. Paul nodded and followed as Dave cleared a path

through the people. Outside, the ped mall was too well lit. Dave led Paul into the alley behind Givanni's.

"Classy," said Paul, gesturing to the dumpsters.

"Do you really care?" said Dave.

Paul was alone in an alley with a guy who might start punching his face at any moment, if he knew. Paul felt his barely noticeable arm hairs levitate. He breathed air like thrilling Mini-Thins through his insides. Dave did a little swaying dance, pulling Paul to him. Paul came up to his chest and had to tilt his head up to see Dave's face.

Dave kissed him then, a sloppy oniony kiss but not too bad. Paul noticed his pussy area was no longer cozy and gregarious-feeling. That would come back, he thought. This was hot! He was totally passing with a straight guy! Dave pushed Paul's breasts up and ran his hands over Paul's miniskirt. Paul guessed this was foreplay. He ran his hands over Dave's pants, and Dave pushed into him, pushed Paul against the gross brick wall and expertly unzipped his own fly at the same time. Paul found Dave's fleshy half-hard penis in his hand, insistent. Dave pushed on the back of Paul's neck, to let Paul know he should bend over. Paul crouched down and rubbed Dave's knobby penis more.

"Come on," said Dave. He sounded annoyed. "Come *on*, just put it in your mouth. You started this."

Christ, thought Paul. *Had* he started this? he wondered. He wanted to finish it, to know that he'd passed. He wanted his spoonful of proof. But this guy was kind of a tool. He put his mouth over Dave's cock head and Dave shuddered. The alley smelled of dishwater and rotting garlic bread. Dave pushed into the back ridges of Paul's throat over and over, which Paul

did not find arousing. Paul touched the ground with one hand to keep his balance and encountered a shallow pool of slime. He moved his hands to Dave's ass, to wipe off the slime and to make this whole thing go faster. He strangely wanted to cry but didn't. What was he even doing here? He let Dave pound his throat sore, and massaged Dave's ass through his pants. When Dave started to buck, Paul tried to get up, to disentangle his mouth from the whole operation, but he wasn't fast enough. Dave squirted yellowish mucus onto Paul's lip and chin. Paul knew his lipstick was completely gone at this point, so he spat, hitting Dave's shoe, and wiped his mouth with his arm like a sailor.

"Another shot?" said Dave.

"Um, no," said Paul. "I have to go find my brother."

"Okay," Dave said. "Want some help?"

"No, thanks," Paul said.

"It was great meeting you," Dave said.

"Totally," Paul said. He wasn't sure how much longer he could hold his body in place in this nasty alley. "We should hang out some time."

Paul walked with unsteady dignity toward the Holiday Inn lobby, where he asked them to call him a cab to the Foxhead. He had to find Jane.

IV.

On the first leg of his trip home for winter break, a puddle jumper to Chicago, Paul sat next to a business-looking man from Cedar Rapids, silently judging. What manner of business could anyone even conduct from Cedar Rapids? Why would you choose to wear pleated pants? Bit early for that lite beer, isn't it? And so on. His head throbbed from the party the night before, which had been a combination send-off and second annual twenty-first birthday party (Jane's idea, because she knew he was vain about his age).

Paul stripped down to his *Nobody Knows I'm a Lesbian Psycho Killer* tee shirt and read with aggressive spaciousness his copy of *Bimbox*, a queer Canadian zine which advocated, through collage, violence toward businessmen.

At O'Hare for two hours, Paul lugged his tightly stuffed backpack and large duffel across concourses. He'd brought all his best clothes and music, just in case. He sat cross-legged against the wall of Gate 22B, listening to the tape Diane had sent him for the trip in the Walkman (Walk*mate*, they said at Michigan) Jane had semi-permanently lent him. Diane's tape was heavy on art rock and country songs he didn't know, with bits of David Bowie and Donovan carefully wedged in, and surprisingly sloppy—cut-off songs, no track listing, snatches of what she'd taped over (Al Green), which he decided to take as a subconscious romance message. He'd gotten the package in the mail a few weeks before, had played two songs and immediately stopped the tape. It was noise and he gave up. But now,

after four hours on auto-reverse, he had broken through its difficulty and found its beauty.

The first tape you ever got from someone was always an adjustment in how you thought of them, an insight into how they saw themselves. Diane was much cooler than Paul had originally thought; she wasn't secretly cool, she was actually cool. She was an artist, not just a fan. He wondered if she'd still like him after they spent six weeks together. She knew some of what he was, but not all.

The intercom called his flight, and Paul stood up. He was entering his last days of boyhood, at least for a while. He'd be in Provincetown with Diane in a few days, right after this quick placating stopover at his mom's house, payment for the plane ticket she'd sent. Maybe he should have gone into the men's room, seen if he couldn't have gotten a farewell handjob. He'd spent the flight unsuccessfully requesting special favors from the flight attendant, who obviously was one of those "Straight-Acting, Straight-Appearing GWM Seeks Same" liars. So much for the mile-high club.

When Paul arrived at the Albany airport, his mom was waiting by the baggage claim. She'd been waiting for an hour but she didn't mind, she said, as if Paul had made the plane late, possibly through his choice of outfit or just through original sin.

"How many bags did you *bring*?" she said. She was so practical, his mother. "I thought you were only staying a week."

"Actually, I'm going to visit a friend of mine in Cape Cod for New Year's," he said, refusing her the satisfaction of hearing him name a female friend. "And then I'm going to fly back from Boston. So not quite a week."

"Well, Ari will be sorry to hear that," she said. "He was really looking forward to some big-brother time."

Paul could not suppress an eye roll. Ari had never once looked to Paul for anything brotherly, hadn't even bothered to come to the airport—and why would he? Being seen with Paul was the last thing a sixteen-year-old kid in Troy would want. His mother shouldered Paul's large duffel. He tried to take it from her and she pushed his hand away.

"And don't you want to spend time with Grammy? I know she wants to see you."

"Mom," said Paul. "Jesus. She doesn't even remember my name."

"Of course she remembers your name, and watch your language," his mother snapped. "You know, Ari visits her every week. He's very devoted. And she always asks after you—how's Paul, is Paul doing a new play? Is Paul a famous actor yet? She never got over your Shakespeare days."

"For chrissake, Mom," said Paul. "It was one play."

"But you were so good."

"Mom!"

Paul closed his eyes in the car, claiming travel-related nausea while his mother filled him in on the goings-on of various relatives he couldn't quite place, over the low hum of public radio. At appropriate pauses he asked, "How *is* Dmitri, still at HVCC?" or "So, what's happening at work?" and let her talk. Jane's old Walkman pressed into his side, clipped to his big white belt. He felt the old desperation. What if he couldn't get out of this town again, was somehow trapped here while all the other fun people were hanging out together somewhere else? He mentally assembled a soundtrack for the depressing stretch

of highway between Albany and Troy—mostly Skinny Puppy or KMFDM—and then for Troy itself, where abandoned liters of Crystal Pepsi tumbleweeded down the empty streets. This required the big guns, the Pogues' "Old Main Drag" or L7's "Pretend We're Dead," which reminded him now of Diane, in the kitchen at Michigan. He remembered driving the streets of Albany the summer after high school, wearing sunglasses in a futile effort to distance himself from Justin Rosenblum, who while nicely chauffeuring carless Paul around town tended to blast the Communards from the rolled-down windows of his Saab.

"Paul," said his mother. "Wake up, my babydoll. We're home."

He opened the car door, now legitimately nauseated and headachey. Nothing had changed—same shabby ranch, same lone sheath of vinyl siding disengaged and dangling off the side of the house, same plastic Santa climbing into the chimney on the across-the-street neighbor's roof, same old Huffy—Paul's, in fact—rusting under the carport. He saw the light on in the basement window, his bedroom—Ari's bedroom now. He should call Justin, he thought, see if he was home for the holidays and wanted to get a proper drink somewhere, like two clever prodigals. Justin probably still had his own car; they could hit the gay bars in Albany. Then again, Justin Rosenblum, like most other twenty-two-year-olds Paul knew, had already graduated from college, and so, logically, was not on semester break, and anyway being Jewish was probably not planning to come home from LA for *Christmas*. Paul followed his mother into the living room, where she'd made up the couch for him. He might have to go to Provincetown early, Paul realized; he didn't know how much more of Troy he could take.

×

In high school Paul had been neither popular nor cast out, but instead alternated between the two states, a comedian and a scholarship boy. He worked just hard enough to maintain his full ride to Albany Academy, to placate his parents and to avoid Troy High, which was chock-full of meatheads he'd known since second grade. Albany Academy was twenty minutes from his house, and a world away. His mom dropped him off on her way to her job as a teacher's aide at Doyle, and he usually made his own way home. His first year he made friends from a variety of circles. He played D&D on Friday nights with a group of guys from Latin class, watched arthouse films up at RPI with Beckett and girls Beckett knew from Emma Willard, made JV soccer, and got himself cast as Puck in the school play. His characters tended to die early in their campaigns, he sat on the bench for four years, and he *had* been cast as a fairy, but Paul felt somehow right in those mahogany halls, surrounded by boys in navy blue blazers, as though he'd finally found the backdrop he'd always deserved.

Then, in Paul's second year, Justin Rosenblum arrived from Atlanta, flaming like a comet. Justin flamed so helplessly and with such a sweet and foreign Southern drawl he was almost tolerated by the other boys, and by Paul's third year, he was willing to meet Justin in the school library to "study," Paul's code for trading copies of gay books they'd found at the used bookstores in town.

Like all underclassmen, Paul was prey to the older boys, especially the hockey players and the Junior ROTC guys and, for some reason, the Model UN members, who coughed "fag" at

him in multiple languages. Paul felt, at those moments, a revulsion for the terrible cliché of high school, a revulsion no number of John Hughes movies or New Wave mixtapes could heal.

Yet those same hockey players and glee club heroes and future Masters of the Universe came to Paul hat in hand when they needed a nickel bag. Paul had learned after his first semester to play up his townie street cred, buying a few dimes at a time from his half-cousin Dmitri with money from summer caddying. He supplied freshmen and sophomore boys too scared to buy from the juniors and seniors. Paul might be small and too graceful, but he knew how to talk like a kid from the projects and scare the shit out of the overgrown Nordic sons of judges and doctors.

In tenth grade, Paul lost his straight virginity strategically, to Heather Federson, sister of one of Beckett's friends, a girl prettier and fancier than a boy in Paul's category could reasonably be expected to date. Heather Federson was the sort of rich girl for whom the effortless things (her beauty, intelligence, and appeal to others) were worth little. She liked Paul's ice-cream-social monologues, his comparative subtlety in the field of high-school boys, and even, he suspected, his girlish looks. They'd bonded over their shared appreciation of Echo & the Bunnymen and the Dead Kennedys and *Heathers.* Paul suspected Heather Federson thought going to her junior prom with Paul was her big Winona Ryder moment, which he did not begrudge her. At the after-prom party at Tom Minard's house in Grafton, they'd found a guest room and locked the door.

Paul was naturally curious about girls; he didn't know how to find a boyfriend; and sex was sex, he thought. Later, other

gay men would find this remarkable; they would make their endless fish jokes, or confess proudly their inability to get hard with some cheerleader. Paul didn't understand that. What was sex but newness? And sensation and conquest and intrigue and desire and romance and fantasy, and specific people sometimes, sure, but not always. Having sex with Heather Federson had been hotter than sucking off the fourth guy he'd ever gone down on. Not as hot as the first three, the newness there trumping their less-appealing qualities. Fucking Heather Federson had been scary and dangerous and even humiliating, and he'd felt brave to do it and protective of her and scared of her and all of that was fun, right? And it was fun to put his dick inside her, a different kind of masturbation, and she was sarcastic and had cute clothes, and so what if he couldn't ever fall in love with her? She didn't love him either, and wouldn't. She was proving something on him too. Boys were harder, easier, more dangerous, and mostly Paul just *wanted* them more, but something was better than nothing, when it came to sex, and always, always he was curious. As a kid he'd been as interested in girls' bodies as boys': the thrill of information versus the thrill of the unspeakable.

What he shared with the gay men he met later was the claustrophobia of doing what everyone else did. He had the prison nightmares of his bedroom shrinking, of living in a ranch house outside Albany with some expectant and then expecting woman asking him to fix the car and mow the lawn and go to a job and come back and never do anything fun. Heterosexuality = marriage = death, Paul knew.

When Paul first fled Troy he didn't get far, just two hours away to Binghamton, home of the safety school. He'd applied

to NYU and Bennington, places he'd heard mentioned in conjunction with gays or artists, but not Vassar or Sarah Lawrence—even expressing an interest in places like those was tantamount to a declaration Paul wasn't prepared to make, not with a full year of high school to survive. In his optimism, Paul discounted the importance of his mediocre grades and junior year peach-schnapps-related suspension.

Binghamton was a comedown, a slap, a reminder of who he'd always be. Paul smarted his way through two semesters before realizing the combination of daily harassment, no interesting film classes, and serious dearth of cute boys meant he was wasting his student loans. He dropped out and planned to spend a summer in Troy, saving money, but when he took the train down to New York City for Pride, he knew he couldn't go back. He crashed for two weeks with a gay guy who'd just graduated from Binghamton, friend of a friend of a friend, who edited a well-known drag-queen zine and rarely left his room. Paul spent a year bussing tables at a series of restaurants in the East Village, sharing a subletted squat on Clinton Street in the Lower East Side and mooning after older go-go boys at Queer Nation demos.

Meanwhile, Kostas left Paul's mother, after seventeen years. She stayed in Troy with Paul's little brother, Ari, and Kostas moved home to Des Moines. He'd gotten a new job as a bookkeeper for a construction business and quietly moved in with his high-school sweetheart, with whom he'd apparently been exchanging letters this whole time.

Paul was more offended by the sentimentality than the cheating, by Kostas's low expectations of life. How could he love someone he met in *high school*? He didn't feel protective of

his mother so much as relieved his baby brother was there to tend to her, to hate his dad for her. Ari was good at that. Paul knew gays were supposed to be super-close to their mothers, confidantes, best little boys in the world, but he had never been close to either of his parents. They were alien species to each other: Kostas, with his secrets and his associate's degree, so happy to be out of Dubuque Works, where his own father and brothers all made articulated loaders (whatever those were), so happy to add up numbers for the physical plant at Hudson Valley Community College, to wear a suit to work, to try to pass as a professor at the diners near campus; his mom with her developmentally disabled students and her night classes and her all-day-every-day *goodness* and disappointment and morning Mass.

Still, when Kostas offered to claim him as a dependent so he could go to Iowa, with its low tuition and its film department, Paul found a way past his scorn. New York would eat him up, Paul thought. He'd already had anal sex one time (insertive) and he knew he'd have it again (receptive) if he stayed and then that would be it for him—waitering and eventual death. He would hide out, instead, in the safe Midwest, the flown-over lands where no plague could find him.

×

During an hour layover at the Providence bus station, Paul ducked into the first stall in the women's room. An elderly lady in a bedazzled white Portugal sweatshirt did a subtle double take, like she might say something, but when Paul came out all breasted-up and began to wash the six hours from Albany

off his face, then apply eyeliner and creamy bright pink lip-
stick, she just looked relieved. He bummed a cigarette from
a solicitous college boy in the parking lot and then reboarded
the bus, waiting to be questioned about the orange plaid mod
sweater dress he knew was just visible beneath his peacoat—
*Wait, you're not the swishy gay boy who was just sitting here! Thief!
Imposter! Where are your pants?*—but neither the bus driver nor
Paul's seatmate batted an eye. People saw what they wanted
to see and wanted to see what they expected to see, and Paul
could do whatever he wanted, like some sort of non-murderous
Raskolnikov. His lipstick tasted rough, chemical, like night-
time. He'd begun *The Price of Salt* earlier in the trip, and now
finished it, tearfully, right as the bus crossed the Bourne Bridge.
He packed up and put on his special amp-up tape of the
moment—*The Best of the Runaways*—for most of the remain-
ing minutes to Barnstable, sneaking strokes of his angora
thighs, imagining Diane's hands. He was going to see his dyke
lover and meet all her cool dyke friends. The bus pulled up to a
darling little clapboard cottage, which turned out to be a Mini-
Mart.

"Next last and final stop on this coach is Barnstable,
Mass.," said the bus driver. "Barnstable, Mass., folks, everybody
will disembark here I repeat this bus will not stop at Hyan-
nis Transportation Center today the next last and final stop is
Barnstable and a happy holiday to you and yours please take
any soda bottles or candy wrappers with you everybody off
Barnstable, Mass. . . ."

So *that* was how you pronounced Barnstable, Paul thought.
He accepted, somewhat flattered, the unnecessary help of the
across-the-way solicitous college boy in retrieving his duffel

from the overhead compartment, and then found himself in a standoff when he tried to let the boy leave first so he, Paul, could check his look one more time in the bus's dark windows. He hoped the boy wouldn't try to talk to him in front of Diane. He really didn't need that.

He spotted her right away, leaning against her VW in a blue flannel under a blue-and-tan western-style ski vest. She looked like the promise of a mustachioed young truck driver who'd take you to IHOP and play Gram Parsons in the cab on the way, minus the mustache.

Diane hadn't seen him yet, so he took a minute to check his lipstick. He looked over at her again. Her dirty dark urchin hair fell out of her watch cap and onto her face. Paul was a snare drum, and somebody played a gravity roll on him. He didn't want to alert her to his presence, wanted to keep watching as she chewed up and swallowed her bit-off nails. She was biting her nails over him, he thought with a mixture of guilt and resentment which he immediately banished.

Diane looked up and saw him—smelled him first, she said later. He waved a little half-wave then walked over to her, trying not to trip on the platform Frye boots he'd "borrowed" from Jane.

When he was close enough, she took his '70s thrift-score Lady Trojans softball duffel and slung it over her puffy blue shoulder like a team captain.

"I guess chivalry isn't dead," he said.

"I can't wait to fuck you," she said right in his ear with her hot breath. Paul also couldn't wait to be fucked and had suffered through nine-plus hours on a stale-smelling bus from Albany to the Cape for that express purpose. He followed her

to a stall in the public bathroom at the back of the Mini-Mart, and they curled their fingers into each other, mouths on necks, backs against metal walls, boots braced against the toilet.

They didn't talk in the car. Diane drove with only her left hand, impressing Paul greatly. She reached over, tucked her right hand down Paul's jeans, causing him to come again almost immediately. He liked this feeling of being subject to Diane and sat nicely in his seat for the rest of the trip, feeling very French, like Genet or Violette Leduc, a *classy* submissive.

He gazed out the window at the romantic desolation of the Cape in December. He'd only been here once before, as a child, to stay in a Hyannis motel called the Shamrock Inn with his grandfather, who'd passed the summer week in the motel bar while Paul shoplifted Sweet Valley Highs from a nearby strip-mall Waldenbooks. It had been one of the best weeks of his childhood. Nothing had changed, he thought.

With laser, almost cannabinoid focus, Paul noted the gradual shift from tidy roadside ranch houses and White Hen Pantries to shuttered fried-clam shacks and snow-coated cottages named for flowers, as if they were traveling back in time, passing the '80s and landing squarely in the '70s, clearly Diane's turf. She pulled into a clearing in what appeared to be a scraggly stretch of woods across from a boarded-up beachfront motel.

"Here we are," Diane said.

"Where?" said Paul. This woodsy isolation was not exactly what he'd been expecting when she invited him to stay with her in P-town for his break. He sincerely hoped he wasn't going to be asked to camp again.

"Don't be scared," she said, smiling in such a way that Paul felt himself to be truly known. She raised one finger, and he

looked up to see a sprawling weather-beaten Modernist house, tucked into a small hill. He could make out Christmas lights strung in the window, the thumping bass of a party in process.

"We don't have to hang out with everybody right now," she said, behind her the vast gray of gloaming light and sea. "They'll understand."

Diane grabbed Paul's backpack and duffel, leading him up the rickety steps, through sliding glass doors, past a blur of girls (*women!*) reclining in front of a fireplace in the open-plan living room, past a low-lit kitchen of half-open wine bottles and recently abandoned dishes, up a set of winding stairs, past a slightly ajar bedroom door through which Paul could just make out a few figures dancing in a black-lit room to what sounded like Digable Planets, past another door festooned with a taped-up sheet of butcher paper graffitied with a women's symbol with fist inside it and the anarchy A, up a second flight of stairs, and into a sort of crow's nest attic room, where they embarked on a thirty-six-hour reunion sex fantasia, breaking only to tip-toe down to the kitchen to retrieve plates of vegetarian lasagna or tofu curry left on the stove by Diane's thoughtful and now-absent housemates.

By Thursday noon, they were ready to breathe outside air. Diane drove them up Commercial Street to the only open restaurant, a little bayside diner called Dodie's, adorned with antique toys, where Paul ordered a giant all-day breakfast of pancakes, eggs, bacon, and sausage. Pleasingly, this was called the "Hungry Woman's Breakfast."

Diane frowned and ordered the tofu scramble. She regarded Paul icily.

"Are you okay?" Paul said.

"I'm fine," said Diane.

"'Cause you don't seem okay," Paul said.

"Well, you never told me you ate meat."

"Um," Paul said. "I eat meat."

"Meat comes from animals, Polly," Diane said. "You should hear how they talk about us. We're like Nazis to them. If you could hear what cows say, you wouldn't eat a cheeseburger ever again."

"Okay," said Paul. "But what about animals that eat other animals? Like cats or wolves or something? Aren't we just like them? Should cats not eat mice? Should lions not eat gazelles?"

"Jesus, Polly!" Diane said. "Don't make a game of this. I'm telling you something about my life."

Paul considered. He could lose her over this, he began to realize. And he liked animals, so why not take the moral higher ground? He'd go vegetarian, at least in front of her.

"Okay, no meat," he said. "But can I still eat eggs?"

"Sure," she said. "If you like eating chickens' periods."

Paul's stomach heaved slightly.

"No eggs!"

He changed his order to the tofu scramble, and Diane leaned across the booth to French him her approval. Paul was soft and acquiescent. He could change for love. There was a right answer. There was a scripted next line, and he could get it right. He was superheroic.

Their delicious vegan breakfast platters arrived.

"Will you teach me to cook vegetarian food?" he said.

Diane nodded happily.

"And if you're vegetarian, you could even maybe move in

officially," she said. "If you wanted. The only house rules are you have to be vegetarian and a woman."

"Hmm," said Paul, licking his fork. This tofu scramble thing wasn't bad with hot sauce. And as soon as he could, he'd sneak off and get a burger somewhere.

<div align="center">×</div>

Paul sat back deep in the couch in his New Year's outfit, intentionally dressed down to signal that New Year's Eve was for amateurs, watching all these cool Provincetown girls pass around an elaborate handblown glass bong in preparation for going dancing. Another carful of shockingly attractive disheveled girls arrived from New York, corduroy-clad and brandishing bottles of Rene Junot. From what he could make out, the new arrivals either currently attended or had recently graduated from Wesleyan, and were engaged in an unspoken coolness-battle with the Evergreen girls. A strapping androgynous Britishy girl (Wesleyan) slid Bettie Serveert's "Tom Boy" into the CD player and was seen and raised one by a girl with a homemade bowl cut and a Kim Wilde cassette (Evergreen). Paul didn't know where to look; Diane brought him a Flintstones jelly glass of wine, which he sipped happily, relishing the protective weight of her arm over his shoulder.

The rival gangs all turned for approval to Gerty, the townie sous-chef who'd rented the house cheaply for the winter and whom everybody else had met at Michigan. Gerty herself didn't engage in the coolness-off, instead holding forth about her plans to open her own restaurant that summer, or maybe

the following summer, all the while eyeing the preening dancers. She was clearly the powerbroker, a little older than the rest, a working-class butch fox in the college girl henhouse. Paul felt annoyed that she hadn't flirted with him yet. He was a college girl, he thought—but he knew those Wesleyan girls had something he never would have.

Diane didn't have whatever "it" was either (a trust fund, Paul thought, or maybe a childhood spent in Westchester), but she had something else, something different from everyone in the room, something different from other girls. Diane was as fascinatingly blank as any man. And as frustrating. A shiny reflective surface and Paul a magpie. The mystery of her cheeks, her dimples ever-shocking when she'd smile at him from across the bed or table. Jane had been the first person to explain to Paul about dimples. It was a category of desirable attribute he hadn't before considered, but now he saw dimples everywhere and—what were her eyes, chocolate syrup? Paul squirmed and shifted until the crotch seam of his cords pressed pleasurably against the soft triangle of his cotton panties. Diane had recently bought a pack of tighty-whities and he saw the yellow-and-blue-striped waistband sneaking out of her workpants. What was she? She was girlish but not womanly, she was an androgyne off the Left Bank, her choppy blunt cut like a WASPy little girl or a Dutch man, her signature red hooded sweatshirt zipped all the way up under her black pleather bomber jacket. Her huddled concentration, her finger in her mouth as she read, her brow furrowed—over what? what *were* her emotions? did she *have* emotions?—

Diane was *Combat Rock*, she was a song building, she was—what *was* that? a fuzzbox—she was Albertine, a tiger's

paw, a marble faun in a pocket garden, a whiskey sour, a traffic light turning red at twilight. Did Paul love Diane for her looks? Yes. *No.* Okay, yes. But what did it mean to love her looks? He could see the contrary position: some family Thanksgiving, the suburban television magazine agonies (too big, not feminine, *too big*, messy, dirty, bovine, slow). Her jaw like a statuary angel, her ears poking out through a sheaf of hair, her bangs in her eyes, her *clavicle* (new word), her broad features, her straight hips and hard small bumps of breasts in her frayed tee shirt. Her melancholy blankness, her hidden stores of thought and pain. Paul stared at Diane, remembered the day he'd met her in the Michigan kitchen, tried to hold onto whatever first invited this compulsion to stare, tried to understand, to puzzle her out, to possess through figuring out, to maintain, to plumb, to ensnare and study. What kind of creature was she, dark and earth-smelling, a rustic, topsoil-encrusted fingernails and all. The musk of her armpits at night, her red lips the texture of rose petals, the hard muscle of her arms, the occasional gray hair he'd find, her eyelashes like tarantulas' legs, she was Zeus's own sweet cow and his tender cupbearer at once, placid slow expanses of skin and what Paul knew to be called big-boned. She was bigger than him-as-Polly or him-as-Paul, a few inches taller and wider. Her shoulders were broader than his. You'll stretch it! he thought helplessly when she'd borrowed his shirt that morning, but no, better, he'd sacrifice his shirts for her. He'd wear the stretched-out shirt thinking *Diane's body was here and I am now inside the space she left, I fit myself inside her shape.*

"Is everybody coming to dinner?" Gerty asked loudly, startling Paul out of his reverie. She gestured with a novelty red

high-heel phone. "I have a table for ten but they'll make room for a few more."

At dinner, Paul and Diane sat squeezed together at the corner of a big table in the back room at Edwidge, an expensive-seeming restaurant upstairs from a pizza place. At least he'd save money if he had to eat vegetarian, he thought. Two of Gerty's performer friends joined them, ordering martinis and generally lording it over the college girls. Paul had begun to work out the taxonomy of Provincetown (should he say "P-town?"—he wasn't sure): performers seemed to occupy a stratum between tourists and townies—weekender tourist, all-summer tourist, short-season worker, long-season worker, year-round worker, queer townie, fisherman townie—but which one he wasn't sure. The performers, a large butch lounge singer in a tuxedo and a glamorous femme comedian, a dead ringer for Sophia Loren, drank copiously but didn't eat, in preparation for their late-evening shows at "the Crown" and "the Pied." Paul was careful to take in but not yet use the local patois. He still had newness to spend but wanted to transition easily and appropriately to authenticity when the time was right. Paul couldn't tell if the lounge singer and the comedian were together, but he could tell the lounge singer was checking him out. He moved his chair even closer to Diane, and made a show of stealing olives off her plate. But the lounge singer had him in her sights, and she fired.

"Honey child," she said, in raspy drag queen sotto voce. "What is going *on* with you two pretty ladies? Who is the *man* in your little ménage? Let Daddy tell you what's what."

Paul could feel Diane flinch; he cast about for a cutting

retort, but before he could say anything the comedian stepped in, with a slow, elegant, but menacing full-body turn in her chair.

"You leave those nice young people alone, Dynelle," she said, Southern honey dripping. "They just want to be free."

The lounge singer wasn't having it.

"Oh please," she drawled. "I'm just trying to mentor here, run a Big Brother Big Sister program to let these children know they can do something besides each other's hair. You know me, I'm a walking public service announcement."

The Wesleyan girls snickered—or the butch ones, at any rate. The femmes knew what Diane was, Paul thought, knew what she and Paul were doing, even if Diane herself didn't.

The waiter came to take more drink orders and the conversation shifted to backstage drag drama—Sahdjie said this and Ryan Landry said that and did you hear about Big Lil! On and on. The Wesleyan girls knew everybody, had waited tables at Café Blasé the previous summer. Paul didn't know any of the people being discussed but enjoyed proximity to any kind of fame. Diane did not seem to be having fun, which worried him. He wanted to go dancing after, and hoped this wouldn't ruin their night. The Evergreen girls began to talk amongst themselves. Diane looked lost.

"Hey," said Paul. "So, what's the story with all the whale watching here? And that coastal studies place, that seems a little fishy."

The lounge singer groaned and the Wesleyan girls ignored him but the comedian smiled generously at Paul.

The lounge singer jumped in.

"The whale watches gather whale data for the center," she said. "And they keep straight people off the streets, after we've taken their money."

"No," said Diane. "That's wrong."

"*Really?*" said the lounge singer, with a quick look of joy. "I'm *wrong?*"

"Yes, you're wrong," said Diane. "The coastal studies center tracks whales to protect them, like when they're beached or whatever. Those whale watches just spew their poison into the water, they don't help. That whole data-gathering thing is just marketing bullshit."

"Oh, I see," said the lounge singer. "An environmentalist. Of course. I bet you're from the West Coast, right? Well, what about the connections between the coastal studies center and the secret navy labs in Woods Hole? What do you say about that, huh? Didn't know about that, did you?"

What a trainwreck, Paul thought. Diane had gone into a sort of thrall state like that rabbit from *Watership Down* and the lounge singer was jabbering at her relentlessly. He signaled the waiter for more drinks, though realistically he should save his money in case there was a cover. Fuck it, he thought.

"That's just a rumor," said Gerty. "There's no military dolphins. Why do you people hate America? Shouldn't we get going?"

"Yes," cried the Wesleyan girls. "Allons-y!"

The waiter dropped the check on the table and the lounge singer grabbed it.

"Forty each should do it," she said. Paul felt a little sick. He looked at Diane, who also looked a little sick.

"This is so fucked up," he whispered, pulling two twenties out of his bra.

"I know," Diane whispered. "Military dolphins. Jesus."

They left in a pack, spilling into the bracing oceanic night. The performers said their loud goodbyes and see-you-laters, and Gerty led the way to the A-House, where they'd probably be the only girls. Everyone was very excited about this; there was a general air of transgression to the proceedings. Paul and Diane hung back a little, Paul chattering away and pointing out special features of the landscape as they passed—*What kind of tree do you think that is? It looks extremely old.* or *Look! A whole store devoted to men's underwear. Can you believe it!* But he could tell Diane was still angry.

When they arrived at the A-House—which was actually, Paul noted, called the Atlantic House, so he was already seamlessly using the inside words—Gerty got them all in for free. The A-House looked like everything else in Provincetown: a stop on some rich person's historical landmark garden tour, with rent boys and leather daddies instead of docents and butlers.

"You wanna see my card, Billy?" Gerty said, flicking the bouncer's leather suspenders. "You wanna see my friends' cards?"

"Friends of yours are friends of mine, Gerty," said the bouncer, queenishly. "But don't go telling Amos I let a bunch of underage girls in for you."

"Our little secret," said Gerty. She really was pulling out all the stops. Why did all the dykes in Provincetown sound like fags, Paul wondered.

Inside was any gay bar Paul'd ever been in, with a lower ceiling and redder light. He felt like he was at a gay rave in

Narnia. Instead of heading to the bar, Diane pulled him deci-
sively into a corner, next to a giant speaker pulsing out bass. She
pushed him up against the wall, kissing and grinding on him
so fiercely he forgot everything but his happiness. They were
almost hidden from view, just visible enough to be exciting.
Diane was surprising; every day she did something he didn't
expect. He would have thought she'd be agonizing over that
stupid lounge singer, or moping, not taking Paul exactly as he
wanted to be taken. He pushed his wet pussy against her thigh,
rubbing himself up and down her like an animal or an unself-
conscious teenager. He wanted what he wanted and he was
getting it—to be girls together with this hot tomboy girl. A
do-over. Right before he came, Diane pulled away and watched
him tremble. She maybe really was a top, he thought. At that
moment he would have done anything she'd asked. Best to nip
that in the bud.

"Let's get drinks," Paul said, miming a bottle. "Drinks!"

"Oh," said Diane, nodding.

She led them to the bar, where they waited and waited. And
waited. Boy after boy came up, ordered drinks, and returned
to the dance floor. That barman was extremely unprofessional,
Paul thought.

A handsome older bear walked up to the bar and stood
next to them.

"Let me help," he said, and flagged down the barman, who
came over immediately. "My friends would like a drink."

"Thank you," said Paul, accepting bottles of beer for him-
self and Diane.

"My pleasure," said the bear, tipping his leather baseball
cap at them before walking away. Paul watched him walk back

to his group of friends, bears all, except for a much smaller daddy–boy couple who both looked familiar. While dancing with Diane, Paul chewed on the question of how he knew them. After a few minutes he realized who the daddy was: Jack Manjoyne, the Falcon star who'd been in all those films with Joey Stefano. This was not an observation to share with the group, but Paul couldn't help taking a few more sneaking looks at Jack Manjoyne's boy-toy. Maybe another porn star? No, that wasn't it. But so *familiar*. Paul realized, with a start, who the boy was—the youth from Chicago! The youth who had definitely been a girl when last they'd seen each other.

Just then, Gerty came up to him and Diane, dancing brashly with Paul. Could no one see that he was with Diane? He danced away, not entirely oblivious to Gerty's charms.

"We're all going over to Jesse's house to party," Gerty said, tapping one finger under her nose significantly. "If you guys want to come."

"Sure," said Diane. Another surprise.

"Let's go," said Paul. He snuck one more glance, tinted now by a free-floating jealousy, at Jack Manjoyne and his boy, who had never once lifted his gaze from Jack. What did Paul care anyway? He was about to try cocaine, probably for free, it sounded like, with the coolest dykes he'd ever seen.

×

Very early Monday morning Diane left for her job on an all-women construction crew with a bunch of Gerty's townie friends. Diane was the apprentice, and the head carpenter was this leather daddy named Bev, who had also been at Michi-

gan and who Paul was pretty sure Jane had mentioned ten or twenty times. He wasn't sure how he felt about the whole Bev situation.

"You'll be okay, Polly? I should be home by four, definitely by five. I'm not sure when they'll let me go."

"Of course! I'll be fine," Paul said brightly, at once bereft and offended to be thought so. He kissed Diane goodbye and watched like a housewife from the sliding glass doors as Diane jumped into the waiting contractor-thick pickup, handsome and unknowable in her painter's pants and splattered boots. The truck drove off and Paul pulled his special maroon satiny bathrobe around him, sipping his coffee. He poked through the house's music collection and popped a Carly Simon tape into the kitchen boom box, letting the trilling heartbeat of its drumline wash over him. This song *was* about him, he thought. He *was* particularly vain! He probably should wear more apricot. He gazed romantically out the window for a moment, but without an audience the pose was both boring and uncomfortable.

"Hey," said a compact little butch who walked down the stairs, yawning. "We haven't met. I'm Zoe, the other housemate."

"Oh!" said Paul, knocking over his coffee. "I'm Polly, Diane's, um—"

"Right!" said Zoe, and handed Paul a dishrag. "Diane's mysterious long-distance girlfriend. I never even met you at Michigan. We've been calling you the Snuffleupagus."

"No, I'm real," said Paul, pleased to have been discussed, and at some length, apparently.

"I'm driving into town in a bit to check my mail, if you want to come with," said Zoe.

Paul decided he should take the offer, check out the scene.

Zoe chatted the whole way, pointing out the few places open in January—the post office, a twelve-step bookstore ("everybody who's here spends the winter either in AA meetings or in the bars"), the Governor Bradford ("the town straight bar"), a pizza place, and the Vault, a basement-level fag bar Paul pretended not to notice.

"They have a backroom down there," said Zoe, in a possibly wistful manner.

"Cool," said Paul, not entirely sure what tone to take.

"Yeah, right? But no girls allowed. There's also the Dick Dock, which is basically right in the center of town on the beach, where all the boys go to cruise at night—even in the winter. Fags have everything good . . ."

"It seemed like a lot of people were cruising at Michigan," Paul said. "It's not like women don't hook up."

"Sure, well, at *Michigan*," said Zoe. "But not anywhere else. I mean, I have *tried*, girl. I have tried."

Zoe said was she going "up cape" to do laundry with her friend Elena and Elena's toddler, and did he want a ride back, but Paul figured he could make his own way. He decided to explore the West End first, then on his way back he'd stop for coffee at the only open café in town. He waved Zoe off, nice as she was, and pulled his peacoat close against the wind.

Provincetown in winter did not look so very gay, Paul thought. How different was it, really, from any closed-up New England beach town? What was he doing here, in a village the size of a University of Iowa dorm, chock-a-block with quaint and gaudy bed-and-breakfasts? At that moment, he happened to glance into the front yard of one of the more gaudy than quaint bed-and-breakfasts, wherein he saw displayed a lush

diorama of bondage Barbies and SM Kens trussed up with ball-gags or resting in miniature slings. Somewhat mollified, he continued westward, which Diane had said was the "more gay" end of town. What did it mean, then, that Diane lived on the East End? He came upon a fork in the little toy road, and neither way appealed to him. He crossed over to the bay side and picked his way down to the beach. He'd walk back to the center of town and if he happened to see Zoe's famous dock, it wasn't as if he'd sought it out. He just liked to know where things were, was all. He thought about Diane, and for a full minute sincerely wished she was with him, wished they could look for the secret dock together.

He crunched through the frozen sand in his Frye boots, the tide a few inches away, nipping at him like a playful dog. Paul stared out at the bay. The bay was not the ocean, he reminded himself dutifully, without understanding. Diane had drawn him a map, showing him the special spiral of the town from a bird's-eye view, offered him a compass and even a quick lesson in celestial navigation, but Paul had no head for directions and promptly forgot everything she'd said. If he headed back toward the enormous phallic monument in the center of town, he'd find his café home base. He moved back up the beach, investigating the boarded-up houses. Who lived there? Rich old gay guys, probably, gone inland for the winter. Gay snowbirds. He had never been anywhere so empty of people before. He hadn't seen a soul in ages! He imagined being here with Diane, walking boldly through the front doors of all these closed-up cottages and rummaging through the owners' belongings. He wanted to do everything he wanted to do, but *with* her. That seemed like a sign of something, right? He wasn't going to have

enough money to pay his tuition bill for the semester, so why not just stay here and avoid his growing stack of Incompletes for a little while? Why not let rhetoric and chemistry fade into pleasant memories, struggles vanquished by time or his own craftiness? Maybe he could transfer somewhere in Massachusetts once he paid off last semester's tuition bill. Jane could mail him the rest of his stuff—tucked neatly away in her hall closet—by book rate, and . . .

He'd made his way back to the post office without noticing any docks. Perhaps another sign from the universe? He left the beach, found himself back on solid sidewalk, back to civilization with its attendant cappuccinos and new people. He pushed into the café, which though very small contained multiple queers as well as a few lesbians and a gay. Sweet relief! He ordered coffee to go from a tall fellow with piratical hoop earrings and a face tattoo and quickly left the place, in order to prolong whatever new-in-town mystery he might possess. He walked back in the general direction of Diane's house. He found a Norman Rockwell drugstore where he bought a few postcards, more for the relief of the transactional than out of a desire to communicate with anyone he'd left behind. He took his time, studied the shop windows—most stores were closed "for the season"; others, like the bookstore, the astrologer, and two fudge stores, only opened on weekends.

The only other open place Paul could find was the library, an old-timey white house set back from the street like a secret. He settled in for a few hours reading a well-worn copy of *Beebo Brinker*. When his ass began to ache, he headed out, stopping on the way to inquire about a library card. The nice old showtunes queen behind the desk advised Paul to send himself a

postcard in order to establish residency. No ID needed! This was indeed gay utopia, he thought, walking back to the house to eat whatever he could find and wait for Diane.

Zoe was already back, and offered him some split pea soup, which he accepted gratefully. She'd run into one of Gerty's friends at the laundromat, she said, this older townie real estate agent who'd offered Zoe a steady job prepping rentals for the season if she could get another person, and what did Polly think?

"It pays decently well and it's under the table," she said. "So we don't have to declare anything. We'd have to clean sometimes but we'd also get to paint."

"Definitely," said Paul. "I used to have a cleaning job." Again, no ID necessary. He'd never have to show anyone in this town his driver's license with its laminated M, its *Paul Polydoris.* How many more signs of welcome did he need? "I'm so in."

"Sweet," said Zoe.

"I don't actually have a ton of experience painting," he said.

"Don't worry," Zoe said. "That's just your female socialization talking. It's easy. I can show you in a day."

"Yeah," said Paul. "Let's do it."

He was in, totally on the inside. Diane's friend liked him, Diane wanted him to stay, he could spend the whole break with all these cool townie dykes. He could be Polly for four weeks straight, he was pretty sure. The longest he'd gone so far was at Michigan, a week, and that had turned out fine. The switching back and forth was the hard part, not so much the being. At first he was always conscious of his concentration, but eventually he'd plateau, he'd hit his stride and maintain. Paul imagined this was how long-distance runners felt. He'd read a book

about running once, or seen a movie title at the video store; anyway, what he knew was that those runners were supposed to be so lonely, but he was less lonely with Diane than he'd been in his whole life.

×

By the end of the week, Paul was stir-crazy. He'd been either painting cottages with Zoe or up in Diane's bedroom with Diane. He felt strange in the living room or kitchen, intimidated by Gerty and her rotating-nightly cast of fancy college-girl visitors, and as a rule, he preferred the street. When Diane proposed they go read at the café in the rain on Saturday afternoon, Paul was suffused with love for her. She drove them down, luxuriously, so Paul wouldn't have to change out of the black crinkled silk Mao-collared dress he'd put on in the morning without taking the weather into account. He could tell she liked that he was girlier than her, liked that she was so much bigger than him, liked to do little things for him, but sometimes he did wonder if she liked liking what she liked.

Inside the cramped, steamy café, they commandeered one of the window tables, defending their territory against middle-aged Boston gays who wandered in unsure of what to do when it rained on their save-the-relationship weekends. Every townie who came in for to-go coffee smiled at Paul and Diane; everybody knew who they worked for—even though they were new, they had been vetted. Old and young townies, queers and fishermen, fags and dykes and daytime drag queens with their plucked-chicken heads—all were aligned against the tourists and willing to accept all comrades. Paul had never lived

anywhere so small; he found the surveillance almost shocking, shades of prep school *in loco parentis*, but also pleasing like minor celebrity.

They sipped their lattes, a gift for Diane from the spiky-haired dyke behind the counter. Paul wondered exactly how well Diane had known her before he got to town.

Out the windows of the café, they watched a glum Spuds Mackenzie dog tender-paw through the rainy street, a muddy ball in its mouth. The terrible lounge singer from New Year's followed a few paces behind.

"That *would* be her dog," said Diane.

"Why, what's that dog thinking?" he asked.

"I don't know," said Diane. "I don't have supersonic hearing. But you don't have to be Aquaman to know that animals need shelter in the rain."

Paul wondered if this was true. Also, he was pretty sure Aquaman did not technically have supersonic hearing—he used sonar or something.

PJ Harvey's voice bounced off the tiny café's high ceiling, the song about wearing leather boots. Paul caught another girl behind the counter checking out him and Diane, and imagined them from her perspective. Did they seem like girlfriends? Sometimes Diane could hold herself aloof. He scootched his chair closer to hers to make their sex vibe more visible.

"So what should happen to all the dogs and cats?" he said. "We can't free them all from human bondage. They'd starve. The streets would be teeming with vicious starving puppies and kittens."

"No," said Diane. "Just the ones people are abusing or testing stuff on."

"Right," Paul said. "No, obviously that's wrong, testing things on animals." He wondered if it *was* wrong to test AIDS drugs on animals. He remembered one thin whiskery ACT UP guy he'd met at a gay bar in the Village who'd lectured him about Americans and how they cared more about animals than gay people. What was that bar? Uncle Charlie's, the Ninth Circle? No, Julius. A lifetime ago.

Rain beat down romantically against the windows. A gray sliver of bay was visible between the post office and Seamen's Bank. Paul suppressed a queeny giggle, as he did every time he saw the bank.

"Want to read?" he said, and Diane nodded and reached into her messenger bag. She was still reading that same animal rights book, the one with the particularly handsome giraffe on the cover. Paul piled his reading material on the table: two new comics (*Sandman* and *Books of Magic*) purchased on a recent trip to the comics shop in Orleans, a small stack of Zoe's Riot Grrrl zines he was trying to like, and a xeroxed Judith Butler article which Jane had sent him care of General Delivery. They read.

After a few pages of *Sandman*, Paul looked up. He liked to forestall the pleasure of finishing something he loved, especially something so short. He had to read in manageable bursts. Diane's dirty hair was in her face and she bit her index finger as she read. He looked at the ring on her middle finger, a silver snake coiled and biting. Diane wasn't scared of snakes. They'd stumbled on an enormous and terrifying rattlesnake-looking eastern hognose (according to Diane) just a few days ago, hibernating in a dune shack they'd broken into. Diane didn't flinch, just politely indicated their nonviolent intentions

while Paul quaked behind her. Paul generally enjoyed hiking with Diane, although he preferred the term "walking." He was a flâneur, not a hiker; he still had standards. Plus people killed lesbian hikers, that was a thing. Diane thought him a bit of a baby, he knew, but she seemed to think it was cute. *She* thought he was a femme.

Diane looked up. She laid her well-worn copy of *Animal Liberation* on the table and sighed.

"What's going on?" Paul said awkwardly. He found himself in the unusual position of wanting to know more about someone's feelings. "What are you thinking about?"

"Just that fucking lounge singer."

"Yeah?" said Paul.

"Yeah, I think she's the one who keeps her dog chained up in this metal outdoor cage thing, and he's *muzzled.* It's medieval. We're working on the house next door."

"That's terrible," Paul said encouragingly. Diane needed a lot of drawing out, which he found simple enough but somewhat exhausting, like bartending.

"Yeah."

He waited a beat, then picked up his comic again, just casually enough to signal his willingness to not read, although he was getting to a good part involving Death, who definitely seemed a little queer.

"Actually—"

"What?" said Paul.

"Nothing. I don't know. I feel like I need to *do* something."

"About the dog?" Paul said. "Okay, well, what should we do?"

"You'd help?" Diane said. "Really?"

"Of course," said Paul, with some trepidation. "I love dogs."

×

"Did you hear?" Zoe asked. "They just murdered a dyke in Nebraska. That's where you're from, right, Polly?"

"Iowa, actually—but I'm not really *from* there," Paul said. He lay down his roller carefully in its tray and took the newspaper from her. "Why do you have the *Times*?"

Paul liked these early mornings with Zoe, driving to the day's job in her truck, stopping for good coffees at Express. Zoe was organized and appreciated Paul's attention to detail, his careful cutting before they painted, his precise touch-ups. They kept up a good rhythm, like yoked oxen. Plus she had turned him on to all these West Coast bands he'd never paid attention to, like Mecca Normal and Excuse 17 and Team Dresch. She had Bikini Kill on right now, and he had to admit that for famous punks they were pretty dancey.

"I heard something on WOMR, so I looked in the dude's recycling and of course he had all these unread newspapers, the poseur."

Paul stared at the words on the page. He'd gotten paint on the paper and felt strangely guilty.

"This is totally fucked up."

"I know," said Zoe. "She was our age, she was twenty-one."

I'm twenty-two, Paul thought. He felt old. "Woman Who Posed As A Man Is Found Slain With 2 Others," the headline read.

"I don't know anybody in Nebraska," he said. "I'm not actually from the Midwest."

Zoe poured the rest of the Navajo White into her paint tray.

"Listen to this," Paul said. "*He was in here all the time with girls, and the girls were hanging all over him, Ms. Gresham said.* He sounds like a total player."

"*She*," said Zoe.

"Right," said Paul. "She."

×

In a remote fishing village at the end of a long spiral peninsula, a bachelor fisherman spent his nights in a rough shack and his days on a small but nice fishing boat.

In his youth, the bachelor fisherman had been unlucky in love—none of the girls in the village had returned his interest, so he grew accustomed to thinking himself ugly. When he was still a sad young man, his father had suggested he see the world. He secured a berth on a ship as a merchant marine and worked his way up to deckhand in his first year, but he hated the ship, which was high above the sea and away from the fish.

At the end of his first year, he received a letter, already a few months old, from a woman in his village. His parents and siblings had all died in a fire. The fire had destroyed their house, and if he did not return the mayor would auction off his father's boat. He left the cargo ship at the next port and returned to his village, where he set his attention to fishing.

The bachelor fisherman had an unusual talent for finding fish, and every day brought his catch in to the market, where

he was paid handsomely. Because he had no wife or family, he spent very little money. He stored his savings in a hole under the floorboards of his shack, and his shiny hoard grew and grew.

One day was much like all other days for the bachelor fisherman, until there came a day that wasn't. On this day, the bachelor fisherman had caught so many fine plump fish by midday that he had no more room for fish in his boat. He decided to explore the coves a few leagues south of his village, and to eat his peanut butter sandwiches in the company of the seals there. He found a rocky spot not far from shore, where seals sunned themselves, and dropped anchor. As he ate his sandwiches, he spoke to the seals, telling them about his enormous catch and suggesting they might find fine plump fish where he'd just been. The seals brayed their responses, but the bachelor fisherman could not understand them.

He fell asleep in the hot sun, and woke to a mournful, almost human, sound. The sky had clouded over and the seals were gone. The bachelor fisherman pulled up his anchor and turned his boat around. Just then he saw a swimmer, very far from shore.

"Are you in distress?" he called out, but the swimmer did not seem to hear him. The bachelor fisherman steered closer.

"Do you need help?" he called out again.

The swimmer raised her head and her bare shoulders from the sea.

"Do you have a towel?" she said. "I've swum too far out and left my clothes on the beach."

The bachelor fisherman cast about on his fishy boat for something clean, and finding nothing, began to strip off his

vest and overshirt, down to his clean-smelling undershirt. He threw the rope ladder down to her, and handed her his undershirt without looking at her nakedness.

"Thank you, kind sir," she said, climbing aboard the boat. The bachelor fisherman looked up and saw that the swimmer, standing before him on his boat and dripping through his undershirt, was a beautiful woman, perhaps a few years older than himself.

"How can I repay your kindness?" she said.

"Allow me to make you dinner," said the bachelor fisherman, surprising himself.

"Gladly," said the swimmer.

At the dock the lady swimmer climbed gracefully out of the boat and followed him up the dunes to his shack. He offered her clean clothes and built a fire on which to cook their fish. He had never had a woman in his shack and now saw how lonely his life had been.

"Would you like to stay the night?" said the bachelor fisherman, and the lady swimmer nodded.

The next morning, the fisherman felt himself to be no longer a bachelor. The lady swimmer had cooked breakfast, had sung a strangely familiar wordless song in his outdoor shower, and had declared him to be her husband.

"Husband," she said. "Will you make me dinner again tonight?"

By this, the fisherman knew the lady swimmer would stay with him, and so she did. Months passed, and the fisherman now returned every night to his swimmer wife, cooked her an elaborate dinner of his day's catch, and woke up every morning to hear her singing in the outdoor shower. She rarely wore

clothes and never worked, but lounged happily in his shack all the day and night, walking down the dunes to the sea and swimming whenever the mood struck her. When they kissed, he could taste the ocean on her lips.

As the months passed, the fisherman noticed his wife was growing larger, and finally he realized that she was going to have a child. He was overcome with happiness at his good fortune.

He began to think about a suitable house for their new family. He wanted to surprise his wife, who had already brought him so much happiness. He took his savings from his hiding place and built a little cottage on the land where his family's house had been, in the center of town. Soon the cottage was finished. Every day he caught more and more fish and he used his earnings to fill the cottage with comfortable furniture, toys for the baby, a real kitchen instead of a campfire, and a closet full of delicate clothes specially made for his wife.

Finally the baby arrived, beautiful and healthy. The fisherman was overjoyed and could barely believe his good luck. There was something that puzzled the fisherman—the baby was covered in a light layer of fuzz. His wife said as the baby grew, it would disappear. The fisherman began to worry that some harm would come to the baby out there in the dunes, so far from the village. Whenever he kissed the baby's face, he tasted salt. He knew babies should not taste of salt. The fisherman decided to move to the village as soon as possible. When the baby was a few weeks old, he said to his wife, "Come with me, my love."

He led his wife and baby down to their dock, sailed them around the cove to the village harbor, dropped anchor, and led them to the cottage in the center of town.

His wife began to weep, very quietly, which he took to be a

sign of her appreciation for him. He lay their baby in the cradle and showed his wife all around the cottage. She did not speak much, just looked carefully at all the preparations he'd made.

"This is all for you," said the fisherman proudly.

"But we'll go home tonight, won't we, husband?" she said.

"We can sleep right here," said the fisherman. "We never have to go again to that shack."

"As you wish," said his wife, and she lay down on the feather bed he'd bought with his savings and went to sleep.

In the morning, the fisherman awoke to birdsong from the cottage's kitchen garden. He listened for his wife's shower-singing or the baby's cries but heard nothing. He looked all around the cottage, but he was alone.

"Perhaps they have gone for a walk," he said to himself, and he walked throughout the village, looking for his wife and child, to no avail.

"Perhaps they have gone to the shack, to fetch the rest of our things," he said to himself, and walked up the path. The shack was empty.

"Perhaps they have gone down to the beach," he said to himself. He walked to the beach and looked for a sign of them but saw none.

×

Paul and Zoe finished up a job early, the boxy Commercial Street condo of some closeted Back Bay lawyer. Zoe was heading to the Governor Bradford for ironic afternoon beers with fishermen but Paul begged off. He needed to go to the bookstore, he said; he'd see her back at the house.

Paul biked down the unusually warm, even balmy, two o'clock streets in his paint-dirty bibs. The rain stopped; a few long-weekenders appeared, walking aimlessly down the middle of Commercial Street. Friday to Monday, Paul had learned, were the days he could count on the relief of seeing strangers, some measure of anonymity.

He went to the post office, picked up his mail, marked General Delivery, at the counter. It was as if this was the '50s, he thought, and he a mysterious drifter. Christopher had sent him a manila envelope containing bills, carefully marked so Paul could see his share; a list of phone messages, including another one from Tony Pinto, oddly enough; and a packet of SASEs requesting *Polydoris Perversity*. Paul reflected on Christopher's reliability as he threw the bills and messages away; he only had room in his pockets for the SASEs, and he didn't have any extra money right now anyway. He'd send Christopher a money order once he got paid, surprise him by rounding up.

Hungry after the day's work, Paul stopped by Spiritus for a slice. He lounged in a booth while he waited, eating pepper flakes straight just for the rush. He read the handwritten blackboard menu, then scouted the restaurant for a copy of the *Banner* with which to distract himself while he ate. He caught the eye of a gray-haired construction worker with a neat little ACT UP goatee and a single earring. Paul had pulled his hair back into a ponytail and shoved it in a baseball cap for work, and so maybe it wasn't surprising that the older gentleman looked, looked away, looked back. Paul took off the cap and shook out his lustrous dark hair like Brooke Shields. He leaned curvaceously into the wall, and smiled at the man.

The older gentleman looked down, paid for his slice, and

left. Gotcha, thought Paul. He'd enjoy reporting on this to Zoe and Gerty, who'd be delighted and a little envious. Better not to mention it to Diane. She'd be home late, he remembered; she was working a job two towns away, in Wellfleet. He ate the last bits of sausage off the paper plate and headed back to the bathroom. Inside, he locked the door and concentrated on letting Polly fall away. At first nothing happened, so he closed his eyes and tried to sense his cock, his boy-nipples, just enough fuzz. When he'd changed back, he turned his tee shirt inside out to hide the Virago Painters logo Zoe'd stenciled so they'd seem more professional. He looked in the mirror—not quite right. He rolled his sleeves up and puffed his biceps out, but not too much. Better.

Paul left the bathroom, left Spiritus, walked his bike (or, rather, Gerty's bike) across the street and down the alley to the beach, a straight line of pure focus. He dropped the bike on the sand and leaned against a post in the time-honored invitation. He unfastened one of his overalls' straps. His bikini-brief underwear were too tight with cock and balls, and getting tighter, the cycle of tightness. He watched men stroll the beach past the dock, eyeing each other with bad intent. Eyeing him. He hadn't been eyed like that in weeks.

A sinewy knife-faced houseboy Paul had seen around ambled by, radiating the timeless allure of the delinquent. He stared at Paul as he lit a cigarette, kept staring as he leaned against a post a few feet away, inhaling with great intention and gazing out at the bay. He finished his cigarette, heeled it deep into the sand, and ducked under the deck.

Paul knew what to do: wait a genteel moment, then fol-

low. He leaned against his post, watching the tide roll in, considering.

×

The first day of the semester came and went, and Paul continued to live his new life of early morning coffee, painting with Zoe, vegetarian dinner parties, and nights in Diane's bed—now their bed, as he'd begun chipping in for rent. Paul had stowed his unused return ticket, along with his license, in his frayed and foxed copy of *A Lover's Discourse*, already bursting with dried lilacs and obsolete love notes and wedged alongside his other books and clothes on the cinderblock shelving in Diane's room. Tony Pinto had said stay, and Paul had left. Diane had said stay, and Paul had stayed. Maybe Paul was growing up.

Diane came in and hugged him from behind.

"Polly," she said. "I've been thinking."

That was an understatement. Diane talked comparatively little but read so much, always political books, books about the environment, books about animals. She was a slow reader, Paul thought, not without a hint of judgment.

"We need to take action," said Diane.

"We should totally fuck up those navy labs where they make soldier dolphins," said Paul.

"Polly, this is serious," Diane said. "You don't mess around with stuff like that. You probably shouldn't talk about it, to be honest. And that's not even what I mean."

"Oh! Okay," said Paul, ashamed of his naïveté. "What are you talking about, then?"

"We need to do something about that dog."

"Which dog?"

"The lounge singer's dog, remember?"

"Of course," he said. "Of course, I remember."

"I think we might need to get him away from her," Diane said.

"Like go to the police?" Paul said.

Diane glared.

"I mean, of course not the police. What's our plan? Should we protest?"

"I was thinking more of a rescue mission," said Diane.

"Wow, okay," said Paul. "Okay. Yeah, let's do that."

He'd do whatever Diane thought best; first he just needed to get a tight black ribbed turtleneck sweater. He could do *Silkwood*-era Cher, maybe, if he grew his hair out. She had really long feathered hair in *Silkwood* and went out with Meryl Streep. He'd heard the Cher thing before, usually more in a *Come Back to the Five and Dime, Jimmy Dean, Jimmy Dean* way. It was his nose. He'd never changed his nose, he realized. He almost said the thing about the turtleneck, but Diane was being serious and revolutionary.

<div align="center">×</div>

The next morning, over coffee at Express, Diane brought up the dog again.

"Hey, Polly," said Diane. "Can you make yourself look like someone else?"

"Like Mystique, you mean? Like take someone else's face? I don't think I can do that," said Paul.

"Oh," said Diane.

"Did you know Mystique was gay?" said Paul. "Her girl-friend was Destiny. They never said it, but it was obvious."

Diane was not interested.

Paul smoothed his skirt down over the growing rip in his tights, and spun around on his stool.

"Come with," he said, gesturing toward the bathroom.

The pretty counter girl smirked as Paul and Diane went in together and Paul smiled back, raising his eyebrows ever so slightly.

"Who should I try to be?" said Paul.

"Well, not me," said Diane. "What about Elena, who you just cruised?"

Paul had noticed Elena, it was true. He often saw her walking through town with her kid. She was not unattractive, he had to admit.

Paul kissed Diane.

"Don't be jealous, baby," he said. "Don't look for a minute, and let me try this."

Elena was more stacked than him, that's all he could remember. He opened the door and skulked another look. She was a little bit darker, maybe Puerto Rican, and a lot shorter. Muscular, with curly hair, long lashes, and a pouty bottom lip. He shut the door, closed his eyes against Diane's scrutiny, and concentrated. He felt his weight shift. He became more solid, packed in tight. He felt gravity in his belly and breasts. He touched his hair and opened his eyes.

"You, with bigger breasts," said Diane. "And curlier hair." She sounded disappointed and impressed at the same time.

Paul looked in the mirror. His skin was maybe a shade

darker, he thought. His lips were sort of puffier or maybe he was just holding them that way. He tried to remember what she looked like. Maybe a picture would help.

"Keep trying," said Diane, pushing him against the bathroom wall and separating his legs with her knee.

"Oh my god," said Paul. He laughed in angry surprise and turned his cheek from her kiss. "You want me to look like her so you can fuck her?"

"No," said Diane. "No. No. That's not it."

Paul didn't believe her. He felt one-down, uncomfortably so. Should he be cool, offer himself like a kinky treat, a birthday blowjob? Could it be that Diane was not his Malone but his Mr. Benson? He let his Polly self return, and made his face seem like he didn't want to cry. Should have followed that houseboy, he thought, and in the background of his mind, he began to rake loose resentments into an armament for later.

<p style="text-align:center">×</p>

When Diane had a plan, Paul noticed, she evinced high levels of organization: she set alarm clocks, transcribed marginal notes to index cards, checked tasks off neat lists, and—most disturbing—delegated.

As a rule, Paul neither had plans nor was organized and while he didn't mind going-along-with other people's plans he did not enjoy thinking of himself—or being thought of—as a sidekick. Paul preferred to think of himself as easygoing, flexible, not tied down. Strictly speaking, however, going along with *was* sidekick behavior. He could do abject (pleasurable flash of Tony Pinto), and he'd certainly bottomed hard for Diane—

the grimy second-floor bathtub, how she stood over him as he fucked her with his fingers, then sucked on her wet pussy and begged her to piss in his mouth, swallowing her ejaculate instead, begging again for her piss. The Governor Bradford bathroom, her no-longer-new fist inside him, a line outside the door, her calm questioning, *Like that? Want more?* In bed, most filthy of intimacies, how she fucked him with her silicone dick and slid her hand in so she was fucking her hand inside him, had lost track of his pleasure, was greedily cumming, was using him for her pleasure, which put him over the edge. But he didn't want to be her sidekick. Eyes on *each other*, he thought—not looking together at something she saw first.

Now she was asking him to make a trip to the hardware store, and he wasn't sure he liked where this was going. Paul had always hated hardware stores, the smell of chemical fertilizers and grease-fingered overgrown gaybashers in the aisles assuming Paul couldn't find a stud in a wall or take apart an engine or whatever. Which he couldn't. Why was she making him go to a hardware store?

Paul was cooking up a fun dinner of fake eggs and fake bacon; what more did she *want* from him?

"Maybe we should wear dog costumes and picket!" he said. "Animal costumes with glitter. I could be an angry glittery puppy. Maybe we should start with a protest."

Diane clicked the Pretenders tape into the boom box on the cinderblock bookcase, still wearing her peacoat. Sometimes Diane would leave her peacoat on for hours after she got home, like a blanket or armor. To warm her or to keep him out, Paul wondered.

He wiped his hands on his *A Woman's Place Is in the House*

and the Senate apron and stared at Diane. He couldn't believe he knew her; she was so pretty and tough. He spelled it t-u-f-f in his mind, calling up images of the girls in *Times Square*, Patti Smith, a girl from any French movie, those Lower East Side dykes in the little collarless leather jackets he and Tony Pinto had so admired. Diane looked like a child sailor, a red-cheeked, creamy-skinned European boy. Eyes like chocolate saucers, he thought. Eyes like bonbons, like brown velvet with black lace, like an alien, like a whale. And she'd chopped a few inches off her lank brown hair in the bathroom last week, hadn't washed in days, maybe a week; her hair was slightly greasy and always good-smelling and soft, sometimes held back rakishly with a bandana. How was it possible Diane was his to stare at so closely, whenever he wanted?

"We need at least one more person," Diane mused, as if Paul hadn't said anything. He felt a stab of shame. Maybe he was superficial. Maybe his true colors were beginning to show. Maybe he didn't have what it took to be a lesbian punk rocker Riot Grrrl activist.

"Yeah," said Paul. The fake eggs were smoking. He put the hot sauce on the table and agreed to go to the hardware store to purchase tarps and kibble and gallon jugs of fresh water for the dog, once they freed it.

After dinner, they went right to bed, confident in their honeymoon right to fuck all the time and leave the dishes in the sink. Paul screwed in the black light and Diane put on the Nina Simone and they drank red wine out of mugs Diane had made in college. Smooth Paul curved two fingers inside Diane like he'd read about, and found a spongy sort of button. He could see it with his fingers, a perfect red circle the spider-

webby texture of lip insides. He pressed on the button and Diane barnacled onto him. Cause and effect.

With Diane, unlike with his other lovers—and who were they, he thought? who were those other lovers? all tricks, numbers, marks on a wall, notches on his lipstick case, excepting Tony Pinto, so say that—with Diane, unlike with Tony Pinto, Paul derived his satisfaction from learning to please. With Tony Pinto, Paul had fallen entirely, fallen down Tony's rabbit hole, fallen into Tony's asshole that one terrifying night, fallen out of his rules and bounds and into Tony's hands, mouth, bed. Paul had been unable to resist Tony Pinto and Tony Pinto had not asked to be resisted, had flown to Iowa and to Paul's bed so that Paul could fall, or more accurately crouch, onto him without resistance.

Whereas Diane was all resistance. What they did with their bodies was just one part of it, for Diane. Diane's mind was elsewhere a frustrating fifty-one percent of the time, by Paul's reckoning, and she wanted him in the elsewhere with her. She wanted more from Paul, more seriousness of purpose. She would respect his process if he were an artist, he thought, but what did he do besides "make commentary" and dress himself variously? His life was superficial, surfaces to be polished and re-seen. He'd painstakingly assemble an outfit that told a story (willful debutante experimenting with heroin, say, or cowgirl gone to town on a Saturday night, or revolutionary princess) and then he'd take it for a walk, possibly rework elements of the outfit on the fly if one of the thrift shops was open, catalog responses both verbal and otherwise. That could be a whole day. A good day. He was happy enough to have abandoned his schooling, greedily reading in a lineage of his

own devising and necessity. He considered putting together a new zine, maybe a girl-power type of thing, though he was a bit old for Riot Grrrl. They were mostly teenagers, three or four years younger than Paul. A cultural eternity. He didn't want to intrude. Was he already intruding on their gender? Maybe, but it was his too, right? His body did whatever he wanted, so he belonged in all the genders.

Paul thought about straight people occasionally, not that he personally knew very many people he could really call straight. Straight culture, he guessed he meant. Movies, books, songs—especially songs. TV shows too, he surmised, not that he watched TV except for *X-Files*, which at least switched up the butch–femme dynamic. Men and women alike confounded Paul; they were so rule-bound. Straight people seemed confused by each other, so anxious to find camaraderie within their gender, so startled by differences between their bodies, always pinning explanations for the inevitable gulf between humans on chromosomes. Diane wasn't like that. For Diane, women were the norm. She never mentioned what she once called Paul's "body of origin."

"Water?" she said now.

Paul took the water glass carefully and drank a tiny sip without sitting up. They watched the sun come up, huddled low on the bed, the window a rectangle of sheer light.

"You never let me get any sleep," Paul said. *He* never let *her* get any sleep, they both knew. Paul thought, if we do it enough times, enough ways . . .

"If you're tired, you should sleep," Diane said.

×

Paul had been Polly now for almost a month straight. He would've been at two months, but then after he'd changed at Spiritus he'd had to restart the clock. After that incident in the bathroom with Diane, he'd decided not to change for her, not that she'd asked him again. Diane, in turn, seemed to have given up her idea of Paul as her key operative, her infiltrator. They'd been tender and avoidant with each other since, at least on the topic of Paul's body.

He'd hoped that if he stayed in Polly form for longer than a month he might have a period, and had bought anticipatory variety packs of tampons and pads. Then she'd trust him. He'd been reading the house copy of *Our Bodies, Ourselves* and had spent an hour in their room with a mirror and a plastic speculum and a flashlight, checking out his vagina. He had all the parts just like in the book, he discovered with relief: clit, pee-hole, fuckhole, g-spot. His insides felt to his fingers like Diane's insides: spongy button, ribbed in some places, smooth in others. When Diane wasn't home, he occasionally fucked himself with his fingers or other implements. He snuck-rubbed out an orgasm or two whenever he could. He snuck-rubbed in the bathrooms at the condos he painted, in their bed while Diane went to pee. One Sunday night when they'd all gone down to eat free popcorn and watch *Mrs. Doubtfire* at the Holiday Inn, he'd jerked his clit to coming in the fully occupied multistall women's room (thighs hard, left bicep pressed against the stall wall, right middle finger pumping, ragged breathing shut into his mouth until he popped with a whippet-style head rush) just to compare it to his tearoom adventures in what he'd begun to think of as his old life.

So far Paul's vagina did everything advertised but bleed:

expanded and contracted; was more or less red, more or less wet, more or less smooth; clamped down and opened wide; emitted a variety of smells; encompassed fingers, hands, silicone implements, a hard white plastic vibrator, a cucumber wrapped in a condom. His clitoris begged for attention if he had to pee or saw an even mildly attractive human or read words directly related to sex or words spelled like words directly related to sex. He didn't seem to have ever had a hymen, if you used blood from fucking as evidence; he'd worried about this until he'd read a Riot Grrrl zine Zoe'd left in the living room and *Susie Sexpert's Lesbian Sex World*, which he'd bought at Ruthie's. Apparently hymens were a patriarchal control myth.

He hadn't female-ejaculated yet, and he thought maybe Diane was scared he'd male-ejaculate if he tried. Everyone else Paul knew was very interested in learning about female ejaculation. Diane female-ejaculated with some regularity, most often in the early morning after many beers and many hours of sex. She'd never done it with anyone else before, and Paul had been proud and a little jealous. He'd drunk whatever of the liquid he could, slightly acrid but not piss-acrid. He'd been camped out at the bottom of the bed for quite some time, pushing his parts against the edge of the mattress while he sucked on her clit and fucked her with one flittering and two curved-up fingers. They were having not very safe sex and would be in trouble if the safe-sex people knew they licked each other without dental dams, used latex gloves only occasionally and then only for fisting. Could you get something from swallowing female ejaculate? Diane had gotten tested after she'd found out about him, he knew. He'd taken all the tests, plenty of times. He was negative, negatory; he was positive he was not

positive. He'd been pretty safe with boys, by doing what the brochures called risk reduction, safer sex, except for those times with Tony Pinto, and they'd used condoms and they'd both been tested every six months afterward and Paul still was getting tested every six months at free clinics under various names and making up a plausible-sounding sexual history for each identity. So far, no one had remarked on anything unusual in his blood. He wondered if they really even looked at the blood, or just spun a board-game wheel. The Game of Life. He made up Social Security numbers on the spot, easy once he realized the first three digits were always the same, based on the state where the holder was born. The easiest lie to tell was the closest to the truth.

But Diane did like to use condoms for easy clean-up, and so Paul continued to pocket free packets at the A-House when they went out dancing. Paul suspected the other dykes they knew were using dildos all the time. One of the Wesleyan girls had worked at the feminist sex-toy store the previous summer and brought over a bag of old display models and stolen cocks to share. Paul picked out the biggest silicone dildo—the Johnny—in black, which seemed nicely neutral and worked well with the pink glitter pleather harness he also snagged. He sterilized the cock, under Zoe's tutelage, in the house spaghetti pot. But Diane thought it was maybe a little exoticizing to use a black cock, so he'd spent a half-week's wages at Shop Therapy on a Doc Johnson Emperor Realistic 8", which Diane seemed to like better for fucking him. He'd whimper, guide her fingers into his asshole, tug at her nipples, get himself filled up. Diane fucked him with it that first night, shyly at first and then with abandon. In all her exploits with various Jennies and Maggies

before him, she'd never used a dildo. He'd been pleased to out-dyke her in this regard, and hinted about his night with the rock star whenever the occasion arose, such as when someone played their CD or mentioned Seattle.

"What if I fucked you sometime, with the *implement*?" Paul said one fine Sunday afternoon as he and Diane strolled to Express, which they'd come to call The Place, as in "Shall we go to The Place?" "Yes."

"Um," said Diane, blushing in her milky skin. In the stark bright daylight she looked like a stranger.

Paul's belly went drop-and-tingle. He wasn't usually toppy with her, but there wasn't any reason he couldn't be. They weren't being butch–femme; they were being tuff girls, which was completely valid, whatever that stupid lounge singer thought. They could switch! Diane said she didn't consider herself a femme or a butch; if she had to put a name to it—which she didn't—she'd maybe say kiki.

"Do you want to?" she said.

"Yeah," said Paul, trying on laconic. He stretched an arm over her shoulder, but she was two inches taller and after a minute she shrugged his arm off and clasped his hand. A passing straight tourist scowled at them, which reunified them for the rest of the day.

That night in bed, Paul asked again, and Diane said yes. He could tell she was hesitant but wasn't sure why. He wanted to do *all* the lesbianism. He strapped the Johnny on himself (better to avoid any resemblance to his own penis) and adjusted, pulling out pubic hairs and crushing the base against his outer labia. Paul liked knowing the words for the parts, even if the words themselves were unappealing. He hovered over Diane,

off balance as he covered the black silicone with a ribbed condom and stared at her.

"Just do it," she said. She reached for his breasts, and as he leaned in to give her more access he accidentally pushed the head of the dick into her. She gasped.

"I'm sorry!" Paul said. "Are you okay? Should I take it out?"

"No," said Diane. She clenched her eyelids shut. "Do it more."

Paul began to push into her, trying to find his rhythm. He hadn't fucked a girl with a dick since Heather Federson, and that had been his own dick. He closed his eyes and found his hips in his mind.

"Yeah," said Diane. "More like that."

Paul pushed into and out of her, awkwardly. Their sweaty bellies made a loud sucking sound, for which Paul apologized.

"Shh," said Diane. She put her fingers in his mouth, wet them, and reached around between his legs. As she brushed his asshole, he pumped harder. He was starting to get what was exciting about topping. The base of the cock slipped between the parts of his pussy and hit his clitoris, hit hit hit it. Diane was starting to come. He could feel her pussy throbbing and grabbing through the cock. How was that possible? He pushed faster and harder, remembered fucking Tony Pinto's ass. He wondered what would happen if he changed back now and came on her stomach, like in the porns, and felt ashamed. He wanted to put his flesh dick into Diane and imagining this along with the rubbing and thrusting and Diane's coming he came too.

"Take it out," said Diane. She sounded angry.

"Sorry," he said.

He arched his ass, pulling out slowly, and began to take off the harness.

"Was that okay?" he said. It had sounded like it was okay, and the bed was soaked, but he'd discovered there were shifting criteria for a rating of okayness. Also, something could be very good in one way and not okay in another.

"Polly," said Diane.

They didn't say each other's names very often. Paul's stomach contracted and his mouth began to water.

"Hmm," he said.

Diane pulled the green wool blanket over herself. Paul lay back on his pillow, the softer pillow, and covered himself with a corner of the blanket. He was crying, he realized in time to hide it. He began to loosen the harness, but had to stand up to do so. He hoped she wasn't watching, because he couldn't get the pleather straps loose from the rings.

"Do you ever want to do it the other way?" Diane said.

"What? No," said Paul, quickly. Did she mean do it with his own dick?

"It just seemed like you were really into it," she said.

"I thought you were," he said. "I don't know."

×

"Jill Schwartz might actually be good to ask," said Diane. "I think she was involved with that needle exchange thing in Boston."

She took a long drink of soy latte, her new treat. There were so many vegans in Provincetown! Paul thought. They kept

inventing treats for each other. He couldn't adjust to soy milk and drank his coffee black around Diane so she wouldn't be sad. She didn't need to know that he still ate microwave cheeseburgers from the Cumberland Farms, that he felt himself slipping away when he didn't eat enough meat, that he was being vegetarian for her.

They were trying to figure out one more person to help with their plan, a getaway driver. Diane rejected all Paul's suggestions for new comrades. Paul was aware he was suggesting only cute people, but he thought if Diane articulated this complaint he could argue it was subtle discrimination to not take cute people seriously. Paul was pretty sure if the Revolutionary Rapture came he would not be one of the saved.

"Yeah," he said. "Oh, and we can ask her at the Governor tomorrow night, at that Dyke TV fundraiser."

Diane's hair had grown into a *Tiger Beat* shag, and she looked like the irresponsible family friend on a TV drama. Paul thought of more things from the '70s he liked: handlebar mustaches, Fire Island, proto-punk, Afros, bell-bottom sailor pants, women's liberation art of fists. Zoe had such a tattoo on her bicep, along with the single blue star under her watch band. Paul considered getting a tattoo but was scared of needles. Also, what would he get? How to decide?

"Who else?" Diane said. She drew a smiling pit bull in her composition book. Paul reached for her pencil, gave the dog a top hat and cane.

"I don't know," said Paul. "Let's figure out what our name should be."

"Jesus, Pol," Diane said. She looked faraway, judgmental,

like a marble president delivering his proclamation. "Can you focus?"

Paul looked down at his burgundy cords, his black Runaways tee shirt (a church thrift shop score in Orleans—how jealous Jane would be) tight over his waffled long-john shirt, his Save the Whales! belt buckle with its fresco humpback. He liked his new look, enjoyed this foray into androgynous style, liked the little fuck-you shadows of femininity he deployed. He wasn't trying to copy Diane, but he did like them to be complementary. He'd managed to find a copy of *Times Square* at City Video and rented it for them to watch together, had tried to explain to her his thoughts on runaway tomboy rocker dyke gender, but she'd been unimpressed. Diane didn't like to talk about gayness very often. Paul estimated he held back two out of five gay-themed comments.

"I don't know that many people here yet," Paul said, which was not entirely truthful. He knew Gerty and Zoe and their various lovers and Diane's painting crew and all *their* friends and lovers. He knew all the bartenders and the coffee shop people he flirted with when Diane was at work. He knew Dottie the window washer, and the oldish lesbians from Gabriel's who stared at him hungrily, and the fag hag girl who worked at the record store. He knew all the year-round houseboys, and the cute young ACT UP fag who kept the books at the Boatslip, at least enough to say hi to.

"Oh, wait! What about that boy who works at the Boatslip?"

"He's cool," said Diane. "But he's a man, ultimately."

Paul got up. He was tired of talking, tired of being wrong.

×

"It's the Hunger Moon tonight," Diane said. "Do you want to go for a walk?"

The Hunger Moon! thought Paul. If only Jane could see him now.

"Sure," he said, putting down Zoe's copy of *Bodies that Matter*, which he'd been futilely skimming for gossipy asides or endnotes. "Where to?"

Maybe he could steer Diane to a post-walk drink at the A-House or even the Governor Bradford. He hated to waste a weekend night entirely on nature when it was the only chance to see strangers in town.

"Let's just walk," said Diane. "It's so nice out."

She waited for him to lace up his boots, then led him down to the bay beach. They crunched through the frozen sand. Paul didn't understand how the night could be both balmy and snowy, but somehow it was—maybe because of the sea? He was almost curious enough to ask Diane, but she'd probably know and then he'd have to listen to the entire explanation.

"Why is it the Hunger Moon?" he asked instead. "Do all the moons have names?"

"Um," said Diane. She didn't handle multiple trains of thought well. "Wait, okay. Hunger Moon, but first there's Wolf and I think maybe Sap and Pink—"

"Pink?" said Paul.

"There's more. Beaver, something else—Barley? I can't remember."

"Pink Moon?" he asked again. "Like Nick Drake?"

"Yeah, I guess," said Diane.

As they approached town, Diane led them up the beach past the Mews, then cut through Lovett's Court, over to Bradford. She managed to avoid town. They saw no one.

"Are we going to the cemetery?" said Paul. "What about the coyotes?"

"They won't hurt you," said Diane. "Coyotes are misunderstood."

"Okay," said Paul. "But do you think we'll see one?"

"I don't know," she said.

He knew he'd be safe with her and he also knew she wouldn't call a coyote pup from its den for his amusement, which he understood as the correct ethical position but still resented. Didn't love mean breaking your own rules? They walked toward the dark West End, house after empty tourist house waiting for summer. Paul felt Provincetown to be extremely rural and longed for the bright lights of Commercial Street, just one block, but also a world, away.

"Isn't the cemetery this way?" he said.

"I just want to go up here for a minute," said Diane, looking for some inscrutable sign, some nature thing. He followed, wishing he'd worn mittens and wondering if Express would still be open when they finished this walk. He stopped to tighten his bootlaces, and when he straightened up, Diane was gone.

"Hey!" he called.

Nothing. He was alone with possible coyotes.

"Hey," he called out again, with some urgency.

He heard a bark and wondered if coyotes barked as well as howled. They were just bigger dogs, right? Diane reappeared, her face flushed and her eyes bright.

"I'm right here," she said. "Hey, do you want to get a hot chocolate at Express?"

Paul could hardly believe his good fortune.

"Sure," he said. "If you want."

Inside the café, they chatted with some townies playing Scrabble. Everyone was getting excited for the summer—Paul was hoping to land a job bartending at the new club opening up on Shankpainter on their women's night. The future opened out ahead of him, an adventure he'd chosen as casually as turning a page.

They took their hot chocolates and sat at what Paul thought of as "their table," the one by the big window looking onto the street.

"Polly," Diane said. "I'm not sure we should do this."

"Oh," said Paul, his relief telling and gigantic. "Yeah, me either. I really don't want to get arrested for stealing a dog."

"No," said Diane. "Forget that. I took care of that."

"What?" said Paul. "Without me? When?"

"You were there," she said. "I just did it. You were great, actually."

"How did you—"

Diane patted her army pants' pocket.

"Bolt cutters," she whispered. "Then I told him to hide out in the dunes and I'll bring him food tomorrow."

"Oh," said Paul. He finished his hot chocolate, now cold.

Diane looked proud and defiant, and Paul felt an obscure sadness.

"So, wait, what?" he said, standing to bus his cup.

Diane looked pale.

"I meant us," she said.

Paul sat back down. Over the café speakers k.d. lang was crooning *just a kiss just a kiss*—

"Let's just go," said Diane. She buttoned up her peacoat, even popped the top button through its loop, which she never did.

Paul started to cry. Not fair to be ambushed while romantic songs were playing.

"Why not?" He inhaled snot.

"I love you, Polly. You know I do."

"Stop saying my name," Paul muttered. "If we love each other, why are you breaking up with me?"

"I didn't say I was breaking up with you," Diane said. "I said this wasn't working."

"You said you weren't sure," Paul said, sniffling. He wiped his eyes with his tee shirt.

Diane sighed, an angry exasperated sigh Paul hadn't heard before. Now he'd done it. Rewind! Rewind! He stared at her. He held his breath.

"I just feel like we don't collaborate well," said Diane.

"Why, because I'm not a vegan? I'm not political enough for you? You know why I can't get arrested."

"I know," said Diane.

"Okay, so that's what this is about?"

"You want to be everything, all the time," Diane said. Her voice caught. "I just want a girlfriend. I'm afraid you're going to get bored of being a girl, and then where will I be?"

"I love being a girl," said Paul. "I don't even know if I can go back now."

"Why, have you been thinking about it?" Diane was crying

too now. Paul felt very French for a moment, crying with his lover at a café.

"No," he said. "No, of course not."

"Seriously," she said. "Seriously, I know you. You even said it yesterday, how mutable you are. What happens in five years, a year even? It's in your nature. I don't want to keep you from your nature."

"I was talking about *astrology*. Sagittarians are mutable fire," said Paul. "It's a *metaphor*. I'm not that mutable. I haven't changed in months."

"But you want to change again sometime, right?"

Paul considered. He had changed, of course, pretty recently, but nowhere near as much as he could have. He probably would want to change again at some point, maybe not back for good. He was only twenty-two. What could he know about the future? He imagined them together in five years. They'd be twenty-seven. Well, she'd be twenty-eight. Old but still hot. They'd never said they were monogamous; he could imagine hooking up with other people and coming back to Diane, but if he was hooking up, he liked to have options. He thought about his penis. He might like to use it again, put it somewhere. Not with Diane maybe, but—

Paul bit his lip.

"Is that bad?" he said.

"Can we get out of here?" she said. Paul pulled on his coat and scarf. Diane was right; they needed to be in bed, site of all important decisions, for this, whatever this was.

They walked home in the moonlight, block after chilly block of not talking or touching. Paul felt the pull of Diane's

shoulder, her hip. When they got back to their room, Diane lay down on top of the unzipped green sleeping bag they used for a blanket.

"Come here," she said. They didn't wait to get their clothes off. But when they were done he knew they were done.

V.

Paul slumped against the plastic window of the California-bound Amtrak, the Zephyr. He alternated between weeping and wishing he'd worn tighter pants. He'd changed when he'd left P-town to take the return flight from Albany to Chicago and was now stuck, a ghost with gangly limbs, a potbelly, his own round chin, too much or maybe too little body hair—all his old inadequacies. He couldn't muster the energy or focus to become a more attractive version of himself. No one on the train was cute anyway. Maybe no one would ever be cute again.

In movies you always met someone on the train, which is why Paul had spent an obscene sum of money on a train ticket instead of just taking the Greyhound like a normal person. The train was a place of possibility, of romance, a portal to a new world, or at the very least an opportunity for a ground score. In *Strangers on a Train*, Robert Walker chatting up Farley Granger in the dining car, Granger smiling, "You don't know *what* you want." Paul knew. Of course, that had not ended well. But what about *Some Like It Hot*? Didn't Tony Curtis meet Marilyn Monroe on a train? For a moment he felt a little better. He'd meet someone who'd take his mind off this endless looping of Diane to Diane to Diane. He was not enough for Diane, was not right and could never be right by virtue of his very malleability, was not right because he could *make* himself right? But then, she had said at one point in the last few days that he was "too much" for her, so what to do with *that*? Paul tried to put his thoughts in order.

The train ride from Chicago to San Francisco—actually, the stop was called Emeryville—took fifty-two hours; Paul had been on the train for twenty-nine hours already and his ass ached from the bristly velour. In twenty-three hours he'd be in San Francisco with nowhere to go, no one expecting him. He possessed a folded-up sheet of loose-leaf with the scrawled names of a youth hostel and three cafés likely to offer bulletin boards, notes from his call to Christopher from a payphone at O'Hare. Christopher had told him just to come back, that he could stay in the living room until the subletter moved out. Paul didn't call Jane. Jane was mad at him, he was pretty sure. She'd never liked Diane, couldn't understand but mostly was just pissed that Paul disappeared when Diane came into the picture. Anyway, he couldn't go back to Iowa City in the middle of a semester, in such obvious disrepair. He needed a place to stash himself for a while. He wished he were a replicant, wished he could unplug himself for a few months. When he did sleep he dreamed of Diane, the worst dream—the dream where she still loved him—and when he woke he was alone again.

Paul was too old to run away but not grown. He'd already spent five dollars on a crappy boxed ham sandwich and needed to ration his money. He had $519 left to his name, $181 of it in cash. He bought a coffee every few hours, just to have an activity, paying in coins so as not to break into his paper money. If he ate something else maybe he could change, could look how he felt, about fifteen. He could work up enough energy if he had a hot dog probably, stomach-turning as the thought might be, but hot dogs were five dollars too. Couldn't some kind train mother open her picnic basket full of cold bottles of

milk and fried chicken and apples and offer Paul food? But the train mothers sat with their sleeping children in their laps, flipping through *Marie Claire*s, drinking individual white wines. If the train mothers were to consider Paul at all, they'd consider him balefully. Paul walked back to the terrible bathroom, held his breath, and applied eyeliner and a heavy coat of Fire & Ice as a last-ditch effort to improve his mood.

Minutes after a roadside sign for Roseville, Morrissey's voice began to drizzle in Paul's ears, his offer to die by the side of his beloved unfulfilled. Paul hit eject to investigate and discovered the glossy brown ribbon snagged, unraveled, useless— mutilated by the act of looking at it.

He managed a few minutes' sleep here and there, crying into his sweatshirt to exhaust himself. Individual train lights pierced the darkness because people had to read. What could they read at a time like this? During one moment of waking Paul pulled down the beige plastic table and wrote a few sentences to Diane on notebook paper, but he had nothing to say so he stopped. He couldn't read. He was unconsoled by the *Vogue* he'd stolen from the train station newsstand. When night returned, Paul brushed his teeth in the terrible bathroom, gathered his belongings, and repaired to the bar car, where, he thought, dashing Cheeverish older men might like to buy him drinks.

He found instead two off-duty train conductors, a red-nosed salesman discussing the frustrations of the office-supply business, and the persistent smell of discount cigarettes and fried onions. Paul fled back to his velour cage, where he tucked his legs primly against the seat and attempted to hold one position indefinitely. Maybe in San Francisco he'd become a monk.

Anything was possible there. He'd never been to San Francisco, but it was a place you could go, a lit-up bulb on the map, the last okay destination.

Paul considered his resources. He'd spent a good chunk of his Provincetown cash on the Peter Pan back to Albany and the train ticket. His belongings were at Jane's. His mom thought he'd gone back to Iowa City months ago. So did Kostas. Everybody in Iowa City was probably mad at him, except maybe Christopher. He had no friends in California or, now, in Provincetown. Did he have any friends anywhere?

×

Theresa liked to tell Paul she'd missed the '60s, she hadn't been cool enough, she was washing diapers for professors and going to bed early, but that wasn't exactly true.

She'd dropped out of Russell Sage after one year, fulfilling her mother's predictions. It was 1969. She liked the classes but couldn't stand the sheepy other girls, so proper and snobby. So *parochial.* Theresa considered herself a citizen of the world, and she wanted to see the whole of her territory.

That June she spent her accumulated life savings on a one-way plane ticket to Paris, where she hoped and expected to meet a combustible but tender painter who'd bring her around to his favorite cafés, where she'd banter with poets in fluent bed-learned French. Instead, she took the first invitation she received and boarded a train for Sienna with an Italian girl she met on the plane. The Italian girl, Rosalie, was from Queens and was very free, Theresa thought. Not like the girls in her neighborhood, or those stuck-up Russell Sage girls.

Theresa wanted badly to be free. On the ferry from Napoli to Palermo, Rosalie met a weedy English playboy who persuaded them both to stay with him at his uncle's place in the Paphos District, on Cyprus. They couldn't refuse, Rosalie had maintained, as she and Theresa conferred in the ferry's rainy stern. How could they live knowing they'd missed the festival of Dionysus? Who else in this life would ever invite them to Cyprus? And so to Cyprus—where they drank the absent uncle's wine, where they climbed the rocky coast to picnic on olives and exotic crumbling cheese, where the English playboy, Reggie, rotated his affections to Theresa, who found herself—woke up to herself—bidding Rosalie farewell at the ferry terminal in the little city. When, two wine-soaked weeks later, Reggie returned to his fancy English life and his fiancée, Theresa stayed on. She extracted from Reggie a guilty offer of a caretaking position, and was allowed to remain at the house until his uncle returned the next spring. She needed time to accommodate this new version of herself, as someone who'd throw over a girlfriend for a boy she didn't like, who'd walk out on a full scholarship to a private college, who'd leave two inept parents alone and drinking themselves to death in the cold upstate winter. She'd left Troy in flames, she thought, making her way through a translation of the *Aeneid* borrowed from the uncle's library.

Was she Dido or Lavinia? When Reggie's uncle returned with his valet (his *valet!*), Theresa packed the Virgil into her small bag and again accepted the first offer that came: babysitting for a German couple, archaeologists too busy digging up the Paphos police station to toilet-train their only child. I'm Lavinia, she thought with scornful self-awareness, but was relieved.

She tried to hide her goodness from herself, pretending she wasn't saving for her ticket home to the States but instead for more adventure. She flew on goodness-autopilot. She told herself the money she'd asked Frau Vogel to hold for her would buy a month in Paris. Meanwhile, Stefan was as charming as any small child, and the archaeologists were kind in their Teutonic way. They drew her walking maps to special ruins on the island, taught her to cook a passable schnitzel, and introduced her to the only other young people they knew: their graduate students and their colleagues' au pairs. Theresa didn't speak French and was intimidated by the graduate students but she established a camaraderie with an Australian au pair called Daisy and they occasionally made day trips to Rhodes. She sent cheery postcards to her parents and picked up their infrequent letters at the post office, thinking all the while, a few more months, a few more months. She waited out the rainy season, diapering and reading and planning her trajectory around the Continent.

One Thursday, the eternal help's-night-off, Theresa met Daisy down at the new bar for tourists, right on the beach in Paphos, to dance by the sea now that the rains had slowed. She'd drunk quite a bit—it was some festival or another—and had danced with no restraint, had felt like Isadora Duncan. She had, she thought later, perhaps made a spectacle of herself, and then an even more spectacular dancer took the floor. For the rest of the night she danced exclusively with this dark stranger, sweat pasting his thin unbuttoned shirt to his chest. Later on the beach Theresa licked the salted sweat from his neck—bold Dido!—and he made love to her right there in the sand. When she reported her adventure to Daisy, who was somewhat less free than Rosalie, she used the words *made love.*

Theresa never saw the stranger again. She didn't know his last name, or where he was from. She knew that he spoke English with an accent she wasn't sophisticated enough to identify, maybe Greek or Turkish. That he had curly black hair and olive skin, maybe darker. That he had no home, was a traveler, like her a citizen of the world. And that, on his thigh—for she remembered not his face but his bare thigh—a scar like a pink worm dripped down to his knee, shiny keloid reflecting the moonlight. Theresa felt herself subtly changed. She began to consider Paris more seriously. She listened to the Vogels' box set of *La bohème* as if she might divine her destiny in Maria Callas's voice.

This is my life now, she thought on Thursday mornings, sipping thick sweet coffee in the café and reading week-old copies of the *International Herald Tribune* left by British tourists. Occasionally a group of long-haired American or French boys would pass through town and Theresa would invite them to spend a Thursday afternoon exploring ruins. Daisy had begun to look up to Theresa as the wild one, the free one. Eventually, Theresa had to admit to herself her two missed periods. When she began to show, she confided tearfully in Frau Vogel, who advised her with an expensive Continental sangfroid that was shocking but also comforting. It was too late to "do something about it," Frau Vogel said, which Theresa knew. They agreed she would stay until the baby was born. Then, of course, she would be on her own.

When the baby came, Theresa sent her parents a postcard of a church, St. Kyriaki's, and wrote a few impressive lines about the dig. She didn't mention the Vogels' fear that the violence in the north would drift down. She didn't mention the baby

or her new job at the café or the morning mass she'd begun to wake up for every day.

When the Turks came for real, five years later, Theresa bundled up her baby—still her baby!—bade farewell to the island and retreated, with the rest of the Americans, to the safe lie of home.

VI.

Emeryville, as it turned out, was not San Francisco.

Paul had to pack himself onto a shuttle bus from the Emeryville station to the Oakland station, which was also not San Francisco. By the time he was back on dry land, it was one in the morning.

The newish green streetlights, a municipal marriage of hunter green and teal, washed the bleak Oakland cement and blacked-out storefront glass. The street had that stage-set emptiness that brought to mind thoughts of Stephen Sondheim. For blocks Paul saw no humans. He hit the end of all streets, saw water. He rubbed any remaining makeup onto his shirtsleeve. He couldn't get much bigger physically—he still hadn't eaten properly and couldn't just imagine himself bigger—so he put up his hood and tried to walk "like a man." The few other people who'd disembarked from the shuttle with him were long gone, on to meet their families or hail their taxis. Paul couldn't find anyone to ask for directions to the hostel, something he hadn't anticipated. He was used to New York, imagined arriving at the equivalent of Grand Central. He couldn't sleep in the train station; the benches were divided by bars every two feet—so homeless people wouldn't stretch out and nap, Paul realized bitterly. Even if one *could* sleep sitting up, which after fifty-two hours on a train Paul could not, fluorescent lights and rent-a-cops would make sleep impossible.

Paul's two small bags gained weight with each step. He passed the same boarded-up Chinese takeout place twice, then

helplessly paced the block three more times before dropping to his haunches in the doorway of a metal-shuttered tobacco shop. A cab whooshed down the street and Paul jumped into the gutter, wild-handed until the cab pulled over half a block up. Paul ran.

"Can you tell me how to get to"—he consulted his sheet of paper—"Kearny Street and Broadway?"

The cabdriver sighed, checked his fake Rolex, and unlocked the back door.

"Fifty bucks," he growled.

"I'm broke," said Paul. "Can't you just tell me how to get there?"

"Gotta drive 'cross the bay. Can't walk it," said the driver. "Or wait. BART starts at 6."

Paul swore in his mind. That would bring him to $131 cash. He could not wait five fluorescent hours in that station. He opened the back door and slid across the vinyl. He tried not to think about the percentage of his total money he was now spending on this cab, couldn't do that math anyway. He tried not to think about how stuck he was in this sad tired old body. Out the streaked windshield the bay was strung with tiny Christmas lights or fairy litter, which didn't make up for anything.

×

Paul spent that whole first night at the hostel scratching his thighs and ears, bedbug-hunting, and then they kicked him out at eight without time for a shower or even a French bath. He

stuffed both his bags in a common-room quarter locker and left with only his Walkman and his remaining $120.

His crappy free tourist map didn't show bus routes or even individual streets, just locations from which one might watch seals or eat "bread bowls." Where was San Francisco? Paul didn't want to ask the straight, probably homophobic, hostel people how to get to the Castro, so he decided to walk until he saw another gay person. He walked and walked. Maybe San Francisco wasn't gay anymore, he thought after twenty fruitless minutes.

He found Market Street, apparently the hub of low-rent commercial activity: cigar stores, hamburger chains, Paylesses. There wouldn't be any gays on Market Street, he thought, but then he saw a peep show. It didn't open until nine, so Paul sat across the street at a diner and made a dollar coffee last. He'd wait until lunch to spend money on food, even though he was spacey with hunger.

When the box-office grate opened, Paul paid his check and left the diner. The haggard queen in the booth drew Paul a walking map to the "heart of Gay SF." He was halfway down the block before he noticed the unsolicited phone number on the paper. Paul was awash in judgment—did he seem so desperate he'd go for a toothless old fag?—before he decided to feel flattered.

He stopped at a Rite Aid and stole double As for his Walkman to listen to a mix Tony Pinto had made him years ago. Maybe he could start over, from then. Rewind, scotch-tape the tabs, tape over his life. He walked and walked. By the time Paul found a critical mass of pink neon triangles and blacked-

out windows with silver-fonted signs, his stomach stung from hunger. He liked that internal buzzing, which burned out stray thoughts of Diane. But he needed to bulk up, or curve up.

He chose the first diner with a good name: Sparky's. A hopeful name. Maybe he could be sparky again, as someone else. He sat at the counter and ate a cheeseburger, and then another cheeseburger, and then a plate of fries with gravy, Iowa-style. His rawboned skinny punk-rock waiter arched an eyebrow after the second burger but didn't say anything.

When Paul looked up, he saw it was raining. He'd definitely ordered expensive-enough food to hang out until the rain let up, but he didn't have anything good to read. He wished he'd sat in a booth, where he could hide from the waiters. His waiter hovered in a tight black tee shirt that said *The Stud*. Paul didn't have the wherewithal to make conversation, even with such an easy opening. He guessed the skinny waiter was cute, even with all the acne scars and patchy sandpaper beard. Or maybe because of the scars. That was a type some people were into, he thought with a detached regard: guys with pockmarks. He wondered vaguely if there was a corresponding hanky color. He missed Diane.

"Coffee?" said the skinny waiter.

"Okay," said Paul, removing his headphones. Liz Phair was playing. He wondered if the skinny waiter picked the music.

"Good album," said Paul. The world was his breakup tape.

"Yeah," said the waiter, busying himself with side work. Paul sneaked a look at the quarter-sized cork plugs in the waiter's earlobes.

"Are you hiring?" he said, to say something. The diner was pretty empty, lulling between breakfast and lunch.

"No," said the waiter with a harsh little laugh. "I doubt it. You need a job?"

"Yeah," said Paul. "I just came here from Provincetown. My girlfriend dumped me. I don't know."

The waiter arched his eyebrow again.

"They're always hiring at Different Light," he said. "But don't mention your *girlfriend*."

"Ex," said miserable Paul. He put his headphones on but didn't press play. If he was Polly right now he'd probably cry. Polly was kind of a crier, something Diane had teased him about. Paul didn't cry. What else did Paul do or not do? He'd have to remember or find out. He could do anything now; he was Teen Runaway Paul. Was it cheating to stay in the hostel? Maybe he should sleep on the streets, hustle like a real teen runaway. Maybe he should make himself way younger, get taken in by Social Services and adopted by a wealthy but liberal older gay couple, start life over. He could ace high school now, get a scholarship to NYU for film . . .

The waiter leaned his spindly elbows on the counter in front of Paul.

"She really broke your heart, huh? Did you wrong?" The waiter had gay voice but punk tone, a rockabilly mixture Paul couldn't help but appreciate. Paul pointed to his headphones and shrugged. He pulled his sweatshirt hood over his head.

"You're a mess, kid," said the waiter. "I've been there. My shift's over in fifteen minutes, if you want to hang out."

Paul sat still for a minute, just breathed. Hang out could mean anything. He didn't want to have sex with this guy, he didn't think. He'd just let the waiter believe he was a straight boy, a rube, get taken care of.

"Okay," he said, piling his thirteen dollars on the check (he was now at $106) and taking off his headphones again.

A half hour later, Paul sat back stiffly on a plastic-covered chenille couch in a bay window three streets over and two floors up, and let the waiter throat his cock, watching his hollow cheeks fill and empty. The waiter's sandpaper chin chafed him. He couldn't force himself to harden up, *wouldn't*, out of loyalty, but he could force himself to ejaculate, just to be done. To Paul's surprise, the waiter swallowed. Paul had only been away for a half a year, but he was pretty sure you still weren't supposed to swallow. He felt a small pinch of commingled disgust and fear in his abdomen.

"Rain's stopped," said the waiter, wiping the bristly corner of his lips. "Come on, I'll take you to the bookstore. I guess you're gay enough for them now."

"I don't know," said Paul, unsticking his thighs from the plastic and pulling up his jeans. "I don't have much bookstore experience."

"What can you do?" said the waiter, whose name was Oscar, Paul now knew.

"I can paint houses," said Paul. "Or bartend."

Oscar smiled. Pityingly, Paul thought. Chickens don't bartend in the big city. Paul *was* a rube. He thought back on the bartenders at the gay bars in New York; he'd have to make himself bigger, butcher, maybe even hairier—all harder work than the other direction.

"Well, come out with me tonight and I'll introduce you around," Oscar said. "Maybe you'll get lucky."

"I have to be back by 11 or they lock me out of the hostel," said Paul, squirming on the couch and rubbing his eyes with

his fists. He knew how he sounded, knew he could get whatever he wanted with this lost boy routine.

Somehow he had let Diane turn him from shark to seal—shiny, fat, sunning himself on a rock—but that was over now. He was back.

×

The bouncer waved Oscar, and by extension Paul, through the door of the dingy punk club on 16th Street that was hosting a drag performance of *Chinatown*. The drag queens kept breaking into Stevie Nicks songs, badly and with no apparent relation to the story. Everything on the minimal set (a folding chair, a table, a potted palm) had been covered in tinfoil, perhaps to indicate a relationship between LA and outer space. Weak, Paul thought.

He watched the Tuesday night crowd mill about, that ancient variety of bike messengers, waiters, students, drug dealers—people who got by outside the work week, the same from city to city. Oscar handed Paul a beer and he drank it down. He handed Paul another beer, and Paul drank that down too.

"I could do that way better," Paul said.

"What?" said Oscar, straining over the Stevie Nicks.

Paul shook his head. What was the point?

Many beers later, Paul walked with Oscar and his boyfriend Weldon back to their house, where he allowed himself to be fondled into a desultory three-way. He fell asleep midway through and when he awoke, he smelled something burning, which turned out to be fresh-roasted coffee. His underpants, already rank, were missing, an embarrassment but not an obsta-

cle. He pulled on his pants and shirt and wandered through the silver and purple halls of the ramshackle apartment until he found the kitchen.

Weldon stood in a royal-blue silk kimono, huffing swears at a coffee maker. Paul posed awkwardly in the doorway until Weldon saw him.

"Oscar said you weren't impressed last night," he said, handing Paul an empty teacup and saucer.

Paul examined the cup's floral pattern, thinking back over the night. What was meant to have been impressive? How had he disappointed them?

"The drag show?" Weldon prompted.

"Oh!" Paul said. He wasn't going to take that back. "Well, yeah. No offense."

"No offense, of course. You could do better, I'm sure."

This was it, thought Paul. Of course, so obvious! He could do drag for money! Drag queens probably made a ton of money in San Francisco, where people knew how to tip.

"Yeah, maybe," Paul said.

"Cheeky," said Weldon, in the manner of someone who'd spent a semester in London or had once had an English boyfriend. "My closet's the first door on the right. Let's see what you got."

Weldon's closet proved to be a small room crammed with freestanding racks of dresses, boxes of shoes and wigs, a makeup table with lights, a three-way full-length, and a cobwebbed disco ball swaying overhead. Paul had rarely done drag and had never *performed*. He was ashamed, abashed—and yet determined, like a young Dusty or Diana—in the face of Weldon's professionalism. He avoided anything he might wear for

real (for instance, a spangly *Barbarella* unitard). He scrutinized the exhaustively vulgar collection of satin dresses, gold spandex cat suits, indeterminate feathery garments. He tried on the smallest dress he could find—Weldon must be what, six foot? a giant—and made his body fit inside the red sequins. He struggled into high-heeled shoes and a blonde wig. All Weldon's wigs were blonde! Internalized racism, Paul thought, but then he liked how he himself looked blonde, the unlikeliness a little punk. He looked pretty good. He looked like a really good drag queen, but better because his face wasn't matte.

He clattered, careful in the heels, back to the kitchen and posed again in the doorway, turning his volume up from shy to ingénue.

"Shit," said Weldon. "You weren't kidding."

"Do I look okay?" Paul made his voice just high enough to be believably coming from a male body. He didn't want to give away his trade secrets.

"You look like a pro," Weldon said, setting down two teacups of coffee on the yellow lacquered kitchen tabletop. "Are you?"

"Amateur," said Paul. "So I can stay eligible for the Olympics."

"Huh," said Weldon. "You're a little weird, aren't you."

"Seriously, mister, can I have a job?" said Paul, turning on his kitten voice. Maybe Weldon would discover him, like Lana Turner. Paul disliked asking directly for assistance but he could see the edges of a plan and needed someone to show him how to fill it in.

"I guess you could do a contest," Weldon mused, without conviction. He peered at Paul's skin, stroking Paul's cheek with

his thumb. "Your *pores* . . . Sometimes there's something at the Endup, maybe this weekend. The pot's usually pretty big. Can you sing?"

"Not really," said Paul.

"Dance?"

Paul shook his head.

"Hmm," Weldon said. "So mostly what you do is look good."

"I guess," Paul said, and felt himself unintentionally blushing. "I could lip-sync, maybe?"

He attempted to lean seductively against the doorjamb and stumbled a bit in his heels.

"Yeah," Weldon said. "Hey, be careful, okay? That's a really expensive dress."

Paul knew when he had been dismissed. He returned the dress to the dressing room, and put back on his own smoke-stenched jeans and semen-crusted tee shirt. He ducked his head into the kitchen as he slid back into his corduroy jacket.

"Tell Oscar I said goodbye," he said.

"Okay," Weldon said, slathering marmalade on an English muffin.

Paul trudged down the stairs and out onto 14th Street. He didn't know which way to go now. He'd imagined he would impress Weldon, who would immediately offer him a lucrative job as a female impersonator. Wasn't that Paul's big talent? And didn't people make money off their talents? What had he done wrong? Oscar had been perhaps a tad too attentive to Paul during what Paul remembered of the evening's activities.

Paul had to have a job. But maybe not drag. He walked and

listed his other known talents: pouring beer without too much head, shoplifting, washing dishes, organizing items, knowing what was going to be fashionable a little bit early, thrifting, clever commentary, introducing people to other people, cutting pictures out of magazines with X-acto knives, knowing when people were open to having sex, having sex, being gay.

Tony Pinto had worked out a whole theory of gayness and promiscuity based on his memory of high-school science: male creatures had a biological imperative to spread their seed and so could not actually be monogamous. Monogamy was unhealthy, possibly even unsafe, Tony had said. Paul wrestled internally with the implications of this logic, but adopted the position anyway, to be closer to Tony Pinto. Interestingly, Diane had shared Tony's conclusions about monogamy: for her it was just another way the patriarchy controlled women's bodies. They'd never been officially monogamous, just provisionally (and actually, for the most part) while living in the same room. Diane. Paul suspected Diane wanted monogamy but couldn't admit this breach in her politics. But what about him? He'd liked it too. He'd liked the dinner parties and the stocked pond and the surprising coziness of occasionally not having sex. He liked somebody telling him what to do.

He experienced a heavy, almost intestinal, crush of despair, and stopped in the park across from a big anonymous stone fortress: high school or jail, he wasn't sure which.

He huddled into himself on a bench, face in his crossed arms. What if Diane knew about his activities last night, yesterday afternoon? How he'd been a boy, gotten sucked off as a boy, cum as a boy, walked through the heart of gay San Francisco as the simultaneous subject and object of the male gaze—

nothing she could share; he was unrecognizable as her lover. Paul couldn't understand desire that could be turned off, a circuit breaker routed through particular body forms. He'd imagined Diane as a boy, and loved her. Unfair! he thought-cried. Fuck her, he thought, proud of himself and a little hungry. He surged with excitement, freedom. He'd go back to the hostel to regroup, and he'd make a sweep of the Castro on his way, scouting for cute people. He was free!

The Castro turned out to be many long blocks out of his way, but Paul felt a call to the duty of surveying his new field; according to any system of logic advocated by anyone counseling the recently dumped, he should be "getting out there" as a form of "taking care of himself." He recalled advising this very course of action to Jane after Stacy had left her for that exotic dancer from Coralville. (Jane! He really should call her.) He decided to trust his pre-Diane self, the self who knew, the uncontaminated truest Paul.

He walked right past the gay bookstore Oscar had mentioned, then reconsidered and turned back. Paul considered real bookstores (as opposed to sex bookstores) the best places for afternoon cruising, the more serious cruising, date cruising. At night you were all set; you found yourself at a bar or party, drank drinks, met a person, and decamped with that person to a second location. Instant date. No need to arrange or plan, and complete flexibility in the likely case you found a more amenable situation at the last minute. Daytime cruising, when not at a tea dance or beer bust, required more finesse and more certainty. First off, both parties had more time to second-guess between the securing of the phone number and the calling of the phone number. Secondly, you saw the person

in the harshest light and without any softening lens such as beer, wine, or whiskey. In Paul's ranking of all possible day-time cruising locations, gay non-sex-shop bookstores ranked at the top: congregants within were most likely to be both out and literate, qualities Paul valued. He thought fondly of the hours he'd spent at Oscar Wilde or the Different Light back in New York or even the HQ76 section of the university library's stacks, though, to his endless disappointment, he'd only ever found library success in men's rooms.

Paul believed in reconnaissance, intelligence gathering, staking out likely targets rather than canvassing broadly. He strongly preferred to have sex with or talk to people who *liked* being queer. He was less excited about people still shaking off the poisons of their homophobic families or small towns, or anybody raised religious who was currently ambivalent rather than angry about that religion: they might be (likely were) dirty and wild in bed but Paul found the shame, self-loathing, obses-sive post-coital showering deeply unhot. He was not curious about other people's families or spiritual beliefs. He was not excited by normal AT&T gays. He did not himself care to assimilate into the power structures of heteropatriarchal white Christian America, was bored and horrified by those who did.

Bookstore cruising was also perfect for his current state: a little slower than bar cruising and thus good for someone with a broken part, like a splint. Paul loitered outside the door, pre-tending to study the posters announcing various benefits and open mics and documentaries of interest to the Gay, Lesbian, and Bisexual community. He filled his lungs with the hunter's sweet air of expectation, and pushed inside.

The bookstore—just as Oscar had promised—had a hand-

lettered *Help Wanted* sign taped to the cash register. Paul filed this information away as he browsed his way through Gay Erotica, Lesbian Mysteries, Gay History, Lesbian Romances, Bisexual Studies, and Postcards. He picked through the zines, wondering why they'd never ordered copies of *Polydoris Perversity*. Maybe he could finally do another issue, sell it here. Without Diane to disapprove, he could return to his publishing empire. He was the only customer in the store and neither of the clerks appealed. Paul ambled through the aisles, reading here and there from books he could not afford but strongly wished to own.

He calculated. He still had $324 in his Iowa City bank account and the $106 cash in his pocket, nerve-wrackingly— just enough to stay at the hostel ($154 total) and eat out for two weeks ($20 per day on food = $280) while waiting for a deus ex machina. Or maybe enough for first month's rent somewhere. He'd wait another week, he decided. Maybe something would happen, the universe would provide a sign. He slouched by the periodical wall, waiting for hot people to come in. He flipped through the most current *Sister!/My Comrade*. The drag queens pictured within were all so beautiful and clever, like a more evolved species. He just wasn't one of them, he allowed himself to know with some regret. His thoughts turned once more to financial matters. What could he do? He was too lazy and willful for prostitution. Without local connections or his old buoyancy he'd never find work as a bartender or vintage shop clerk. His best option was the bookstore. He reexamined the bookstore staff. Tattoos: check; hair dyed in Play-Doh colors: check; playfully unclear genders: check; overalls with glitter tube tops: check double check. He could work with these peo-

ple. He knew he'd get the job if he tried for it, in the same way he knew when someone was about to agree to sex.

He walked up to the counter and procured an application from a languid clerk in a Power Breakfast tee shirt, then repaired to a corner to fill in the blanks. Using a coffee-table book of Mapplethorpe photos as his desk, Paul considered his experience. He'd spent quite a bit of time at the campus bookstore at Iowa where Jane had worked. Paul visited her and stole books with her approval, even worked there for a week during rush one semester. So that was bookstore experience. He marked Jane's name down as his manager. He was as good as hired, he thought.

"Come back when you have a phone number," the clerk told him, glancing down at the paper before tucking it under the cash drawer and clicking the register shut.

"Oh," Paul said. "Okay. Yeah, I'll come back."

Maybe in San Francisco they called references. He'd have to warn Jane. That was going to be complicated.

A wiry fag with mutton chops and a backwards baseball cap walked in, but now Paul occupied the liminal space between worker and customer: he was a supplicant, a possible object of surveillance—too weak a position from which to make any play. He left the bookstore and began to walk in what he hoped was the direction of the hostel.

The sky darkened and the streets smelled lightly of garbage and cotton candy. Night was coming—how had that happened? The whole day gone. He stopped at a lonely fluorescent taqueria and ate the cheapest rice-and-beans burrito, forcing himself to read an abandoned business section of the *Chronicle*.

He struggled through an article about the North Ameri-

can Free Trade Agreement, which managed not to call to mind thoughts of Diane.

Back at the hostel, another $11 down, and a rugby-shirted gang of French backpackers had colonized the main bunk room, making weak bilingual fart jokes and mock-punching each other. Weren't *Americans* supposed to backpack through *France?* Paul thought. And anyway, weren't French boys supposed to be like Giovanni, waiting gaily for you in their rented room and actually Italian? *Quel dommage.*

Paul lay down fully clothed on the most remote bunk he could find, turned fetally to the wall, and hugged his duffel. The French hostelers looked dangerously American to him, dubbed-over frat boys. This was San Francisco? Paul knew he could not remain in the hostel. All night he hovered just above sleep: missing flights, retaking the SATs, boarding express trains going in the wrong direction. When the first alarm bell rang, he sprang up and claimed the one single-stall shower. He dressed in the stall, stripped his bunk of its pilling sheets, returned his dirty linens to the front desk, and checked himself officially out.

Today he'd hit the café bulletin boards, get dimes, make some calls. And if he couldn't find an apartment to move into by night, he'd sleep in the park. Paul had gone west, as the Pet Shop Boys had advised, and he was new. He needed to be where the new people were.

×

At Café Flore, Paul spent $1.25 on a coffee plus a buck in the tip jar. He arranged a temporary office for himself by the phone.

He'd taken only the little xeroxed rectangles and could no longer match number with gay-friendly roommate situation, so he ordered the slips by handwriting, artiest first. A tired or else stunningly jaded fag answered on the first ring and invited Paul over immediately; the apartment was a few blocks away.

Paul scooped up his coffee, wishing he had a scarf to toss jauntily over his shoulder. He made his way to the apartment, which turned out to be both prohibitively expensive and rife with cats. Paul counted six but smelled more. His potential roommate—bald, disheveled, in his forties—oozed needy troll energy, another strike. Paul drew the line at living with trolls. Some people would, for instance in the situation where the troll offered free rent. Paul dared not take the chance; uncoolness was contagious and no one was immune. The troll worked as a graphic designer, apparently, which accounted for the misleadingly nice handwriting.

Paul made his polite refusal and walked back to Flore, which is how he'd overheard a sparkly boy on the street refer to his new base of operations. The country-punk counter girl smiled at him. He left more messages on more answering machines, leaving the payphone number for callbacks. He'd used up all his numbers and all his dimes and now he'd have to guard the payphone against other customers. Paul smarted at this unfairness of apartment hunting: you needed an apartment with a phone to get an apartment with a phone, like you needed a job to get a job, or money to get money. But worse—you needed a phone to get a job, so you actually needed an apartment to get a phone to get a job, so the apartment was first, but you needed a *job* to get the apartment. Paul felt an incisive critique of capitalism coming on and ordered an expensive latte as a

distraction. When he tried to pay for the latte, the counter girl waved his money away.

This, thought Paul, buoyed, *will be my city*. He left the full price of the drink in the tip jar, $91 left in his pocket.

He and the counter girl smiled at each other in pure true friendship. When he finished his delicious latte, Paul knew he had to leave. He could come back the next day, but he couldn't order anything else here today and he couldn't linger. The balance was delicate. He could say one more thing, though, to cultivate. He approached the counter, snapping his jacket closed.

"What's this song? Who *is* this?" he said, with a hand gesture of subtle rapture.

"Oh my god, right?" the counter girl said. "It's Echobelly."

"Oh, cool," said Paul. "PJ Harvey's drummer's new band?"

"Yeah."

"So good."

Paul stood tip-tapping his fingers on the counter for another minute.

"Hey," he said. "Do you know anybody who's looking for a roommate?"

"Weird," said the counter girl, with her big-toothed Scandinavian smile. "I actually do."

She wrote out name and number in graffiti-style letters, and pushed the napkin toward Paul.

"Does that say Ruffles?" Paul asked, modulating his intonations carefully: too much emphasis said hickish surprise and no emphasis said hickish gullibility. He raised one eyebrow ever so slightly.

"Yeah," said the counter girl, laughing. "That's his name. He's cool. Everybody in that house is cool."

"Cool," said Paul.

"Say Suzy gave you the number."

Paul made a sharp little salute of thanks, high on conquest-adrenaline and expensive coffee, and went back to the payphone. Ruffles answered and invited Paul to come over to check out the house, located in the very butch-sounding Alamo Square. Out on the street, Paul stood briefly with his tourist map, attempting to find Alamo Square, before he gave up and decided it would be more fun to just ask people.

Alamo Square was more a lawn than a park, flanked on all sides by tumbledown gingerbread houses. Paul rang the bell of the most tumbled-down of all the houses and a scarecrow fag in very snug silver bell-bottoms, a shaved head, and two very large hoop earrings answered. Paul could hear Shirley Bassey's mellifluous laugh in the background, then horns.

"Paul?"

"Ruffles?"

"Come in, darling," Ruffles said. He was maybe in his thirties, and so stylish Paul couldn't breathe properly at first. The counter girl must have thought he was cool enough to live with Ruffles, and a proud calm infused Paul's body.

Ruffles led him on a tour of the house: two floors, a room just for bikes, something called a water closet which turned out to just be a bathroom without a shower. The kitchen had wallpaper, which Paul found exotic. The Shirley Bassey was coming from a record player. The living room, Paul was surprised to discover, was not thrift-store ironic but instead sunny and wood-floor minimal, with a view of the pretty red bridge.

They sat on facing couches and Ruffles explained the situation: five people lived in the house, but one was going to Berlin

for a couple months and needed to sublet her room, conveniently the cheapest, located in the basement. She planned to leave it furnished but would pack up most of her stuff. Would Paul mind using her furniture? Was Paul vegan? Could Paul agree to not eat meat in the house? Was Paul cool with possible SM-related noises? Was Paul very quiet in the mornings? Did Paul have any pets? Did Paul smoke? How soon could Paul move in and start paying prorated rent? Paul was cool with everything, the other roommates were cool with Ruffles deciding, Ruffles was cool with Paul. They shook hands, for fun.

"We're going to just *eat you up*," said Ruffles, slipping the Shirley Bassey record back into its sleeve and putting on Herb Alpert and the Tijuana Brass. Ruffles was clearly a tastemaker. Maybe Paul could sit at his feet and learn, an ephebe to Ruffles's Socrates.

"Would you take a check from Iowa?" Paul asked.

"Can you get a money order?" Ruffles countered.

Paul agreed to come back later that evening with the money order and get his key then. Ruffles said Paul could move in the next day. He hadn't asked where Paul was staying, and Paul hadn't volunteered. Sitting out the night at a twenty-four-hour diner beat having Ruffles think him a friendless waif. Ruffles was *not* the kind of gay who rescued puppies, Paul could tell.

Paul walked shin-splintingly fast to a bank machine, then to a check-cashing place on Divisadero where he purchased a money order for $162, which he then delivered to Ruffles. After the prorated rent plus the ATM fee ($1) and the charge for the money order ($5), he had $156 in the bank and the $91 still in his pocket. He was going to make it after all.

He met two more of the roommates: also disinterested, also

older punk-rock royalty—a photographer of hardcore bands who worked at Flax and a playwright who managed a small experimental theater in the Mission. Paul privately decided to bone up on hardcore and experimental theater, two areas of study he'd never before considered. The roommates were very polite and about to leave for a trip to Joshua Tree, which Paul pretended to have already known was a real place.

Ruffles handed Paul a key attached to a pink two-tone rabbit's foot, and they all agreed Paul would move his stuff in the next morning. Paul hoped it wouldn't seem strange that this "stuff" consisted of two bags. He left the house trying to imagine how Holly Golightly would handle the situation. He should maybe get big sunglasses, he thought. He should definitely go to the movies.

He splurged for one movie (*Crooklyn*) and then snuck into two more (*Bandit Queen*, *The Crow*) at a cineplex on Van Ness, and emerged bleary-eyed and melancholy at midnight. Which world was this, he wondered. He couldn't believe how sad it was that Brandon Lee had died during the filming; anyone so gorgeous was undoubtedly gay. He felt a little tragic, with the night so long and open before him.

He still had at least ten hours to kill until he could honorably "move in." He walked to the Castro, where packs of happy business gays pranced through the streets complaining loudly about the sullen waitress at dinner or tsking the street kids outside the subway station.

It was very hard to break into the avant-garde without a place to live, Paul thought. Back at Flore, Paul's new friend wasn't working, so he sat and nursed a succession of coffees and wrote multiple unsatisfying drafts of a letter about crows to

Diane, punctuated by guilt postcards to his mother, Kostas, his little brother Ari, and most guiltily of all, Jane. And to Christopher, who had sent him a letter care of General Delivery in Provincetown, itemizing his share of the bills and listing his phone messages (including another one from Tony Pinto).

He walked to the Safeway at 3 AM to look for a cheap meat snack, and found a novelty-size marbled composition notebook. Paul loved functional tiny things; he loved how they turned him into a temporary giant, how he could have everything he needed in the palm of his hand. He surged with pleasure and excitement—maybe it was the coffee or maybe it was being able to go to a supermarket at three in the morning. He loved the city. He wandered the aisles with the tiny composition notebook, gazing in wonder upon all the California foodstuffs. He decided to pay for the notebook, if only to have some kind of interaction with the cashier.

Back at Flore, Paul arranged his copy of *A Lover's Discourse* on the table, careful to keep all the various Polaroids and pressed lilacs inside. Someday he would actually read the book all the way through, not just skim sections until he found a pretty idea which then overwhelmed him. He drew crows in his new notebook and dabbed coffee in between the lines for a watercolor effect. By the time the sun came up, he had reached a pitch of exhausted agitation and packed up his little office.

He had seen a miniature park with benches on the other side of the Muni tracks, so he walked there in the chilly spring air. He curled up on the bench and dozed off the coffee until the noise of upstanding citizens with their dogs forced him awake. He let his mind empty, watching the dogs smell each other. Dogs, like everything else in life, were better with Diane.

He thought of how intently dogs stared at Diane, sometimes pulling their owners down streets to follow her.

He'd gone as his scruffy girlish-boy self to Ruffles's house, had introduced himself as Paul—a mistake, he now saw. What if Diane wanted to get back together? But at least he'd have a phone number for that bookstore application. But then if he got the job, he'd have to go to work in his boy body. Everything was impossible and his stomach hurt. The coffee crash had begun.

×

An hour or so later, back at Alamo Square, Paul rang the buzzer and knocked. When no one answered, he let himself in. Heaven, he thought—a house to himself. He clattered down to the "garden" level and found his new room, maybe a little dustier and smaller than he'd remembered. He unpacked quickly and then sneaked looks behind his new roommates' closed doors. He canvassed the kitchen for food he could eat without anyone knowing, and made himself a little sick on a breakfast of crackers, pickles, peanut butter, spoonfuls of tomato sauce, and—the big score—two large bites of cashew chicken from a takeout container. He had many tasks to accomplish today— thrift-shopping for sheets, giving his new phone number to that bookstore, buying groceries. Where to begin? Definitely a shower.

Paul couldn't remember the last time he'd taken a long hot shower in a clean bathroom. He washed and conditioned his hair a few times, sampling all the different products, from Aussie Mega to Finesse and finishing up with Aveda. He exfoliated

with that apricot face scrub that smelled like the beach, slapped his face with Clinique toner, and carefully worked a dab of Sebastian Molding Mud into his hair. He took the smallest amounts of the products, samples really; no one would notice.

Finally clean and fresh, Paul reclined on the living room couch with a stack of old but high-end fashion magazines (*i-D*, *Photo*, *Vogue Italia*) he'd found in the "water closet." He doubted they belonged to Ruffles, but anything was possible. Gay men were so full of contradiction, he thought, as he began systematically paging through a *Bazaar* for pictures of the holy trinity of supermodels: Christy Turlington, Naomi Campbell, Linda Evangelista. Paul understood the feminist critique of the fashion world. He too was anti-fur and pro-positive images. He agreed models were too white and too skinny, but he loved these strange beings, their lost boyishness and their ennui and their dioramic emotional rearrangements.

Linda was his favorite. He took the most delight in finding her in some crowded mise en scène. Linda allowed her form to appear in shocking configurations; Paul imagined these as vaguely collaborative, desultory acquiescences to some high bidder. When she'd said she wouldn't get out of bed for less than $10,000, let alone do whatever was being proposed—what was she wearing when she'd said that, he wondered. He liked her Chanel campaign well enough but what hooked him was her editorial work: the Peter Lindbergh pieces in *Vogue Italia*, the Steve Meisel shots of her as blonde bombshell or Catholic schoolgirl or Catholic schoolboy or Linda as a girl poised to kiss Linda as a boy. Naomi was the smart one, Paul thought, and Christy was soft, Christy you might actually want to talk to about your problems or make out with, but Linda was the

cunning fox, the trickster, this generation's Stephen Gordon in French cuffs, Linda the Artemis to Christy's Aphrodite and Naomi's Athena. When he lived in New York he'd steal old magazines from rich people's tied-up recycling on his way home from the bars and hunt through the back pages for clues about Linda's natural habitat. She might be at Nell's or the Tunnel or some VIP room at Limelight, and he'd only have to get past a bouncer to meet her and—then what? Even in his fantasies he never got past just seeing her and basking.

Back in high school Paul had taped George Michael's "Freedom '90" video off *120 Minutes*, and for years he watched it over and over, absorbing the drug of Linda, new every time. If anything, the high improved upon repetition, potency rebuilding during the rewind. First, drums and a tambourine. Next, flashes of Linda, short hair, in pants, sitting alone in a hallway. Romantic! Then Linda mouthing words, intercut with Naomi dancing in underwear, confusingly sexy—then back to Linda, and I mean, come *on*, thought Paul. She is totally singing to Naomi! On film Linda seemed almost vulnerable, softer but not soft, one of Fassbinder's sailors, soft with malice, singing, "Heaven knows I was just a young boy, didn't know what I wanted to be . . ." Singing with her eyes closed, singing about someone else. Even in the fantasy, you couldn't have her. Anyone could see her vulnerability but it wasn't for you. To watch her was to watch the girl you loved fantasize about someone else. "I was every little hungry school girl's pride and joy, and I guess it was enough for me . . ." she mouthed, over and over, then intercutting with Naomi and a jolt! they both opened their eyes. Then the chorus, and Christy comes sweeping through the loft, naked under a sheet like a wedding dress, Christy seemed

sad, what was it about her sadness that made Paul want her? But he wanted to *be* Linda. Now a motorcycle jacket was on fire! Christy knew what George Michael was singing about, Christy was the nice girl who felt bad that George Michael had to be such a closet case, who felt bad that Linda Evangelista had to be secretly in love with her, who felt bad that Naomi Campbell was secretly a genius not being taken seriously. Christy was full of love, Paul thought. But Paul loved Linda, who was tortured and mean and hard and the kind of gorgeous that hurt, all angles and rage, she walked the catwalk in pain she was too proud to show. Never feminine, if feminine meant at all soft. Never pretty.

In Iowa City he'd tried to play down his love of supermodels, had diluted his Linda wall shrine with drag-night club flyers and museum postcards. At Diane's, he'd been restrained, hadn't put anything on the walls in his effort to conform to her admittedly superior minimalist aesthetic. She'd tack one fading flea-market snapshot to the wall and be done with it. Now all that was the past. Who would he be here, in this high-ceilinged city? He split the binding of the *Bazaar* and carefully removed a Versace ad featuring Linda with a pompadour. He'd hang it up in his new closet, for old time's sake.

×

A bookstore was really no different from a bar, Paul thought when he arrived, ten minutes before anyone else scheduled for the night shift. More public, better lit, but the same seaside question of what might wash up today.

Now that he'd been at the bookstore for a few weeks, Paul

had amassed preferences, was settling in. For one, he preferred opening, being alone with his light sweet coffee and dominion over the tape player. He disliked arriving late, but no one else minded. The store, the owners, the workers, the customers—everyone was on Gay Time. Paul liked the late shift well enough; nights often meant readings, and readings were efficient: anyone attractive was almost guaranteed to be smart and interesting, and anyone old enough to be unattractive might be famous.

While his coworkers trickled in and out, Paul fussed the racked postcards into alignment, marking off items for reorder according to his own missionary sense of what the gays actually needed (less Joan Crawford, more Divine; less *Desert Hearts*, more *The Hunger*; less "I Can't Even Think Straight," more "Kissing Doesn't Kill"). Next he organized the rainbow rings jewelry, with a moral superiority he didn't even try to quell. The bookstore sold way more crap than books; the crap subsidized the books, so Paul was okay with it (the crap was called "sidelines," a detail Paul resented knowing), but still judged the crap-buyers. Buy a book, for the sake of all that is holy, he thought at them. Fussing was the equivalent of side work at the bar: chopping lemons, refilling maraschino cherry containers, marrying bottles of well liquor. When his coworker showed up, Paul moved into shelving (the equivalent of barbacking). He was a perpetual motion machine, stacking books alphabetically and with a carefully emptied mind scooting around, slipping books between books. Everything in its place. Before he tired of this task, Divya asked Paul to take over the register, which was the pouring drinks equivalent. Paul chatted up everyone, training his romantic attention fully on each postu-

lant, whether money-giver or lingerer; he drew little maps for lost homosexual tourists, bantered winningly with the friends of the money-givers, admired new haircuts and jewelry made from cock rings, wondered aloud about the provenance of certain special tee shirts or belt buckles. Paul the temple prostitute took pleasure in satisfying others' unspoken, even unknown, needs. He was a healer today. Most days. He was like Annie Sprinkle, he thought, a sex priestess.

Everyone had a role. Malcolm, tall as a ladder, maintained the book orders; he was the slightly Machiavellian power behind the owners' throne, and Paul found himself in an unplanned thrall, not in the least attracted but flirting regularly. Divya was worker-focused; she all but ignored customers, preferring to draw cartoons of the regulars and leave them taped up behind the counter. Sometimes she brought experimental baked goods: carrot cake laced with hemp oil, or pot turtles; she was sort of a hippie, a wake-and-bake mural painter with black hair to her ass and no evident politics. Paul hadn't even been sure Divya was gay until her sweet-cheeked girlfriend had appeared at closing one night with an anniversary picnic in her bike basket. Bike picnics were so the Mission, he thought, envious.

Handsome skateboarder Franky was the medium-sized muscle of the place, nicely but firmly kicking junkies out of the bathroom and always unloading the boxes on delivery days. Silver, pretty and skittish, held tight to the role of store DJ. Paul had expected great avant-gardism from Silver based on her half-shaved green hair and face piercings, but left to her own devices, Silver played *ABBA Gold* or the *Priscilla, Queen of the Desert* soundtrack on auto-repeat. Once Paul opened the

wrong paycheck by accident and saw Silver's legal name and since that moment had felt a tenderness toward both Silver and the neglectful store owners.

Thom, whom Silver and Malcolm sighingly called Thom of Richmond, was the manliest bookstore clerk Paul had ever met. Thom also worked the early morning shift for UPS and one time, late to the bookstore, Thom had changed out of his damp brown uniform shirt behind the counter, revealing the textbook musculature-plus-paunch of a real working man. Paul and all the customers in a twenty-five-foot radius swooned from such heady authenticity. Sales were very good that afternoon.

A few other people worked at the store, maybe one shift a week, and Paul didn't know their faces, just their names from the time sheets: Marcel, Rusty, Gabriel, Toby. They acquired the status of Mystery Shoppers or indifferent gods: they could be casually surveilling Paul anywhere, in the store or walking down Valencia; he could have met any or all of them in one backroom or another. Paul thrilled at this vulnerability, the sheer sense of possibility in these unknown connections. He'd already been at the bookstore for a month. For a startling instant, like emerging from a swimming pool for air, Paul remembered college, Jane, seasons, time passing—then another lovely androgyne placed another hardback copy of *Written on the Body* on the counter and Paul returned to the smooth cozy green deep of San Francisco.

×

Paul walked up 14th Street toward Guerrero. The guy whose house he'd woken up at had told him the streets to get home

233

and Paul repeated them in his mind. He had to go to work, but not for a couple of hours. His clothes stank with what he had done, his dismal life. He'd lost Jane's Walkman somewhere between the Eagle and the first party, so he was all alone. He passed the crepe place, Ti Couz, and saw a patch of curly hair in the line. He knew that hair, that shape of head, like a childhood memory.

He kept walking, worrying the image in his hungover brain. Zoe! As in Diane's Zoe . . . Paul felt his heart banging in his chest. He stopped—he should talk to her, this was obviously a sign from the universe—and then he remembered what she'd see if he approached her. He knew of an only slightly skanky taqueria bathroom a half block away; he could Clark Kent it there. What if Zoe left? Maybe a doorway? Nothing private enough in this achey California daylight.

Pancho Villa smelled enticingly of the roasted pork Paul had recently learned was called carnitas. The bathroom had an out-of-order sign, but the knob turned, so Paul sneaked in. He found his inner Polly, made her manifest for the first time since he'd come to San Francisco. He was dressed a little more butch than he usually dressed in Provincetown, but Zoe would probably approve of that. He tried not to run back; he jogged the block in spurts, then walked casually up to the café, rehearsing his backstory: just came to get some coffee, on the way home . . . from something fun? No. He wanted Diane to know the truth (his loyalty, pining, and loneliness) but not the details (his rainbow of boring, terrible, and semen-drenched assignations). He approached Zoe, telegraphing heartbreak in her direction. Zoe turned under the weight of Paul's thoughts—who wouldn't—and startled, then smiled, then looked like she had gas pains.

"Polly!" Zoe sounded happy to see him.

"Hey," said Paul, affecting an initial stiffness he then allowed to melt into her hug. All responses appropriate so far, passing functions operational, correct behavior module activated.

"It's so good to see you!" Zoe said. She was standing with a crew of rowdy dykes, who cursorily checked Paul out then went on with their conversations. "How are you?"

"Good," said Paul. "No, I'm good, I'm—"

"We all miss you, you know?"

"Yeah, no, I miss you all too." Paul's voice cracked, unintentionally, on the *all*. "How's—"

He stopped talking, felt a sob on its way up, felt his face heat up.

"Come on," said Zoe kindly. She pulled him away from the line, into a space between parked cars. Her eyes looked sad or maybe compromised, and Paul's stomach went sour.

"I messed up," Paul said.

"Polly," she said.

"I should have been more—"

He couldn't say what really happened, of course; who even knew what Diane had told Zoe or anyone else for that matter.

"I don't think it was you," said Zoe.

Paul burst into tears, his arms stiffly at his sides.

"Would you give Diane a message for me?" he said, when he could talk again.

"Oh man, I don't—"

"No, you're right. I'm sorry."

"She misses you, Polly. I shouldn't say it, but—"

Paul nodded. Zoe talked more. She was driving cross-country to Olympia to pick up the last of her things from stor-

age before the P-town season started, and had stopped in San Francisco to meet some friends from Michigan on the way. They were leaving that afternoon.

"Maybe don't tell her you saw me," said Paul impulsively.

Zoe looked relieved.

"Our secret," she said, hugging him goodbye and going back to her friends. They looked over for a minute, then reintegrated Zoe into their cell.

Paul gathered himself and walked up the block, sucking in the last of his sniffles as he crossed the street. He'd been doing fine, great even; then he'd been socked in the gut. And now look at this, coming down the sidewalk—two more lovebird dykes, shoving their happiness in everyone's faces. Wait, was that . . .

"Diane?" Paul heard his own voice, like an animal's involuntary yelp. The two dykes stopped, disentangled, and turned into Diane and the pretty counter girl from Express, Elena. *The single mother*, Paul remembered. That's what they used to call her, he and Diane; she was famous to them for being a hardcore vegan and having a toddler.

"*Polly*," said Diane, but Paul was still walking. He boarded the first bus that pulled up on 16th and Guerrero, didn't check, and so rode the 22 all the way to Pacific Heights and would have to walk many blocks back down now but what did it matter. *Single mother*, he thought over and over as the bus bumped and rolled.

Back at the house, nobody was home. Nobody was ever home, Paul thought. Someone, probably Ruffles, had left a pot of crusty lentils on the stovetop overnight but Paul wasn't hungry anymore. Afternoon sunlight flooded the living room.

Paul moved through the air and sun and into the cave of his room, where he lay on the futon on the floor and bit his nails down to the cuticles. How could he compete with a *mother*? She was fixed like a photograph, effortless and uncomplicated. He was helpless. Maybe he could physically bear a child, he thought. Maybe he could use his own sperm to fertilize his own eggs, who knew? But Paul didn't *want* to be a mother. Not ever. Or a father, for that matter. Wasn't the whole point that he didn't have to do those normal things? Paul sucked the blood off his thumb and shook his hand to ameliorate the sting.

×

Over a month and Paul still couldn't properly read the bus schedule. He walked to the next bar on his list, out of the Castro and all the way down Market in the drizzle, blocks and blocks of his own head and *Incesticide* because Kurt had just died, which Paul couldn't even understand. When he'd heard, he'd wanted to call Diane but restrained himself with whiskey.

The first three bars had been a bust, full of stupid fags so excited about their gym memberships and still squealing when Dee-Lite came on. Not a single hot guy. Maybe Paul was looking too tender. He'd fended off would-be daddies in their Dockers and braided belts, their pastel plaid short-sleeved shirts *tucked in*. None of them even offered to buy him a drink. Too much like actual daddies, if your dad liked Bette Midler and hydrangeas and tanning and was a little bit cheap.

The strangers he'd like to know were probably at the Box tonight, which he was avoiding since running into Diane. He'd been avoiding his roommates, his roommates' friends, the

punk-rock queers he saw on Mission Street, avoiding the muscley bike messenger dykes and the twiggy tattooed fags and bi-curious boys who'd be with the dykes, as cover. He avoided everywhere he knew the cool kids were: the Bearded Lady, the Endup, Unleash the Queen. He avoided El Rio, Muff Dive, Club Jesus, Josie's, even Café Beano; he ignored flyers advertising bands he'd like to see; he avoided Adobe, Reckless, Osento. Avoid, avoid, avoid. If he met people he'd like to meet, he'd be here, this would be real; he'd be as alone as he was.

Paul had a written list of gay bars where the boys he liked wouldn't be, culled from the *Damron Guide* at the bookstore—where he was working only one day a week, until they figured out the new schedule—and he was making his way down. If at any of these crappy bars there was anyone he could stand to look at, he'd let them do whatever. He walked and walked, from the Castro down to the other side of Market, down to the leather bars. He didn't bother to make himself into a big hot cub or a dirty boy scout or a young dad type. Fuck it.

He walked up to the Eagle like a wet mutt, dripping rain on the floor of the foyer. The bouncer gave Paul a pranking look—a *you little fish let's see how they bite you* look—and let him in. The bar was maybe half-full, and Paul stood for fifteen minutes while the bartender poured beers for much manlier men and polished shot glasses. A frail old guy as out of place as Paul came up and stood next to him. Paul side-glanced the guy, noted chicken-skin poking out of his leather vest. But at least the old guy had appropriate clothing. Paul wasn't even dressed right. His Levi's were cords and he wore Diane's old Revolution Girl Style Now! shirt, which had smelled of her when he put it on but now just looked campy. No wonder the

daddies weren't interested. They probably had petulant teenage daughters at home they were trying not to think about while they looked for boys half their age but legal. Their daughters' boyfriends! How gross, thought Paul. He finally caught the bartender's eye.

"We don't serve lite beer, *miss*," the bartender said, in high dudgeon.

"Do you have Jack Daniels?" said Paul. Of course they had Jack Daniels. He meant to say it toughly ("Jack, dude. Make it a double"), but was taken aback by this forgotten experience of chicken oppression and squeaked instead.

The bartender rolled his eyes and poured Paul's shot. He counted out singles and left the tip in quarters. He knew better but it was all he had. The jukebox was playing "Margaritaville." These big tough leathermen needed to prove how much they didn't care about music by playing terrible radio songs, trying to act how they thought construction workers would act: picking Jimmy Buffet songs on purpose, pissing in troughs, beating each other up and off, drinking shitty beer, and hazing losers like Paul. He sipped his shot. Once he finished it, he wouldn't have anything to do with his hands. The shot had been a strategic mistake; he could have had two cans of PBR for the same price. He looked around for a smoker. If he bummed a smoke while he still had a drink, the legitimate overlap would buy him the time it took to finish the cigarette. He screwed up his courage and asked an approachable-seeming boy in a dog collar and jockstrap. The boy fished in the waistband of his jock for a soft pack of Marlboro Reds and carefully handed Paul one cigarette, then turned away.

Paul turned back to the bar, retrieved a pack of matches

from a bowl next to the condoms. His hands shook a little. He finished the rest of his shot quickly. In normal circumstances none of this would be hard—this was Paul's métier, going into bars alone and making friends. True, he'd never entered a leather bar as himself before and he didn't have the energy to leave, change clothes, change body, and return. If only he could remember himself, put himself back together . . .

He had only one move left. Facing the bar for privacy, he focused on his cock, keeping it semi-soft and growing it down his leg. He'd have to go bigger than Jeff Stryker to get anyone here to look past his skinny chest, flabby torso, round face, too-soft eyes.

He turned around to show off, to no avail. No one was looking at him. He felt like Andie at the beginning of *Pretty in Pink*. He could stroke his pants to gather attention, but the gesture seemed un-hot in tan corduroy. He spotted a pitcher of water and poured himself a plastic cup, then another. The bartender looked his way, mustache sneered up. Paul put out his cigarette, faking a punk disdain, and ambled awkwardly across the room, cock strapped by his pants to his mid-thigh. The bathroom—thank god—was what he'd expected: a giant trough along one whole wall and at least a dozen men standing around. He didn't really even *have* to pee. He found a space, unzipped—the zipper itself a travesty, an insult to leathermen everywhere!—and fumbled out the penis like a garden hose or a stethoscope. His heart was pounding. He wasn't supposed to be here. He pushed deep inside himself, tried to find the pee with hidden inside muscles. He kept his eyes down. He had to act like he didn't know the penis was large, or his plan wouldn't work. He found his piss-reservoir and began to drain it as slowly as possible

while demonstrating a strong flow. Thank god he'd read all that John Preston and so knew how to act. How long could he keep peeing? He stopped and started again, cultivating the sound of his stream against the side of the aluminum trough. He kept his head down. Was anyone looking? He started again, stepping back from the wall so more guys could see the length. He wasn't used to aiming something this big, lost control briefly and splashed the floor. Now he heard something in his periphery, a something of not-talking, of crowding closer. A grizzled but fit old man with silver chest hair under a buttery-looking black vest, a young cub guy in a collar, and an old-timey clone in a flannel and 501s flanked him. Paul kept peeing and when he splashed the cub's boots the next time he meant it. The cub was "hot" like a dancer on a Pride float, with a black chest harness and leather chaps, shaved head, trimmed beard, cherry lips. The older men stepped back to watch, like children at a zoo. What would the baby polar bear and the baby otter say to each other?

"Um," said Paul, turning to the cub.

"Wow," said the cub.

"Holy—" said the older man.

Paul shook the gigantic half-hard penis and put it back in his corduroys. He left the bathroom and returned to his place against the bar. After a few minutes, the bartender grudged a shot onto the bar.

"From that dude," he said, cocking his head at one of the old guys from the bathroom and shrugging, unimpressed.

Paul slammed the shot glass into his mouth and gulped, retrieving some part of himself in the harsh sugar.

Later, in the back of the bar, in the room behind the room, Paul thought about his own new room, with the last occupant's

futon, the kelly green sleeping bag he'd bought at Community Thrift, his collection of pocket trinkets arrayed on the windowsill, his no-lamp, no-lease, no-dresser, no-desk, no-chair cell, and how he'd already paid his $200 for the month and was free. He kept his eyes closed, let his body float. He was a stage diver, he was held aloft by invisible *Belle et la Bête* hands, he was a product to be constructed by this assembly line of deft fingers. He thought about the blue walls, he thought about the morning sunlight through the barred window, the lemon tree in the backyard, the taco cart on the corner, the honeysuckle alleys. He imagined pulling the sleeping bag up to his chest, how he'd add the day's bus ticket to the careful pile under his stack of unreadable books, how he'd go sleep there later tonight or tomorrow, alone and cold, how he would probably sleep in his clothes, too cold to undress, how no one had heat in San Francisco, how bone-cold it was, how cold.

×

San Francisco was not Provincetown, was not Iowa City, was *really* not New York. New York was punk, harder, more fatal. What bad thing could happen to a person in San Francisco? On the 33 Paul avoided the eyes of the wasting men who took the bus up to the free clinic in the Haight. Was he immune or did he want to die? Paul didn't know, not at night when he drank shot after shot at the Eagle, welcome now as that scrawny kid with the horse cock, that staple of porn fantasy, no uniform needed. Paul opened his throat for the shots and the beers, drank them down then headed to the backroom or the bathroom and let some man touch him, suck him. Paul didn't

touch them, those professor-age men, or the jocky guys in their twenties, or the hardcore eternally forty leather guys with their graying temples, or the regular mustachioed clones, or the side-burned ACT UP clones. Paul went limp everywhere but his cock, like a Mustang in a car wash. You couldn't catch anything from getting blown or fondled, he thought. No matter what the flyers said. He refused to fuck anyone (too much work) or to get fucked (still too much work) or to blow anyone (unclean). In the daytime at the bookstore Paul drank coffee after coffee to keep his mind fast. Just forward motion, go go go to the next night with the buzz in his forehead and then the shots to turn it off. In the mornings he emptied his pockets of the little slips of paper with phone numbers and names, shoving them into an empty tomato-sauce jar. The fuller the jar, the hotter he was. He never called the numbers, didn't want to see those men again. After two months he was ⅓ of 14 ounces hot. He was 4.66666667 ounces hot. And he was completely supporting himself from the bookstore. Sometimes he let older men take him out to dinner, but they didn't count toward hotness; they just helped him live within his means. He let these men—whom he met at the bookstore, usually—give him career advice, in the time-honored way of older fags. They liked to take a young guy out to dinner, Paul knew, and they liked it best when you didn't have sex with them. That way they believed they were mentors, that the relationship was non-transactional. They believed Paul was baby-them and told him what they thought they would have liked to have heard: go to law school, don't be so promis-cuous, be more promiscuous, quit being a lawyer, your father loves you, start working out when you're young. Most of them stuck to some variation on "follow your dreams," and Paul took

manly scavenger bites of rare steak and tried not to think about how cliché these men sounded, which he felt was inhospitable while he dined on their tab. As a point of honor, for the duration of each meal Paul made himself believe anything his host said, and only afterward—maybe watching a Bette Davis video with Ruffles—did he indulge his critiques.

×

Paul was five blocks from the Gang Way, an old queen's dive, with an hour to spare before he was to meet up with his coworker Franky for their first outside-work hangout. Paul began to get himself obviously lost; he went so far as to remove a blank scrap of paper from his pocket and consult it elaborately while squinting at building numbers. Paul liked having an alibi. After a few turns around the blocks, he realized he was dangerously close to his destination. Nothing worse than hovering desperately in front of a place you're going to have to enter later, looking like you're too scared to go in alone or too much of a loser to have friends, a real greenhorn. So he avoided the street the bar was on. He had another forty minutes to kill. He began to hunt for a little black book, a pocket-sized address book—covered in black leather with gold-leafed pages—in which he might keep phone numbers for future use, like James Bond or Helen Gurley Brown. Paul knew an address book of this type would be essentially impossible to locate in the Tenderloin at 10:30 PM on a Wednesday night, but he broadened his circuit to include a gas station and a couple bodegas. At each store, he'd first look, then engage the clerk in his quest. He completely absorbed himself in this project, feeling such

a deep invented need for this little black book that he eventually bought a package of three coverless memo pads wrapped in plastic in order to appease the last clerk, a helpful woman whose babushka'd hair reminded him, with a startling embarrassment, of his yaya, Kostas's mother.

Paul strode more purposefully down Larkin toward the bar, packet in hand. A block away, the spell broke. Paul realized he couldn't enter the bar with a packet of notepads, like some errand boy, some Bartleby. He set the packet carefully between the metal bars of a shuttered limousine service office. What would they make of this in the morning? He imagined all the things he could leave in the night, to be found by bemused but grateful morning people. Night-Paul the package fairy! Those morning people would feel but not understand the superiority of the night—who would leave such strange packages all around town, they'd think, berating themselves for their lack of imagination before returning to the soul-crushing jobs they didn't understand they could just leave!

Paul was now only fifteen minutes early, which was exactly the amount early to be. He pushed open the flimsy door, performing a quick "Just looking for my friend" check of all the nooks and crannies.

No one particularly interesting yet. He bought himself a bottle of the sale beer, which he swigged while pumping quarters into the only game they had, Space Invaders. Video games didn't showcase his ass and hips the way a vigorous game of pinball could, but Paul knew Space Invaders well enough to make two quarters last for five minutes (Level 6). He liked Space Invaders better than most games because you basically shot little sperm bullets at various moving targets. Pump

pump pump! He also liked Ms. Pac Man, because of the name (Ms. Man! Ha!). Paul's other bar skills included darts (decent), pool (mediocre), breaking up fistfights (okay), taking keys from drunks (excellent). He finished his beer and left the bottle. He took a place at the bar, so when Franky walked in, he'd see Paul just ordering his first beer. Paul preferred to keep his numbers private if he didn't know a person. He remembered the after-bars in Iowa City, that fraternity of drinkers-to-excess. He thought in succession of a boy named Joshua who wore glasses, of the enthusiastic bisexual stripper from Dubuque, of the winter-long naked showering craze Paul had ushered in at a particularly banal condo party on the Coralville strip. He missed Iowa, where necessity had mothered such charming invention.

Paul ordered his next first beer, a nicer beer so Franky wouldn't think he was cheap. Paul theoretically believed in starting with top shelf and switching to well when he was unable to discern the difference. In practice, however, when he was forced to buy his own drinks, Paul's concern was for quantity; he privileged the always-full glass. Paul liked to know the right position to espouse on various topics. He had a store of drink-combining wisdom (beer before liquor, never been sicker; beer before grass, flat on your ass; beer before wine, feeling fine) and adopted opinions (blended Irish whiskey beat blended Scotch whisky; the only good bourbon was Knob Creek; single-malt Scotch could be drunk all night; good whiskey must never be diluted by ice or soda whereas bad whiskey can be salvaged with a little ginger ale; never drink well vodka or any gin because of the impurities; a Bloody Mary will fix a hangover better than whatever one had drunk to get there). And there was Franky,

skateboard tucked under his arm, plaid shirt buttoned all the way up.

"Hey," said Franky, nodding.

"What's up," said Paul, expansive with secret beer. He wanted to hug Franky but didn't. Paul looked him up and down for girl, but couldn't find any tells. Paul had never met a transsexual guy before Franky. He'd known his share of butches who passed and lots of young girlish queens and the occasional transsexual lady. But Franky was a guy; Paul wouldn't have ever known Franky was anything other than a cute indie fag if Malcolm hadn't gossiped. At first he wondered if Malcolm had lied, but then he'd seen Franky palling around with one of the Lusty Lady girls. And Franky had once mentioned that he'd seen Paul's zine when he was at Santa Cruz. Paul wondered briefly if Franky was like him, but somehow he thought not. Franky knew what he wanted forever, Paul thought. That was the difference between them. Paul knew what he wanted at any given moment, for sure. Right now he wanted more to drink.

"What's your poison?" he asked Franky, folding a ten-dollar bill and holding it over the bar so the bartender could see he had money for a tip. He mysteriously wanted to impress and treat Franky, even though they were the same age and had the same job. He wanted to extend the blanket of his hospitality so it enveloped Franky. This wasn't necessarily flirtatious.

Paul followed Franky to an empty spot along the wall. The music was loud and bad and exciting despite itself, bassline pumping into Paul with every sip of beer. He was beginning to feel like himself again—*there you are!* The real Paul didn't feel pain. He pushed away a nudging thought of Tony Pinto's voice on his answering machine, the strangely formal message ask-

ing him to call. Paul considered the question of whether or not to have sex with Franky tonight. He thought not, but he could be persuaded. How had Tony Pinto gotten Paul's mother's address? They drank more beers and Paul focused his attention back on the important discussion of who was hot.

"Over there," Franky said, lifting index finger from bottle to indicate a man with hair clippered to a 2, close-trimmed salt-and-pepper beard, a single 12-gauge earring in his left earlobe.

Paul nodded supportively but lost a small measure of respect for Franky. The beard guy was a little perfect, too obvious. Paul scanned the room for the more unusual-looking people, the finds.

"*That* one," he said, leaning into Franky's ear.

Together they studied the big-nosed white boy gangling by the jukebox in a Stryper tee shirt. Paul always appreciated the jolie laide. Plus a good sense of humor, Paul thought. And bold fashion sense. Paul liked to pick out the secretly cool people, people too cool to flash their coolness. The cool people were not always or even usually the same as the shiny people. Often someone shiny was too conventionally good-looking to be cool but they were still compelling, in terms of sheer wattage. Paul knew he wasn't good-looking enough to be shiny, but he could be cool in certain contexts. Cool was relational and conceptual; cool took work, cool was a meritocracy which, with all its flaws, he still preferred to the aristocracy of genetics.

As they made their evaluative way around the room, Paul enjoyed not knowing if he was Franky's type, or vice versa. Underneath the cruising-buddy patter they held another conversation, a trading of clues about the future, hunter to hunter.

ANDREA LAWLOR

Both could swing lots of ways, which they signaled to each other by indicating which men they found attractive or hideous.

"You only like older guys?" Paul said, knowing this was not the case. He swiveled his body so that his erection would brush Franky's leg and held himself still for a moment. Yes. Electrical surge. He moved an inch away.

"No," said Franky, his eyelids heavy like a cat's.

"Let's do shots," said Paul. A shot would make them both officially drunk, which would be the abracadabra to open the door to the rest of the night.

They each did a shot, Franky sitting wide-legged on a bar-stool, and Paul standing sideways in between his legs. Franky stood up, curled his finger through Paul's belt loop, and pulled Paul toward the black-lit backroom.

"I think you want me to fuck you," said Paul.

Franky looked shy, like Paul might say such a thing and then not do it. Paul admired this pose. Franky was either really new or incredibly skilled.

"Yeah," Franky said.

They made out for a while, Franky's hands stretching all over Paul's impostor man body. No one else was in the back. Paul knew what Franky wanted, to touch something uncomplicated. Not that he could tell Franky he knew this without ruining Franky's good time. Paul felt something pressing on his thigh—Franky's cock. He clumsily unzipped Franky's pants until Franky took over, turning around, and Paul pulled his own hard dick out of his pants, nudging it up to Franky's now-bare ass. He saliva'd a finger and opened up Franky's hairy asshole, guiding his dick inside. The music from the bar pulsed in. Paul

had Jägermeister in his veins, thought of mercury rising and his cum rising and he pushed into Franky hard and mannishly, to be nice, thrusted like a high schooler, which he thought Franky would appreciate, the realness—until Franky jerked to standing, squeezing Paul's dick out of him. Paul stuffed his cock in his pants, felt a hot drip of pre-cum on his thigh.

"What the fuck, Paul?"

"What?" said Paul.

"Dude, were you just wearing a rubber?" Franky said.

"No, of course," Paul said. "Of course I was."

"Shit," said Franky. "I'm sorry. I'm so drunk. Keep fucking me, man."

"Let's just go," said Paul, cold with shame. "The moment's passed."

The light in the bar was different now, icy and blue. Paul ordered another bourbon, though he was already full. He controlled his gag reflex and let the liquid settle down his throat into its secret headquarters, from which it spread its message of world peace to all points Paul.

<center>×</center>

Paul woke up with drymouth and staggered to the bathroom to drink from the tap and to pee. He stank of cigarettes, old sperm, bar grime. Beer-sweat emanated from his pores. His mouth watered and he swallowed acid down into his stomach.

He surveyed the damage in his room—jacket and boots flung willy-nilly, balled-up plastic bags, dirty dishes, a mysteriously empty peanut butter jar. He picked his jacket up off the floor, reaching into the pocket to check for money (where was

all his money?) and stuck his middle finger into what turned out to be a used rubber. Where had he gone after he'd ditched Franky?

He had to stop picking up random people. What he should do now was shower and walk to the bookstore to pick up his paycheck before his shift, so he could mail the check to his bank in Iowa City for deposit. It would take a week to clear and rent was almost due. But he couldn't face work, didn't deserve a shower. He had to stop going to bars. He would definitely stop going to bars.

He went back to bed to get warm for a minute before work then fell asleep. When he woke up again hours later, he was disoriented and late. He called the bookstore from the phone in the hall and told Divya he had food poisoning—which other people did all the time, so didn't he get to do it once? but what if they fired him, what would he do then?—and crawled back into bed in his warm fermenting clothes. What he really should do was apply to SF State, but he had all those Incompletes. He would stop changing, stop picking up randoms. He would get his shit together.

Paul lay flat under the covers and listened to Ruffles and the roommates move about upstairs then leave the house in a loud happy group. The phone rang and the machine picked up. He rolled over and stared at the wall until sleep took him once more.

×

Paul's mother had always said things would seem better in the morning. Paul woke up to another rainy day, which should have been romantic but just felt cold and clammy. He showered and

pulled on clean jeans. He was okay. His mom was right. He just needed sleep. He borrowed Ruffles's bike so he wouldn't have to waste money on the bus, and sped up Market as fast as he could go. He saw a driver's-side car door opening but couldn't stop in time and took the door into his side.

"Watch where you're going, faggot," the driver yelled. "Or whatever you are!"

"Fuck you," Paul said, falling half off his bike. The bar menaced his soft sad balls, the threat of pain as bad as the pain itself. He got back on his bike before the guy could come after him. He turned from a safe distance and hollered, "Asswipe!"

Paul biked more slowly now, stoned on adrenaline. The pounding ache in his side felt good almost, clarifying. The bike seemed a little wobbly, and he thought about how much it would cost to fix. He got to the bookstore and chained the bike to the fence out back.

He saw through the window that Franky was working. This day was just getting better and better.

"Hey, Paul," said Franky. His eyes had that soft look. What eyelashes. Paul hadn't seen him since the Gang Way. This was why you don't shit where you eat, he thought.

"Hey," said Paul. Did Franky *like* him? Even after the other night? Maybe gay guys really all were masochists. Now he'd have that mess on his hands. He headed straight back to the office and pocketed his check.

"Glad you're feeling better," Malcolm said. "Food poisoning's the worst."

"Yeah," said Paul. "Can I help with that order? I mean, if you want to go up front. I kind of want to learn."

"That would actually be great," said Malcolm. "You don't mind being back here?"

"Nope," said Paul. He settled into the comfortable office chair.

×

STORY NAME: The Uncanny Ex-Man

PAGE ONE

PANEL 1: Establishing shot. Medium shot. Cargo ship off the coast of Cyprus.

CAPTION: Off the coast of Cyprus, early summer 1985. A ship carrying a mysterious cargo makes its way from Europe.

PANEL 2: Close-up of two French-looking sailors on deck doing something reckless. Maybe a little gay. Wrestling? They jostle a barrel marked with skull & crossbones.

PANEL 3: Close-up of the barrel marked with skull & crossbones falling overboard.

PANEL 4: Below the previous panel. Close-up of barrel opening, mysterious radioactive substance seeping down to where a Moray eel is swimming by.

PANEL 5: Close-up of Moray eel swimming by, getting doused in mysterious fluid.

CAPTION: The MORAY EEL, a species of marine fish in the family Muraenidae, is a nocturnal, cave-dwelling carnivore known for its evolutionary cleverness—in a pinch, the Moray eel can CHANGE its SEX. The Moray is thought to be vicious but is, in reality, shy & only attacks when provoked.

PANEL 6: Moray eel swims to undersea cave near shore to hole up. Hotel sign in distance.

PAGE TWO

PANEL 1: Establishing shot. Medium shot. Paul arrives at the airport in Paphos, Cyprus, as guest of his friend Justin's rich family.

CAPTION: That same day, at the Paphos airport . . .

DIALOGUE:

> *Justin's dad:* What a flight! My head is killing me. I think that stewardess put something in my drink.
>
> *Justin's mom:* Stop it now, David. We're on vacation! Lighten up for once in your life.
>
> *Justin:* [whispers] I'm so glad you're here, Paul. My parents are driving me crazy.

THOUGHT BUBBLE:

> *Paul:* I can't believe I finally got out of TROY!

PANEL 2: Later that night, Paul & Justin sneak out of their hotel room.

CAPTION: That night . . .

DIALOGUE:

> *Justin:* [mooning after Paul] I can't believe we're in Paphos together—did you know this was where Aphrodite rose from the sea foam?
>
> *Paul:* Yeah, I know. My mom used to live here. Come on, I think the party's this way! [pointing to the beach]

PANEL 3: Medium shot. Bonfire on a beach. Paul tries to chat up Handsome College Boy while Justin looks miserable & twee.

SFX: Music notes.

DIALOGUE:

> *Paul:* We'd love to come see your dig tomorrow! Right, Justin?
>
> *Justin:* Yeah, sure.

PANEL 4: Medium shot. Morning. Archeological dig. Handsome College Boy takes Paul & Justin to see a recently uncovered mural of Orpheus & the beasts.

CAPTION: At the dig site where archeologists have recently uncovered an early mural of Orpheus singing to the beasts.

DIALOGUE:

> *Handsome College Boy:* In Ovid's *Metamorphoses,* Orpheus was not only the best musician in the world, but he also brought the love of boys to Greece. You guys should really read it.
>
> *Paul:* I will totally read it.
>
> *Justin:* [rolls his eyes]

PANEL 5: Close-up. Architectural dig. Handsome College Boy gives Paul a small trinket from the site (what should this be?), as he leaves with arm around Pretty College Girl.

DIALOGUE:

> *Handsome College Boy:* Here you go, kid. A souvenir of Paphos.
>
> *Paul:* Thanks! Maybe we'll catch up with you later.
>
> *Justin:* [squiggly line? something to denote being bummed out] What a . . .

PANEL 6: Medium shot. Paul puts the trinket in his Jams' pocket as he & Justin walk toward the beach.

DIALOGUE:

> *Justin:* Let's go swimming. The water looks so pretty!
>
> *Paul:* Sure, whatever.

PAGE THREE

PANEL 1: Close-up. Justin & Paul in the water, Justin looking at Paul, Paul looking away.

DIALOGUE:

> *Justin:* [small voice] Paul, there's something I really want to tell you . . .
>
> *Paul:* Oh, look over there! Are those dolphins?

PANEL 2: Medium shot. Paul swims away toward cove, trinket falls out of Jams' pocket & down . . .

PANEL 3: Medium shot. Underwater. Trinket falls down into a pocket of sand/undersea cave.

PANEL 4: Close-up. Underwater. Paul, diving down, sticks his hand in the cave to retrieve the trinket, is bitten by eel.

SFX: Ow!

PANEL 5: Medium shot. Beach. Paul shows Justin his hurt hand.

DIALOGUE:

> *Justin:* Let me kiss it.
>
> *Paul:* [annoyed but feeling a little strange] Dude, I'm fine.

PAGE FOUR

PANEL 1: Medium shot. Hotel room, later that night. Paul & Justin sleeping in twin beds. Paul falls asleep holding the trinket [?]. Dream bubbles to next panel . . .

CAPTION: Later that night . . .

PANEL 2: Wide shot. Dream bubble. Handsome College Boy asks Paul to prom, Paul turns around & sees self in mirror = girl in dress.

DIALOGUE:

> *Handsome College Boy:* Would you like to come to prom with me?

Paul: I'll check my schedule. I'm kidding. Of course I'll go to
 prom with you.

PANEL 3: Close-up. Paul's bed, morning. Paul wakes up, touches
 his body, he IS a girl.

THOUGHT BUBBLE: What the!?! Justin? Can this really be hap-
 pening? Must . . . change . . . back . . . Got to . . . hide . . .

PANEL 4: Medium shot. Hotel room, morning. Justin asleep in
 other bed. Paul panics [how to show?], changes back [not
 sure how to show—maybe motion lines?].

CAPTION: TO BE CONTINUED . . .

<div align="center">×</div>

Paul threw his keys on the futon and went up to the kitchen to
get a glass of water.

"Someone's really trying to reach you," said Ruffles, stir-
ring eggs and tamari and garlic very slowly in a cast-iron pan.
"Someone's *pursuing* you, my dear."

Paul decided not to tell Ruffles about the bike yet; he'd get
it fixed first. He glanced at the answering machine. He took a
bottle of beer from the refrigerator, forgetting entirely about
the glass of water, and retired to his room to drink, which was
both cheaper than going out and less likely to end in trou-
ble. He put *Greetings from Asbury Park, N.J.* in the boom box
he'd borrowed from the living room. He took out the bottle of
Bushmill's he kept for guests in his dresser drawer and poured
himself a shot to go with his beer, then another.

He knew what was on that answering machine. He'd heard
Tony Pinto's voice in his head all week. There was only one

thing Tony Pinto could want with him, had ever wanted with him.

One more shot, then he'd play it. Maybe two more shots. The other side of *Greetings* was Joni Mitchell's *Blue,* Diane's doing, a time-release intensity bomb of feelings. The whiskey went straight to Paul's eyes and leaked out. He wiped his face and licked the salt off his finger.

He needed the exact right message-listening outfit. He chose a pair of tight navy blue Levi's cords with a slight bell and a beige striped wide-collar shirt in a sort of thin suede, left open to the third button across his flat chest. He found his wide tan leather belt, the one with two rows of grommets which reminded him of childhood, the closest he'd come to the wide white rough leather belt which would transport him back to 1974, that perfect year. He took off the cords, removed his underwear, and put the cords back on, admiring his lines. He drank one more shot, the burn like cock-gagging—a means to an end, yet so sexy in and of itself. He padded back upstairs to the living room. He felt bridal in anticipation.

Paul was ready; he hadn't thought he was ready, but he was ready. He spread his naked toes into the shag carpet, steadying, steadying against the fulgent whiskey warming his chest.

He pressed play.

"Hey, Paul," said the pinholes of the machine. "This is Tony. Can you please call me?"

That was it, the whole message. That and a 212 number that Paul didn't recognize, but then he hadn't talked to Tony Pinto in months. Well, more. Seventeen months? Eighteen? He pressed play again.

"Hey, Paul, this is Tony again. Call me back, okay?"

Paul listened to the message again. The voice was different in the second message, maybe a little colder? Was he having second thoughts about asking Paul to come back?

There was another message. Maybe it said *Forget it, Paul. I don't know what I was thinking, don't bother to call.*

Paul pressed play again. Better to rip off the band-aid.

"Hey, Paul, listen, you have to call me back. I can't talk to your machine. This is Tony."

There was only one more message. Paul pressed play without breathing. Ruffles's friend Tyrone boomed an invitation for the whole house to a Reclaiming Beltane ritual, whatever that was.

Paul tried to figure out what time it was in New York but his math skills were weak. He knew it was pretty late to call casually and he wasn't about to show his hand first.

He padded back downstairs to his room. He decided to get his nipples pierced next paycheck. Tony would like that. He preened in the mirror, trying on different outfits and finishing the bottle of whiskey to brake the race cars zooming around his head. He fell asleep to Bruce Springsteen singing sweetly to him of the times he and Tony Pinto used to have, would have again.

<div align="center">×</div>

When Paul awoke, fully clothed, it was still night. The whiskey had worn off, replaced by coursing, unlocatable panic. He brushed his teeth, donned his tight Levi's jacket and his boots, and left the house as if chased. Just to the corner store, he thought. Just going to get a beer.

But the corner store was closed, so he walked a few more blocks of the sleeping city, then a few more. All the gay bars were closed by now; by this hour all gays had paired off or grouped off or decamped for secret after-bars whose locations changed nightly. Paul was the last little kid in Hamlin. He walked and walked but could find no gays.

He found a bar on Haight still serving and ordered a well bourbon. "I have to work in the morning," he said over and over, which seemed to result in more laughter and fellowship with every repetition. He didn't have to be at work until early afternoon, but he'd said "morning" the first time by accident, then repeated it for poetic effect. Paul drank with the real drinkers now, accepting a gratis whiskey sour from the rickety barmaid, accepting first a cigarette then a bump of medicinal coke from the liver-spotted fist of a retired cop in the bathroom, accepting an invitation to a party on Capp Street from the crusty punks who showed up at last call begging for sixes to go.

The crusty punks now comprised his escort through the night. They clapped him on the shoulders and encouraged him to fuck his job.

"Just quit," they said. "Come live with us!"

At the Capp Street party, they introduced him around as Bob, which he found unnerving. Did he look like a *Bob*? Heaven forfend.

He escaped into the bright kitchen, where a clean-looking tough girl in a flannel shirt offered him a jelly glass of tequila from a stash in her backpack. Her boyfriend had just left her for a lesbian who danced at the Gold Club, she told him, and now she was smoking again.

"That's lousy," Paul said. He liked that word, felt noir-ish saying it.

"They're getting married," said the girl.

"Lousy," repeated Paul. "Of all things."

She nodded glumly.

"I don't know any of these people," Paul confessed, gesturing loosely at the doorway.

"Me neither," said the girl, smiling a tight little smile. "I live downstairs." She started a new cigarette with her old one.

"This lighting is bringing me down," said Paul. "It's so Bukowski. Do you want to get out of here?"

"I love Bukowski," said the girl. She slumped on the fake wood of the table.

"What's up, Gay Bob?" shouted one of the crusty punks from the living room. "Who's your friend? We should play Hi Bob with her!"

"What's Hi Bob?" said the girl. "Who's Gay Bob?"

"You need to go home," Paul said. He had been in his bed and now he was in this appallingly lit parallel universe.

"Yeah," she said, without sitting up. "Home."

"Okay," said Paul. He tugged her up by her flannel and scooped up her backpack. "Let's go."

The girl was steady enough to walk downstairs, which was good because she was significantly bigger than Paul and he didn't think he could carry her. When they arrived at her locked door, she became very helpless and Paul had to fish around in her backpack and then her pants pocket to find the keys.

"Roommates," she mumbled angrily. "Shhh!"

Paul lay her down on the living room couch and she began

to snore. He felt his good citizenship keenly and finished off the bottle of tequila. He took stock of the impersonal living room, with its impersonal black pressboard shelving unit and impersonal *Calvin and Hobbes* omnibus on the impersonal fake wood coffee table. He felt sick at the thought that a city as beautiful as San Francisco could contain this kind of placeholder apartment. How could the girl stand it? She had seemed human enough, with human needs for beauty and goodness. He ran out of the apartment and down the stairs, smiling wildly at the sex workers flicking their long nails on the corner by the warehouse. The air! The air! He sucked it all in as he walked the dark streets, his head clearing with every footfall. Maybe things were going to be okay.

<p style="text-align:center">×</p>

Paul turned onto Mission and stopped outside a shut-up dollar store. Light was coming up on the world through a misty sky, and hark, what was that? A man wearing only a leather utilikilt was playing a mournful bagpipe song on actual bagpipes.

Paul tried to remember all the substances he'd ingested: no hallucinogens, he didn't think. He was pretty sure this was really happening, in consensus reality, happening in such a way that other people could also see and hear a barefoot man playing bagpipes. Yet there was no one else on the street, as far as he could see. No people or cars. Paul watched the bagpiper walk toward the 24th Street BART station—in the middle of the street, no less—playing his funeral song. Paul considered following the piper, but to what end? You don't chase an oracle.

He stared across the street at Magic Donut. Were the donuts within magic? Maybe things were what they claimed to be; maybe magic hid in plain sight, mystical bagpipers only Paul could see, etc. He crossed the street and used all the change in his pockets to buy two Boston cremes. He leaned on the counter, eating his donuts out of the bag. Paul liked any food that exploded into his mouth: grapes, Freshen-Up gum, soup dumplings. There was something pleasing, something orderly, about swallowing a mess.

Paul finished the donuts and scrounged futilely in his pockets for more money. He had seven dollars in the bank, last time he'd checked, and he knew of a bank machine on 25th that gave five-dollar bills, but that was the wrong direction. He walked instead to Dolores Park to watch the rest of the sunrise. He could watch in Alamo Square, but no one interesting would be up at this hour. Maybe an adult walking a dog. The magic people were in the Mission or the Castro, more likely. Magic could be anywhere, Paul knew, but the odds were better in certain places.

Paul stretched out on a bench at the top of the hill, watching the sky, the rosy light underneath the clouds. *The rosy fingertips*, he thought. Down by the fat-trunked palm trees, a few homeless guys had set up a little pioneer camp inside a circle of shopping carts. He didn't see anyone lurking up by the J Church, but he couldn't be sure. His buzz was wearing off, and he was too tired to check the bushes for desperadoes.

A white guy with disorderly blonde dreads under his rasta cap leaned over Paul.

"Can I sit here, man?" he said.

Paul looked at him; he was weirdly maybe cute. He could be cute to somebody, at any rate. Paul sat up. He noticed, as he made room, that the next bench over was empty.

"What's in it for me?" Paul said, dropping his voice a register and modulating the obvious come-on with surliness. This was standard defensive cover with trade, when he could pass as trade.

The hippie guy smiled a big-toothed smile, the smile of someone with a history of good dental work, sat down with legs akimbo, and produced a slender joint. Paul patted his pockets for his Zippo and lit the joint, cupping his hands to protect the guy's hands from the wind. When the guy passed Paul the joint, their fingers touched. Paul left his a second too long, playing chicken. The hippie guy moved his hand just quickly enough for plausible deniability, and Paul relaxed into knowledge. Or maybe that was the pot.

"This is really good shit," he said. He knew hippies liked to be complimented on their weed, not that he cared or could even tell kind from unkind.

"Mos' definitely," said the guy.

Paul cringed inside, but he knew hippies were sexually promiscuous and he needed ease, something to help him regain his confidence, something to laugh about later or turn into an impressive tale of derring-do or fetishism for Ruffles. He took another big hit, and coughed.

"You okay, little buddy?" said the guy. Paul wondered how old the guy was, how old he thought Paul. Paul knew he looked pretty young, but the guy seemed like he was Paul's age. He knew looking girlier meant looking younger, but hadn't thought he looked that girly right now.

ANDREA LAWLOR

"I'm good," Paul said. "You don't cough, you don't get off, right?"

They laughed, the easy laughter of comrades. Paul checked out the guy's loose worn army pants, which were definitely bunched at the fly. Maybe a half-chub, Paul thought, getting himself into hippie guy mode. He decided to be bold, maybe just say his move. He could run to 18th pretty fast if the guy was not amenable.

"Do you—"

"Do you—"

They laughed again.

"You go first," the guy said. He reached down, picked a blade of grass, and stuck it in his mouth.

Paul thought of all the dogs who peed in the park. The moment was gone.

"No, you," he said.

"I was just going to say, do you like nature? I was thinking about going up to the park in the Upper Haight."

"Oh," said Paul. He was pretty high. "I'm pretty high. I was thinking we could just go up to the bushes by the train and you could suck my cock."

He waited a forever minute, awash in cold adrenaline. The word "cock" floated between their bright faces. He could feel his heart beat in his dick, swelling his pants leg. He would either get his face punched or his ticket punched, he thought, turning the phrase over and over. Paul stared right into the guy's eyes. He had thought he was going to say, *let me suck your cock*, and then look what had come out of his mouth. He laughed. They were underwater. Paul was a merman, a very bold fishy. He remembered how he was magic, and the guy stood up.

265

"Okay," the hippie guy said, showing those expensive teeth again, and loped up the hill. Paul walked slowly after him, like a panther knowing he's about to sink his teeth into a nice fat antelope, then broke into a run. His legs felt amazing. He was a powerful beast. He followed the guy into the bushes. They were close to the street but totally hidden. Paul released his cock into morning air, then warm mouth.

The hippie guy bent over at first, then sort of knelt on one knee. Paul felt a little embarrassed for him, and closed his eyes so he wouldn't have to see the bobbing rasta hat. He knew he shouldn't be rewarding this guy's fashion with sex.

"Am I not doing it right?" the guy asked.

He looked like he might cry. Paul didn't know what to say. With the chase over, Paul's excitement flagged. He tried to think of things to make the experience hotter. He could ask for more stuff; that might work. Or he could distract the guy. He pulled the guy up and reached into his army pants, down the loose waist. No underwear, kind of gross but also hot. Paul was not high enough to put his mouth on that, so he pulled the guy's cock out into the air and stood on his toes so they both fit in his hand. He jerked them together, and the guy spewed almost immediately, which Paul found hotly jejune and which was worth a few drops of his own juice. Paul had a little bit of a premature ejaculation fetish; a person must be really attracted to him if they came that quick.

The hippie guy tried to kiss him but Paul was done with that. It didn't matter if Paul was gross or rude or non-reciprocal; he would never see this dirty hippie again and plus most guys liked gross, rude, and non-reciprocal. He pushed the guy down to his knees and slowly fucked his mouth, just a few thrusts

with his eyes closed; Paul didn't even try to pull out. When he was done, Paul stuffed his dick back in his pants.

"Thanks, man," he said.

He brushed pine needles off his shirt.

"Wait," said the hippie. "Would you want to get some breakfast?"

Paul calculated. He had the morning off, but there wasn't much food at his house. He could get breakfast and then just go home and crash until his shift. Maybe the guy would even pay.

"Okay," he said.

They walked silently toward the street, then up to the Castro. The hippie guy's name was Jim and he was a political science major at SF State and he was from Walnut Creek, which was accessible by BART. Paul nodded and said uh-huh at appropriate intervals, like a cyborg learning how to be human. He wanted to get away, but was hungry. They ended up at Sparky's; Paul hadn't been back to the diner since his first day in town, even though the bookstore was only a few blocks away. He felt relieved when he saw Oscar wasn't working, and he slid into a booth. The hippie guy reached over the menus, awkwardly moving his hand toward Paul's. Paul pulled away. He didn't want to hold hands right now but especially didn't want to hold a grimy-nailed hand. Maybe he was a bad gay; he just couldn't work up a hotness for dirty fingernails.

After they ordered, Paul listened to the hippie chatter, now about the great genius of the band Phish and now about the terrible situation in the redwoods, which were being clear-cut. Paul understood that he should care about the redwoods and the predatory practices of the timber industry and if Diane were here he would care with less effort. But he was so tired!

He ate his eggs sleepily, trudging forkfuls up to his mouth and trying to keep his eyes open.

When he chanced to look up and across the diner, he saw Franky ordering coffee at the counter, his soft faded Flipper tee shirt hanging loosely over Ben Davis pants in that way Paul could never achieve, that casual perfection which came from actually skateboarding for transportation.

Oh, now Paul was awake, awake and alive with a biting shame as if a miniature dragon was burying its pointy teeth into the tender flesh of his side. Franky spun around on a counter stool, and saw Paul seeing him. He nodded.

"I have to go," Paul said to the guy, this Jim. Jim looked crushed; he'd already paid the check, conveniently, although now Paul wished he could toss some bills on the table to buy back his freedom and dignity.

"Wait up," said Jim. "I can drop you someplace, if you want. I have a car."

Paul could see Franky watching.

"I'm good walking," he said.

"Or I could walk you wherever you're going."

"Really," Paul said, a little harshly. "I'm good. Thanks for breakfast."

He walked out, Jim catching the door behind him, and headed toward Market. He hoped Franky wasn't still watching, but he didn't dare look back. Jim walked a few paces behind like some kind of *servant*. Paul realized he was going to have to say something mean. Sometimes that was the only way to get free.

×

The answering machine's red light blinked its red 1, 1, 1—a heartbeat. Fuck it. Paul walked over and pressed play.

"Hello," said an awkward voice with a flat New England accent. "This is a message for Paul Polydoris. This is Maria Pinto; my son Anthony wanted to talk to you—"

Paul went cold. He pressed the pause button so he could get warm first. Why was Tony Pinto's mother calling? He knew and he didn't know. He sat back down on the couch with the afghan but it wasn't enough. There were more blankets on the other couches and he gathered them all and lay down on the couch and piled them on top of himself. He was shivering. He better call Tony. He was still cold but he reached out for the phone, exposing his bare arm to the freezing air. No fucking insulation in San Francisco, why hadn't they learned? What would it take for that technology—storm windows even—to make its way west?

He pulled the phone by its curly cord to the couch, dragging the answering machine on the floor. He covered his head with the blankets. What was the number again, the number Tony Pinto had left yesterday or whenever he'd called? Paul rewound and listened to the first message twice to remember it because he was too cold to get a pen and where would he get a pen from anyway? He dialed and the number rang.

"St. Vincent's, please hold."

Paul hung up and redialed, moving his cold fingers more carefully, as if they were remote-controlled sausages.

"St. Vincent's, please hold." Same voice, more irritation.

Paul hung up again. He couldn't listen to that message again. He dialed directory assistance for Waterbury, Connecticut, and the street name—what was it, Hawthorne? They now

connected you automatically from Information, so he didn't need a pen. Progress was good. He thought about Thomas Edison and how his own grandfather had worked for Ma Bell, and Alexander Graham Bell, who was that, what had Alexander Graham Bell done? Buzz buzz buzz.

"Hello," said a man's stern voice.

Wrong number. He hung up, cursing in his head, and went through the whole process again because he didn't have the number written down.

The same stern man answered the phone. Of course. It must be Tony's mean dad.

"Who is this?"

"This is Paul Polydoris," Paul said, lowering his voice to heterosexual man levels in case Tony's dad still didn't know. "Is Tony there?"

"No," said the man. "There's no Tony here."

Paul held the phone, listening to the dial tone. The man had hung up on him. Tony Pinto was in trouble; his father had found out he was gay and he was in deep shit and he needed Paul—he'd called Paul, out of all the friends he could call. Paul would call back again until the bastard put Tony on the phone or he'd go there, go to that crappy city where Tony had grown up and rescue him.

He redialed in a righteous fury.

"I know he's there," Paul said. He didn't wait for the man to talk. "I know he's there. Put him on." He couldn't believe he was talking to an adult like this.

"Is this Paul?" It was a woman's voice now. "Are you Paul?"

"Yes," Paul said. He was freezing cold again. His name sounded strange to him. She must mean someone else.

"He's gone, Paul. He died last night."

Paul listened to his heart beating, studied the reddish black insides of his eyelids.

"I know you were his friend. And he wanted to talk to you especially, he had the phone in the bed with him—"

Paul couldn't hear the rest. He could tell she was still talking and he let her talk and then he hung up and walked covered in blankets to his room and drank the second bottle of whiskey he had stashed in his drawer, his emergency bottle, swallow by swallow, under the blankets, in the bed, freezing cold.

×

Paul lay in bed, trying to figure out who to tell. He should call someone; it seemed like basic human courtesy to announce what had happened. Paul considered his mother, who thought he was still in Iowa City. She was too sad. He couldn't call her. He called Jane instead, planning his apology, but as soon as he heard her voice, he began to sob.

"Don't be mad," he said when he could talk.

"Oh honey," Jane said. "What's going on?"

He told her about Tony, but not about the messages, not about what Tony's mom had said about the phone.

"He was my boyfriend in New York," said Paul. "I mean, kind of."

"I remember," said Jane. "You told me about him."

"I did?"

"Yeah," Jane said. "You knew him from ACT UP, right?"

"Well, mostly from the Pink Panthers," Paul said, annoyed at Jane for acting like she knew anything about Tony Pinto.

"He actually came to Iowa City to see me, the semester before I met you. I think he was in love with me."

"I'm so sorry," Jane said.

"Whatever," Paul said, roughly. "It's fine. We weren't in touch."

"Honey," said Jane, clucking.

"Just tell me about what's going on there," he said. He couldn't take the clucking. "Please."

Jane complied. Apparently her dissertation director, a famous medievalist who did queer theory as a sort of sideline, had told Jane to read the French feminists, which had led Jane to Derrida, which seemed to be leading to a nervous breakdown the kernel of which was the evidence that nothing *meant*, and what was more, why was Jane doing a film studies dissertation with a medievalist anyway? Martha, the dissertation director, considered film a passing fad, and focused her theoretical lens on queer readings of French convent literature, and wasn't that practically criminal, that refusal to pay critical attention to the world around them, that privileged retreat into the apolitical, a practically Modernist solipsism and (probably racist) reverence for some impossible golden age, unusual only in its locus of medieval France? And Jane's new date, a sporty older butch about whom she was ambivalent anyway, was not being supportive.

Paul listened docilely, agreeing when he should, murmuring all the right outrage. He needed to get off the phone but he needed to stay on the phone; the phone line physically connected them: from his hand, through the curly cord, to the plastic box, to the wall, to the ground outside, up those tall wooden posts, over the miles to Iowa, to South Johnson, up the

side of the white shingled house and through Jane's apartment wall, down into Jane's hand and head. They were touching. He pressed the yellow receiver into his ear until it hurt.

"But Paul, I feel bad talking about this!" said Jane, with the wrung-out disbelieving gratitude of someone who's been unexpectedly allowed to monologue for an hour. "Tony *died*. How do you feel?"

"Oh, shit, other line," Paul said. "Can I call you back?"

"Of course," said Jane. "Of course!"

She sounded guilty. Paul tucked that away, without intention. He sank into the living room couch and waited for something to change. He waited on the couch for fifteen minutes and then reached out to the special bottle of ouzo Ruffles kept on the mantelpiece. He felt the thrill of stealing a drink, the thrill of drinking a special occasion drink on an ordinary occasion, the thrill of the afternoon drink, the thrill of the solitary drink—all the thrills of a bad act broken down into component parts—and he poured himself a tumbler, the final thrill of disproportion. He liked ouzo, experienced what he thought of as racial memory in its sweetness; ouzo was from Cyprus, like him. The ouzo went down fast into Paul's empty stomach, cough syrup for his soul. His soul had a cough. That made him laugh a little as he flipped through Ruffles's vinyl collection, drawn mostly to what Ruffles called the Quiet Storm: Dionne, Al Green, Barry White. Or maybe older jazz vocals? He held *Billie, Ella, Lena, Sarah* like an altar boy. Then he saw the Sandra Bernhard *Without You I'm Nothing* concert album—

×

—Paul remembered staking out the Cubbyhole with Tony Pinto because Madonna and Sandra Bernhard had once had a date there in 1987, or kissed, or something.

Paul remembered staying up late to watch Madonna on David Letterman, never daring to believe anything gay would happen on *television*.

Paul remembered Hudson Street in the rain.

Paul remembered the porn store on the corner, looking at vintage physique magazines, those long-gone men in leopard skins and posing jocks.

Paul remembered Tony Pinto making muscles to distract the shopkeeper while Paul stuffed an old *Drummer* down his pants.

Paul remembered three-packs of old gay porn mags, the good ones on the outside and the crappy third stuffed inside like a grab bag, the newsprint stories and letters signed A Reader in San Diego or Horny Midshipman.

Paul remembered *Blueboy, Numbers, Honcho, Freshman.*

Paul remembered the case of the tape Tony Pinto made for him, the second time they met, Tony's scratchy handwriting marking out the song titles, original artists in parentheses when the song was a cover. Who said gay men always had beautiful handwriting? Tony Pinto had spent his boyhood rolling six-sided dice and sketching elves, and it showed.

Paul remembered "Bizarre Love Triangle" and "A Little Respect" and "TMT♥TBMG."

Paul remembered the first Saturday of the month dances at Columbia, crashing the Ivy League, being early, walking around the block ten times, the Greek diner in Morningside Heights, cheap bad coffee.

Paul remembered coffee breath.

Paul remembered C. Howard's "violent mints."

Paul remembered the night he met Tony Pinto, smoking on the steps of Earl Hall, trying to tell who belonged, Tony Pinto stretching his Gumby arms in a terrible imitation of a voguer.

Paul remembered lights up, finding his stashed coat.

Paul remembered the Meatpacking District, clubs which changed sex according to the night (Clit Club Fridays, Meat Saturdays, or Jackie 60?), same cinderblock walls painted black.

Paul remembered 4 AM bagels with bright pink lox-flavored cream cheese at the bakery on the corner.

Paul remembered the Christopher Street pier at night, fourteen-year-old queers in tube tops and short-shorts, cigarette cherries reflected in the oily water.

Paul remembered saying, "How fast they grow up," and Tony Pinto shaking his head ruefully and saying, "Kids, what're you going to do?"

Paul remembered drinking at Max Fish with Tony's straight goth friends from Fordham, walking west for miles with Tony until they hit the water, sitting on a broken concrete pylon and kissing for hours, hands down each other's pants even though Tony had a serious boyfriend of two months.

Paul remembered the sunburn Tony got at Pride that year, how their older friends carried sunblock, Tony's wounded red-brown chest and back, like a soldier wearing pukka beads, some older lesbian with a crew cut and a squeeze-tube of aloe vera, sitting in the shade on the steps of a church which was really a bar, far enough away from the fray, in the shade, laying Tony across his lap so he could think *Tony lay across my lap like a*

pieta. And Tony's serious boyfriend of two months rounding the corner laughing.

Paul remembered giving Tony back.

Paul remembered sharing grilled cheese sandwiches with Tony and that girl, what was her name? Glynis? Yes, Glynis with the gay mom. From the rap group for gay teens at the Center, the three of them college kids, older and not from the city, maybe a little too old to be in a rap group but officially still teens, still youth.

Paul remembered the working group he joined because Tony Pinto was joining, meeting at an apartment of a much older gay man with a job and a leather couch and crudité in the living room while they made plans to die in the street.

Paul remembered the aching hall of the Center, those Monday night meetings in the belly of the whale, the incomprehensible reports from the Treatment Action Group and the meeting's incomprehensible response, what Tony Pinto called "the grown-ups fighting."

Paul remembered carrying store-bought frozen soup to a man he didn't know, with Rina, somewhere in Gramercy, one of those high-rises that made him feel like he was in 1970s Poland, leaving the soup on the dusty kitchen island, feeding the man's tropical fish while Rina changed the sheets on his hospital bed, all the while *Days of Our Lives* continued as if nothing were different.

Paul remembered the men lined up in green plastic chairs at the Center, young men with canes and liver spots.

Paul remembered the cheery rattle of day-of-the-week pill-box compartments.

Paul remembered the smell of orange medicine soap, sulfur

and sweet, the gash on his palm from a fruit-salad can lid—
how was it possible to get a fruit-salad injury?—wanting the
sliced cherry, glimmer of fear in the eyes of the receptionist at
the Center who sent him to the free clinic, fear of his blood,
now contaminating the can.

Paul remembered colored condoms.

Paul remembered a condom stretching over him like a bal-
loon animal, unlubricated, Tony squeezing out two free packets
of Probe.

Paul remembered Tony's pockets, his backpack, always full
of giveaways and liberated rolls of toilet paper from restaurant
bathrooms, Tony stopping in the foyer of every bar to fill up,
the top of the cigarette machine, wherever they kept the bowl,
Tony collecting condoms in all flavors and brands and colors
like baseball cards, his shock and horror at the condom stapled
into the *Bimbox* page "Straight-Acting Straight-Looking WM
Seeks Same" not because he didn't agree that self-hating ho-
mosexuals should fuck off and die but because that exact con-
dom was wasted, and some proud and out queer might need it.

Paul remembered flannel shirts with the sleeves cut off.

Paul remembered Tony's black leather motorcycle jacket
with its rectangular stickers bragging FREQUENTLY FEMME
and BASICALLY BUTCH and SAFE SEX STUD in neon green,
his black hair shagging over the collar like a Portuguese Lief
Garrett, how was anything ever so smooth as Tony's just slightly
too-long hair?

Paul remembered Tony's serious boyfriend of two months,
then three, four, five—David, unsuitable David, the WASPy
Jewish guy who'd played lacrosse at Andover and loved John
Cheever, older but recognizable to Paul, his easy law-school

ways, his embarrassing obsession with any dark-skinned man, how he'd settled for Tony Pinto who was not dark enough, how he'd cheated on Tony Pinto over and over again, how he'd once at a demo outside St. Patrick's run his index finger down Paul's chest, down to his navel, dipping then turning away from Paul, who was enraged, flattered, humiliated, and never mentioned it to Tony.

Paul remembered asking his friend Jimmy—how proud he felt to say his friend Jimmy about Jimmy Battelli, the kindest and most handsome man in ACT UP, an older man who preferred older men and that he'd allowed himself to be befriended by Paul was a miracle—Paul remembered asking Jimmy Battelli where he'd been, why he'd missed some meeting and Jimmy shrugging, *oh another memorial service darling you know,* Jimmy turning away from Paul kindly even in his despair, Paul's relief to be so young, his nineteenth year a talisman, the word containing the word *teen* itself protection from what the older guys, those memorial-weary men in their twenties, thirties, forties, what they were losing—

×

—and then the phone rang, as it will. Paul moved upstairs in drunk-time, watched himself miss the last ring, watched the miniature-tape mechanism click into action and rewind when the caller hung up just after the beep. Leprechaun tapes, Tony Pinto called them. Paul didn't have any real friends here. He stretched his body out onto the couch and lay without sleeping or moving until Ruffles came home and fixed him a box of

macaroni and cheese, which he set on the floor next to Paul's couch. But then Ruffles left for his mysterious office job suspiciously early, clearly avoiding, clearly back to master-tenant distance. Paul's troubles were not his troubles; Ruffles had a full trunk of loss, room for nothing new.

Who did Paul even know? He couldn't call Franky or Christopher or Silver, all for their own specific reasons unable to help or listen, or he was so in debt to them he couldn't ask. He couldn't call his mother or Kostas; he hadn't talked to either of them in months. He thought momentarily to call Justin Rosenblum, but he could hardly call the boy he rejected in high school to cry about another boy he'd rejected. He would have liked to call Diane, but that was the worst possible idea. The only person he could tell was Tony Pinto himself, who was not only dead but probably mad at him for not calling back. Paul was oarless in a boat on a river of factory runoff. He poured himself another tumbler of ouzo. He'd have to replace the bottle; he might as well finish it.

Paul stood up on his liquid legs, spun over to the record player and carefully unsleeved the Doors' *Greatest Hits*, another Tony Pinto band. He hovered the needle over "Break on Thru" then released, and when the song was over, he played it again. Tony Pinto loved what he called "babysitter music": Led Zep, the Who, Pink Floyd—all the music those long-legged long-haired coltish girls played while eating plastic-wrapped cheese slices from the fridge and talking to their boyfriends for hours on the phone. Tony Pinto loved babysitters, pointed out dykes they knew or women on the subway who could have been babysitters once. Babysitters were of a particular age in rela-

tion to oneself—seven years older, usually—and a particular temperament—maternal, crafty, teasing, a little jocky, mean to men but nice to boys.

Tony loved one such girl in particular, a dyke they knew, his neighbor Griselda. She lived around the corner on Clinton and waited tables at an Italian restaurant in Soho. She brought Tony leftovers, which he refused to share with Paul, who was so charmed by Tony's adoration of Griselda he forgot to feel jealous. Griselda only ever called him "Tony's friend," as in "Hey, Tony's friend, will you get me a beer if you're up?" Paul accepted this as mild flirtation, though in his heart he knew Griselda was of the rare breed of person completely immune to his charms. Sometimes he walked by her work, hoping she had an outside section so he could study her.

Griselda had a roommate, Rainier, as gorgeous as his name, gorgeous as a buck, all tawny shining fur and rippling muscles, deep sad eyes always looking for his dead boyfriend. Rainier didn't have a job; he sat around being beautiful and sad, and older men paid his rent, or he had a trust fund. No one envied or begrudged Rainier. He had earned a life without work by being handsome and tragic. He rode his bicycle all over, from the East Village to the West, and men would stop and stare as they went out to get flowers for a party. Men would drop their bouquets in the streets when Rainier pedaled by, shirtless, one overall strap hanging loosely off a perfectly shaped and tanned and muscled shoulder. And Griselda, the most beautiful lesbian on any rooftop on the Lower East Side, near Rainier like a cat, the only person to whom Rainier looked for approval, Patti to his Robert—the real star, the true man of the two. Tony Pinto was their son, their rescue puppy, their friendship

project, someone for whom they could break out the blinis on New Year's Eve, someone who would exclaim in pleasure and present himself to be taught. Paul had no place in their little family but was seduced into its periphery. He lounged on the dusty hardwood floor of their sixth-floor railroad, listening to Dionne Warwick records and watching Griselda and Rainier marvel over Tony Pinto, as Paul too marveled—Tony Pinto's boyish delight in gossip, his dance-floor transformations, his earnest guided tours through Forbidden Planet's metal figurine collection, his unironic reverence for the dawn.

Now Paul was Rainier. No, that wasn't true either because valiant Rainier had lost his boyfriend after a year of fighting with pharmacists and applying cold washcloths and lotioning bedsores. And Paul? Paul had abandoned his first love to the stinking deck of the beautiful plague ship, had fled in coward-ice, had insult upon injury fallen in love with Diane, had not listened to his fucking messages.

Paul force-finished the second tumbler of the once-delicious ouzo and wobbled up. He'd go out into the night, find someone to beat him tender. He'd swish up and down Divisadero, taunt cops or college boys, move their fists on him like marionettes. He left the house without a jacket, succeeded in crossing the street to the park, face snorkeling the air currents. He located a bench and allowed his body to collapse. He was limp but everything was spinning, so he closed his eyes. A wall of vomit, one wave in a great sea of vomit, pushed up through his mouth and over the park bench; he was hanging half over, more throw-up in his mouth and on his shoes. Everything started. He threw up his heart and his liver and some palm trees and a cowboy hat, widening his mouth to disgorge

the brim. He threw up Rainier and Griselda, Dionne Warwick, the gray plastic answering machine. He threw up Franky, a box of stale Lucky Charms he'd apparently eaten; he threw up years of beer and the afternoon's ouzo. He didn't want anything. He wanted to be with Diane; he wanted the bed of their morning-breath love, the comfort and safety of her babysitter arms. Or he wanted to be with Tony, for it to be before, back before any of this, before Tony had written him that ultimating letter after the Iowa visit, before Tony had given up on him, before Tony had been right to give up on him.

Paul went back in the house thinner, brushed his teeth, took a shower, and walked over to the Mineshaft before happy hour ended. Whatever there was for him tonight was outside, was another mystery, this mysterious universe with its mysterious purpose. He leaned his corduroy hips against the long wooden bar and ordered a Negroni, Tony's drink, adopted after watching the young Warren Beatty down them in *The Roman Spring of Mrs. Stone.* Tony had thought Negronis classy and European. Paul savored the Campari as if it were Tony's blood, as if he were a vampire and could drink Tony to death. He understood that he had failed the test. What do you do after you fail the test and you're still alive?

×

Paul woke in the mid-afternoon, disoriented and still a little drunk. He walked unsteadily to the bookstore, sweating out the drink and grateful to have someplace to go. At the end of his shift, he asked Franky if he wanted to get something to eat, but Franky said no. So Paul borrowed a store copy of a paperback

that caught his eye, *The Motion of Light in Water*. On the cover a shirtless young man languidly cradled a guitar, obscured by white words and a rainbow scrim. He took himself to Orphan Andy's for dinner, found a booth toward the back, and pulled out his book. The guy on the cover looked like New York to Paul, intense and toppy. He was maybe Black, maybe Puerto Rican, and Paul felt some obscure kinship in not knowing. As Paul read, he still didn't know. Was it the science fiction? The passing? One hunter's recognition of another?

Delany knew what he was, Paul realized—yes, married, but a man who *loved men;* light-skinned, yes, but a light-skinned *Black* man; writer; native New Yorker; intellectual. Delany was so certain, had always been certain. He'd busted through everything in his way, and on the other side he'd found morning orgies inside trucks by the docks. Delany at nineteen had seen hundreds of men fucking and had jumped in, had been pure body. Paul at nineteen had seen hundreds of people lying down in the streets, dying-in, and had run away.

The next day, Paul snuck out *Borderlands/La Frontera,* then *Close to the Knives,* then *Sita,* then *Love, Death, and the Changing of the Seasons,* then *Zami: A New Spelling of My Name,* then *The Devil Finds Work,* then *The Naked Civil Servant,* then *In the Life,* then *Violet to Vita,* and on and on through every queer life on the shelf.

For the next five weeks all he did was go to work, come home and read, get up and go to work. He buried himself in books as he hadn't since he was a child. He was careful not to turn down any pages or read in the bath. He brought Ruffles's bike into a collective bike shop run by one of the Lickety Split dykes. He picked up a replacement bottle of ouzo.

"You're a changed man," said Ruffles one morning, desultorily pouring cornflakes into a bowl.

"I'm not a man," said Paul.

×

One mid-morning in mid-June, Paul sat in Café Flore, gazing prettily at the rain while taking a break from Frank O'Hara's *Lunch Poems,* cover for his systematic cruising of the room. When he saw a particularly comely boy, Paul stared directly at him, and when the boy noticed and blushed, Paul feigned spaced-out thoughtfulness, made a show of focusing his eyes, and smiled. The boy was *very* comely, brown ringlets of hair in his eyes, like a little lamb. But the blush was enough and Paul returned to his book. Sometimes Paul preferred catch-and-release.

The café door opened, and a gush of rainy wind heralded a newcomer. Paul looked over and everyone else in the café seemed to look over as well. Who *was* that? The newcomer, an impish person with a black bowl cut, shook an umbrella. That was all. And yet Paul was caught.

He made certain fast surmises about the stranger, based entirely on palette, but he wanted to prove himself right and for that he needed to get closer. He took quick stock of his money and approved his own emergency request for another beverage. Very casually, and in the exact time it would take to arrive naturally behind the stranger in line, Paul approached the counter. Who *was* this familiar ineffable personage?

"Girlfriend!" said the counterperson, a faggy butch with— to Paul's dismay—a septum piercing, like a *bull*. Paul believed

everyone should do their part to beautify public space; this butch was letting the community down.

"Darling!" cried the stranger in delight.

Paul stood close but within acceptable gay proximity to the stranger and still wasn't sure if the stranger was male or female, *as if he, Paul, were some clueless straight person.* This stranger was excellently talented. Paul surreptitiously cataloged the usual tells: pores, throat, hands, feet, hips, chest, package, eyebrows, knuckle hair—all inconclusive. He studied the wide shirt lapels, the French cuffs, the jacket slouched with a sloppy schoolgirl grace, the fall of the cuffed trousers, a delicate pin-stripe visible only from this distance, the tropical-weight wool verging from navy into purple, the burgundy ascot. Paul noted every detail with simultaneous admiration for the wearer and for his own sensitive eye. The stranger was fancy, and not originally from California, Paul decided. Paul waited for his turn to order, twirling a forelock in a manner he hoped would register as "distracted by important French thoughts."

An image tugged at Paul's jumpy rabbit mind, a turned-over card looking for its match—wait . . . *Chicago. The A-House.* The *youth*! What were the odds? Paul felt heavy with meaning and intuition.

Everyone ended up in San Francisco. He heard vampire Catherine Deneuve: *There is no escape, my darling,* and felt fatalistic, immortal, jaded.

"We *have to* hang out," minced the counter butch to the youth. The counter butch noticed Paul and nodded perfunctorily. Paul silently judged her mincing; he disapproved of fake gender-bending, those butches who tried to act more campy than they were and called you "sister-friend" and those fags

who tried to front as if they cared about the changing fortunes of football teams when they really longed to don a cheerleader uniform.

Paul purchased a small cappuccino, holding his shoulders in such a way as to advertise his shyness and paradoxical approachability. The elven young person—it *was* the youth! it had to be!—made no sign of noticing Paul, but concentrated on inscribing what looked like a telephone number onto a napkin in artful block characters, folding it delicately and handing it to the counter butch. The youth then walked out of the café clutching a coffee, draining all excitement from the room. Everyone went back to their newspapers or conversations, limp but satisfied. The youth was a very powerful magician and Paul had not made an impression. He retreated to his window perch in defeat.

<div align="center">×</div>

Now Paul began to be out and about, hoping to see the youth around town, which he did: walking a brace of pretty Italian greyhounds down Valencia, leaving the Endup just as Paul walked in, sitting in a reserved aisle at the gay film festival where Paul ushered for free admission. Paul was always alone when these sightings occurred, and he began to wonder if he'd invented the youth.

It was June, and like everyone else Paul made himself extremely busy going to queer art openings and queer punk shows and queer spoken word showcases and queer evenings of performance art. He was exhausted and broke from being so queer, and briefly reconsidered sex work to supplement his

meager bookstore income. The rent boys who haunted the magazine racks waiting for their beepers to go off seemed like a fine sort. Poets, mostly. What was stopping Paul but an obsolete bourgeois objection to working for a living? Why was sex so different from everything else? He'd given it away plenty. But he couldn't make himself excited about sex without conquest. So he ate a lot of peanut butter and stole steaks from the Safeway.

Mid-month, Jane called to say she was coming to San Francisco for Pride.

"Well, officially I'm coming to use the Pacific Film Archives," she said. "They're totally paying for my plane ticket."

"But really you're coming to see me," Paul crowed.

"But of course," said Jane. "And I'm getting in Saturday afternoon, so if you pick me up we can go right to the Dyke March."

"I have to work," said Paul.

"Just take it off," said Jane. She sounded annoyed.

"I'll try," Paul said, but he didn't want to give up a shift. "Don't you have some friends who live in Berkeley or something?"

Jane arranged for her college friends to pick her up from the airport in their car; they were a couple who'd been together since they were juniors, something like five years. Forever! And now they were lawyers or doctors. Maybe one of them was a publicist? They had jobs with titles.

Paul closed the store at eleven on the dot. He'd been receiving eyewitness reports of the Dyke March all night, mostly from older gay gentlemen who'd been unnerved by the sight of so many lesbians on the street. Paul grew more vexed with every passing minute. He had thought it would be cooler *not* to go,

like Pride, but now he realized he should have tried to get the night off. He called his machine from the phone in the office and wrote down Jane's destination, a Noe Valley address which proved to be a party thrown by rich lesbians, who had perhaps not expected such a turnout, if the ravaged plates of brie and grapes were any indication. Paul wandered pleasantly through the rooms of the small house, not seeing anyone he recognized. He had nourished a hopeful thought that the youth might be at this party, but knew from the Burmese shadow puppets on the wall that the youth would not be seen here. What could be less cool than a party of white cultural-appropriator lesbians? Occasionally Paul asked if anyone had seen his friend Jane, but only if someone was looking askance at him. Soon enough he found Jane in the backyard, downing tequila shots with the college friends; she promptly disappeared with her college roommate and left Paul stuck with the roommate's lawyer girlfriend, whose caustic wit he enjoyed. Eventually the lawyer went to find her girlfriend, whom she discovered in flagrante with Jane in a stairwell. When Jane returned to Paul's staked-out area of the garden, brandishing a half-full bottle of Jack, she informed him that the couple had relocated to a street corner to process. Oh, dyke drama, Paul thought. He'd almost missed it; he'd settled so easily into his rock-and-roll fairy life here. No one had made him talk about feelings in months.

"I guess they *weren't* non-monogamous," said Jane, admiring the chips in her dark red nail polish. Jane always passed the femme test without even trying; she never curled her fingers inward, always stretched them out.

"Is that Vamp?" said Paul, grabbing Jane's hand for closer inspection.

"My cousin works at Chanel now," she said. "I'll get you a bottle."

Paul stood next to a short lemon tree, toying with his ball-bearing necklace and lazily scanning the crowd.

"So tell me everything!" he said. "Has *so* much happened?"

"I thought you'd never ask," Jane said. "I'm burning with my latest hate-crush. I can't stop thinking about her."

"*Everything!*" said Paul, interjecting encouraging mumbles and small affirming noises as Jane related the story of one Bitsy Bennett, new lesbian grad student in the English department who had commenced to make Jane's life entirely miserable by existing, and with that haircut! And of course she was sniffing around Jane's dissertation director.

"I don't want to say 'uplift the race,' but uplift the race, Bitsy, my *god*," Jane said. "I'm literally exhausted by her sweatpants, which she wears in public. I cannot believe I am made to be associated with her by shared accident of homosexual birth. Maybe I expected too much when I saw her name? It's so *The Group*. You know I can't resist that. And now she's sneaking around Martha's office hours with cupcakes—"

"Oh my god!" said Paul. "You *slept* with her. Don't deny."

Jane blushed mightily and looked, for a moment, Midwestern.

"I have poor impulse control," she agreed, lighting a cigarette. "I think this might be a *shame* crush, which I didn't even know was possible."

"Possible?" said Paul. "Story of my life, my unspeakable high-school years. Remember that med student who showed up at my house that time with the ironing board? I *still* can't stop thinking about him. His name was actually Randy Plummer. Like, from birth."

Jane passed Paul the cigarette. He could taste her lipstick on the filter.

"Is this Chanel, too?" Paul said. "So creamy."

Jane nodded happily and Paul understood for a moment that she was lonely. He French-inhaled and continued to look attentive.

"And then there's Christopher, who has come unhinged without you, I fear. He never leaves the house except to jog self-righteously or go to class or the library or the health-food store," Jane continued. "We might want to stage an intervention. Hey, what's going on with your zine?"

Every time someone walked out of the house and into the garden, Paul's head jerked. He could not stop himself, though he was beginning to feel like a neurotic dog. He knew Jane didn't mind; she did the same. Over the years most of their conversations had taken place side by side.

"My zine," he said, tapping his head. "It's all right up here."

"Frog's here," Jane noted.

"Here? Like here? Or here, like in San Francisco?"

"Here here."

"Ah," said Paul.

"I am going to get me some of that."

Shit, he thought. He should have known he'd run into those Michigan dykes. Duh. What had he been thinking? He was about to be clocked, big time.

"Hello, Jane," said Frog, striding up to them in chaps, five feet two inches of pure phallic energy. "You look like you've been doing something very naughty."

Not again, thought Paul. Get better dialogue! This was one of Paul's biggest complaints about the SM lifestyle. Plus he

didn't like pain. Fetish, yes; outfits, yes! Pain, no. But back to Frog and his current quandary. He tried to think fast but he had too much whiskey in him.

"Hey," said Frog, squinting at Paul with the casual boredom of an alpha dog meeting an omega. "Oh, hey, Polly. You ladies need drinks?"

Paul relaxed. Frog was drunk! It was dark!

"You should move here," he said with a feeling of relief at Jane's presence.

"I know," said Jane. "I'm completely ruined for Iowa now. I can't believe how many cute girls are at this party alone."

Frog returned, handing Jane a beer. Uh oh, thought Paul. Jane's going to be hurting tomorrow. He took the beer from her hand and drank most of it, to be helpful.

In short order Jane announced she was leaving with Frog. They were taking a taxi to Oakland, and Paul found himself trudging up Market, where they'd nicely dropped him off, wishing he'd worn a jacket, wondering where the youth spent the evening. He remembered his first Pride in New York. Smoking a jay on the ramshackle Christopher Street pier with that tiny drag queen—Crystal? Esmeralda?—and that goth girl Jill carrying a boom box blasting Dead Can Dance through a freak rainshower. Tony Pinto grabbing his hand as they ran across the West Side Highway. Marching with the Pink Panthers. His drunkard sunburn that lasted a week. If it wasn't hot, it wasn't summer. This was fake summer, summer in name only, he thought.

In the morning, Paul wound through the pre-Pride streets on his way to the bookstore, childishly delighted to see so many gays in one place even if it was so commercial now. Legions of

homosexuals were already camped out on the sidewalks, setting up impromptu chorus lines, vending morning beers from illegal coolers, selling homemade tee shirts with clever slogans and rainbow rings (still fashionable among the amateurs), fondling each other's new piercings, writing sex words on chests in eyeliner. Paul stopped at a corner store to buy some cheap rolls and a medicinal Coke for breakfast; even the corner store guy seemed gay today and excited for the parade. Closer to the Castro Paul heard the familiar strains of "MacArthur Park" from an upstairs window and imagined a party of middle-aged fags primping over mimosas. He consorted briefly on the sidewalk with a passel of drag queens in nuns' habits and high heels, and accepted a handful of condoms and dental dams. Everywhere he looked he saw red ribbons and leather thongs, sometimes red ribbons pinned to leather thongs.

At the bookstore Paul had to wait outside until the owner showed up to unlock the door, but he didn't mind because so many new boys were walking by, wearing so little and looking at him with such impersonal hunger, as if to say, *If I see you later, then maybe . . .* The owner had a brunch and left Paul alone to open; the phone rang and rang, coworkers calling to apologize for waking up in the Sunset or having a flat bike tire, while customers began knocking belligerently on the windows. It was a tee shirt emergency! He let them in and settled into work mode. Eventually Silver appeared.

Paul could feel the pounding from Uncle Bert's down the street, the ever-present bassline turned up for this day which was different from all other days. Paul could hear the parade passing by and wanted to run down the block to watch the Dykes on Bikes at least but was waylaid by having to clean up

a pile of vomit at the front door while Silver took the culprit under her wing and brought him to the hair salon upstairs to sleep it off. They put out a tip jar, which was quickly filled with singles courtesy of an army of vacationing bank managers from Toledo. Paul sneaked across the street with the tips to buy forties, which they drank on the fire escape during their breaks.

Jane picked him up after work and they roamed the city streets. All the good parties had been the night before because the business gays had to work on Monday. They ended up eating burritos and discussing the three-way to which Jane had been invited that very night; the college roommate's girlfriend had had a change of heart as a result of all that processing. Paul agreed such an invitation was worth pursuing, especially since Frog was busy. He dropped Jane off at BART and walked home in the opposite direction listening to a handmade Colourbox compilation he'd taken from Ruffles's giveaway box, not exactly disappointed by the weekend—he was too old for that; it wasn't as if he expected to find his true love at Pride—but somehow melancholy. Not once had he spotted the youth.

×

Jane left and then it was July, as cold and damp as Cole Porter had promised. But all was not bleak. Paul finally spotted the youth, while in the company of Ruffles at the 16th Street BART station. A scrappy crew of dykes with a video camera was filming a person in a bubble-wrap spacesuit. The station security guard stomped up to the improvised set and when the astronaut removed a papier-mâché helmet, Paul turned to Ruffles:

"There!" he said. "Who *is* that?"

"Oh, that's Robin Suarez," Ruffles said, laughing at some private joke.

"Robin," said Paul. "That's who I was talking about before."

"I don't think you're Robin's type." Ruffles refused to comment further, just twinkled merrily.

Over the next fortnight, Paul asked around. No one—not even omniscient Ruffles—knew any hard facts about Robin, but everyone knew Robin. "Oh, yeah, *Robin Suarez*," said everyone, knowingly.

Paul stalked his mark subtly through the alleys and night-clubs and parks. He sifted through clues, including Ruffles's offhand remarks. A report of a Robin-sighting at the Zeitgeist, the insinuation that Robin consorted with bike messengers, Robin's picture on an old Junk flyer on someone's refrigerator. He collected innuendo: Robin was an escort, Robin bartended at the Top of the Mark, the SF MOMA was interested in Robin, Robin was a secret Kennedy heir.

Hunters must wait, and so Paul waited.

×

When it finally happened, Paul was caught off guard. He was deep in Reckless Records on a Wednesday morning right after they opened—the best time for record stores. He didn't have to be at the bookstore until four, so he came in to flip through CD bins systematically, starting at the As. Paul liked Adam and the Ants, in no small part because through them he'd learned the word *adamant* and he couldn't help admiring a man who made such a clever and obscure pun so publicly. Apparently Adam and the Ants had been an actual punk band at one time

before they charted. Maybe he'd read this somewhere, probably *Rolling Stone,* before he knew he should read *Interview* or *Paper* or at the very least *Spin.* When he was in high school his mom and Kostas had given him a subscription to *Rolling Stone,* which Paul had studied for clues about New Wave. What was the difference? How could you trust your own taste? Even Justin Rosenblum had known his own taste, no matter how the other boys mocked him for it. Paul never listened to the Smiths or the Cure in high school. That would have made him seem more gay than he already seemed, so he decided to think they were no good. Justin made him tapes with music Paul had never heard of, like Billy Bragg, Michelle Shocked, Laurie Anderson—all music with some quality of gayness, music Paul rejected. All that wasted time! Paul in record stores tried to rewrite his high-school years, casting himself as cooler—which now meant gayer—than he had been.

"Oh, I have this on vinyl, but I don't want to wear it out," he'd explained as he bought his first Velvet Underground and Nico CD in front of Ruffles weeks before. He hated not-knowing. How do you know if you like something because the corporate radio brainwashers want you to like it or because it's actually good and you have an internal sense of what's good, which is a sign of your essential worth as a person? Paul's strategy was to figure out who was cool and to copy what they did. He skipped the Bs so he wouldn't have to see Bikini Kill and Bratmobile and the Breeders—Diane lived in the Bs. The Cs were also dangerous: he could get caught up in Cher and Carole King and forget all about Camper Van Beethoven or the Circle Jerks. He was making a mixtape for Jane, as an enticement for her to move to San Francisco. She could write her

dissertation from anywhere, he was pretty sure, and he needed a wingman. His plan was to reel her in with a sampler of all the music they could go see every night: Pansy Division, Team Dresch, Tribe 8. Oh, look at that: he had drifted to the Ts and had entirely skipped D to S. That wouldn't do. He strolled back. He'd forgotten he wanted to see if they had anything by this singer Ruffles kept talking about, Darby Crash, who supposedly influenced every punk band ever and then died.

He was thinking about influence and the genealogy of punk when someone tapped him on the shoulder.

"There you are," said Robin Suarez.

"Here I am?" said Paul.

"You've been following me," Robin said.

Paul didn't know what to say. Behind his back, he stealthily returned the Germs CD to its bin. He didn't want Robin to know he'd just discovered them.

"Didn't you once chase me through the streets of Chicago?" said Robin, smiling.

"I wouldn't say chase, exactly," said Paul. He couldn't believe he was talking to the *youth*. He looked at Robin's boots (fawn suede with leather tassels), Robin's ears (somewhat pointed), and the packages (wrapped in butcher paper and blue painter's tape) Robin was holding under one arm.

"Yes, you did," said Robin. "And wasn't that you, staring at me on New Year's at the A-House, with your girlfriend right there?"

"Um," said Paul. "We broke up."

"That's too bad," said Robin. "But now you're going to come have hot chocolate with me, and tell me all about yourself."

They walked up the hill without speaking, Robin pushing a green Raleigh ten-speed.

In a courtyard garden behind a yellow stucco building, Paul sat cross-legged on neatly trimmed grass. High walls surrounded a little garden of carefully tended flowers, an orange tree, a green bench, and various statues of animals. Although the house was surrounded by other houses, none looked over into the garden. You'd have to be in an airplane to see in, thought Paul. He felt private, which he imagined was how Robin intended him to feel. Paul felt the same relief he felt after the first significant returned look from a potential trick: he wasn't crazy; this was happening, whatever it was going to be. This was Paul's favorite part.

It was a bright chilly July morning and Robin poured hot chocolate into glass teacups. Paul sipped his drink, which had spices in it. He tried not to stare at Robin's delicate hands, so like his own.

"You like San Francisco," said Robin, with royal generosity.

"I do," said Paul, stifling the urge to thank Robin for allowing him to live here. He had the sense of being interviewed. Robin in private was much less animated than Robin in the world, and Paul modulated his own high spirits to match.

"But you're also hiding here," Robin said, and sipped the chocolate.

"Not really *hiding*," Paul said.

Robin smelled a sprig of honeysuckle and handed it to Paul.

Paul sniffed the white petals. The seasons in California were mystifying. Was this spring or summer? Why were there

flowers in hot chocolate weather? How could fruit grow on trees all year long?

"Have you lived in this place a long time?" Paul asked.

"Oh, I don't live here," said Robin, gathering up the teacups. "My friend is out of town. He asked me to take care of his place."

"Cool," said Paul. He was back to knowing nothing about Robin. Why not say "my friend Lance" or "my boyfriend" or "a guy I know," any of which would make completely clear the nature of the relationship, but no: "my friend." Paul didn't think this was some '70s-style "is *your friend* coming to Thanksgiving?" Robin hadn't seemed like a closet case, on Jack Manjoyne's leash in Provincetown. So there must be a reason. But what? *My* friend. My *friend.* The reason tugged at Paul; he left the line in the water and turned away, back to Robin.

"You want the tour?" said Robin.

An adult lived here; Paul could tell immediately by the unframed but deliberate paintings in the bathroom, the chocolate-colored walls of the living room, the brass bed, the pristine cow skull lit up in a presentation nook, the *guest* room. Paul followed Robin through the flat, thinking at each doorway that Robin would pause to give Paul his opportunity. But Robin walked through the halls like a realtor, extolling architectural virtues and remarking on niceties.

Standing across from Robin at the butcher block, Paul felt the first doorway in the air, that telltale closing-in, always the same, the softening, the familiar force field. Paul swayed forward without stepping, a half-inch closer, if that. Robin said nothing, but leaned visibly back on the ball of one foot, and looked up at Paul through a fringe of black hair. Paul moved

very carefully now. He braced his arms against the edge of the butcher block, ready to pounce, and the phone rang, knifed open the tent of the moment.

"Excuse me," Robin said. So polite! So correct!

Robin spoke softly into the receiver, and Paul—interrupted mid-hunt—anxiously scanned the room. He saw by the clock on the stove that if he didn't leave now he would be late for work. The force field was disturbed and now he was out of time. Paul gestured at his nonexistent watch. Robin shrugged in elegant helplessness and reached toward Paul, who kissed the offered cheek in farewell and rejoined the honking bright flow of the street.

×

Paul sat at Flore, sipping his milky coffee and gazing about in satisfaction. He'd met Robin Suarez and Robin had basically acknowledged that they had business with each other. Paul was both triumphant and calm, and turned his attention to his studies. He examined the crew-cut dyke behind the counter, having already arrayed his books and papers on the table as cover, and now periodically fussed with them. Maybe he'd get it together to read the application for SF State, but first he needed to thoroughly investigate the situation with this counter person.

There was no way the counter girl was butch, even strutting to and fro in her Levi's and poly-blend Colma Tigers Little League uniform shirt. Her crew cut framed her face too prettily, her eyelashes were too long, the shirt too snug. She did not achieve that true androgyny some butches have, where

you look once and see a boy, look again and see a girl, look again for the pleasure of the trompe l'oeil. No, this girl was one of the many femmes who'd moved to the city and cut off her hair in order to participate fully in the urban pleasures. A dyke with short hair was noticeable even from across a street; any woman with short hair was worth a second glance. A femme with long hair wouldn't register in a quick scan, unless of course she was high-femme, picking her way down Valencia at 10 AM in heels and dark lipstick, carrying a shopping bag of performance art supplies. A regular femme with long hair, you'd have to cross the street—but how would you even know to do so? Her signifiers were so much subtler, harder to decode. To wit: baggy 501s = butch, whereas baggy overalls = femme. A crew cut = butch, a crew cut with ten or twelve silver hoops piercing the top of one ear = femme. One or even two silver piercing hoops could still signify butch, of course, but then you were also getting into SM territory, and SM butch in some cases = less masculine butch. There was something a little faggy about someone who made a point to identify as a top, instead of just *being* a top. All of which was to say, you had to be a particularly good reader of signs to find a femme by sight alone.

Paul bobbed his head to the music: they were playing the whole Queen Latifah album, which he hadn't heard in months. He caught the counter girl's eye when she walked around wiping down tables. He wondered with minimal self-interest if she was looking for anything, what that might be. He could be a butch, he thought, bulking up his biceps and breasts under his jacket, then shrugging it off to reveal his cut-off flannel. He spread his legs and bit one thumb thoughtfully, and the

counter girl, walking by with a rattling bus tub, took a second glance his way.

A new crowd of people walked in, and as they fanned out Paul sensed Robin among them, as if the air around Robin had a texture. Paul busied himself with his papers, a model of concentration. When Robin sat down at Paul's table, Paul appeared surprised, happy enough to see Robin yet insouciant. He breathed carefully, regulating his heartbeat so the adrenaline wouldn't pump.

"Hey, you," said Robin, setting down a copy of the SF *Weekly* and leaning over to kiss Paul on the cheek. They were kissing on the cheek now.

"Hey," Paul said. He noticed a smell, light and musky and floral at once, like songbirds and pink frosting with a hint of wolf. Paul looked into Robin's big brown eyes and knew his every thought was printed on his face; as usual, Robin had the upper hand. Still, Paul reveled momentarily in the new attention of the counter girl and patrons. Paul was a player in the city, a dark horse. He became worth noticing the minute Robin approached his table. Paul fussed more with his papers as Robin squeezed next to him on the bench.

"What are you up to?" said Robin.

"I don't know," Paul said. "I'm applying to State?"

"Oh, well, don't let me distract you."

Distract me! Paul thought, but Robin was off, stopping by the table with all the cool people. Paul tried to concentrate on the question *If you could have dinner with one person, living or dead, who would that one person be?* Who could possibly answer that question, who had ever loved? The overlords of San

Francisco State University's transfer admissions did not want to hear about Paul's desire to have dinner with Robin, of this he was fairly certain. Paul held his fingers up to his face in a pose which both looked thoughtful and allowed him to watch Robin more thoroughly, for longer.

×

Many years ago, a fleet of currachs bearing poor farmers and their beasts sailed neatly across the small mild sea. The people on the mainland greeted the farmers happily, for they had land to spare and a delight in the new. They intermarried, traded goods, and learned to speak each other's tongues, and all was easy in the little kingdom. Even the old king welcomed the newcomers; his own mother had once left the other world for this one, and the lilt of the farmers' speech made him wistful for his childhood.

One day, the king's eldest son took off riding with his royal companions. They rode for hours and hours, far out into the land. The prince grew tired of his companions and their dull talk of serving girls and farmers' daughters. When his hounds tore off into a grove of oaks, the prince broke from the others and followed the echoing howls.

The young prince came finally to a clearing, where he found his hounds baring their teeth at another pack. The stranger dogs, handsome in their fine red collars, were feasting on a freshly slain stag. The young prince reared back his horse and brandished his sword, and the handsome stranger dogs ran off. His own hounds set upon the stag, pausing only to gaze up at the prince in bloody-mouthed gratitude.

Before his hounds could finish their meal, the prince heard a powerful galloping, then a horn. A medium-sized man, clad in velvet robes and a simple but elegant coronet, rode a sleek black palfrey into the grove and stopped in front of the young prince.

"Your dogs have stolen my stag," said the unknown king. "How do you propose to atone for their crime?"

"Oh," said the young prince. "I suppose you should tell me what I must do."

"Very well," said the mysterious king. "I have heard of your prowess as a fighter. If you defeat my rival in one sure blow, I will consider your obligation fulfilled."

"Very well," said the young prince. "I accept your challenge, sire."

"There's one more condition," said the mysterious king. "You must defeat this rival in my own form."

The king snapped his fingers in a special formation in the direction of the young prince, who shivered and shook his head involuntarily. When the young prince looked again at the mysterious king, it was as if he were gazing in a mirror—the prince saw his own thick black hair, his own aquiline nose, his own scarred cheek. He looked down at his newly soft hands, felt his breeches suddenly loose around a smaller man's thighs.

"What have you done?" said the young prince.

"Don't worry," said the mysterious king, handing the prince his own coronet and robes. "Now take off your clothes."

×

Paul was going to be late for the drag fashion show in that warehouse on Harrison. On the way out of the house he rum-

maged unsuccessfully for his striped scarf. He had the idea that Robin might attend this fashion show and he wanted to arrive on the early side, to position himself to be run into. He had already declined invitations from Ruffles and Silver to go together, but felt cozy knowing they'd be there and happy to see him.

As Paul biked down Hayes and through the Mission, he loved the city painfully. He didn't want to jinx anything or ruin a moment through expectation, but even the whisper-image of Robin was husky and thrilling, deeply meaningful in a completely obscured way.

Like being in love but not, Paul thought, experimentally articulating the thought he'd incubated for weeks now. He waited a few beats to see if his feelings would change immediately after exposure to air, cycling slowly past the strung-up lights of Community Thrift and down 18th Street. Oh San Francisco, land of treats and portals. Robin was more a portal than a person; if Paul could get through Robin he'd know something new on the other side.

Paul watched the traffic lights change from red to green in the blue-gray dusk. The contrast made him think of Nan Goldin photographs and he wanted to tell someone, to marvel at the beauty with someone at whose beauty he could also marvel. Tony Pinto. He turned his mind forcibly to Diane, feeling around for the edges of that pain. But no, he was alone amid all this beauty.

He thought of Robin, a test thought, and a surge of feeling shot through his fingertips, chest, and inner thighs. After a few more blocks he coasted a bit down Harrison and stopped to check the address on the flyer. He was close.

Paul vaguely knew the people who'd organized this fashion show; they all lived together in a squat and were in a band. That Ruffles was bothering to go meant the organizers were connected, old-timers. Ruffles only went out to reunion events, where he could catch up with people from the days when *really* interesting things had happened. Any party Ruffles attended was worth having gone to, even if it seemed boring to the untrained eye. Paul knew he could have racked up a certain amount of reflected cachet by showing up with Ruffles, but he wanted to keep a lower profile. He hadn't dressed up, either. He couldn't compete and so dressed like a designer or photographer; they always looked schlumpy, scowling out of the back pages of *Paper* or *Outweek*. Paul wore a navy blue zip-up hooded sweatshirt with the sleeves cut off under a cheap, cracked leather vest, Levi's, black engineer boots, and his Iowa Hawkeyes Wrestling cap backwards. He locked his bike to a chain-link fence in the parking lot of the warehouse and pushed through the heavy metal door into the throng and thrum and dim lights.

Ruffles was like a radio tower, pulsing out his signal, and Paul landed next to him silently, listening to Ruffles talk with a gathering of older and more subtly tattooed friends. Apparently two of their acquaintances had been hospitalized with a flesh-eating disease. At first Paul thought they were talking about an opportunistic virus, a variation on the theme of plague, but as he stood nicely listening to the grown-ups, he discovered they were talking about a different new terrible disease junkies could give each other. Ruffles knew a lot of junkies, Paul was discovering, and was angry at them. He wondered when people had the time to take heroin, let alone procure it.

Paul was already so busy with drinking, sleeping, cruising, and standing around the bookstore he barely had time to keep up with the monthly issues of *Sandman,* let alone go to school or make future plans, and forget questing for drugs. He didn't believe in doing something painful in order to get a pleasure reward. Except maybe for anal sex, where the pain did feel sort of good, at least when Tony Pinto had done it to him, partly because he also felt Tony Pinto's good feeling, hadn't separated the two. Ruffles's friends continued to talk and no one seemed to mind Paul standing there quietly, like Ruffles's valet, or second in a duel.

Paul spotted Robin across the room and centipeded his way there, moving by indirection to his target. A few feet away he felt nervous and very unlike a hunter and hid in a group of short people who were trying to see over a group of tall people. Their inadequate and asynchronous movements acted as camouflage. Paul worried he'd overplayed his hand; maybe it was too soon to see Robin again. He began to practice banter-y means of preemptively addressing the situation. "I've been stalking you," he could say with a winsome smile. It wasn't creepy or desperate if you knew it; obvious stalking could be bold. The story could be *Paul was a person who knew what he wanted and went for it.*

Robin sidled up next to him, and Paul pretended surprise.

"I thought I might see you here," Robin said.

"Cool," said Paul.

He felt a slight panic rising; he was off script and would have to improvise.

"I was actually hoping I'd run into you," he said, experimenting.

They smiled at each other for a minute, which seemed like a public eternity. Who would break first? That was the power move, Paul knew, but he didn't want to stop smiling or stop looking at Robin's smile. He silently conceded Robin's power, but found himself looking away first anyway.

The volume in the room decreased and a slinky mistress of ceremonies bounded into the center of the room, which was clearly intended to be the stage. Paths in the crowd appeared, like spokes from a bike wheel. Small creatures covered in white feathers floated down each path to converge around the mistress of ceremonies, looking like a pack of oversized lhasa apsos.

"What *are* those?" Paul whispered to Robin.

"Dogs in bird outfits," said Robin. "On wheels."

"Naturally," said Paul. Very magical, San Francisco, he thought. Well played.

A feather drifted past Paul's nose, and he reached out. The feather was synthetic, he realized, and was briefly sad. Maybe fake feathers were nicer, he thought; Diane certainly would have approved. What would Diane think of Robin, he wondered.

Tonight Robin was inhabiting the archetype of the San Francisco Black-Haired Girl, clad in a plaid Catholic school uniform skirt, tight white button-down, and black lace-up boots, even a bad-girl platinum streak and bright red lipstick. Robin's breasts pushed out into the conversation, a tiny gold cross riding the waves. Paul remembered the girls he'd known who went to Catholic Central, their shoplifting and cigarette-smoking and petit-bourgeois rebellions. Paul burned with pride in and envy of Robin's authenticity. Robin's eyes were like little slits, but not piggy. How was that possible? Paul wanted

to plumb the mystery of Robin's sometimes-slitty-sometimes-saucer eyes.

Robin interrupted Paul's reflections to offer him a menthol cigarette. Menthol! Was Robin unstoppable?

The fashion show had begun. The rule, of course, was break-the-rules, so anyone butch in a dress, anyone femme in a suit. Paul yawned. *Victor/Victoria* was so late '80s. He'd expected San Francisco fashion to be more daring than that of Iowa City, but the ped mall had been a nonstop fashion safari: punk-rock drag queens and dyke fashion models and boy poets in tight polyester Sansabelts and all those rhetoric or painting graduate students with their unpredictable fabric combinations. Maybe you had to be more inventive in the country; you had to learn to hem and rip and sequin, to sift through the cast-offs of the exotic manual laborers of middle America, those corn-husking teens, cereal factory third-shifters, and Monsanto janitors.

Then a herd of space-child androgynes in Angela Bowie jumpsuits giraffed by, and Paul had to admit he was impressed. Robin's face betrayed nothing, a mirror looked into from an angle.

"Do you want to get out of here?" said Paul.

"Not really," said Robin, turning a high-watt smile on Paul almost as an afterthought.

Robin did what Robin wanted, and Paul had misjudged his own currency. He remembered how Kostas had once had his credit card rejected at the Red Lobster in Albany. The waiter said, "What would you like to do, sir?" and then just stood there, mask of service fallen away. Paul would never have a credit card; he didn't like to do math, would rather just keep track of his holdings.

He attempted to recover his balance by pretending he hadn't made a play. He cupped his mouth conspiratorially, using a finger across his nose to subtly point out one of the models to Robin, as if they were straight girlfriends or fag-n-hag.

"Look at that *fantastic* top hat," Paul said, in such a way as to leave unclear his true estimation. The music was very loud guitars, and Paul wished he could go somewhere private for five minutes and cry, just get it out of his system before he was poisoned by his own sincerity. He needed a green room.

"I'm going to go say hi to Candice," said Robin, placing a friendish hand on Paul's shoulder.

"Oh, cool," said Paul.

He started to say "Me too" and bit the words off just in time. This was not an invitation. He didn't actually know Candice, and possessed, in fact, too much information about this person he'd never met. He knew, for instance, that Candice hung around with a group of long-haired metalhead butches, and that they all drove trucks for Veritable Vegetable and drank at the 500 Club. He thought he'd heard that Candice was from the Bay Area originally (always notable for a queer), maybe Daly City, maybe had been kicked out by a homophobic Filipino family? Candice was definitely working class, had come by the studded belts and dirty boots honestly.

Paul had never seen Robin on the prowl. He wasn't even sure he was seeing the prowl now, just something urgent in Robin's movement toward Candice. Robin was somehow magnetized, feline—predatory and muscularly vigilant. Was Paul now discovering some truth about Robin, some revealing taste? He watched Candice buddy around with those other butches, jockish and tall and black-haired themselves, a little gang of cool boys

practicing punches. They had it down, shouldering one another, strutting about in their caddishly askew or earnest forward-pointing trucker caps and Bad Brains tee shirts. Butches must be working class, ideally also vaguely alcoholic, with an undercoat of physical menace, whereas femmes could be—maybe even *should* be—from privileged backgrounds, slumming it in collective houses. Robin approached for the parlay like a general of the opposition forces, and the butches pretended not to see. Robin punched Candice's shoulder in the universal greeting of tough girls to tough boys, and the others fell away into a horseshoe, a rakish chorus line. Paul wanted to be Robin *and* Candice, couldn't choose. He didn't have that in him, he thought. They were playing at a much higher level. He watched them leave, Candice tucking one motorcycle helmet under one sturdy bicep and carrying another, free hand languidly cupping Robin's hip. Paul felt himself both truly provincial and hopelessly effete; what made him think he could compete with a motorcyclist?

"Dear heart," said kind perceptive Ruffles. He draped a long auntly arm around Paul, and led him right up to the makeshift stage area. "You're going to love this!"

Should he stay or should he go? The fashion show had evolved logically into a combination of fat femme burlesque and old-time drag performance, as if the entire space was eating a flourless chocolate cake of glamour.

After the show, Ruffles's friends moved outside and Paul moved with them, like a teenage leopard following a pride of tolerant lions. In the dark, in the lee of the warehouse, they passed a pipe containing a tiny ball of hash, and then another. Paul gazed upon Ruffles and his friends without his Terminator goggles; they were guardians not to be defiled with his

hunterly eyes. He accepted their gifts, pushed his bike with
them back through the drifty warm streets of the Mission
to Dolores Park, where they sat on the swings kicking their
legs. Paul played his role, letting himself be swung or pushed
on the carousel. He noticed, with his hash-enhanced senses,
Ruffles's shaved head, the brown contours of his skull. Ruffles
was maybe losing his hair. They were all going to die. He had
thought Ruffles kept his head shorn for wig-wearing purposes
but now realized Ruffles was trying to preempt the inevitable.
Paul would not have to shave his head. He was full of grace.

×

After closing the next night, he went for drinks with his cowork-
ers and found himself at Uncle Bert's, which was hosting yet
another benefit for ACT UP Golden Gate. They sat awkwardly
at the bar naming zines they liked (*Mousie, Slant, Brat Attack,
Queer City, I Heart Amy Carter, Whispering Campaign*).

Paul drank his first beer quickly, his coworkers gossiping
around him. He recognized a lot of people, fags he knew from
the bookstore or the street or the bars, a couple of the cool
Wesleyan girls from Provincetown, even that confrontational
gay poet from Iowa City—normally any of them would be a
welcome opportunity for adventure. But Paul said hi to no one.
He was being a stoic butch. His coworkers drifted away into
their friend groups and now he was in the position he liked
best: surrounded by people he sort of knew, but alone. He was
only two beers in so he ordered a whiskey, no harm there.

The theme of the benefit was County Fair. Booths ringed
the tiny dance floor: a penny pitch, a water-pistol shooting

game, a balloon and dart game, a wheel of fortune, a ticket seller. Paul bought a few dollars' worth from a drag queen in red gingham and ponytails, and looked around for a game to play. He decided on the makeshift bowling alley set up in a corner.

"Three chances for a ticket," said the diffident boy at the booth, a brown gingham shirt under loose overalls, a flower in his moppy hair, a *Silencio = Muerte* pin on his one done-up overall strap. The boy was not much of a salesman; he had picked the corner of the room for a reason. Paul thought he had seen the boy around the Castro, flyering by the BART station or buying juice.

Paul handed over his ticket. He concentrated on his bowling form, adding a little kick at the end like he'd seen on *Laverne & Shirley*, and knocked down two pins on his very first try.

"You're not very good," observed the boy.

Paul aimed more carefully. With his second ball he took down a total of zero pins. The boy raised one eyebrow. He handed Paul the last ball.

"You can do it, tiger," he said, in the lightest of quotation marks, without any hint of camp.

Paul let loose and hit three of the remaining pins.

"Hmm," said the boy. "I think you've earned a Most Improved prize."

"I agree," Paul said. "I am very much improved."

He accepted a small stuffed pig-dog from the boy, and raised it in the air in a victory salute.

"Thank you," Paul said.

"Any time," said the boy.

Paul walked back to his coworkers, making a point of standing next to Divya and not Franky. As unobtrusively as

possible he looked back at the boy. The boy caught Paul staring and Paul waved a tentative wave. Why was he tentative? He had no idea. And then Robin walked in and the brass section blew its bold angelic chorus, a great unseen remote changed the channel of the universe. Robin walked directly over as if they were friends, as if Robin was meeting Paul here, as if they had an *assignation*.

"Hey," said Paul. He patted the sleeves of his new blue workshirt in a short stroking motion he hoped might call subtle, as if unconscious, attention to his musculature. He might not have a motorcycle, but he could be butch. Or at least tuff. He flexed a little, straightening his shoulders and widening his stance.

"Cute shirt," said Robin, touching his sleeve admiringly before scoping out the room. "Hey, did you see who's here?"

Robin named a famous butch performance artist whose show Paul had seen at Luna Sea on Ruffles's recommendation. Robin had touched his sleeve, which was universally known to be a good sign. But also Robin thought he had good taste in shirts, which was a mixed sign. Paul followed Robin's gaze to a short person with very spiky hair accepting adoration from a circle of young dykes. Famous people really were always short, Paul noticed for the millionth time, pleased with his own compactness, which he knew would come in handy someday.

"Ooh, also—" Paul nodded in the direction of a handsome photographer, notorious for portraits of chickens with chickens. The photographer wore a pair of Levi's with a giant rip in the ass. Paul admired one bare sculpted butt cheek. He must be an inherently special person, Paul thought, to have such finely muscled ass cheeks.

"*That's* a little desperate," said Robin, following Paul's gaze.
"Oh, yeah," said Paul. "Totally."

He wished he weren't so agreeable, such a suck-up. He tried to think of something slightly disagreeable to say, something independent, but he was entirely blank.

Robin had premium gossip on the performance artist, a complicated and funny story also involving a hotel room, the lead singer from a famous all-girl pop group from the '80s, and a broken toe. Paul felt vicariously famous even hearing this story. He scanned the bar for people about whom he might comment. He noticed the bowling-pin boy, now being leaned in upon by a peroxide-blonde gym bunny. He indulged his prejudice against blonde men and butches, and combined this with his long-held but only recently articulated disdain for professionally colored hair.

"Let's get out of here," Robin said, and just like that led Paul, who resisted a backward glance at the bowling-pin boy, through the street-lit sidewalks of the Castro to an enormous flat inhabited by a sleepy old spaniel whose owner was on a spoken-word tour of the South. Robin switched on scarf-draped lamps all over the living room. Paul helped, wondering all the while exactly what kind of sex he and Robin would have. He would have liked to have seen the rest of the flat but instead stood and examined the flat-owner's CDs (lots of Prince but also Melissa Etheridge and Two Nice Girls, clearly a white lesbian) while Robin poured kibble in the kitchen. He cupped his hand to his mouth and covertly checked his breath. Okay, not great.

"Wow," Paul said, frowning, and placed his bowling alley

pig-dog on the glass coffee table. He sunk into the cracked leather sofa. "Nice place."

"She has a trust fund," said Robin, handing Paul a glass filled with a thick green liquid from a cut crystal decanter. "I like your stuffed toy."

"Thank you," Paul said. "His name is Aloysius."

"Of course it is," said Robin.

Paul smiled involuntarily, then tried to compose himself, embarrassed by his pleasure in having his reference appreciated. Be cool, he thought. He suspected he was now blushing. He bit back the also-embarrassing question rising up in him—was this Chartreuse or absinthe?—and looked around the room for something on which he might remark wittily.

"So, you are more than you seem, Paul," said Robin. "You are hiding in plain sight."

To buy himself time Paul pretended to not understand, arranging on his face an expression of humble naïveté. He would know what to do in a minute.

"Don't you want to show off for me? Show me something nice."

He accidentally chugged his drink. "Like what?"

"Oh, we both know what we are," Robin said, sipping gracefully. "Don't let's be coy with one another."

Okay, thought Paul. This is happening now. He could feel the absinthe (Chartreuse?) settling in.

"Hang on." He found the bathroom and inhaled deeply. He squeezed a dab of toothpaste on his finger and rubbed his teeth quickly, then concentrated on being younger: a peppering of acne, two or three stray facial hairs, wider eyes, fatter face.

More fat and grease. To all appearances, Paul hoped, he was fifteen. He walked back out.

"I'd card you," Robin said.

Paul shrugged, with a hint of youthful brattishness, and ducked back into the bathroom. He salted his hair, let his cheeks sag and his skin weather; he overrode his own vanity and allowed himself to manifest graying stubble and a more pronounced paunch: early forties? Aging was harder: waxy, a little gross, but also cozy.

"Never needed an ID," said Paul, back in the living room. He reached for his glass.

"It is one of the benefits," Robin said, suddenly older, stern Deneuve-ian mien broken by the hint of a smile.

Paul laughed.

"It's really all benefits," Paul said. "Right?"

Robin gave him an appraising look.

Paul shrugged.

"Hmm," said Robin. "What else can you do?"

"Lots of things," Paul bragged.

"Let me watch," said Robin.

Paul fumbled open his workshirt. His mosquito bite breasts poked at the ribbing of his A-shirt. He knew Robin would see his dark nipples through the white, and went bigger, his breasts heavy against the cotton. He absorbed his extremities, slurped in facial hair, body hair, cock, balls, and stood loosely in the doorframe.

Robin matched him, but sweeter, more feminine. Paul couldn't look away, couldn't believe he was being allowed to look.

He shifted into leatherman: darker arm hair, a bulge in

his crotch, muscles popping. Robin shifted too, slight but wiry, some lucky young matador. Paul saw a small mound grow in Robin's pants, just the soft presence of a penis, and felt his own pants tighten in response. Paul's arousal was a simultaneous source of pride and helplessness. He did not look at Robin, but let his wrist drop between his legs suggestively.

Robin didn't seem to notice, and Paul let the moment be, content to watch. He'd never seen anyone else change before; he could watch the manifestations of Robin all day, revel in Robin's mystery.

He wanted to say *do more*. He wanted to say *but what are you!* He wanted to press the buttons of Robin's jukebox, *that was a pretty one, play it again!*—but he knew he was not in charge.

"So what else?" said Robin. "Can you look like someone else? Can you look like me?"

"Like the T-1000? No," said Paul. "Why, can you?"

"What are you? I mean, ethnicity."

"Irish mother and Greek father," said Paul. "I think. Maybe Turkish."

"You don't know?" Robin said.

"No," said Paul. "I'm a bastard." He enjoyed the rakish connotations of the word. He was, he felt whenever he said this word, a *lucky* bastard; he had been born outside the patriarchy.

"And you?" he said. He thought probably Robin was Mexican but didn't like to assume.

"Cuban," said Robin. "Well, half. My mother came over from Cuba. My father's Irish."

Paul decided this new coincidence must be a sign.

Robin reached one arm over to Paul's. As they watched

each other, Robin began to sprout freckles, to lighten by barely a shade.

"Try," Robin said.

Paul felt shy, lavatorial; he let his own freckles sink deep into his skin. He'd never done that before; it had never occurred to him to change his freckles. They were a part of him.

"No, that's good, close," said Robin.

"I can't really," Paul said apologetically.

He looked up, and Robin was gone. Paul was looking at himself, a version of himself. Or was he? Maybe he had switched bodies with Robin and *was* looking at himself? He was a little dizzy. He touched his face, cradled his nose for a minute—familiar, yes, his—then checked his right hand for the stitches scar from the broken wine glass at the restaurant. He looked at Robin/himself. He looked cute in Robin's bright blue polyester Cubs uniform shirt. He watched "himself" check "his" ironic radiating baby Swatch and felt a disturbing genital blankness, almost revulsion. Change back, he thought fiercely. Be you again.

"So?" said Robin.

"That's amazing. You know that song—'You be me for a while and I'll be you'?" Paul wanted to stop talking. All his references were so mainstream and earnest; he was devolving or perhaps revealing some profound truth about himself. He simmered in his shame. "Or *Sweet Valley High*! Can you teach me? We could totally do that and trick people, like Jessica and Elizabeth Wakefield."

"Sure, sometime," said Robin, not unkindly.

And then Robin changed back, was Robin again, and Paul was the only Paul.

"I should probably . . ." Robin said, stretching.

Paul started.

"Oh," he said. "Yeah. Me too."

"My boyfriend's coming over to walk the dog with me," said Robin. "I have to get ready."

×

Paul walked home via the tracks behind the Safeway then looped back around onto Church, then Webster, rambling out of his way to take the quiet streets. *Boyfriend,* Robin had said. Paul mulled over the word. Boyfriend. He remembered all the stupid talking he'd done, how he'd wasted what might be his only opportunity to talk to someone like himself.

The rain stopped. He had no idea where he was, and then saw the entrance to a pocket garden he could never find when he was looking for it—like Brigadoon. He entered, and there was the bowling-pin boy, sitting on a bench with his eyes closed.

Paul soft-shoed over to the bench, sat next to the boy, and closed his own eyes. He smelled jasmine, or was it honeysuckle? Something sweet and light.

"Oh, it's you!" he heard.

Paul opened his eyes.

"Hi," he said. "Yeah."

He tugged the ear of the pig-dog out of his shirt. The boy smiled.

"What's his name?" he asked.

"What's your name?" Paul countered.

"Derek," said the boy, extending his hand somewhat formally.

"Paul," said Paul. He shook Derek's hand.

"It's so pretty here," Derek said. "This is my favorite place in the city."

"I know! But I can never find it," Paul said. "It's like one of those unmarked dungeons where you can't remember the address."

The boy looked at Paul oddly, and Paul felt embarrassed. He had never been to any actual dungeon, marked or not. Why did he need to brag? Plus he'd sounded queeny without intending to. He was losing the moment; his tricks were not working. He wanted to impress this boy, this easy target, and felt a little nonplussed that he hadn't already.

Paul sat his pig-dog on the bench between them. Derek smiled.

"What's your secret?" Paul asked.

"How do you know I have one?" said Derek.

"Do you always answer a question with a question?" Paul said.

"Why do you ask?" he said.

"Should I ask a better question?"

"Why don't you?"

They smiled at each other in the night air, street light peeking above the hedges. Paul admired again the boy's brown gingham shirt ('60s Levi's with pearly snaps, hard to find), his silky hair, his prominent Adam's apple, his dark stubble. He was lovely and doe-eyed without being androgynous in the least. Paul wondered what to say next to unlock this boy. He tried his trusty method of starting to talk without knowing what would come out.

"So, hey . . ." he started.

"Hey," said Derek, smiling.

Paul had nothing. He smiled back.

"Okay," said Derek. "I guess I'll see you around."

Paul stood up out of an almost natural chivalry.

"Good night," Paul called out as Derek walked out of the garden and in the opposite direction of Paul's house.

A few paces away, the boy turned around, and Paul waved. As he strolled home he had to make a conscious effort to not snap his fingers like Riff in *West Side Story*. He was better than that.

×

The girl he was subletting from was maybe now coming back, Paul's transfer application was due, he still had to pay off his old tuition bill so they would release his transcript from Iowa, there were messages from Jane to return, and when was he going to see Robin again? He had to call his mother. But today was poetry inventory day, which Paul loved—he could legitimately spend his whole shift sorting through chapbooks and slim volumes of homosexual verse, skimming lines off the tops of poems and following one poet to the next via a dense web of blurbs, dedications, and acknowledgments. From Delany's memoir, he recognized Marilyn Hacker, then Auden (Auden was gay! He knew it!), who led to Frank O'Hara, who led to James Schuyler, who led to Eileen Myles, a celestial firmament hovering above the pages.

Silver walked by with an armful of Naiads.

"This is so great," Paul said, clutching *Not Me* as he sat surrounded by a stack of O'Hara *Selected*s and Schuyler *Collected*s.

"You know who you'd like?" Silver said.

"Who?" said Paul. "Turn me on!"

"Ted Berrigan," she said. "He was friends with all those guys."

Paul looked under B.

"We don't have any," he said.

"Yeah," said Silver. "He was straight. You should check him out, though."

"Cool," said Paul. He didn't have time to read straight poets but he wanted to be nice.

He read one of Myles's poems, the one about being a Kennedy; he was fairly certain but not positive that she was *not* a Kennedy, and this ambiguity thrilled him in a way that reminded him of Robin.

As Paul was thinking through the Robin situation, who should walk in and plop *Close to the Knives* on the counter but the bowling-pin boy, Derek.

"You work here?" Derek said.

"I work here," Paul said, ringing up the purchase with great professionalism.

Derek was wearing a vintage purple Tuffskins jacket and green jeans from which Paul could not look away. That combination should never have worked. How had Derek gotten away with it? Paul had the feeling of having learned something profound, like suddenly understanding one of Foucault's sentences.

He smiled at Derek. Derek smiled back. They stood smiling foolishly across the counter until an elderly gentleman collapsed in one of the aisles. The entire store, staff and customers, sprang into action: Thom administered CPR, Divya called a

gay-friendly EMT she knew, community-minded johns stood by panting with civic concern. A customer gathered four or five oranges that had escaped the man's bag in the fall.

"I should go," Derek said. "You're busy."

"Oh, okay," Paul said. Thom and Divya totally had the situation under control. "Yeah, I should help."

Derek left the store. Paul walked over to the situation. He noticed purple blotches on the man's distended neck; the man was perhaps not elderly. As Paul moved closer, he was rebuffed by the scrum of early responders. He returned to his post at the register. Somebody had to mind the store, he thought. The ambulance came and took the man away. Divya went on break and Thom retired to the office to do paperwork. Paul spent the rest of his shift at the register, out of sorts.

Toward the end of the day, Paul leaned on the counter, pretending to organize the pink triangle jewelry but really staring out through the glass at the dark Tuesday night quiet of the Castro. He had forty minutes left, an eternity to stand at a register alone.

The door opened. Derek came in.

"This might sound forward," Derek said. "But would you want to have dinner when you get off?"

Over burritos, Derek and Paul compared notes on New York, where they'd sort of overlapped. Derek took the Metro-North from Vassar on Monday nights to attend ACT UP meetings at Cooper Union with his friend Kenny, whom Paul thought he remembered. They traded notes on ACT UP celebrities, that *Village Voice* reporter and the famous photographer. Paul remembered the vehement bald lesbian who'd once scolded him for giggling. "People are dying, Paul," she'd said,

and he'd been embarrassed until he saw Tony Pinto cracking up behind her back.

Derek told Paul how he'd been so happy to study dance in college—his childhood dream deferred by a homophobic father—but he'd been too old at eighteen and too short at 5'7" to make it as a professional ballet dancer, so he'd majored in the infinitely more practical art history. Paul, impressed by Derek's tragedy, accepted an invitation to smoke a little weed at Derek's apartment, mere blocks away from the bookstore. After-dinner bong hits led to frottage and an exotic sleepover that dumped Paul back on the street when Derek left for work in the morning, biking out to the De Young for his job as something called a program assistant. Paul would have to ask Malcolm or Ruffles what that meant.

When Derek stopped by the bookstore the next evening to suggest a second date, Paul agreed but couldn't help wondering what Derek saw in him. Derek was so fancy.

The next morning, he came home to an answering-machine message from Robin.

"Hi, Polly, it's Robin. I haven't seen you around for a while. Come over to my studio tomorrow if you want. Around noon."

Paul played the tape over and over, first writing down Robin's address and then attempting to isolate the faint Spanish inflection in Robin's voice. He pictured that green lace-up shirt, the chase through the streets of Chicago. *Robin,* he thought.

×

Paul perched awkwardly on a cot, watching Robin hammer small black furniture tacks into blocks of wood, to what end

Paul could not determine. He surmised this craftiness was a new artistic direction for Robin, whose extant sculptures, though handmade, appeared to have been assembled by robots.

Robin's studio looked severe in the thunderstorm darkness, fluorescent overheads casting a sinister supermarket light. Paul appreciated the avant-garde realness of Robin's décor choices: dirty white walls; butcher-paper plans held up by bright blue painter's tape; a worktable made from filing cabinets and a door; a cot that doubled as couch, covered by a neon-pink-and-green granny-square blanket. Robin would never carefully tape up pictures of supermodels to the wall, unless it was to detourn them.

Robin paid Paul no attention but moved around the studio with a sense of purpose. Paul noticed Robin's particular slightness, accentuated by a faded army-green mechanic's jumpsuit and large black lace-up boots. How effortless Robin looked, how sui generis.

"There's beer in the fridge," Robin offered.

Paul pushed himself off the cot and dutifully opened two beers from the minifridge. He offered one to Robin, who refused. Paul shrugged and lined the two bottles up on the saw-dusty floor. He picked one up and drank most of it in one gulp.

Paul had not thus far been able to bring himself to ask Robin any of his burning questions—why are we like this? are there others? can we get sick? Being with Robin should be answer enough; to ask more would be gauche.

"I'm going back to Iowa," Paul said, experimentally. Until the words came out of his mouth he hadn't even considered this retreat.

"Really," Robin said, precisely tipping over a coffee can of

tacks and standing back to study the pattern they made on the butcher paper. "Seems like a good place to go."

"I might go to State instead," Paul said. He knew he was grasping now, far off the script.

"SF?" Robin said, carefully extracting one last tack from its lip holster.

"Yeah," said Paul.

He looked at his shoes.

"Robin?" Paul said. "Can I ask you a question?"

Paul was immediately disgusted with himself. He sounded insecure, asking if he could ask—just the sort of dumb question he himself had so often railed against. But Robin just nodded, seemingly unperturbed.

"What are we?" Robin supplied.

Robin turned the hammer around and began removing tacks from wood.

"I mean . . ." said Paul.

"You want to know what I really think?" Robin said.

"Yes," Paul said.

"We're like everybody else, only more so."

"No, seriously," Paul said.

"We're just what we are. You're asking the wrong questions, Polly."

Robin disappeared into the hand-built closet in the corner and reemerged with a small box.

"Do you like candy?"

Paul nodded.

"My grandmother sends me a box of turróns every year to my father's house, and my father just crosses out his address and writes in mine. No note."

Robin offered the box to Paul.

"The orange ones are the best," Robin said, pointing out a choice piece wrapped in wax paper and tied up with a piece of orange string.

Paul unwrapped the sticky white candy, which tasted like nougat and seemed like something Tony Pinto would have eaten.

"I never met my father," said Paul, between bites.

"I can't decide if we should be lovers or best friends," said Robin, as if Paul hadn't spoken.

I already have a best friend, who I owe a phone call, Paul thought. Friends were too much work.

"Lovers!" Paul said. He had a sugar rush from the turrón, and reached for another.

Robin laughed, with a shrug, that laugh of recognition without amusement.

"Of course that's what you'd say."

×

"What happened with Robin?" Ruffles asked Paul one morning a few weeks later, after Derek had gone home to change for work and Paul sat about aimlessly drinking coffee and flipping through an old issue of *Deneuve*. He might not be a lesbian right at this very moment, he thought, scratching at a patch of dried semen on his boxer briefs, but he liked to stay current.

"We're friends," Paul said.

"Uh huh," said Ruffles, helping himself to the rest of Paul's French press.

"Did you know Meshell Ndegeocello is gay?" Paul said. "I love her!"

"Jade's experiencing a grand passion, by the by," said Ruffles. "She's staying in Berlin indefinitely. I thought you might like to know."

"Meaning?" Paul said, raising one eyebrow. He knew Ruffles preferred him as a roommate to Jade, who sounded with every anecdote more and more like a domestic tyrant.

"Yes, my pet," Ruffles said. "You may stay on indefinitely."

"My favorite word!" said Paul. They toasted with their coffee cups.

The universe was conspiring to keep him here, Paul thought.

×

Later that same week, Paul cooked dinner at Derek's for the first time. So far Derek had cooked every time they ate together, as Paul's specialties ran from scrambling eggs to ordering well, and Derek preferred, unfathomably, not to spend money on restaurants.

Paul did like to cook an elaborate meal occasionally, and he decided to impress Derek with a capon out of *Mastering the Art of French Cooking, Volume 1.* He banished Derek to the living room to pick out music and open the wine, and consulted the recipe he'd hidden in his pocket. Derek periodically ducked into the kitchen with little questions about Paul's early life, about his parents and schooling and extended family. Paul deflected most of these, offering a noncommittal tidbit and then, "But what about *you*? Were *you* out in high school? Who was *your* first boyfriend? Are your parents cool?"

Was Derek actually curious about Paul's past? He seemed

to be running down a list of "dating questions," almost like an interview. He seemed pressingly interested in Paul's future, which Paul suspected was born of Derek's not-very-well-hidden embarrassment that Paul hadn't finished college and worked in retail. Although a bookstore wasn't retail, not really. It wasn't like he was a *shop girl.*

Derek was apparently close to his mother (shocking) and scared of his surgeon father (again, who would have imagined such a thing, for a young gay aristocrat?). He had a sixteen-year-old sister to whom he spoke by telephone nearly every day.

Paul thought of his own brother, who'd turn seventeen in a month. When was the last time they'd actually had a conversation? Not last Christmas, certainly. Probably before Ari hit puberty. Paul had sent him a funny postcard of the crookedest street in the world a few months ago. Ari was probably better off without him, Paul thought, but silently vowed to make him a birthday mixtape this year. He tuned back in to Derek's story about his Latin tutor in Grosse Pointe, whom Derek had always suspected might be gay.

Paul stared at Derek from the doorway, all that earned muscle under his clothes, his bare feet stony from years of hardwood floors.

"You should really finish your application to State," Derek said, carving the capon because Paul didn't know how. "And why not apply to UC Berkeley while you're at it? You'd have in-state tuition either place, so you might as well go to the better school."

"Good idea," said Paul, thinking *Yeah, right,* and *They call it Cal.* Derek was the sort of person who could have gotten into Cal without even knowing its name.

×

For weeks, then months, Paul and Derek went on dates to see the buffalo in the park, to film festivals, to modern dance shows choreographed by Derek's friends, to lackluster demonstrations in front of government buildings or pharmaceutical company headquarters after which they got coffee. They attended and hosted dinner parties made up of other handsome young college-educated gay couples of all nations. They had a gentle and cuddling sex life, mostly what Paul called side-by-side love. He used to mean it snidely but was learning to appreciate its pleasures. Sometimes they gave each other minty-safe plastic blowjobs, smoking pot first for extra focus. Early on, Derek articulated his objection to anal sex on both safety and cleanliness grounds. But despite his heightened attentiveness to personal hygiene Derek was possessed of a supremely filthy imagination. Always up for a role play, he'd happily indulged Paul's Edward II and Gaveston fantasy, seeing Paul and raising him one—Kid and Tak, Clinton and Lewinsky, Catherine the Great and her steed. Derek stopped by the bookstore most nights Paul worked, bringing him sandwiches and staying to chat. He was impressed by how many books Paul had read, and Paul tried to find poems or passages Derek might like, to read out loud in bed.

×

When Derek's friend Kenny got a positive test result, Derek cried for two days straight, canceling rehearsals and watching marathons of daytime TV.

"I just at some fundamental level don't understand," he said to Paul, who'd stopped by before his shift. "He works for needle exchange, for Christ's sake. He's always safe."

Paul kept his own counsel, having seen Kenny enter more than one backroom on the heels of one or another old white guy. Paul remembered something Diane had said, some hoary lesbian chestnut—"Don't pathologize your desires." That had been good advice, even if she hadn't taken it herself. Paul wondered why Kenny liked those older guys, why they had to be white. Kenny's boyfriend wasn't white or old.

"He's still alive," Paul said. He felt a righteous monologue about the entitlement of rich boys from Grosse Pointe coming on and squelched it, resulting in a sentence that sounded, even to his own ears, wise and compassionate.

Derek pressed his thumb against the square of flesh between his eyebrows.

"Yeah," he said, and Paul could see the ghost of Derek's boyhood. He swallowed his rage.

"It's okay," Paul said, picking up and softly petting Derek's free hand. "Everything's okay."

They sat like that for a few minutes and then Derek curled up on the couch. Paul muted the television.

"I wish I didn't have to go but I do," he said, covering Derek with a blanket. He needed to get back on the street.

"Paul," said Derek, as Paul fiddled with the deadbolt.

"Yeah?" Paul said. He turned around.

"I love you," Derek said. He looked at Paul with tender eyes and a raw red nose.

They'd never said this before, and Paul felt sick and a little

violent at the thought of what he was about to do, what Derek was making him do.

"I love you too," he said, and went to work.

×

At the store, Paul found himself shadowing Silver, mesmerized by her always slightly pursed lips, the dimplish folds which appeared at the side of her mouth when she spoke in her whisper-soft voice. He wondered if she pursed her lips intentionally, to make them fuller, more girlish. Silver was talking a lot today, maybe because it was just the two of them in the store. She'd found one of the regular street kids nodded out on the back patio when she'd opened; she'd made sure he was alive and sent him on his way but now she needed to talk to her AA sponsor, who, Paul came to understand, was not returning her phone calls.

"What do sponsors do?" Paul said. "Maybe I can be your substitute sponsor."

He'd never known anyone else who'd stopped drinking before, though of course he remembered the rock star in Iowa City and all the hubbub about sober space at Michigan. And he'd seen those Sober Dances advertised. Poor Silver. Now she'd have to go to Sober Dances.

"Well," said Silver. "First off, you'd tell me to have an attitude of gratitude."

"Okay!" Paul said. "Ready? 'Have an attitude of gratitude.'"

"Thanks," Silver said. "Now tell me to make a gratitude list."

"You better make a gratitude list," Paul said sternly.

Silver nodded and started writing on the back of a flyer.

Paul thought of the bumper stickers bought by so many lesbians and really old gay guys in drawstring pants.

"Hey, Silver," he said. "Hey. Ready? I have more. 'Take It Easy!' 'Keep It Simple, Stupid!'"

"Basta!" Silver said. "You're on my list already."

"Look who's a salty dog," said Paul, and applied himself to the unpacking and shelving of the weekly delivery of porn mags. He knew that street kid, the one who spent hours at a stretch reading *Portrait of a Lady,* slipped into copies of *Honcho* to preserve his appeal for the johns. He decided to make a gratitude list himself. He'd have to thank Derek—"My lover Derek," he'd say. He pictured the camera panning across the audience, as if it were his Oscar acceptance speech—Susan Sarandon's supportive face; Tom Cruise, intrigued. But what would he thank Derek *for*? Derek had, it was true, turned him on to John Cage and Merce Cunningham and Yoko Ono. Derek got him into museums for free. Derek encouraged the tender shoots of Paul's academic ambitions. Derek had given him a first edition of *Dancer from the Dance,* with the original dust jacket. But Paul couldn't help wondering if Derek secretly thought of him as the earnest and wifely Italian truck driver. Derek had introduced Paul to his whole circle of college chums, the exact sort of nice boys Paul could never be friends with on his own. And Derek made efforts—accompanied Paul to Klubstitute and valiantly tried to hide his fear of the brash dykes therein, bought him trinkets, laughed at his witty asides, told him he was pretty. Derek was a good boyfriend, and with every passing week, Paul felt himself also to be a good boyfriend and to have numerical proof, in days and weeks and months. No

need to reveal Paul's thoughts when he'd spotted Robin at the Box—where he'd only gone to drop off flyers for Derek's show, of course—leaning over to flirt with a pretty bartender.

<div align="center">×</div>

"So you've been with Derek for what?" Robin asked.

"Like four months?" Paul paused on the stepladder, rainbow wind-sock in hand.

Robin had stopped by the store just as Derek was leaving, which made Paul nervous. He didn't like them to talk to each other, preferred to keep his worlds separate.

"You haven't told him, have you?" Robin watched Paul rearrange the window display, occasionally handing him a miniature disco ball or novelty penis snow globe.

"Does Jack know?" Paul countered.

"Of course," said Robin.

"Hmm," said Paul.

<div align="center">×</div>

Derek decided to quit his museum job and start a dance company. He had, he told Paul, reached the age of majority in regards to some money left him by his grandfather, a rich industrialist, and he'd grown weary of office life. Derek had always insisted on paying 70/30 when they went out for dinner or to Russian River for the weekend—"the socialist payment plan," he'd called it, officially proposing this arrangement to Paul. Paul hadn't known what to think but now realized Derek

must be rich in a way Paul hadn't imagined. Paul liked Russian River, lounging in hot tubs while older men admired him and Derek from a respectful distance.

He'd certainly found himself more and more in the company of boys who'd attended better all-boys prep schools than he, better colleges—boys who thought of Paul as poor and casually fetishized his "working-class authenticity," boys who sold their Ivy League mouths for life experience and coke money, boys with emergency J. Press suits in their cedar-lined closets, boys with five-year plans. Paul realized he'd been cast as David Copperfield to Derek's Steerforth and worked to bolster this perception among these boys, Derek's friends, presenting himself as the hardscrabble, up-by-the-bootstraps, disadvantaged intellectual, a role he'd first auditioned for with the young professors at Iowa, now on its national tour.

For Paul's twenty-third birthday, Derek threw him a dinner party but didn't give him a present. Weird, thought Paul, his feelings hurt. He drank more wine than he had in months.

"Bedtime for you," said Derek.

Paul let himself be walked into Derek's bedroom. He saw an envelope on the bed and flared with disappointment. He liked to have a box to open, preferably multiple boxes.

"Thanks," he said.

"Open it," said Derek.

Paul sat on the bed and opened the envelope. Derek had drawn, beautifully, a picture of Paul's little pig-dog Aloysius. Who knew Derek could draw?

"I want you to have what you need, Paul," said Derek.

Inside the card was a check for $500.

"You can pay off your tuition bill and transfer to State."

Paul traced the drawing of the pig-dog with his index finger. The picture would have been enough, he thought. Maybe in a frame.

×

Once Paul passed Robin on Castro in the company of Jack Manjoyne. Paul did not stop to say hello, as Jack was discoursing on what seemed to be an important subject, and Robin was listening attentively, even deferentially. Robin looked so small and young—such smooth cheeks, such thick eyelashes, an Ivory-soap urchin. Their eyes met for a second and Robin smiled at Paul, then turned toward Jack.

×

Paul liked how Ruffles kept so many plants in the living room, watered them and kept them alive. The air smelled better than normal air, wetter and heavy, the air was like drinking cake. Ruffles was a good person.

Paul leaned back on the couch and wrapped the neon-pink-and-black afghan around him. He felt fresh after a shower. People said you could get lost in California, never come back to reality; people warned about lotus-eating. Paul thought maybe he didn't mind so much. He could stay here forever, and time would stop, and he wouldn't have to choose anything.

×

A few days later, Paul pushed the uncashed check through Derek's mail slot with a little note. He walked out of Derek's building into the cool bright light. He had practically the whole day free until his shift and the crackling air smelled like flowers. He walked and walked, looking up at the attic windows and roofs of renovated Victorians, the treetops, a congregation of pigeons on the web of train wires over Market Street, the big Western sky. Sunlight seeped into his head, sunlight down through his eyes, down his throat, and spreading out. He came to Duboce Park and lay down on the grass, his head on his backpack and his fingers in the dirt. He saw a little kid in a faded tie-dye call out nonsense words to a bird-nosed man. He saw a crusty spare-changer share a sandwich with her yellow dog. He saw a handsome older gent running for the train. He saw the counter girl from Flore, reading a paperback copy of *A Wizard of Earthsea* on the bench. He saw a violet pushing up through a disintegrating Muni transfer. He saw the city, as good-smelling and various as himself.

Acknowledgments

I am grateful to all workers, teachers, and fellows of both RADAR Labs and the Lambda Literary Foundation for creating true communities of queer and trans writers. My most special thanks to Michelle Tea, Ali Liebegott, and Beth Pickens of RADAR Labs, and to Jenn Reese, Tony Valenzuela, William Johnson, and Sue Landers of Lambda.

Thank you to my esteemed teachers Chris Bachelder, Dodie Bellamy, Jedediah Berry, Samuel R. Delany, Peter Gizzi, Noy Holland, Kevin Killian, Kevin Kopelson, Sabina Murray, Sandra Newman, Carter Sickels, James Tate, Carla Trujillo, and Dara Wier. And thank you to my students, who teach me what writers can do.

Thank you to my beloved Rescue Press family: Hilary Plum and Zach Savich—most thoughtful, generous, patient editors and dear friends—and also, always, my deep gratitude to Sevy Perez, Caryl Pagel, Danny Khalastchi, and Alyssa Perry—what good fortune I have had to be in your company. And thank you to Jeremy Wang-Iverson of Vesto PR, you hero!

And thank you to my lovely new traveling companions! Thank you to PJ Mark, the coolest agent in the world, Virgil to my Dante. Thank you also to Ian Bonaparte and everyone at Janklow Nesbit; to the sage Jason Richman and to Nora Henrie and everyone at UTA. Thank you to everyone at Picador UK. I'm so grateful to the excellently-named and silver-tongued Paul Baggaley, who first took a chance on me;

to my brilliant, kind, and supremely encouraging editor, Kish Widy-aratna; to the bold, intrepid, dedicated, and generally wonderful Grace Harrison; to Mel Four for her cover design; and to Hannah Dualeh, Camilla Elworthy, and Paul Martinovic (also excellently-named).

Thank you to Eileen Myles, Maggie Nelson, and Michelle Tea, benefactors and sources of inspiration.

Thank you to my beloved comrades Cathy Halley, Sara Jaffe, and M. Milks for reading so many drafts and talking through so many big and small decisions with me.

For excellent advice in various pinches, thank you to Alexander Chee, Naomi Jackson, Tayari Jones, Adam Reed, Sarah Schulman, Char-lotte Strick, Michael Taeckens, Lindsay Williams, and Rebecca Wolff.

Thank you to all the reviewers, list-makers, interviewers, editors, curators, reading-series organizers, and booksellers who've given this book its life in the world—I appreciate your labor every day!

Thank you to all the workers at Mugshots, Amherst Coffee, the Hay-market, the Roost, the Woodstar, SIP, Rao's, Northampton Coffee, Thirsty Mind, and the Smith College Student Union Café; to the librarians at the Jones Library, the Frost Library, the W.E.B. DuBois Library, the Neilson Library, the Williston Memorial Library, and the Free Library of Philadelphia. Thank you to all independent book-sellers and librarians everywhere!

Thank you of course to all the friends and family who've read drafts, fed and housed me, encouraged and sustained me over the years:

Acknowledgments

Samuel Ace, E.R. Anderson, Ari Banias, Emily Barton, Julia Bloch, Jennifer Blowdryer, Kera Bolonik, Cooper Lee Bombardier, Tisa Bryant, Marcy Coburn, Stephanie Corrales, Bobby Cortez, Christy Crutchfield, Cedre Csillagi, Dennis Cunningham, Luke Dancona, Roberta Danza, Steve Dillon, Steve Dolph, Mark Ewert, Michael Fauver, Margaret Foreman, Judy Frank, Elizabeth Freeman, Mel Friedling, Melisse Gelula, Tracy Hobson, Mary Hoeffel, Xylor Jane, Tara Jepsen, Tim Jones-Yelvington, R.E. Katz, John Krokidas, Zack Leven, Jeremy Leven, Robin Coste Lewis, Luce Lincoln, Gustavo Llarull, Amy Martin, Anna-Marie McLemore, Delia Mellis, Miranda Mellis, Dori Midnight, E.E. Miller, Sarah Miller, Eileen Moyer, Sonny Nordmarken, Miller Oberman, Katherine O'Callaghan, Alvin Orloff, Allison Page, Luke Phelan, Michael Polydoris, Corinna Press, Barb Rands, Frances Richard, Blake Riley, Nicolas Sansone, Deb Schwartz, Mark Shea, Aretha Sills, Gina Siepel, Kate Singer, Sara Smith, Dean Spade, Eirik Steinhoff, Elliott Vanskike, Heather Varnadore, Shawna Virago, David Watkins, Betsy Wheeler, Johnathan Wilber, Rebecca Yaffe, Dov Zeller, and Eileen Zyko.

Thank you to my BFF Jordy Rosenberg: good buddy, kindly uncle, stellar introducer, true reader and advisor and talker-down-from-ledges. Dude.

And thanks to my parents, Bridget and Donald Mariano, who surrounded me with books.

My deepest appreciation, beyond measure, to Bernadine, Shugie, Sleeve, and T'other—my loves, my home.